JOURNEY

Books by Angela Elwell Hunt

FROM BETHANY HOUSE PUBLISHERS

Gentle Touch

LEGACIES OF THE ANCIENT RIVER

Dreamers

Brothers

Journey

JOURNEY

ANGELA ELWELL HUNT

BETHANY HOUSE PUBLISHERS
MINNEAPOLIS, MINNESOTA 55438

Published by Bethany House Publishers
A Ministry of Bethany Fellowship, Inc.
11300 Hampshire Avenue South
Minneapolis, Minnesota 55438

Printed in the United States of America.

Library of Congress Cataloging-in-Publication Data

Hunt, Angela Elwell, 1957–
 Journey / Angela Elwell Hunt.
  p. m . —(Legacies of the ancient river ; 3)
 ISBN 1–55661–609–0 (pbk.)
 1. Egypt—History—Eighteenth dynasty, ca. 1570–1320 B.C.—
Fiction. 2. Bible. O.T.—History of Biblical events—Fiction.
 I. Title. II. Series: Hunt, Angela Elwell, 1957–   Legacies of
the ancient river ; 3.
PS3558.U46747J68   1997
813'.54—dc21
                                                      97–21116
                                                          CIP

There are two kinds of adventurers:
those who go truly hoping to find adventure
and those who go secretly hoping they won't.

William Least Heat Moon
[William Trogdon]
Blue Highways: A Journey Into America

ANGELA ELWELL HUNT is the award-winning and bestselling author of over fifty books and a thousand magazine articles. Among her books are three historical fiction series for adults, three series for teenagers, and bestsellers like *The Tale of Three Trees*. She and her husband have two children and make their home in Florida.

Contents

Prologue

SHE HEARD THE MURMURING SOUNDS OF WATER, FELT the deck under her feet rise and fall, and knew she was dreaming of her death. Again.

Borne by an insistent wind, the ship that carried her through the dream pressed forward, slicing through the silk black water that ran along its side. Jendayi clutched at the railing, then lifted her hand and held it before her widened eyes. She could *see* every line of her palm, scrubbed and cleaned, her fingers tipped with the neatly trimmed nails of a musician.

She shifted her eyes to the glassy surface of the inky river and felt the wings of tragedy brush lightly past her, urging a shiver up her spine. The images of this place did not mesh with the faded visions of her mortal memory. When the gift of sight had been hers in life, she had looked out upon a bright and vivid world, but a crimson hue tinged everything in this region, as if the fiery malevolent eyes of Ammit colored everything in his domain.

The boat slid silently onto a mounded levee, rocking with a soft thump that nearly knocked her from her feet. Jendayi reached out for the railing as the bark began to turn and drift. Massive black rocks jutted up from the water's edge; no grasses, crocodiles, or hippos lived along the shore. This, after all, was the realm of the dead, a place of gods and spirits.

She heard the soft sound of sandals moving toward the ancient river, then tiny pairs of invisible hands locked on to her arms and gently propelled her from the boat. She gasped at the first shock of coolness on her bare feet as she stepped from the bark into the water, and someone laughed, a strangely indulgent sound. The little beings pulled her forward through the water toward the soft sand where a pair of enormous pillars aggressively thrust themselves out from a pale and gleaming stone structure.

Jendayi swallowed, trying to steady her erratic heartbeat. Strange that she should still feel it beating in her chest. Stranger still that she could feel and yet not see the impish beings who propelled her forward. But she was not afraid of the dark. Being blind had taught her not to fear anything . . . on earth.

The crimson darkness around her felt heavy and threatening, and yet she padded after her ghostly escorts, straining to maintain her fragile control. As she neared the twin columns, the dank fungus smell of sun-starved stone filled her nostrils. The hands gently urged her from the soft dampness of earth to the paved portico of what seemed to be a temple. The twin pillars, carved to resemble the eternal lotus blossom, loomed directly before her, a gaping black void between them. Two torches, one thrust into the wall beside each pillar, pushed at the gloom. Some immortal inhabitant of this place had inscribed the columns with passages from the Chapters of Coming Forth by Day, but Jendayi could not read all the hieroglyphs.

Her invisible escorts withdrew, and she suddenly sensed that she stood alone. A silence settled around her, an absence of sound that had about it a physical density. Of course. Each being must take his place in the silent halls of death unaccompanied; no one could reckon with the gods for the soul of another.

A doorway had been carved into the wall between the two pillars, and its edges seemed to glow as she considered the yawning emptiness beyond.

"We will not allow you to enter past us," the doorjambs whispered, their voices buzzing in her ear, "unless you say our name."

Jendayi paused, searching her memory for the myriad lessons she had been forced to learn. "Accurate Plumb-bob," she whispered, her voice fainter than air, "is your name."

A fiendish giggle rent the stillness, sending a little spasm of panic across Jendayi's chest, but she pressed her lips together and waited. They could not trick her.

"I will not allow you to enter past me," said the right lintel of the door, gleaming phosphorescent in the dark, "unless you say my name."

"Pan for Weighing Truth is your name."

More sinister laughter broke out, and Jendayi steeled herself against the sense of inadequacy that swept over her. She had learned the answers to these questions. She was prepared for death. She would not give way to fear.

"I will not allow you to enter past me," said the left lintel of the door, glowing softly, "unless you say *my* name."

"Offering of Wine is your name."

More laughter, hoarse and bitter.

"I will not allow you to pass over me," murmured the threshold, bright against the dark floor, "unless you say my name."

Jendayi did not hesitate. "Ox of Geb is your name."

"Aha! She may pass!" The diabolical voices dimmed. The doorway shone with an even brighter brilliance, and Jendayi took a step forward, then paused as the floor beneath her bare feet flashed red.

"I will not allow you to tread on me," said the floor, its voice a sleepy purr. "Unless—"

"You are the Hall of the Two Truths," Jendayi interrupted.

"Yes," the floor answered, its tone coolly disapproving, "but I do not know the names of the feet with which you will tread on me."

"Flames of Ha," Jendayi whispered, "is the name of my right foot. Wnpt of Hathor is the name of my left foot."

"You know us," the voices of the door recited in unison. "Enter then in over us."

She walked forward, compelled as much by her dislike of the fiendish guardians of the hall as by her wish to be done with what lay ahead. As she walked, the floor suddenly brightened, spreading outward in a wave of golden tiles that culminated abruptly at black walls to her right and left. Shadows canopied the distant ceiling, and a progression of thick-set columns appeared in front of her, each inscribed with the name and image of a god, each pillar glimmering with a radiance all its own. She knew the columns and images were supposed to overawe her, to intimidate her into confessing her wrongs. Jendayi refused to look up as she passed through them but walked with her eyes focused on her hands, forcing her mind to avoid the interview that lay ahead. Her hands were nothing special, merely a composite of bones, connective tissue, and flesh, yet they had served as her greatest asset in life. . . .

A sudden bright light flared before her, and she instinctively threw up her arms to shelter her face, then slowly lowered them. A cold knot formed in her stomach when she recognized the chamber into which she had wandered. She stood now in the judgment hall where the immortal ones waited, called from their duties to hear her confession.

Shadows wreathed the spacious chamber. In the wavering light cast by a series of rush torches, the images of Egypt's gods danced on the painted walls. The images did not frighten her, but every nerve leaped and shuddered when she saw the three gods. At one side of the room sat Thoth, the scribe of the gods, a reed stylus in his hand, his black eyes glowing fiercely as he stared at her. A man with the head of the ibis, he waited to transcribe the results of this interview, to record for all eternity whether Jendayi had passed into eternal life or suffered the second death. She knew she ought not fear him, for he loved virtue and hated abomination. He would record the truth.

But behind Thoth sat Ammit, the Eater of the Dead, a creature with the head of a crocodile, the foreparts of a lion, and the hindquarters of a hippopotamus. If Jendayi failed the gods' test, Ammit would devour her body so that no part of her might pass into the otherworld.

In the very center of the room, behind the golden scales, stood Anubis. The ears of his black jackal's head twitched slightly as he stared at Jendayi, and his man's hand lifted and gestured slightly as if to draw her in. In the gesturing hand he held the ankh, the symbol of eternal life; in the other he gripped a walking stick. As the Opener of Roads for the Dead, he would send Jendayi on her way to eternal joy or to everlasting damnation.

She stepped forward, her heart thumping madly, knowing they wanted her to confess her sins in their presence. Pharaoh's priests had taught her the words to say when arriving at the Hall of the Two Truths. She had also been forced to repeatedly recite the phrases that would purge an individual from all the evil he or she had committed.

Those words rose to her tongue now, tripped over her fear, then tumbled out of her mouth. "I have not acted evilly toward anyone; I have not impoverished associates. I have not done evil instead of righteousness; I do not know what is not correct. I have not committed sins. I have not set tasks at the start of each day harder than I had set previously. I have not reviled the god. I have not robbed the orphan, nor have I done what the god detests. I have not slandered a servant to his master. I have not made anyone miserable, nor have I made anyone weep. I have not killed, nor have I ordered anyone to execution. I have not made anyone suffer. I have not diminished the food offerings in the temples, nor have I damaged the bread offerings of the gods. I have not stolen the cakes of the blessed. I have not indulged in fornication. I have not increased nor diminished the measure. I have not diminished the palm. I have not encroached on fields. I have not added to the weights in the balance. I have not taken milk from a child's mouth. I have not driven herds from their fodder. I have not snared birds for the harpoons of the gods; I have not caught the fish of their lakes. I have not stopped the flow of water at its seasons; I have not built a dam against the flowing water. I have not extinguished a fire in its time. I have not failed to observe the days for offering haunches of meat. I have not kept cattle from the property of the god. I have not opposed the god at his procession."

She paused, breathless. She knew some of her statements were not entirely true, for every man and woman sinned at some time, but the gods would overlook her faults if she had recited the formula correctly. And another, more telling test was yet to come.

The ebony eyes of the jackal looked at her, then blinked.

"No evil shall befall me in this land . . . in this Hall of the Two Truths," Jendayi stammered, recalling the rest of the ritual, "because I know the names of the gods who exist in it, the followers of the Great God."

Anubis moved his head ever so slightly. She thought she saw approval in his jet black eyes. From where he sat, Thoth the scribe did not look up but scratched on his papyrus, the stylus making tiny tsk-tsk sounds in the silence of the great hall.

Behind Anubis, Ammit the Eater growled impatiently, then opened his mouth in a slow, intimidating yawn. Jendayi shivered at the sight of so many jagged crocodile teeth, at the expectant light in his savage eyes.

She stepped forward toward the golden scales. In the left pan rested the feather of Ma'at, the symbol of cosmic harmony, justice, order, and peace. Into the right pan Jendayi must place her heart.

She lifted her right hand to her left breast and was not surprised when a cold and solid substance slid into her palm. Her heart was no larger than her fist, a stone organ of veined marble, slightly pink in the red torchlight of the chamber.

Anubis dipped his head slowly, his rounded eyes intent upon her movements, and Jendayi gently lowered her heart into the empty pan of the scale. As it clattered there, Thoth and Ammit lifted their heads. The feather of Ma'at twisted slightly on its pan as if blown by a breath of wind, then the horizontal arm of the scale began to creak. As Jendayi watched in horror, the beam shuddered, tilted, then the weight of her heart sent the pan crashing to the marble floor.

Jendayi's blood slid through her veins like cold needles as a gouging, ripping mayhem of noise filled the Hall of the Two Truths. Anubis lifted his jackal head in a mournful howl. Thoth looked down at his papyrus and cawed in dismay. Ammit the Eater roared in fiendish glee. Even the floor and doorways seemed to wail in horror.

"Your heart is a stone!" A voice filled the hall, a stentorian rumbling unlike anything Jendayi had ever heard. She wanted to cover her ears, to run and hide within the darkness she had known in her mortal life. But that darkness had always been inside her. She could not hide in it now.

"The principles of Ma'at are not in you," the voice roared on, quaking the pillars of the chamber, "for your heart is dead!"

"I cannot help it," she whimpered, pulling her hands to her cheeks. A rush of cold air brushed the backs of her legs, and beneath the heaviness of her wig her scalp tingled. "The gods have not dealt fairly with me. They took my sight. They took my freedom. How can a heart live within a slave in Pharaoh's house? Within a blind harpist?"

"Foolish girl, be silent!"

She lifted her hands to cover her eyes, preferring the familiar darkness, then realized that the gesture might anger the Great God further. Gathering her slippery courage, she timidly peered through her fingers. Thoth, Ammit, and Anubis stood silent and still, awaiting orders from the unseen entity who roared from the walls.

"You have loved nothing. You are nothing. You have nothing! I leave you, foolish child, to Ammit! You shall not enter the otherworld!"

Caught in the grip of terror, Jendayi breathed in short, painful gasps as the monstrous Eater of the Dead lumbered forward. She struggled to retreat, to run, but the treacherous floor held her feet. Falling backward, she felt her thin arms hit the tiles. Then the floor imprisoned her hands, too, holding her more tightly than the graveclothes of a mummy. She threw her head back, opened her mouth to release a guttural cry of terror. . . .

And felt the tiles beneath her hands soften to the texture of linen sheets.

The familiar embrace of her own bed and the nighttime sounds of the slaves' chamber slowly made their way back into her consciousness. Jendayi lay back and drank in deep breaths, silent but for the pounding of her grateful heart.

EPHRAIM

Now it came about after these things that Joseph was told, "Behold, your father is sick." So he took his two sons Manasseh and Ephraim with him.

Genesis 48:1

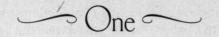

One

THE GILDED BARGE TRAVELED AS SWIFTLY AS AN ARROW down the ancient river that was the heart and soul of the Black Land. Common folk from the settlements at Hermopolis and Herakelopolis paused along the banks to admire the golden vessel; fishermen on their small papyrus skiffs raised their hands in salute as Zaphenath-paneah, the Father to Pharaoh and the Bread of Egypt, passed by.

Sitting beneath the barge's brightly emblazoned canopy, Joseph brooded over the thoughts that whirred above the rhythmic pounding of the drummer who urged the oarsmen to unity. The message from Reuben in Goshen had implored Joseph to hurry. Their father, Jacob, now called Israel, lay near death. He waited only for Joseph and his sons to arrive before he would pronounce his final blessing and depart for paradise.

The barge passed the entrance to a lagoon, black and heavy with the flood's fertile silt. On the mounded bank a pair of young boys waved and shouted as the barge flew by like a giant dragonfly, its oars shining wings in the sun. *The air is warmer here than in Thebes*, Joseph thought. *A bright light is about to leave this earth, and yet still the sun hovers overhead like a steady, unblinking eye.*

The background noise provided by the chanting of the oarsmen and the pounding of the drummer could not penetrate the silence enveloping the barge's passengers like a heavy mist. Manasseh and Ephraim sat beside Joseph under the canopy, their eyes fixed to the muddy banks sliding by, their thoughts far away. Whatever they were thinking, Joseph was certain his sons' thoughts were not at all like his.

He sighed in satisfaction as his eyes moved again to the flooded riverbanks. The seasons of desperate drought and famine had passed. For the last twelve years God Shaddai had allowed the Nile to bless the kingdom, and the Black Land had blossomed green from Goshen to the southern reaches of Nubia and beyond. God had brought Joseph's family to his door for preservation in the time of hunger, and they had remained near him, protected and secluded in Goshen, for the past seventeen years.

His eleven brothers seemed content to remain in the fertile pasturelands of the Delta where they herded flocks of sheep and goats and raised cattle. In his inner heart, Joseph wondered if they remained because they truly enjoyed living in the area or if guilt compelled them to linger so Israel could spend his remaining years in fellowship with the son they had sold into slavery. But their motivations did not matter. God Shaddai had led the sons of Israel to the Black Land, and Joseph, as part of Egypt, had been their salvation in the time of famine. They owed their lives to him, but Joseph suspected many of them would rather die than admit it. Most of his brothers despised Egypt as devoutly as they had once despised Joseph, for it was a hedonistic kingdom, one given to idolatry and wine and the continual search for happiness.

Happiness had never come easily to the sons of Israel, but they had been quick to accept help from Egypt's bountiful fields and generous granaries. And, after begging forgiveness for their harsh treatment of Joseph so long ago, they had accepted their brother and his place in the royal Egyptian society.

Joseph's mind curled fondly around thoughts of Pharaoh Amenhotep III and the Royal Wife, Queen Tiy. He had been the current Pharaoh's tutor, guardian, and counselor for nearly thirty years. He had nurtured Amenhotep through the death of his father, through numerous rivalries and crises at court, and through the threat of war. He had even advised the young king to marry for love when it became apparent that Amenhotep's heart had fixed itself upon Tiy, a commoner.

One of Joseph's many honorary titles was "Father to Pharaoh," but God Shaddai had wrought it in word and deed. Perhaps, Joseph thought, his eyes straying to the strong profiles of his own sons, he was more a father to Pharaoh than he was to the two young men who rode beside him now.

But God Shaddai had placed him in Pharaoh's life and had seen fit to keep him in the royal throne room. He had lived fifty-seven years in the shadow of El Shaddai's guiding hand, and during that time he had seen the best and worst that life could offer. And because he was as certain of his calling as he was of the sunrise to come, Joseph's heart brimmed with peace.

But what feelings stirred in his sons' hearts, he could only imagine.

———

The sun was not shining over the Delta.

The bilious black clouds over Goshen, blown from the Great Sea, hung so low that they seemed to compress the earth. Several knots of men, Jacob's sons and grandsons, huddled outside the patriarch's tent, their heads lowered as if they sought to escape the thunder to come. As Joseph and his party approached on the trail from the river, Reuben lifted his hoary head and nodded in a grim greeting.

"He waits for you and your sons," he said, moving toward Joseph in stiff dignity. "He will not rest until he has spoken to you."

Joseph forced a smile and nodded tensely, then lifted the flap of his father's tent. Joseph's sister, Dinah, and her daughter, Tizara, stood inside, their faces breaking into relieved smiles as Joseph entered. Dinah moved away toward the brazier where glowing coals held back death's coldness, but Tizara bowed herself to the ground.

"Rise, Tizara," Joseph said, momentarily annoyed by his niece's gesture of supplication. His eyes flitted over the still form on the fur-lined bed. "Are we too late?"

"Of course not, my lord." Tizara lifted her head from the floor. "He has tremendous strength, and he waits for you. I will wake him."

Moving as softly as a shadow, she reached out and placed a gentle hand on the old man's bare shoulder. Jacob's cheekbones jutted forth like tent poles under canvas. The fullness of his lips had shrunken to thin lines of gray. Yet an inherent strength remained in his face, and when the heavy eyelids lifted, the faded eyes were still compelling.

"Grandfather Israel," Tizara whispered, "your son Joseph has come."

With a visible effort, Israel gathered his strength and sat up in the bed. Squinting through the dim light in the tent, he peered in Joseph's direction. "My son?"

"Yes, Father." Leaving the dignity of his own authority behind, Joseph stepped forward, once again a dutiful son waiting to hear his loving father's wishes.

"I am glad you have come." Israel's words came slowly, as if drawn from a deep well. "Listen carefully to what I will tell you, for I am old and will soon join my father and his father."

"I am listening," Joseph answered thickly.

A look of tired sadness passed over Jacob's features. "God Shaddai was seen by me in Luz, in the land of Canaan. He blessed me and He said to me: 'Here, I will make you bear fruit and will make you many and will make you into a host of peoples. I will give this land to your seed after you as a holding for the ages!' "

He paused, gathering strength. "So now, your two sons who were born before I came to you in Egypt—they are mine. Ephraim and Manasseh, like Reuben and Simeon, let them be called mine! But any sons you beget after them, let them be yours, by their brothers' names let them be called, respecting their inheritance."

Joseph nodded silently, understanding. By his words Jacob had indicated Manasseh and Ephraim would share Jacob's inheritance equally with the other eleven sons—in effect giving Joseph the double blessing due the firstborn and immediately passing it on to Joseph's children. Reuben was Jacob's eldest son, but Joseph was the firstborn of Rachel, whom Jacob had always considered his true wife. Even though after Rachel's death Jacob had come to love Leah, his second wife, he never forgot he had intended for Rachel and Joseph to hold the favored legal position of the first wife and firstborn son.

The patriarch squinted past Joseph. "Who is with you?"

Joseph gestured behind him. "The sons God gave me here in the land of Mizraim."

The point of the old man's tongue slowly moistened his underlip. "Pray bring them over to me that I may give them my final blessing."

Immobilized by the shock of grief, Joseph could not turn, but

Manasseh and Ephraim had heard and were already moving toward their grandfather's bed.

Israel lifted trembling arms and searched for the strong shoulders of his grandsons. When his fingers had firmly grasped each young man, he pulled them to him, kissed their cheeks, and embraced them.

"Oh, Joseph, my son." His voice echoed with awe as his arms encircled Joseph's sons. "I never expected to see your face again, but God has let me see your children as well!"

Joseph stumbled forward to kneel at his father's side, and Manasseh drew back to make room. In respect for Israel's age and position, the young men bowed their foreheads to the ground while Joseph clasped his father's hand and wept. The flash of joy that had ignited in his soul at their reunion had not dimmed in seventeen years. Too soon he would again endure the wretched suffering of parting!

"Now," Israel said, his voice fragile and shaking, "bring your sons to me so I may bless them."

Standing, Joseph motioned to his sons. Ephraim had been about to approach Jacob on the left side of the bed, near Jacob's right hand, but Joseph snapped his fingers and gestured sharply, indicating that the young men should switch places. Manasseh, as the elder, should receive the greater blessing, traditionally bestowed with the right hand.

Joseph's heart swelled with fulfillment as his two handsome sons fell to their knees to receive the blessing. Israel closed his eyes, lifted his hands toward heaven, and began to speak in a voice that rang with command: "The God in whose presence my fathers walked, Abraham and Isaac, the God who has tended me from the day I was born until this day, the messenger who has redeemed me from all ill fortune, may He bless the lads!" Israel then crossed his arms. The right hand, which should have fallen upon Manasseh's head, fell instead upon Ephraim's. Apparently unaware of his mistake, the old man continued: "May my name and the name of my fathers, Abraham and Isaac, continue to be called through them! May they teem like fish to become many in the midst of the land!"

"Wait, Father," Joseph interrupted, stepping forward. A cold, thin blade of foreboding sliced into his heart, for he was watching a travesty in the making, history repeating itself. Jacob stole Esau's rightful blessing, Leah usurped Rachel's rightful place. Second-born Ephraim should not be favored above Manasseh. . . .

"Not so, Father." Joseph took hold of Jacob's right hand, intending to lift it from Ephraim's head and place it on Manasseh's. "Indeed, this one at your right side is the firstborn. Place your right hand upon his head."

"No, son." Jacob stubbornly held his hands in their position. He lifted his pale eyes, and Joseph saw the light of intent shining in them. "I know what you are thinking. The firstborn will be a people. He too will be great, yet his younger brother will be greater than he, and his seed will become a full measure of nations!" He lowered his gaze to his grandsons. "By you shall the children of Israel give blessings to one another, saying: 'May God make you like Ephraim and Manasseh!'"

As his spidery hands fell from the boys' heads, Jacob leaned back in exhaustion, but contentment shone on his face. "I am dying." He looked up at Joseph. "But God will be with you. He will return you to the land of your fathers. And I give you one portion over and above your brothers." He paused, his chest heaving. "Call the others, for I must speak with them before I depart on my final journey."

Stunned by the sound of weakness in his father's voice, Joseph darted to the tent doorway and hoarsely summoned his brothers.

———

Manasseh stood silently in the shadows with the women as his grandfather pronounced his final blessing upon his sons: Reuben, Simeon, Levi, Judah, Zebulun, Issachar, Dan, Gad, Asher, Naphtali, Joseph, and Benjamin. Many of the uncles wore puzzled looks, Manasseh noticed, as blessings and warnings poured from Jacob's tongue. Simeon and Levi seemed to wilt beneath their father's harsh words. But the blessings Israel bestowed had little to do with the men as Manasseh knew them, and he wondered if the old man's words were intended to be taken literally. Would God Shaddai bring Israel's predictions to pass? And what had Jacob intended when he gave Ephraim the blessing of the right hand, the blessing that rightfully belonged to the firstborn?

Perhaps he shouldn't allow the gesture to bother him. After all, what was a blessing? A dying man's words, a heartfelt wish for prosperity. Ordinarily the firstborn would receive double the inheritance of any other children, but he and Ephraim would share Jacob's estate evenly with their eleven uncles. So the blessing wasn't a matter of property or inheritance. Jacob had said that Ephraim would have more descendants, but what did that matter in a man's lifetime?

Yet his younger brother will be greater than he. The memory of those words burned in Manasseh's brain. He and Ephraim had always engaged in the typical battles and contests of sibling rivalry. Until recently, Manasseh had been two years smarter, two years stronger, two years taller than his brother. But now that he was twenty-five and Ephraim twenty-three, maturity had evened the ground from which they competed. In time he would be two years slower, two years weaker, two years nearer the tomb. . . .

Why should a blessing bother him? Looking around, Manasseh noticed that none of his uncles seemed terribly upset by their father's predictions. Simeon and Levi, for instance, whom Jacob had practically cursed for their fierce anger, stood in the back of the room, now composed and quietly awaiting their father's eternal passage to paradise.

From his couch, Jacob rallied his strength again as the women helped him sit up. "I am about to be gathered to my kinspeople." His breath rattled in his throat, and his eyes closed as if he did not have the energy even to look around the room. "Bury me by my fathers in the cave that is in the field of Machpelah, which faces Mamre in the land of Canaan. There they buried Abraham and Sarah; there they buried Isaac and Rebekah; there I buried Leah."

He murmured a few other comments in a voice too low for Manasseh to hear, then Jacob lay back, curled upon the bed, and breathed his last.

A pain squeezed Manasseh's heart as his weeping father threw himself upon the patriarch's body and kissed Israel's sunken cheeks.

———

Jokim, son of Shelah, son of Judah, sat outside by the fire, joining a circle of weeping men. Though none of them were so foolish to think that a man one hundred forty-seven years old could live forever, Jacob had always been among them, the one constant in a sea of change and trouble. Jacob was the one who decreed that they should always live in tents so they could move when and wherever God Shaddai commanded. Jacob heard the voice of God Almighty in the night. Joseph would be the patriarch now, for he had inherited the blessing of the firstborn, but Joseph seemed as distant as a mountain on the horizon. He kept himself in the city of Thebes. He would forever be drawn away by his duty to Pharaoh.

Jokim looked over at his father and grandfather. Pain had carved merciless lines on Judah's face; his heavy white beard was streaked with tears. Jokim's father, Shelah, drew his lips in thoughtfully and stared at the fire as though the mysteries of Jacob's life flickered there. Silence, thick as wool, wrapped itself around the mourners as each man strove to imagine the days to come without Jacob's pervading influence.

Uneasy in the somber heaviness of the group, Jokim slipped away from the old men and wandered among the tents. The women had no time to mourn. Their hands were busy preparing food and making beds for the guests who would soon descend upon them. The Canaanites traditionally mourned for thirty days: three days of tears, followed by seven days of lamentation, followed by twenty days of receiving those who came to pay their respects and offer condolences. Jacob of Hebron had been well known and respected in the land of Canaan. Kings and princes from the entire civilized world would soon begin to wend their way to Goshen in order to acknowledge the great man who had begotten an even greater son.

Jokim stopped suddenly at the sight of Manasseh and Ephraim near the animal pens. The two brothers, both of whom were about his age, Jokim supposed, were strikingly handsome, even though they dressed and painted themselves in the manner of the Egyptians. They wore fine Egyptian wigs, neatly trimmed and anointed with oil, and the white of their kilts dazzled against the somber hues of Jacob's tents and the Hebrews' dyed tunics. Manasseh, the elder, had a lean and narrow face. His smooth olive skin stretched over high cheekbones, and his carbon black eyes seemed to pierce whomever they studied. A healthy beard had begun to shadow his chin and upper lip, and Jokim supposed that the Egyptians had not had time to shave before boarding the barge that brought them to Goshen.

Manasseh's brow was furrowed in thought, his hands tight upon the rail of a pen that confined a group of lambs too young to swim through the encroaching floods.

"Hello, cousins," Jokim said, approaching cautiously. He did not know his Egyptian relatives well, for Joseph and his sons spent very little time in Goshen. Manasseh and Ephraim rarely accompanied the vizier on the infrequent occasions when he did visit, and Jokim could not recall speaking to his kinsmen more than once or twice in his lifetime. But here they were, of the same age, and apparently caught up in the same flood of confusing emotion that faced him.

Manasseh inclined his head in a formal gesture, but Ephraim flashed Jokim a heartfelt smile. "Hello! Jokim, isn't it? You are Shelah's son?"

"Yes." Jokim tried not to let his relief show in his face. Joseph's sons were nearly Egyptian royalty. He had heard that they often dined with Pharaoh's children. Joseph's wife, their mother, had been a beautiful Egyptian noblewoman, so Ephraim and Manasseh had inherited attractiveness and position from both parents.

Ephraim, Jokim decided, must have received his mother's looks. His face was not as narrow as Manasseh's, his eyes not nearly as direct or piercing. At his neck a black curl escaped from under the straight tresses of the Egyptian wig, and his smile was wide, quick, and bright, immediately putting Jokim at ease.

"Shall we sit?" Ephraim pointed to the rail fence. "We would like to hear what has happened in the last few days. Unfortunately, in Thebes we do not often hear reports from the Delta."

Jokim smiled, realizing that Ephraim was being tactful. Most people in Thebes cared nothing about what happened to the Hebrews who dwelled at Goshen.

He shrugged and perched upon the top rail of the pen. "The

weakness came upon Israel gradually. He grew weaker and more feeble, and two nights ago he told the women to send for Joseph. My grandfather Judah saw it coming—for the past week he has said that the end was drawing near."

Jokim tilted his head slightly and studied Ephraim's expressive face. "Can you tell me what went on inside Israel's tent? My mother said I should not go in."

Ephraim shot a quick glance at his older brother, who muttered something in the Egyptian tongue and walked away, crossing his arms.

"Israel bestowed his blessings." Ephraim lowered his voice as his brother left them alone. His left eyebrow rose a fraction. "He included me and Manasseh among his sons. We did not expect that, of course, but the most unusual thing—" He paused, as if weighing the wisdom of his words.

"What?" Jokim leaned closer. "What unusual thing happened?"

"It probably won't mean much to you," Ephraim said, nervously moistening his well-formed lips, "but he placed his right hand on *my* head, even though I knelt at his *left* side. My father sought to correct Israel's mistake, but Grandfather insisted that he meant to do it." A hint of boastfulness crept into his voice as he finished. "Israel said I will be mightier than my brother."

"Truly?" Jokim leaned backward, surprised both by the news and by Ephraim's casual delivery of it.

"Yes." Ephraim lifted both brows as his handsome face split into a wide grin. "Oh, the drubbing I can give Manasseh now! He always held it up to me—his being the elder, of course. But he'll never say anything again, because I can answer him with Israel's own words. I am to be a mightier man, and from me will come a tremendous nation!"

Jokim stared in amused surprise. The boast would have sounded impertinent coming from anyone else, but Ephraim uttered it with such bold indifference that it did not seem untoward or tactless.

"What do you think Israel meant?" Jokim asked.

"I don't know," Ephraim answered, slipping from his perch on the rail. "But I will have a merry time with Grandfather's words while I can. It is not every day that I manage to better my elder brother."

～ Two ～

WITH HER FELLOW MUSICIANS IN THE QUEEN'S CHAM-
ber, Jendayi lowered her head at the conclusion of the song and
waited for a cue from Akil. The queen's companions, whoever
they were, fell silent during the lull in music, and Jendayi wondered why they did not speak. The silence in the room was uncomfortable, an almost palpable reminder that the enslaved musicians were people, too. They needed time to think, to regroup,
to rest strained fingers and breathless lungs.

Akil snapped his fingers three times, and Jendayi pulled her
harp closer, ready to play again. In work she found a mindless
solidity that helped disguise the deep heartache of loneliness
that colored her days and nights. Ever since she had been abandoned as a small child, she had grown accustomed to pain and
loneliness walking with her in the dark.

The music began and Jendayi's fingers plucked the strings of
her instrument. She faced a lightless future, a life of nightmares
and boredom and slavery. Her one joy was her music, but it was
a bittersweet pleasure, for the love and joy embodied in the notes
she played only reminded her that she would never experience
these things for herself.

She attacked the harp with nimble fingers and a burning
heart, giving voice to the agony of her despair. The women in the
queen's company would undoubtedly listen to her music . . . and
think it beautiful.

Queen Tiy, Mother of Upper and Lower Egypt, Follower of Horus, Guide of the Ruler, and Favorite Lady, shifted in her gilded
chair, bored by the music and the gymnastics of her pet dwarf. The
ladies of her court, all of whom had dressed and painted themselves in an obvious effort to outshine the others, laughed and gig-

gled uproariously at the slave's antics, but Tiy pressed her lips together and smothered a yawn. She allowed herself one hour with her ladies merely to fulfill the role the royal court expected of her. In reality she had no patience with others of her own sex. Only Sitamun, her eldest daughter, held any fascination for her, and Tiy suspected she tolerated Sitamun only through maternal affection.

"Hail to you, my lady!" A courier at the double doors of her throne room prostrated himself, his broad hands slapping the tile before him. Tiy looked up. Breathless from running, the man's chest heaved like the flank of an exhausted stallion. Tiy quirked an eyebrow upward and signaled the musicians to be silent. Such haste was unusual in Pharaoh's orderly household.

"Rise and tell me what news you bring." She extended her hand in pardon for his intrusion. Her ladies twittered like birds as the elegant slave approached, and Tiy rolled her eyes, annoyed with their adolescent yearnings. Life in the palace had spoiled them. Her, it had hardened.

The messenger bowed again, about to lower himself to the tile and repeat his salutation.

"Remain on your feet and speak," Tiy said, resting her elbows on the arms of her chair. She steepled her fingers and gave the man a properly gracious smile. "What news brings you breathless into my court?"

"The Vizier of Upper and Lower Egypt, the great and noble Zaphenath-paneah, stands outside your door," the messenger said, a blush burning his cheek as she stared through him.

"Zaphenath-paneah is here? He wishes to see me?" She lowered her hands as a curious, tingling shock ran up her spine. The vizier rarely sought her company, but he spent every morning with Pharaoh, regularly crossing the river to Amenhotep's new palace at Malkata.

Stricken dumb in her presence, the messenger wagged his head.

Tiy glanced around. She must give the vizier her prompt attention, but she would not receive him before these foolish, simpering women, nor would she subject him to the ridiculous antics of the dwarf.

"I will speak to Zaphenath-paneah in my garden," she said, rising from her chair. "Escort him to me at once."

Leaving her retinue to their vapid entertainment, she slipped out a hidden door.

————

After returning from Goshen with Israel's body, Joseph had charged Ephraim with the care of Jacob's remains while he proceeded directly to the king's palace at Thebes. He knew Pharaoh would not be in residence at the Theban palace, but Tiy would be holding court. Joseph did not feel up to the task of wading through the king's harem in order to bare his heart and speak of Jacob.

Though women abounded in the king's life, no one doubted that both his heart and his trust safely resided in the formidable Queen Tiy. Amenhotep had built Tiy a vast and imposing palace at Malkata, but she preferred to spend most of her time in Thebes, receiving courtiers and overseeing the care of her royal children. They had a peculiar marriage, Joseph thought, following a guard through the gleaming marble halls of the queen's chambers. The royal pair seemed bound as much by distrust as by affection.

The messenger stopped suddenly at a passageway opening to a roofed and columned portico. Nodding his thanks, Joseph stepped through the opening. Tall columns, painted in stripes of green and gold and mounted by lotus blossom capitals, dwarfed his own substantial height. High above his head, the ceiling had been painted a deep blue and emblazoned with the white gold images of stars. Polished alabaster tiles under his feet reflected his image. A landscaped garden and quiet reflecting pool lay beyond the portico. But he did not see the queen.

Joseph locked his hands behind his back and advanced slowly, not wanting to surprise Pharaoh's Great Wife if he had caught her unprepared. The queen tended to be an overwhelming presence, strong and forceful, intense and intelligent. Joseph supposed that some of her sharpness sprang from her acute awareness of her lowly pedigree. As the daughter of Yuia, a provincial priest of Akhmin, and Tuia, a servant of the Queen Mother, Tiy had been married to Amenhotep when they were both little more than children. Though Tiy probably felt she had to prove her worthiness and ability to reign, Joseph could not help but believe that the hard edge she brought to an inbred dynasty would improve the royal lineage.

"Zaphenath-paneah." Tiy's piercing voice cut through his musings, and he whirled to face her. Apparently pleased that she had surprised him, she smiled and folded her hands at her waist as she stepped out from behind one of the pillars. "To what do I owe this pleasure?"

He politely lowered himself to the ground and sighed in relief when she told him to stand.

"I have a most urgent request," he said, his eyes meeting hers as he stood. A small woman, barely five feet tall, her face was marked with a pointed chin, deep-set eyes, and a firm mouth. He would not have called her beautiful, but her complexion and clothing were immaculate, her headdress regal and imposing. No royal wife in his memory had appeared more conscious of her august status.

"Your request?" She tilted her head slightly. A small smile shadowed the corners of her mouth, and her voice softened. "You know I would do anything in my power to please you."

He heard something in her voice—an intimation of desire—and he frowned, unsettled by the thought. Over the years, especially since the death of his wife, a host of bored, silly women had offered themselves to him for purposes of matrimony or simple pleasure, but Joseph had managed to elude them and keep his mind on his responsibilities. Ordinarily he would resort to an artful cat-and-mouse game that dissuaded attention-starved women, but today the matter of his father's burial pressed upon his mind.

"If you would please me," he said, bowing slightly as if he'd been honored by her attention, "know that my father, Israel, has departed this life and gone to his fathers. I have charged my physicians to embalm him, and we have entered into our days of mourning. But if I have found favor in your eyes, please speak to Pharaoh for me. As he lay dying, my father bade me swear that I would bury him in the site that he dug for himself in the land of Canaan. So if you would be kind, beg Pharaoh to let me go to Canaan, bury my father, and return."

A tremor touched her smooth, marblelike lips. "Your father? He has died?"

"Yes, my Queen."

"I am so sorry to hear it." An uncertainty crept into her expression. "If you have a difficult journey, you may be gone for some time."

"A small caravan can make the journey in seventeen days. A larger party will be slower, but I do not think we will be gone more than two months."

Leaning her head back slightly, she gazed fully into his eyes. "What if some harm should befall you? Pharaoh cannot risk losing you, Zaphenath-paneah. You are more than a father to him."

Joseph bowed his head. "Once the days of mourning are passed and my father is buried, I know that God Shaddai will hasten my return. My lifelong duty is to serve Pharaoh—and you, his queen."

Satisfaction pursed her mouth. "Then I will speak to Pharaoh for you, and you may go bury your father. We will see that your journey is well made. With you shall go all of Pharaoh's chief servants, the elders of his household, and the governors of Egypt. The world will see, and know, that one of Egypt's mighty ones has passed into immortality. And thus his name will live forever, as will he."

Joseph bowed from the waist. "I thank you, my Queen."

An inexplicable look of withdrawal had come over her face when he looked up at her again. Strong emotion flickered in the deep wells of her eyes. "I will mourn with you," she whispered, lifting a hand as if she would touch his shoulder. But she did not, and after a moment she turned, the wind stirring her wig as she abruptly moved away.

Tiy immediately ordered a barge to carry her across the river to the complex at Malkata. The name meant "Place Where Things Are Picked Up," and Tiy was not certain if Pharaoh had meant to refer to the clean look of the place or to his habit of acquiring women for his harem.

From the deck of the barge, Tiy could see the pink granite palace rising from its exalted strip of earth. Before Malkata spread the river, now swollen to its height. Behind Pharaoh's house rose the western mountains, which concealed the burial places of ancient kings. The barge turned into the T-shaped harbor, dredged especially for Malkata, and to her right Tiy caught a glimpse of the lake that Amenhotep had ordered his architects to dig in her honor. On festival days the waters of her lake rocked with barges and boats dedicated to the sun god, Aten.

A narrow canal, camouflaged by thickly growing reeds, broke off from the lake and skirted the entire complex before doubling back to the Nile. Tiy hated the canal, convinced that it served as an ideal nesting place for snakes and rodents, but many of Pharaoh's top officials and couriers used it as a secret entrance and took pride in knowing of its existence.

The late afternoon sun streaked the water crimson, and Tiy fretted at the railing, eager to be off the ship. When at last the gangplank was lowered, she hurried past the guards and entered through the pink-tinted columns of the entrance gates. The buildings around her, built of sun-dried bricks and lavishly painted with scenes of life along the Nile, shimmered with the rich colors of life.

Malkata was not merely one palace, but several, a sprawling combination of compounds, each with its own administrative chambers, houses for court officials, reception halls, chapels, and lavish apartments. Homes for the most deserving and skilled artisans had also been erected on the site, but the average people of Egypt had been forbidden to settle on this western shore of the Nile.

She hurried along the pathway, ignoring the fawning slaves and officials who fell to the ground like paddle dolls at her approach. The palace built for her son, Crown Prince Neferkheprure' Wa'enre', rose at her left hand, but the complex to which she hurried was far larger and more elaborate than the prince's. It was home to the king's vast harem.

Pressing her lips together as she walked, Tiy remembered a dispatch she had found from Amenhotep to his provincial governors. "Send beautiful women," the king had boldly instructed. "But none with shrill voices. Then the king your lord will say to you, 'That is good.'"

Her husband preferred love to war. During his reign he had married additional Egyptian women as well as two princesses from the Mitanni kingdom, two from Syria, two from Babylon, and one from the kingdom of Arzawa in Anatolia. One of the Mitanni princesses arrived with three hundred seventeen ladies-in-waiting, many of whom Amenhotep was pleased to add to his harem.

Slaves and guards scattered like chaff as Tiy swept grandly into the House of the Women. She found her husband seated in the reception hall, a trio of dancing girls before him, an all-female orchestra behind him, and a pair of concubines at his side. For an instant her temper flared as it had in the early days when it became apparent that Amenhotep preferred the company of many women to that of one, then she carefully reeled in her anger and hid it away. She forced her lips to part in a carefully curved smile as his gaze met hers.

"Life, prosperity, and health to you, my lord!" she murmured, prostrating herself on the floor as did every mortal who entered into the king's presence.

"Tiy?" Amenhotep's voice cracked in surprise. "I didn't expect to see you today."

Obviously not. She lifted her head and boldly met his eyes. "I have had a visit from your vizier, Zaphenath-paneah. His father has died and he begs your permission to journey to the land of Canaan to bury the one we knew as Israel."

"My vizier's father is dead?" With the back of his hand Amenhotep absently pushed one of the concubines away, then straightened himself in his chair. "The old man? I thought he would never die! None of Egypt's pharaohs ever lived so long."

"Zaphenath-paneah says his god loved the aged man," Tiy answered, lowering her eyes in false humility. "The god's blessing rested upon him."

"As it has rested upon Egypt since my vizier's arrival." Amenhotep's jaw clenched, his eyes narrowed slightly, and Tiy knew what he was thinking. As a child, when Zaphenath-paneah had been Pharaoh's tutor, Amenhotep had dutifully given lip service to the vizier's invisible and Almighty God. But as he grew older and fell under the influence of the priests of Amon-Re, Pharaoh decided that Zaphenath-paneah's ideas were too restricting, too conservative. And so he had widened his allegiance to a host of gods, placating both his people and his priests, and Egypt had not seemed to suffer for it. Indeed, after the famine the land had grown greener than before, and due to the vizier's ingenuity, all the land in Egypt now belonged either to Pharaoh or to the priests. Whether this rich blessing had fallen upon the Black Land because of her Pharaoh or her vizier, Amenhotep could not say, but he suspected the latter, for his father, Tuthmosis IV, had filled the sacred annals with words of praise for Zaphenath-paneah and the Spirit of God that rested upon him.

Amenhotep might be vain and hedonistic, but he was not a fool. He would not risk the future.

"What did you tell Zaphenath-paneah?" Pharaoh asked in a lower, huskier tone.

Tiy stood to her feet and clasped her hands. "I knew you would not want him to be unhappy, my King. So I told him to go and bury his father in Canaan. He had sworn to do it."

"You sent him away?" Pharaoh gripped the arms of his chair. "Tiy, what are you thinking? What if he does not return?"

"He will, my lord." Tiy smiled in the calm strength of knowledge. "I am sending the best of Egypt with him—the elders of your household, the priests, a royal escort, a fleet of chariots, and warriors. Such a show of support will bind his heart to yours and will guarantee his safe return."

Pharaoh sank back in his chair, tenting his hands, then cast her a glance of pure admiration. "My clever Tiy," he murmured, his eyes lazily appraising her. "Beautiful as well as scheming. The gods were good when they sent you to me." Masculine interest radiated from the dark depths of his eyes as he leaned forward and extended his hand to his queen. "Will you eat dinner with me?"

Tiy felt the corner of her mouth lift in a wry half-smile. Ignoring the dancing girls, the musicians, and the concubines, she met his hungry eyes and defied them. "My king, I must see to the particulars of our vizier's journey." She lifted one shoulder in an elegant shrug. "If you would keep Zaphenath-paneah in Egypt, you must allow me to refuse your kind invitation."

"Of course." He abruptly dropped his hand. "Go, then, and see to it that our vizier is happy. We must not risk his departure from the Double Kingdom."

"Fret not, my husband, I will not allow him to leave." She turned to go but added a thought under her breath as she slipped through the doorway of the royal chamber: "I would not risk his departure for anything."

~ Three ~

ONCE THE PATRIARCH'S BODY HAD BEEN WASHED AND loaded onto the barge for transport to Thebes, a heavy mournful mood settled upon the Hebrews around the encampment's central fire. They sat and wept for nearly a full day without speaking, some rocking back and forth, some kneeling upon their cloaks, staining the fabric with their tears.

Reluctant to confront the superior smirk Ephraim had worn since Israel's final blessing, Manasseh did not return to Thebes with his father and brother but chose to remain in Goshen until the days of mourning had passed. Feeling very much like an outsider, he hunched around the fire with the others, his arms drawn close to his chest, his eyes downcast. He had not spent much time with his grandfather, for the demands of Egypt had prevented Joseph and his sons from regularly visiting Goshen, but Manasseh held a deep and abiding respect for the man his father had openly adored.

As the sun sank toward a livid purple cloud bank piled deep on the western horizon, Reuben stood, wiped his tears, and folded his hands. Facing the circle of men, he let out a long, audible breath, then began to recite the story of two babies who jostled each other inside their mother's womb. "God Shaddai told Rebekah that two nations would be divided from her belly," Reuben said, depth and authority in his voice. "One tribe would be mightier than the other, the elder servant to the younger. And when her days were fulfilled for bearing, twins were in her body. The first one came out ruddy, like a hairy mantle all over, so they called his name Esau, Rough One. And after that his brother came out, his hand grasping Esau's heel, and so they called him Jacob, Heel-holder."

Reuben stood silently for a moment, then sat down. In the silence that followed, Judah rose stiffly to his feet. Leaning heavily on his staff, he told the story of how Esau sold his birthright to Jacob for a serving of boiled red stew. "Therefore they called him Edom, Red One," he said, raking wisps of windblown hair from his forehead, "and Jacob gave Esau bread and boiled lentils, and he ate and drank and arose and went off. Thus did Esau despise the right of the firstborn."

When Judah had finished, Dan rose to speak of the time Isaac and his sons had moved to dwell in Gerar in obedience to the voice of God Shaddai. "And God said to Isaac our grandfather, 'Do not go down to Egypt; continue to dwell in the land that I tell you of, sojourn in this land, and I will be with you and will give you blessing,'" Dan recited, his dreamy eyes sweeping over the men in the circle. "And God said, 'I will make your seed many, like the stars of the heavens, and to your seed I will give all these lands. All the nations of the earth shall enjoy blessing through your seed, in consequence of Abraham's hearkening to my voice and keeping my charge: my commandments, my laws, and my instructions.'"

After Dan had spoken, Simeon stood to tell of how Rebekah and Jacob had deceived Isaac and stolen the firstborn's blessing from Esau. His thunderous voice boomed over the gathering, rueful laughter punctuating his words. Jacob had been a wily deceiver in his youth, but Esau had already demonstrated his contempt for his father's blessing. If Esau did not receive the firstborn's birthright, Simeon's uplifted eyebrow seemed to say, he got what he deserved.

On and on the stories continued, acknowledging Israel's vices even as they celebrated his virtues, focusing Jacob's image in their memories, reviving the old man's youth, his yearnings, his yieldedness to God's commands. Manasseh sat like a statue through it all, surprised again and again by his grandfather's unpredictable encounters with El Shaddai. He had never heard such stories! He had grown up with the tales of Egyptian gods and goddesses, legends of Horus and Isis and Osiris and the primeval waters from which the world was supposedly formed, but he had never felt any personal connection to such outlandish accounts. But now his uncles revealed his own history, unmasking the rivalry between Jacob and Esau and explaining the trickery that brought Leah, the elder daughter, into Jacob's tent though he loved Rachel, the younger.

"In a similar way our father Jacob displeased Joseph before he died," Benjamin told the gathering. "Israel crossed his arms so that Ephraim and not Manasseh received the blessing of the right hand—"

Manasseh colored fiercely when he heard his own name, and Benjamin stopped abruptly, apparently recalling that Manasseh had not returned to Thebes.

"Go on, Uncle, it is all right," Manasseh murmured, the misery of the previous day still haunting him. "I'm not sure what Grandfather meant by his gesture."

"He meant nothing." Simeon leaned forward from across the circle and gave Manasseh an almost playful smile. "So what if Ephraim has more children than you? Rejoice! You will have fewer mouths to feed in your lifetime and less worry when you are dead. Count it a blessing, my nephew!"

Simeon's words brought a measure of comfort, and Manasseh managed a tentative smile as he listened to the other stories that poured from the lips of Israel's sons. He learned of Jacob's frantic flight from Hebron after the artifice that cost Esau his father's blessing, of the death of Rachel at Bethlehem, of Jacob's stunned amazement when his sons told him that Joseph lived as vizier of all Egypt.

Reuben stood up, his deep voice rumbling like thunder as he began to recite yet another oral history: "And El Shaddai said to Abram, 'Go you forth from your land, from your kindred, from your father's house, to the land that I will let you see. I will make a great nation of you and will give you blessing and will make your name great. I will bless those who bless you; he who curses you, I will curse. And all the families of the earth will find blessing through you.' "

Reuben paused, his eyes raking the gathering. "And just as El Shaddai spoke to Abram, later called Abraham, thus did He speak to Israel in the night: 'I am the God of Abraham, your father, and the God of Isaac,' He said. 'The land on which you lie I give to you and to your seed. Your seed will be like the dust of the earth; you will burst forth to the sea, to the east, to the north, to the Negev. All the clans of the soil will find blessing through you and through your seed! Know this, I am with you. I will watch over you wherever you go and will bring you back to this soil; indeed, I will not leave you until I have done what I have spoken to you.'

"After this our father woke from his sleep and said, 'Why, God is in this place and I did not know it! This is none other than a house of God, and that is the gate of heaven!' And so our father Jacob started early in the morning, and he took the stone that he had set at his head and set it up as a standing pillar and poured oil on top of it. And he called the name of the place Bet-El, meaning 'House of God,' but Luz was the name of the city in former times."

"The House of God?" Manasseh murmured to Jokim. "Where is Bet-El?"

Jokim shrugged. "I've never been there. I was born in Hebron, and we moved from that region to this one when I was young."

"Don't you want to visit that place?" Manasseh asked, nudging his cousin. "And Shechem, where our uncles slaughtered the city? And the site where Rachel is buried? How can you hear stories of these places and not want to see them for yourself?"

Jokim gave him a sidelong glance of disbelief. "I've heard stories of Sheol, too, and I don't want to go there! Would seeing these places help me be a better shepherd, or make my goats give more milk? No. What makes one desert or stretch of pasture different from another?"

"Apparently God has made them different." Manasseh spread his hands as he fumbled for words. "That other land is the one God promised to our people! Canaan is where Jacob wanted to be buried! If one land is like another, why did Israel make my father swear to bury him in Canaan?"

For that Jokim had no answer.

Miles away, in Thebes, Ephraim stood in silent respect as the corpse of his grandfather entered through the gates into the small temple within the vizier's villa. Pharaoh's own physician-priests had been dispatched to tend to the patriarch of the Hebrews.

While Manasseh lingered in Goshen with Jacob's sons, Ephraim agreed to help Ani, the steward of his father's estate, oversee preparations for the vast funereal procession that would return Israel to the land he loved. As busy as a fly with his unexpected responsibilities, Ani assigned Ephraim to the job of overseeing the crucially important embalming process.

Ephraim knew that the people of the Nile had elevated physical preservation to an art form. The Egyptians believed that when a person died, his *ba* and *ka*, elements of the soul, escaped from the body and lived on in the tomb. The *ba* watched over the living family and friends of the deceased, while the *ka* traveled back and forth from the body to the otherworld. In order to enjoy true immortality, the *ba* and *ka* had to be able to recognize the body throughout the ages or they could not return to it.

Though Ephraim did not agree with these elements of Egyptian religion, if Jacob's body were to withstand the long days of mourning and a tedious journey into Canaan, it would have to be embalmed. And so Ephraim followed the corpse, slipping into a dark corner of the small temple to watch the priests of Amon-Re commence their work.

Israel's body, which had been enfolded in sheets of linen, was stretched out on a slanted embalming bed within the temple, then carefully and reverently unwrapped. After positioning and cleansing the body, the priests allowed the water and fluids to drain away through holes in the marble slab. Ephraim watched in fascinated interest as the physicians then used a chisel to break through a resistant bone at the back of the nostrils. With an iron probe, they extracted several cupfuls of a semiliquid gray substance. The brain material, considered worthless in this life and the one to come, was thrown away.

Over the course of the next several days, Ephraim rose with the sun, breakfasted with Ani, then joined the physicians in the little temple to observe the continuing process of embalming. After removing the brain, the physicians made a slit in the left side of the body just above the joining of leg to trunk. Working from this cut, the embalmers removed the liver, lungs, stomach, and intestines. After carefully cleansing these organs, the priests rolled them in powdered natron, a grainy, salty substance gleaned from deposits in the Nile, then placed the organs in separate canopic jars for the journey to the tomb. The heart, the seat of the emotions, was removed, sprinkled in natron, and replaced inside the body.

The physicians carefully cleansed the interior and exterior of the body with scented oils, then packed the body cavity with linen and bundles of natron. As they neared the completion of this first phase of the long process, the physicians chanted prayers and began to stitch across the gaping cut.

As he watched the priests work on Israel's remains, Ephraim marveled that the Egyptians displayed such reverence for this father of the Hebrews. A decree from Pharaoh himself urged his people to observe the passing of the vizier's father, and for the past thirty days the citizens of Thebes had mourned Israel as thoroughly as had the Hebrews in Goshen. Many nobles of the court sprinkled ashes upon their wigs each morning and beat their breasts outside their houses in public acknowledgment of the debt they owed Israel, progenitor of their beloved Zaphenath-paneah, the Bread of Life and Father to Pharaoh. Though twelve years had passed since the great famine, most Egyptians remembered that the vizier—and his God—had brought them alive through the Years Without the Flooding of Hep-Ur, the ancient river.

Why shouldn't the Egyptians and Hebrews work together? Ephraim wondered. He and Manasseh, the offspring of a son of Israel and a daughter of the Black Land, proved that such a mingling could bring honor to both peoples. Ephraim and his brother had been reared among the glories of Egypt, enjoying the fullness of its splendor and access to its vast treasures of knowledge. They spoke both the Egyptian and the Canaanite languages and could write the hieroglyphs as easily as the twenty-two consonants of the Hebrew tongue.

And Israel blessed us equally with his other sons, Ephraim thought, studying the wizened face in repose on the embalmer's slab. *And he blessed me with greater favor, with his right hand. . . .*

Finished with the suturing of the body, the embalmers stepped back. Chanting prayers to the gods of the underworld, they lifted painted bowls and began to ladle powdered natron over the corpse. They continued ladling and chanting until the powder lay heaped over the body, enveloping it completely.

Ephraim breathed a sigh of relief. The natron would cover the body for forty days, desiccating it completely. Until the end of the drying time, Ephraim's duties were certain to be less gruesome.

———

The sun had already begun to melt behind the walls of the villa when Ephraim left the temple. The guards at the gate of the villa stirred in a flurry of activity, and he shaded his eyes to see through the bright glare of the setting sun. A pair of camels stood there, joined by lead ropes to a straggling pack of donkeys. A small group of men, clothed in the linen garments of the desert-dwelling Bedouins, had dismounted to speak to the guards. Ephraim turned away, satisfied that the visitors were traders from the north, seeking to curry the vizier's favor before the day's business was done.

"Ephraim!" Manasseh's voice rang out across the courtyard, and Ephraim turned in surprise. He had not heard from his brother since they parted in Goshen, but now Manasseh ran toward him, his head turbaned in linen, his slender body disguised by a long tunic. Manasseh's eyes snapped in greeting. "I have such news!"

"What a surprise!" Ephraim greeted his brother with a quick slap on the back, then stepped back and rested his hands on his hips. "What can possibly be happening in Goshen?" He flashed his brother a teasing smile. "A new lamb, perhaps? Or has Reuben found a way to make his cattle grow as fat as Benjamin's?"

Manasseh ignored the sarcasm. "Sleepy Goshen will never be the same, my brother." He slipped an arm around Ephraim as they walked toward the villa's wide portico. "The entire world comes to mourn Israel. Kings from Jericho, Kadesh Barnea, and Gaza. I never dreamed our grandfather was so well known! Though Father often referred to him as a prince, it has been so many years since Israel dwelled in Canaan that I did not think the kings of the world would remember him. But within a week of your departure, the horizon filled with caravans, men who had traveled many miles to reach our settlement. They came; they offered words of comfort; they told stories of Jacob that stirred my blood like nothing I have ever felt before!"

"*Our* settlement?" Ephraim lifted a mocking brow. "Do you live in Goshen now? You speak as if you are one of them." He stepped back and eyed Manasseh up and down. "You even *look* like you are one of them."

"How can you think you are not?" Manasseh flushed with sudden anger. "The Hebrews are our people. If God had not called our father out from among them—"

"They would all be dead," Ephraim interrupted. "And you and I would not exist. But we do. And we are not only Hebrews, we are Egyptians, too. This is the will of God, and Israel confirmed it before he died. God himself married the sons of Israel to Egypt, and we are the first generation offspring."

Manasseh's dark eyes narrowed and hardened, but Ephraim did not give him a chance to speak. "Do not let tales of desert barbarians turn your head, brother, for such stories are not your only heritage," he said, grasping Manasseh's elbow. "Your past lies in the glory of the pharaohs, the splendor of Egypt, the strength of the Nile. If God can bless a straggling pack of nomadic shepherds, how much more can He bless those who have the resources of the world's mightiest empire at their disposal?"

Manasseh did not answer but glared at Ephraim in irritated silence. Shrugging, Ephraim dropped his brother's elbow and walked away, a little surprised at his own temerity. Never before in his life had he spoken so forcefully to his older brother, and never before had Manasseh let him get away with it.

He tucked his hands into the belt at his kilt and began to whistle. Perhaps he was the mightier man after all.

———

Stunned by Ephraim's train of thought, Manasseh shook his head as his brother walked away. Only the sweet grace of understanding had enabled him to hold his tongue, for he had reminded himself that Ephraim mourned *here*, in the heart of Egypt. He had not spent the last month sitting by the fires of the Hebrews, listening to the stories of Abraham and Isaac, Sarah and Rebekah.

And what did Ephraim know of his heritage? Nothing! For the first time in his life, Manasseh felt as though he fully understood the legacy of his ancestors. The knowledge that he and his people had been chosen to bless the world had left Manasseh slightly shaken and more than a little awed.

Setting thoughts of Ephraim aside, he bounded up the portico steps two at a time and wandered through the vestibule. The front hall where his father routinely received guests and suppliants stood empty, but the room had been deserted only recently, for the fragrance of incense still hung heavy in the air. Manasseh moved easily through the halls toward his father's private chambers. A pair of guards stood outside a wooden door, confirming his expectations.

"Is my father inside?"

One of the guards answered with an impersonal nod.

"May I enter?"

Another stiff nod. Tarik, the captain of the vizier's bodyguard, encouraged his warriors to be stern of demeanor and limited in speech.

Manasseh pressed the door open and stepped into the room. Like a demiking in his own personal realm, his father sat in an elevated chair next to a tray loaded with papyrus scrolls. Ani, forever the dutiful steward, hovered near like a watchful guardian.

Ani's beaked face spread into a grin at Manasseh's approach. "Master! Look who has returned from the north!"

Suddenly self-conscious, Manasseh lowered himself to his knees, then prostrated himself on the floor. After a month of the Hebrews' easygoing familiarity, the gesture felt awkward and stiff.

"Rise, Manasseh." He lifted his head as his father smiled. "It is good to see you, son." One of the parchments upon the tray suddenly curled and rolled onto the floor, and Joseph looked away and frowned as Ani scurried after it.

"I trust your uncles took good care of you?" Joseph's handsome face, lined now with weariness and the passing of many years, seemed to gentle as he turned back to his elder son. "How are they faring in the north?"

"They mourn, Father," Manasseh said, straightening. He shifted uneasily and felt his cheeks burn at the honest welcome in his father's eyes. Ani, who had retrieved the parchment, stopped and affectionately clasped one of Manasseh's hands.

Manasseh gave the old man a grateful smile, then turned again to his father. "They mourn, but they are comforted by a stream of visitors from Canaan and beyond. A band of Esau's people arrived just before I left."

"Edomites?" Joseph's brows shot up in surprise. "Imagine that. I suppose Esau's sons will forgive the past for an occasion such as this." He glanced again at the parchments on the tray. "So," he said, clearly distracted, "tell me what you have done during your time with your uncles."

"Father, I have learned so much!" Manasseh struggled to curb his excitement. "The stories they tell are unbelievable, and they are all true! Jokim assures me that these things are so, and yet I find it hard to believe that an angel of God could stop Abraham's hand as he prepared to sacrifice Isaac, and that Sarah could give birth at ninety years of age."

"El Shaddai has always been a God of miracles," his father answered, reaching for the parchment Ani had retrieved. "From the beginning of the world until this day, He has not taken His hand of blessing from us."

"I know, Father, but—" Manasseh paused, hesitating to share the thoughts that had been echoing in his heart for days. "If these tales are so wondrous, why haven't you shared them with us? Jokim could not believe that I had not heard the stories of Rachel and Leah, or Jacob and Esau."

He stopped, afraid to reproach his father further, and saw that Joseph's attention was riveted to the parchment in his hand. He had not even heard the question.

"Peace and prosperity to you," Manasseh said, formally bowing his head. "I think I'll go wash and change into something—more Egyptian." He gave Ani another smile. "Ephraim seems to think I look like a goatherd."

Ani laughed, and Joseph's face wrinkled in an automatic smile. "Yes, go clean up." Joseph dismissed Manasseh with a wave of his hand. "Perhaps I will find you at breakfast tomorrow."

"Perhaps." Manasseh lowered his eyes in disappointment as he backed out of the chamber. "But I will understand if you do not."

Four

FORTY DAYS PASSED. THE GLISTENING SHEETS OF WA-
ter left by the inundation thinned but remained on the fields,
brilliantly mirroring the cloudless blue sky above. As the vizier's
servants went forth to reset the flooded boundaries of his fields,
Ephraim met again with the physician-priests. After greeting
them in the villa's temple, he stepped aside and allowed the men
to begin their work. While lifting rhythmic chants to Amon-Re,
the embalmers used palm-frond fans to blow the piles of natron
from Jacob's physical remains. When the last of the white powder had been blown, brushed, and swept away, the dried,
shrunken body was sponged clean and wiped again with oils,
ointments, and spices.

Ephraim sat on a stool in the corner of the tiny temple, his
fingers pressed over his mouth as the priests went about their
work. The physicians reopened the body cavity, removed Jacob's
heart, now shriveled and dark from the natron, and placed it inside a special jar. One priest inserted a stone scarab, an amulet
in the form of a beetle associated with the rebirth of the sun, in
the heart's former position. As the sun climbed across the sky
outside, the priests stuffed the body with new packets of fresh
linen, then plugged the eye sockets and nostrils with beeswax.
Crossing the patriarch's arms, they covered his fingernails and
toenails with specially designed caps of gold. With silken thread
the priests sewed the embalming cut together again, then covered the wound with a golden plate engraved with the protective
Eye of Horus.

After adorning the body with necklaces, rings, and bracelets
of gold and precious stones, the physicians reverently and carefully bound the body with long, narrow linen strips. With infinite patience they individually wrapped fingers, toes, arms, and
legs. With the care they might have shown Pharaoh himself, the

embalmers inserted protective amulets—images of the lotus, the symbol of rebirth, and the ankh, a sign of life—between the layers of binding, then glued every few layers with resin.

The process of wrapping required two weeks and over four hundred forty-five square yards of fine linen. But after twenty layers of binding, Ephraim was relieved to see that the shrunken body had resumed its normal size.

A portrait mask covered the mummy's bound head, a most decidedly un-Egyptian rendering of a bearded man with black fathomless eyes. The physicians bound the mask in linen, then sealed the entire body with a final coat of resin. When the resin had dried, the embalmers stepped back, folded their hands, and looked to Ephraim for approval. Jacob's mortal remains were ready for their final journey.

Impressed with their reverent care, Ephraim bowed to the physicians, then went into the house to report the news to his father.

⇀ Five ⇀

MANASSEH'S MOUTH TIPPED IN ANNOYANCE WHEN HE learned that Pharaoh and Queen Tiy had requested the vizier's presence at the palace for a banquet before the burial procession could depart Thebes, and his annoyance flared to irritation when he heard that he and Ephraim would be expected to attend the royal dinner. He was eager to join his kinsmen on the journey to Canaan, but one thought assuaged his impatience as he shaved and dressed for his audience with the king and queen: the banquet would be held in the palace at Malkata. If all went well, he might be able to speak with Jendayi, the only girl who had ever made an impression upon his heart.

He had first met Jendayi ten years before. He had been a lad of fifteen, still ungainly and uncertain of himself, but his heart had melted when he encountered Ani leading a new group of slaves through the vizier's courtyard. This was a special group, Ani explained, escorting the newly acquired servants to the squat brick building where the slaves slept. They were musicians, and most talented ones. He had spent a hundred deben weight of silver to acquire them, but they were worth every ounce, for the vizier's house should offer the finest music in the land. The slave broker had assured him that no orchestra in all the world was more talented than the group Ani now led through the hot sun.

Manasseh's eyes had swept over the other women and focused upon her. Only a child, Jendayi was a petite girl of seven or eight, delicate, with skin as pure as alabaster and hair as dark as velvet night. The desert wind had whipped color into her cheeks, and even from a proper distance Manasseh could see that dark thick lashes swept down across her cheekbones. A tattered and bruised lotus blossom had been tucked into the fabric of her belt, an incongruous bit of adornment for a slave. Even then her gentle and overwhelming beauty sent his spirits soaring. Though she had to be frightened at her change of circumstances, she wore an expression of patient endurance, while her posture spoke of strength and determination.

Look at me, he had silently urged her, fascinated by the way she held the arm of another slave, a bald robust man whose heavy cheeks fell in worried folds over the broad collar at his neck. But she kept her eyes downcast, even when Ani stopped at the edge of the portico. The stalwart man halted, too, but the girl took two more steps, running headlong into the woman in front of her.

Then Manasseh understood why she kept her eyes lowered. She was blind.

He backed away in wordless surprise, stunned by the realization. He had never seen a blind child. Blind babies were usually tossed to the crocodiles of the Nile, for the Egyptians considered anyone with a physical imperfection accursed. She must have lost her sight at some point past birth, Manasseh mused, and she still lived because she possessed some talent or quality that atoned for her weakness and prevented her from being a burden.

Over the next few days, Manasseh learned the secret of Jendayi's salvation. As talented as she was lovely, Jendayi was a child wonder, as skilled a harpist as he had ever heard, more inventively musical than even the famed harpists of Pharaoh's court. The bald man, Akil, served as the orchestra's chironomist, a singer who directed the musical ensemble with gestures. Manasseh noticed that Akil gave particular, almost fatherly attention to the girl, urging her to play beyond her pain and confusion, to give her full attention to the music.

Apparently she heeded his counsel. The first time Manasseh heard her play, he nearly forgot who and where he was. The occasion was a banquet his father had hosted for a group of Egyptian nobles. On a lark of inspiration, Ani suggested that the master's new musicians be invited to perform during the meal. Zaphenath-paneah agreed, and the small orchestra tucked themselves into a corner of the room to provide soothing music to spur the flow of the guests' conversation.

As chironomist, Akil presided over the orchestra. He sat before them, his back to the room, his eyes toward his musicians.

With one hand on his bent knee, Akil softly beat the rhythm, with his other hand he indicated the notes to be played. The inclination of his arm specified the pitch, the position of his fingers told the musicians whether their sounds should be abrupt, smooth, loud, or nearly silent. Since she could not see the director, Jendayi stood in the midst of the others, feeling their movements, listening to their breaths, seeming to anticipate the movement of Akil's arm even before the others could respond to him.

Along with Jendayi and her harp, Akil's all-female orchestra consisted of women who played the lute, a double oboe, a lyre, and a tambourine. For the most part they performed gentle, unremarkable music that did little but support Zaphenath-paneah's dinner until a lull in conversation gave Akil the opportunity to lower his arms and hoarsely whisper Jendayi's name.

Even through the veil of memory, Manasseh could recall the sparkling clarity of the notes she played. The harp broke through the heavy silence of satisfied banqueters like the shattering of crystal, then trilled in a melodic passage that brought the dinner to a veritable standstill. The nobles seated around Zaphenath-paneah stopped eating; the servants paused in their circuitous routes to the kitchens and stared, astounded, as the wellspring of sound swept through the hall and over the assembled diners. No one had ever heard such magic from either a harp or a human throat, and the effect astounded every soul present at the vizier's dinner.

Sudden tears burned Manasseh's eyes as the music spilled through the room. One minute heavy and boisterous, then suddenly sweet and light, the singularly poignant sounds touched places in Manasseh's heart that no human had ever been able to reach. The melody grew bittersweet, brightening the faded memory of Manasseh's dead mother, then rushed on to lift his soul to the hope of sunrise and the joy of warbling birdsong. Finally the music softened to echo the sibilant whispers of the spirits of the Nile and the whirring insects in the tall river grasses. Manasseh covered his mouth with his hand, afraid lest some inadvertent sound slip out and spoil the effect she'd created, then the girl pressed her hand across the vibrating strings and the sounds ceased.

The silence that followed was like the hush after a whirl-wind, when palm branches hang limp and the earth seems to catch her breath. As worn out as if he'd been running, Manasseh clung to the edge of his chair and stared at the slip of a girl who sat as silent as the Sphinx. A strange and tangible whispering began to move through the air, like the trembling breaths of a hundred simultaneous astonishments. "Who is she? Where did she come from? Has a god inhabited her fingers—or her harp?"

Akil, as master of the orchestra, stood and took a bow, then placed one hand across his breast and gestured to Jendayi. Manasseh burst out in spontaneous applause, echoed by his father and the other guests. The girl, apparently aware that the attention of every eye in the room had suddenly focused on her, stiffened as twin stains of scarlet appeared on her cheeks.

On that day Manasseh had fallen completely in love with her. He would bide his time, he had decided, and wait until she was of a marriageable age, then he would approach his father and ask if she could be his bride. But within three years of her arrival at the vizier's house, news of the musical wonder had reached even Pharaoh's ears. As a gesture of loyalty and love, Zaphenath-paneah sacrificially offered his harpist and chironomist to Pharaoh's service, and shortly thereafter, Jendayi and Akil, together with the others of the orchestra, left the vizier's villa for Pharaoh's pink palace at Malkata.

Though the turn of events left Manasseh feeling bereft and desolate, God had not been entirely unmerciful. Over the years Manasseh had relished his occasional visits to Malkata, not because he rejoiced at Pharaoh's invitation, but because he adored sitting in the same room with Jendayi. A mere ripple of her fingers across the harp had the power to bring tears to his eyes, and the sight of her diminutive form moving carefully through the halls set his blood to pounding in his temples. He did not know how he would one day make her his wife, but he would. He would never marry unless he married Jendayi.

That determination had only grown stronger through the years. On the afternoon of Pharaoh's banquet before the departure to Canaan, Manasseh dressed with special care, then joined his father and brother at the gate of the villa. After crossing the Nile on the vizier's barge, a litter bore the three men from the docks to Pharaoh's gleaming palace.

As a pair of Pharaoh's elite Medjay warriors escorted them through the maze of palace passageways, Manasseh reflected on the king who now held Jendayi's fate in his hands. Amenhotep was not unreasonable, and many held him to be Egypt's greatest and wisest Pharaoh. He neither taxed his people unfairly nor spilled their blood on foreign fields. He had sired a host of royal children and married a woman who had proved to be not only fruitful, but capable.

Of course, Pharaoh did have—Manasseh grinned, searching for the words his father would use to describe the king—*unique* characteristics. In addition to his inordinate fondness for women, Amenhotep possessed an enthusiasm for building that was as strong as his predecessors' passion for war. Along with the palace at Malkata, he had built a large addition to the temple to Amon-Re at Karnak and a larger temple, flanked by an avenue of Sphinxes, to Amon-Re at Opet. Though no one could say which project was the more daring, beautiful, or enduring, the most mysterious work had been accomplished at his mortuary complex. Through some magic of design and situation, Pharaoh's builders had erected a pair of colossal stone statues engraved with Amenhotep's image. Precisely at sunrise each morning, the two sixty-five-foot statues produced haunting musical sounds.

Pharaoh's chief chamberlain met Joseph and his sons outside the gilded doors of the king's throne room and immediately prostrated himself before Zaphenath-paneah. "Pharaoh and the Mother of All Egypt are in the garden," the chamberlain told them after Joseph gave him permission to rise. "You are to join them as they finish their game."

"What game are they playing?" Joseph asked as the chamberlain began to lead them toward the garden.

The chamberlain's broad face cracked into a smile. "Hounds and Jackals," he replied, thrusting his hands behind his back.

Manasseh cast Ephraim a puzzled glance. Hounds and Jackals was a trivial entertainment usually employed by wealthy Egyptians as a way to pass long hot afternoons. He could not imagine the divine Pharaoh and the Mother of All Egypt being bored enough to indulge in a mere board game that he and Ephraim had not played since childhood.

His father must have guessed at his thoughts. "Pharaoh and Queen Tiy have erected a life-size game board in the center of the king's garden," Joseph explained, casting the words over his shoulder as they walked. "The fifty-eight golden circles on the game board have been represented by fifty-eight golden tiles along the garden pathway. And instead of a splotch of blue paint to represent an oasis on the game board, Pharaoh's men have situated a real pool between the two garden paths."

Players of the game had a simple objective, Manasseh recalled as he and Ephraim followed their father and the chamberlain. One player managed a team of hounds, the other a team of jackals. To begin, each player rolled the knucklebones, and the first to roll either a one or a six could set out on the trail, moving from tile to tile. The first player to land exactly upon the shenu, the royal insignia, won the game.

The challenge of Hounds and Jackals lay in managing the two serpentine trails that connected opposite sections of each pathway. If a player landed one of his tokens at the junction of a tile and one of the serpentine paths, he had to follow the secret trail, either moving ahead by several tiles or falling back by the same distance. To further enliven the game, five special tiles were marked with the ankh, the symbol for eternal life. A player fortunate enough to land on the ankh could roll the knucklebones again and take another turn.

As they neared the garden, Manasseh could see that Pharaoh had made a great production of the game. Two winding paths had been cut into the garden on opposite sides of an enormous reflecting pool. A gigantic shenu, a tile engraved with the king's divine name and decorated with gold, red carnelian, and lapis lazuli, rested on the ground directly in front of the garden pavilion.

At that moment an official yelled, "Three!" Pharaoh, who watched from the pavilion, pointed at a slave on the path reserved for hounds. The slave, dressed in a furred headdress and a silver collar, ran forward three tiles. At once a dozen slaves burst from behind a screen of greenery, a replica of the sacred bark of Amon-Re upon their shoulders. The boat, a small model of the bark upon which the god sailed to his various temples, featured a curved prow and stern carved with the image of the ram-headed god. Long poles supported both the craft and the fluttering banners painted with the god's sacred insignia.

The grinning hound, delighted at Pharaoh's good fortune, climbed into the boat while the bark-bearers carried him over one of the hidden paths to a tile much closer to the shenu and the finish line.

From the security of her elevated chair, Queen Tiy frowned. Stepping up to the rope that separated the playing field from the observers, Manasseh noted the position of the players. If his good fortune held, the king would win.

Tiy nodded toward her representative, who tossed the knucklebones into a gleaming bronze pan.

"Two!" called the official.

With a decided frown, the queen pointed toward one of her men—a jackal, Manasseh decided, since he wore a black headdress painted with pointed ears—who promptly stepped forward two tiles. But his move placed him at the exit of one of the secret paths, and as soon as the servant settled on the tile, a pair of priests lifted the lid on a woven basket. As Manasseh stared in mystified amazement, a cobra slithered out and hissed the queen's player back to the beginning of the course.

"Don't worry," the chamberlain whispered as the reptile wriggled away. "It is an old creature whose fangs have been removed."

Triumphant laughter echoed from the king's chair. "Ah, Tiy, I shall beat you yet!"

"We shall see, my King." The queen laughed, too, but her laughter had a sharp and brittle edge.

Pharaoh rolled the knucklebones again, and the spectators broke out in polite applause as he moved another hound forward six tiles.

The queen shot her husband a twisted smile, then gestured to the official. "The bones," she commanded, her spiderlike hand extended. "I will throw them myself."

The official bowed and gave her the knucklebones. Pharaoh leaned back and cupped his hand around his chin, watching his queen. Tiy rolled the bones in her hands as if to get the feel of them, then suddenly splayed her fingers. The bones spilled uselessly onto the ground.

"Tiy!" Disappointment dripped from Amenhotep's voice. "You dropped them! You have forfeited the game!"

"Alas, apparently I have." A smile crawled to Tiy's lips and curved itself there like the undulating cobra. "But I would rather surrender to you, mighty Pharaoh, than be beaten by you. Besides, this is not an appropriate time for games. Our guests have arrived, and they are in mourning."

Pharaoh's expressive face stiffened and became almost somber when he caught sight of his vizier. "Zaphenath-paneah," he said solemnly, his voice suddenly doleful and troubled. "I am glad you have come. I wanted to spend this day with you, to strengthen your heart as you once supported mine as I prepared to bury my father."

Now that the royal gaze had fallen upon them, Manasseh followed his father's example and prostrated himself on the ground before the pavilion. "Rise and kiss the royal foot, most excellent vizier, my Zaphenath-paneah." Pharaoh's voice sounded thin and hollow in the open air. Joseph rose to his knees and crept forward to brush his lips across the tops of Amenhotep's red leather sandals. A great honor, this kissing of Pharaoh's feet. Only a select few noblemen were allowed to touch the divine king.

"You and your sons may stand," Pharaoh called, and Manasseh slowly rose to his feet. Lifting his chin, he assumed all the dignity he could muster, but he always felt like a child in Amenhotep's presence. Though Joseph was the king's most trusted counselor, Manasseh and Ephraim had not spent enough time in royal company to feel truly comfortable in the king's audience. Perhaps no man ever could.

At thirty-one, Amenhotep III stood proudly before the world as a man in the prime of life. Even from this distance, Manasseh felt the power that coiled within him, an energy that could not be disguised by the king's air of studied relaxation. Like the other nobles, Pharaoh wore a linen kilt, girdled at the waist by an elaborate beadwork belt, but there the resemblance to other noblemen ended. From Pharaoh's belt hung a sporran of beaded strings, each topped by a gold cow's head pendant, a symbol of the goddess Hathor.

Since he could never be seen with his head uncovered,

Amenhotep wore the *nemes* headdress, a piece of stiffly folded cloth held in place by a gold band across his forehead. Two striped lappets fell forward over his smooth chest. A model of the serpent goddess Wadjet protruded from the front of the head-dress, and under the *nemes*, the king's profile was sharp and confident. His face, bronzed by the wind and sun, was pleasant enough to be thought handsome, Manasseh supposed, but his eyes smoldered with the intimidating and fiery pride of Egypt's kings.

"Your sons have grown into comely men." Pharaoh nodded with a taut jerk of his head, then stole a slanted look at his wife. "What do you say, my dear Tiy? I believe the young sons are as pleasing in form as their father."

Manasseh felt an unwelcome blush creep onto his neck as the queen rose from her gilded chair. He had avoided glancing in her direction, for Tiy's sharp, restive features and direct gaze had always reminded him of a vulture spying for carrion.

Dragging her pet dwarf on a golden leash, Queen Tiy advanced to Pharaoh's chair. She inclined her head toward her husband in a deep gesture, then swung her gaze over the trio standing before him, her dark eyes lazily seductive. "The sons can never equal the father, for beauty divided could never equal the whole." Her nasal voice cut through the silence like a hot blade. She cast a slight smile in Joseph's direction. "But they are fine sons, my King, and any man would be proud to claim them."

"So I thought." With an abrupt nod, Pharaoh gestured toward his chamberlain, then rose from his chair. "I invited you today for a banquet, Zaphenath-paneah, so let us forgo formalities and retire to my chamber for dinner. I want to hear the details of your coming journey without the distractions of the court. Let my wife and my eldest daughter entertain your sons while you and I enjoy private discourse."

Manasseh felt his heart constrict a little at the king's words. If the musicians played for Pharaoh, he would not have a chance to see Jendayi.

But Queen Tiy stepped forward and slipped her arm through his. "Come, young man, and escort me to my chambers where we shall relax and talk of interesting things." Her smile did not reach her eyes. "My daughter waits for us there, along with food and music sweet enough to soothe whatever trouble stirs behind those restless eyes of yours."

Music! Smiling in the hope of better things to come, Manasseh inclined his head in a gesture of honor, then led the queen from the king's garden.

————

His smile broadened in approval when he discovered that the queen had spoken the truth. The banquet she had prepared was simple, quiet, and intimate. The four diners—Queen Tiy, Manasseh, Ephraim, and Princess Sitamun—sat in tall chairs that had been arranged so that each diner faced one of the others. A steady procession of servants brought in bowls of steaming meats, delicious fruits, and tender vegetables. These dishes were presented first to the queen, who sampled them and then instructed the slaves to divide the food among her other guests.

Manasseh found himself sitting across from the queen, a position that unnerved him until he realized that the musicians, if and when they came, would sit directly behind her. He thought he might be able to appear to give the queen his full attention while he studied Jendayi, but after studying Tiy's bold black eyes, he decided she would not be easily fooled. She would know if something other than her royal presence occupied his thoughts.

For an hour they ate and carried on a pleasant and unremarkable conversation. As Ephraim's tongue loosened he began to tease Sitamun, a spoiled and pampered princess of sixteen. Tall and slender, with a narrow face, the girl possessed such heavy eyelids that she seemed perpetually on the brink of falling asleep. But those eyes gleamed as she bantered with Ephraim, and her wit proved as sharp as her tongue. More than once Manasseh shot a smile in her direction when she scored a point against Ephraim in their gentle sparring, and before the first hour had passed, he realized that the conversation between his brother and the princess had evolved from common small talk to the verbal fencing of flirtation.

Apparently Queen Tiy noticed the shift, too, for the faint beginnings of a knowing smile hovered around the edges of her mouth. Manasseh was about to distract her by asking about the king's plans for restoration work on the gates of Thebes when a curtain parted and Akil entered the room.

Manasseh's mind floundered and his stomach dropped like a hanged man. Behind the chironomist came the oboist, the lutist, the woman who played the tambourine, the lyre player, and finally, Jendayi, led by a handmaid.

Manasseh stared at the little harpist in a paralysis of astonishment. He had not seen Jendayi in several months, and then only from a distance. How lovely she had become! No queen, surely no woman in Pharaoh's harem could rival the girl's beauty. She wore a full wig now, as did all Pharaoh's servants, but the young woman under the wig seemed more delicate and ethereal than ever. The hand wrapped around the wrist of her handmaid was slender, her fingers strong and slim. Her throat looked warm and shapely above the bodice of her dress. The softness of her young body seemed to melt against the linen of her gown. The eyes she lifted toward the windows were as gray and wild as storm scud, but Manasseh knew that a passionate, intelligent woman lived behind the facade of those eyes, that perfect face. One had only to hear her play to know the depths of the soul that lived within her and to want to join with that spirit.

He took a deep breath and felt bands of tightness in his chest. How could any man look at her and not want her? How did Akil work with her every day, hear her voice, look upon her face, and not want to partake of her sweet innocence? And Pharaoh! How did he, with his exquisite taste of beautiful women, resist this lovely flower living in his house?

For the briefest instant his eyes met Queen Tiy's. A smile nudged itself into a corner of her mouth, then pushed across her lips. "Has anyone ever told you, my young friend," she lowered her voice to the vaguest of whispers, "that your thoughts shine in your eyes like stars in the night sky? From the look on your face, I know that the king's musicians have entered the room behind me. And"—she leaned toward him—"the light in your eyes tells me that you have found some sight for which you yearn. Since most of the women in Pharaoh's orchestra are waspish, unlovely creatures, the gleam in your eyes must be inspired by— dare I say it? The little harpist."

Manasseh stared at her, tongue-tied, but Tiy's smile told him she understood. "The girl *is* lovely, isn't she? A rare treasure, she possesses both beauty and talent. She is, I'm afraid, one of Pharaoh's favorites." She paused for a moment, her paint-lengthened eyes studying him, then pressed her hand to her swanlike throat. "But do not be alarmed by what I am telling you. Though our king has a fondness for music, the women in Akil's orchestra have never been invited to join the royal harem."

Manasseh felt his heart swell with relief. A thoughtful smile curved the queen's mouth as she regarded him. "I had almost forgotten that such innocence could exist, Manasseh, son of Zaphenath-paneah."

"Innocence?" He allowed his eyes to drift back to Jendayi. "Surely God never created a more innocent creature."

"I was not speaking of the harpist. I meant you."

Manasseh knew his flush had deepened to crimson.

"Do not be embarrassed, my dear young friend," Tiy purred, whispering toward him. "And do not lose heart. Pharaoh is not completely attached to the harpist. With the right encouragement there may come a time when he would be willing to release the girl . . . to a man he wishes to honor." The queen allowed her words to hang in the silence for a moment, then she lowered her gaze fully into Manasseh's. "There may also come a time when you may be of service to your queen, my young friend. Perhaps in the future we can help each other."

Though the queen's words hinted at some sort of mystery, Manasseh was too thrilled by the prospect of winning Jendayi's release to do more than nod in agreement.

———

Ephraim dipped his fingers into the tiny water bowl on his dinner tray, then dried his hands on a perfumed square of linen and studied his brother's face. Manasseh's unruly eyes were trained upon the harpist again, the sentimental fool! Did he not know that Tiy was a jealous queen? She would not take kindly to being ignored. Furthermore, Manasseh's mooning over a royal slave was a waste of time. The girl would never be freed from Pharaoh's service, nor would she be allowed to marry. She should consider herself fortunate that she seemed to find joy within her music, for most of Pharaoh's slaves knew nothing of happiness outside Pharaoh's will.

"Ephraim." Sitamun tugged on his arm again, her hand lingering a moment on his skin.

"How may I serve you, Princess?" he asked, returning his attention to the girl across from him. Sitamun was a demanding companion, never happy unless he was smiling at her, but she was pretty and intelligent, gifted with her mother's genius and her father's persistence. And she was sixteen, ripe for marriage and a not altogether distasteful specimen of womanhood. Though, if truth be told, he would prefer a creature of lightness and beauty like Manasseh's angelic harpist. But the blind girl would never bear heirs to a royal throne. Sitamun would. And though the Crown Prince stood to inherit Amenhotep's kingdom, life was tenuous and the future uncertain. . . .

A smile ruffled Ephraim's mouth as he listened to Sitamun prattle on about the latest court gossip. Why shouldn't he marry a princess? Jacob's right hand had fallen on his head, and what better way could he lead the sons of Israel to greatness than through an alliance with Egypt? His father had begun a mighty work. Ephraim could continue it.

He adjusted his smile and leaned his head on his hand, studying the pleasant princess before him. "Has anyone ever told you"—he pitched his voice so that it would not reach the other two diners—"that your eyes blaze like the heavens above when Sirius is at its brightest?"

———

Though any observer would have thought Akil intent upon the music he directed, his thoughts were concentrated upon the small circle of banqueters behind him. He knew the sons of Zaphenath-paneah, their natures and desires, and he distrusted them. The eyes of the elder, Manasseh, burned Akil's shoulders even now as he stared at Jendayi, and the younger, Ephraim, seemed altogether too glib and attractive for Akil's comfort. During the three years he and his charges had lived in the vizier's villa, he had not been unaware of Manasseh's longing looks and Ephraim's bold flirtations with his child wonder.

But he had managed to shelter Jendayi, the most blessed of the gods, from the boys' attentions. Her blind eyes had never been able to see the open heart Manasseh revealed on his face, and Akil had usually been able to keep a wide distance between bold Ephraim and the beautiful youngster. Only once could Akil recall having shirked his duty—the afternoon Ephraim had discovered Jendayi in the garden and impetuously kissed her. Fortunately, Akil had happened upon the pair before the situation could advance and had immediately led his stammering ward back to the slave quarters. Ephraim, cheeky as always, had merely grinned and walked away, probably to find a more willing slave upon whom he could foist his attentions.

Akil cast a discreet glance over his shoulder. A soft and loving curve lay upon the elder son's lips as he stared at Jendayi, completely unmindful of Akil or the queen, but the younger man seemed intent upon Princess Sitamun. Good. Let him cast his nets after the slippery princess. Those two deserved each other. And, may the gods be praised, as long as Jendayi remained sightless, she would not see the look of love in the other man's eyes.

Akil turned back to his orchestra and gave his sighted performers an approving smile. The song they played was an unremarkable tune in which Jendayi did little more than strum an accompaniment to the oboe. Good. He would not draw undue attention to her tonight.

For he had long known that in Jendayi lay the key to his own prosperity and happiness. As long as the little harpist retained the gift of the gods and remained in Pharaoh's court, Akil would continue to be her musical interpreter. Though Amenhotep had access to the best musicians in the kingdom, he called for Akil's orchestra at every great occasion, both personal and private. As long as Jendayi's harp continued to thrill the king, Akil would remain secure in the exclusive inner circle of Pharaoh's favor, and he would be summoned to play for the queen.

There was no higher honor, no more beautiful or deserving woman. Tiy was the brightest and most brilliant star of Pharaoh's world, a paragon of virtue, intelligence, and cunning. Akil willingly gave his loyalty and service to Pharaoh, but his adoration he reserved for Tiy, the Mother of Egypt and his own Favorite Lady.

She may never know that I would die for her, Akil thought, lowering his hands to end his musicians' song. *But she will never have cause to doubt my loyalty.*

———

Manasseh's soul burned with impatience as the queen's slaves carried their dinner trays away. They still had to endure the ritual chants to thank the gods for their prosperity, then Queen Tiy and Princess Sitamun would take their formal leave and quit the chamber. The musicians might leave before the royals, so he would have precious little time to find Jendayi before the guards would arrive to escort him and Ephraim back to the docks. One did not wander through Pharaoh's palace unescorted.

But he had to speak to Jendayi. He and his family would soon be leaving for Canaan, and it might be weeks before he received another invitation to Malkata. His silent heart had spent years yearning for her, but now she was old enough to hear of his love, to know that he wanted only the best for her and would stop at nothing to obtain it.

The servants finished clearing the room. A bald priest entered and chanted a ritual hymn of praise and thanksgiving. When the priest had finished, Queen Tiy rose from her chair in a smooth graceful motion. "We bid you farewell," she said, her voice shrill and crisp in the stillness.

Taking her cue from her mother, Sitamun stood as well. A small suggestive smile touched her lips as she inclined her head toward Ephraim. "A pleasure to speak with you," she murmured, a sweet edge to her voice. The dark hair of her oiled wig glistened like polished wood as she transferred her gaze to Manasseh. "You both must come again when you have completed your journey to bury your grandfather."

"We thank you for your invitation and yearn to accept it," Ephraim answered, not bothering even to look at Manasseh. "My brother and I will fly to your side whenever you command our presence."

Manasseh folded his hands behind his back. Let Ephraim accept Sitamun's invitation. He would be pleased to accompany his brother if only to catch another glimpse of Jendayi. "Yes." He nodded toward Sitamun. "We would be honored to see you again."

"So be it, then." Sitamun's smile relaxed measurably. "I will implore the gods to grant you a safe and uneventful journey."

Ephraim and Manasseh bowed in respect, then Tiy led her daughter from the room. When both the queen and the princess had gone, Ephraim turned to Manasseh in a burst of excitement, but Manasseh stalled him with a touch on the shoulder. Leaving Ephraim in the center of the chamber, he hurried toward the corner where the musicians were gathering their instruments. Jendayi had already disappeared through the doorway, but perhaps the chironomist would call her back.

"Master Akil," Manasseh said, his voice a great deal shakier than he would have liked.

"May I help you, sir?" Akil turned. The musician wore a frown, and his brows had twisted in a brooding knot over his eyes.

"I am Manasseh, elder son of Zaphenath-paneah." The words rushed together as he hurried to identify himself. "If you would summon Jendayi, I would like to speak to her—"

"I know who you are," the chironomist interrupted. "But we are no longer the property of your father, the vizier." The man barreled his scrawny chest. "We belong to Pharaoh."

"I know." Manasseh nodded abruptly. "But if you will call her—"

"Jendayi cannot speak to you. It would not be proper. You are a nobleman's son, and she is a slave. You must leave. The guards are even now at the door."

Manasseh glanced over his shoulder. The man had spoken truly. A pair of armed warriors had entered the room and waited to lead him and Ephraim through the winding halls back to the docks.

"But I wish only a word—"

"No! Take yourself away, young sir, or you will make trouble for both of us!" The older man would not be persuaded.

Manasseh stepped back, driven not by fear of Akil, but by the knowledge that any rash action might endanger his future invitations to the palace. The chironomist was a stubborn and possessive fool, but Manasseh had allies in higher places. Queen Tiy herself had intimated that she would help in his quest for the harpist's hand.

"Later, Akil," Manasseh called, backing out of the chamber. "I will see you again."

Jendayi followed her handmaid through the palace halls and tried to deny the sour feeling in the pit of her stomach. It was good that Pharaoh would not be summoning her to play tonight, for nothing but loneliness, longing, and pain could pour forth from her harp now.

She heard Akil's quick shuffling steps behind her and lowered her head, knowing he would be angry if he read her feelings on her face. "Why do you long for things that can never be?" he constantly chided her. "Be happy where you are. You live in the grandest palace of the most glorious king of the most powerful kingdom in all the world. And you are a favorite of Pharaoh's. The gods have blessed you, child. No one can equal you, so rejoice and be content."

She tried to be content, but the dream persisted in haunting her. Her nightmare of death and the Hall of the Two Truths had not lost its power to frighten her. She awoke every morning drenched in a sweat, recalling the fervor with which the god condemned her: *"You have loved nothing. You are nothing. You have nothing!"* The eyes of Anubis' gaunt jackal face rose before her even now, and with a shiver of vivid recollection, she pressed closer to her handmaid's side.

Life itself haunted her, for living seemed an exercise she often heard about but would never really experience. She ate, slept, drank, and played in the lonely blackness of the blind. Every day looked like every night. Each time she rose from her bed, she slipped into a tunic that felt like the one she had worn the day before. The voices that rose and fell around her were the same ones that had kept her company since the days of her childhood. The people who moved along the fringes of her world raised their voices when speaking to her as if she were deaf, or they were quick to assume that because she did not make eye contact with them, they could not make any contact with her.

Pharaoh, the queen, the men and women of the royal court lived and laughed in *the world*. Jendayi and her companions were forever isolated behind the veil of slavery, urged only to perform well and then scurry away like rats behind a wall. Her experiences had been as uninteresting and bland as warm water, and her stomach knotted at the thought of a lifetime of emptiness, long years of loving nothing, having nothing, being nothing. . . .

She had been given one gift—an ability to hear and create music. Sometimes in the quiet of an afternoon one of the other slaves would tell her a story of love or hate or jealousy, and Jendayi would struggle to interpret those emotions through her harp. But even at her best, she knew the tones that flowed from her hands were nothing but shadows of the genuine passion that gripped and motivated the rest of the world. Her fingers strove to speak of love and succeeded only in imitating the delicate warble of a mother bird that coos to its young, hidden in the river grasses. She was an imitator, never an artist. Anubis was right. She was nothing.

"We are here, mistress." Kesi, her handmaid, turned abruptly, pulling Jendayi with her. Jendayi lifted her head and smelled the sweet scent of lotus blossoms the lutist had arranged in a bowl the day before. They were back in their room, one of many chambers in the slave quarters behind Pharaoh's palace.

"Thank you." Jendayi released Kesi's arm and held out her hand, waiting for the staff she used to guide her steps while in the slave quarters. Within a moment Kesi had slipped the smooth stick into Jendayi's palm and moved away, probably anxious to be rid of her dependent mistress. Tapping her way through the room, Jendayi counted her way past three beds, then sank down upon the fourth, carefully placing the staff beneath the bed frame. Once she was certain no one would trip over it, she curled on her side and placed her hand under her cheek, pretending to sleep.

But she could not sleep, for the dream might come again. Would she ever be able to silence Anubis' mournful howl? Could her cold heart find love? Her mother had abandoned her soon after it became apparent that Jendayi's weak eyes had succumbed to the disease that robbed her of sight. She had no real memories of her mother, nor of the slave market where she had been deposited. In her childhood she had been fed, bathed, and tutored in various aspects of servanthood until her gift for music was discovered. But had she ever been loved?

The other women slaves treated her with gentle concern but no real affection. Akil cared for her, she supposed, but he was more a teacher than a father, more her guardian than a parent. Jendayi suspected that she was the most talented musician in the orchestra, but Akil said she had done nothing to deserve her extraordinary ability. The gods had gifted her, he said, and they could easily rescind their gifts—hadn't they stolen her sight?

Her life seemed as bleak and formless as the darkness surrounding her, yet occasionally a magic moment disturbed the monotony. Years ago in the vizier's house, one dull afternoon had fired into unexpected vitality when a boy, smelling of sweat and youth, had pressed his lips to hers and pronounced her beautiful. Akil had promptly chased the boy away, of course, scolding him as if he were a naughty puppy, but Jendayi had been profoundly affected by the experience. Human flesh upon her lips—the same lips that gave sound to her words and brought her food and drink. Anubis was Lord of the Lips, for lips were the doorway to life, and this boy had placed his upon hers! Did he love her? Surely he did, or he would not have kissed her.

From that day on she had listened closely for the boy's voice and waited for his scent. She learned that he was Ephraim, the second son of the vizier, a refreshingly candid and openhearted lad. When the orchestra moved to Pharaoh's palace, she thought that her dreams of him would come to nothing, but tonight she had heard his name again! He had been a guest in the queen's chamber. He had undoubtedly heard her play.

Jendayi's hands had trembled over the strings of her beloved harp at the thrill of knowing that the one who had dared to touch her life with his had listened tonight in the darkness. Akil must have seen her discomfiture, for he had not asked her to play alone.

Before she left the queen's chamber, she had heard the visitors promise to return to Malkata. So Ephraim would hear her play again. And if her music touched his heart, perhaps he would remember his kiss and feel kindly toward her. And if she was very virtuous and made the proper offerings to the gods, Ephraim might dare to approach Pharaoh and procure her as a slave for his own house. She could be his servant, perhaps even his concubine. Then, if the gods were willing, she would finally experience love, and tenderness, and honest emotion. Then the gods could not say that she had loved nothing; they could not condemn her to eternal death.

The next time Ephraim heard her play, she would be ready. She would compose a song like no other, one that would expose all the hidden feelings in her heart. She would bare her soul before his and see if he possessed courage enough to hear all that she wanted to say.

MANASSEH

So Joseph went up to bury his father, and with him went up all the servants of Pharaoh, the elders of his household and all the elders of the land of Egypt, and all the household of Joseph and his brothers and his father's household; they left only their little ones and their flocks and their herds in the land of Goshen. There also went up with him both chariots and horsemen; and it was a very great company.

Genesis 50:7–9

⚊◗ Six ◖⚊

DURING THE FIRST MONTH OF THE EMERGENCE, WHEN the days of mourning for Israel had passed, Pharaoh Amenhotep III summoned to Thebes the governors of all the nomes of Egypt. These nomarchs, along with a great host of servants, priests, elders, and other important officials, gathered at the royal palace where they were designated as Pharaoh's representatives on the journey to Canaan. If any of them were disappointed to learn that they would spend the next few weeks journeying through the wilderness, they wisely refrained from showing their displeasure. Pharaoh himself elected to remain behind at Malkata, citing his persistent toothache and fever as an excuse not to travel.

But even though the king preferred to remain behind, he made certain Zaphenath-paneah would not feel slighted for lack of royal attention. Tiy had urged Amenhotep to bestow great honors upon Israel for the vizier's sake, and every tribute that could be dreamt of had been awarded. The finest physicians had embalmed Israel's mortal remains. The most sacred stone had been used to fashion the canopic jars that held the old man's precious inner organs. Pharaoh himself had approved the design of the carved chest that would house the jars. Inscriptions and relief work adorned the chest's exterior; rich blue pigment filled the hollows of the carving. Fashioned of purest alabaster, at its four corners the chest featured raised figures of the goddesses Isis, Nephthys, Neith, and Selkis, their wings extended to enclose and protect the chest's priceless contents.

Surely even Zaphenath-paneah's invisible and almighty God must have approved Pharaoh's labor, for the day of Israel's departure from Thebes dawned in a spectacular burst of blue. From his private balcony Amenhotep could see the Nile rippling as bright as new silver in the sun, and a cooling zephyr rushed up from the receding river. He hummed quietly to himself. It would be a good day. Zaphenath-paneah would be pleased. Tiy would be content with Amenhotep's efforts, and the soul of the Hebrew patriarch would rest secure in the otherworld.

Behind the king, one of the priests who tended him every morning coughed discreetly. Amenhotep turned from the river view, ready to begin his dressing routine.

———

Thebes had never seen such a funereal procession. Not even Egypt's pharaohs, who rode in grand style from the valley temples to their vast mortuary complexes on the Nile's western bank, would undertake so long a final journey. Israel would leave Thebes in full splendor, travel to Goshen to gather his children, and then depart for Canaan. On the journey the funereal contingent would travel through often hostile lands populated by fierce peoples. Though Egypt had formally subjugated the kingdoms from the Mediterranean to the Euphrates as far north as Syria, to guard against any possible aggression, Pharaoh had ordered that two squadrons of charioteers and an elite corps of troops accompany the vizier.

The members of the procession had been assembling in Thebes since morning, and Amenhotep had expressly commanded that they move slowly as they passed Malkata so that he and his family might smile with divine favor upon them. A cloud of dust now stirred along the riverbank to the south, and the king settled back in his chair, pleased that his wishes had been carried out. A pair of slaves knelt at his side, ready to do his bidding; a pair of guards lingered in the doorway behind him. His daughters Sitamun, Ast, and Hentmerheb, who usually lived in Thebes with their mother, now sat at his right hand. Tiy, for some inexplicable reason, had demurred last night when he asked her to remain at Malkata. She preferred to oversee the procession at Thebes, she told him, and she would extend Pharaoh's farewells as Zaphenath-paneah departed from the docks.

He glanced at Sitamun, whose eyes betrayed her feelings. The night before she had dared to suggest that she might join the Crown Prince on the journey with the Hebrews to Canaan. Amenhotep had stalled his answer, and later Tiy explained their eldest daughter's sudden interest in the journey.

"She fancies herself in love with the vizier's handsome younger son," Tiy said, her pointed face creasing into a sudden smile. "At our banquet, he captured her heart. He is quite charming."

"Should I let her go?" Amenhotep had asked, searching his own feelings on the matter. His deep fondness for Zaphenath-paneah sprang from nostalgia for his childhood and his mother's high regard for the man, but he had long ago learned the folly of consistently showing more favor to one counselor than the others. Jealousy hissed like a serpent through the royal throne room, and even Amenhotep had felt the effects of its sharp bite. The priests of Amon-Re, whom he sometimes thought held altogether too much power in their hands, had grown more resentful of Zaphenath-paneah's success as the years passed. Amenhotep had heard reports—though he was reluctant to investigate should such a shameful thing prove true—that even the history of Egypt had been rewritten. The priests of Thebes, unable to believe that an invisible and unknown God had saved Egypt, had recorded in the annals that Amon-Re, "Greatest of Heaven, Eldest of Earth," had saved the Black Land from famine during the early years of Amenhotep's reign. As the people who lived through the Great Famine passed into the otherworld, the truth would gradually disappear like the ruins of the most ancient Egyptians, buried by yet another layer of shifting sand.

Sitamun sighed loudly, interrupting his thoughts, and Amenhotep silently congratulated himself for having insight enough to listen to his wife. Tiy had suggested that Sitamun remain behind, and now he saw the wisdom of her suggestion. If Sitamun journeyed to Canaan with the Hebrews, the priests would see significant and dire omens in the swirling waters of their divining cups. They would read all sorts of dark meanings in Pharaoh's intention. Even now they grumbled about the expense of this great show of favor for the Hebrew patriarch.

The usual assortment of fishing boats and papyrus skiffs on the waters vanished like grain before the scythe as the royal chariots approached, fierce and fast, two lines moving in perfect rhythm on the banks of the swollen river. The levees had been reinforced for the chariots' passage because the muddy soil could not normally withstand the weight of so large a procession.

The gold-plated vehicles gleamed in the afternoon sun as the charioteers turned their faces toward the pink-washed palace in salute. Pharaoh sat forward and studied them intently.

Between the chariots on both riverbanks, a host of wide stately barges floated upon the water, each flying the standard of the nomarch represented aboard. The Egyptian officials vastly preferred traveling by boat than by land, and Pharaoh lifted his chin in case any of his governors were sharp-eyed enough to catch a glimpse of his divine presence on the balcony.

After the nomarchs came the royal barges, which carried members of Pharaoh's own household: the Crown Prince, nearly half of Pharaoh's counselors, priests from the leading temples of Thebes, and a company of scribes to record the wonders of the journey. At one point Amenhotep had considered sending Queen Tiy with them, then decided against it. A journey through the wilderness was no pleasure trip. The heat, grumbling camels, frequent sandstorms, and the inconveniences of uncivilized life combined to make the journey a weariness to the flesh from inception to end. Tiy would not find the wilderness to her liking, and Amenhotep would not soon forget her displeasure if he insisted she go.

Other boats now moved into view, and Amenhotep shifted in his chair and leaned forward on his elbows. He recognized a half-dozen barges and feluccas belonging to the vizier. These were undoubtedly populated by trusted members of Zaphenath-paneah's household: his steward, the captain of his guard, a few other indispensable servants and counselors. Across from these boats on the eastern riverbank marched a corps of tall Nubian drummers who progressed forward in a steady morose beat, thumping a mournful dirge.

"Look, Father, at the dancers," Ast said, pointing. Scooting forward, the eager child clasped her hands together. "What story are they telling?"

"I don't know, my dear," Amenhotep answered, craning his neck for a better view. A host of dancers postured and posed on the wide deck of an oncoming ship, and with a start of surprise, Pharaoh realized that Zaphenath-paneah had employed a group of mimes. In order for the illiterate and uninformed common folk who watched from the riverbanks to understand the significance of the procession, the dancers were paid to pantomime the high-lights of Israel's life. Pharaoh rubbed his chin as a bearded mime, undoubtedly intended to represent Israel, beat his breast while another was led away in chains.

Pharaoh sat back in his chair and pressed his hand to his cheek. "They are telling the story of how Zaphenath-paneah was sold into slavery," he told his younger daughter. "The man in the long robe is Israel, the vizier's father."

"Who would sell our vizier?" Ast asked, aghast.

Amenhotep smothered a smile. "No one today, dear one. But long ago, when our vizier was a boy, only his father and his god recognized the seeds of greatness in him. His brothers, you see, were jealous."

Amenhotep paused, regarding the floating drama with somber curiosity. Strange that he, a man without equal, should know how the brothers felt. For though he had always thought of Zaphenath-paneah as a father, on many occasions he had felt the bitter sting of envy when comparing himself to his vizier.

Shortly after Amenhotep's ascension to the throne, the priests had taught him that Amon-Re consulted with the other gods to see who should bear Amon-Re's child. Thoth had suggested Tuya, the wife of Pharaoh. And so Amon-Re assumed the form of Tuthmosis IV and visited Tuya in the night, therefore Amen-hotep was conceived as the son of a god.

Why, then; did Zaphenath-paneah possess more godlike qualities than Pharaoh himself? Amenhotep was all too aware of his own shortcomings. His wife was a more able diplomat and ruler than he, and Zaphenath-paneah possessed wisdom far above any displayed by the king's counselors, priests, or astrologers. And though no counselor, slave, or priest would dare to lift a voice against the divine king, Amenhotep had seen countless hundreds of eyes glaze over when he offered his opinions. But those same eyes, even Tiy's, blazed with the fire of exhilaration when Zaphenath-paneah spoke.

Giving himself a stern mental shake, Pharaoh directed his attention back to the funereal procession. The professional mourners were advancing now. Clothed in the blue gray color of sorrow and their faces daubed with dust and mud, they beat their breasts and trudged with heavy steps along the riverbanks, their loud wails reaching even to the king's balcony. Between them, on flower-strewn boats, other servants of the vizier stood guard over baskets of food and supplies for the journey, a rich testimony to Israel's worth.

"Ah, here it is." He cast a quick glance at Sitamun. The girl had been pouting all morning, undoubtedly wanting to join her brother on the journey, but this glorious spectacle would lift her out of her black mood. "Look, daughter—the mortuary boat."

The mortuary boat, which Zaphenath-paneah had designed especially for Israel, cut through the water as smoothly as a knife, apparently guided only by the pair of slaves who stood at the bow and maneuvered the graceful craft with slender oars. The tall mast of the stately vessel moved into view, and Amenhotep smiled, impressed with the efforts of his vizier. The sides of the boat had been painted in bright reds, yellows, and black; images spelled out texts from the Chapters of Coming Forth by Day. In the center of the boat's deck, adjacent to the single mast, a shrine cabin had been adorned with lotus blossoms and palm branches, symbols of the resurrection. A few mourners rode atop the cabin, pulling at their hair while they wailed, and a host of ritual priests stood at the stern of the vessel: the *sem* priest who wore his traditional white linen robe and leopard skin, and the embalmers who had prepared the body for its eternal rest. They had been entrusted with guarding and overseeing the physical remains until the point of safe interment in the tomb.

Through a series of windows in the shrine cabin, Amenhotep caught a glimpse of the dull gleam of green stone and knew that he was seeing the granite sarcophagus especially commissioned to guard Israel's mummy. The sarcophagus alone had cost Pharaoh's treasury over three hundred deben weight of silver, but such a tribute seemed small in light of the debt Egypt owed Zaphenath-paneah.

Immediately behind the mortuary boat floated the elegant bark carrying the vizier and his sons. Sitamun leaned over the balcony railing, trying to catch a glimpse of Ephraim, and Amenhotep felt himself stiffen, half-convinced Zaphenath-paneah would know whether or not he was paying proper attention. The vizier always seemed to know what Amenhotep was thinking, another unnatural ability for which Pharaoh had no explanation and the vizier had no rival.

Sitamun sighed in disappointment and sank back in her chair. No one moved on the deck of the vizier's boat, and Amenhotep guessed that the vizier and his sons had entered the small cabin to be alone with their feelings. It was appropriate. A man ought to be able to mourn in private. Some emotions were not meant for public display. Women, good food, and gentle music could do much to relieve the heaviness of a man's wounded heart—

Music. Where were the musicians?

A few other boats followed the vizier's, but none of these flew the royal standard. Undoubtedly they carried slaves and servants who would be needed to tend to the officials on the arduous journey.

Amenhotep lowered his stern gaze to one of the slaves who waited like a statue at his side. "Akil and his orchestra are supposed to be en route with the vizier. Send guards at once and make sure he has departed."

The slave nodded and hastened away as swiftly as a cat.

Satisfied, Amenhotep stood and clasped his hands behind him. As the caravan gradually melted into the northern horizon, he gave his vizier a curt nod of farewell. He had done his part to honor Israel. Israel's God should continue to honor him.

———

Irritated by the close confines of the cabin, Manasseh pressed his lips together in annoyance. Their father sat silently with his legs crossed and his back to the wall, not moving. His eyes were closed either in contemplation or simple weariness, for the planning of this procession had consumed all his energies for many days. Ephraim, on the other hand, had done nothing to warrant special treatment, yet he lounged on a small cot, his head propped on his hand, his entire face spread into a smile as he energetically attacked a bowl of figs. What in the world could he find to be so disgustingly happy about?

"Stop eating so noisily." Manasseh gave his brother a black look. "You've been gobbling on those things for an hour, and my stomach is beginning to churn. Your manners are deplorable, and what if someone sees you? This is a funeral, not one of your festival parties.''

Ephraim lifted an eyebrow in amused contempt. ''You think my manners deplorable? You are the one who has suddenly fallen in love with goatherds! Besides, no one can see me, for we are quite alone in here. If I displease you, go outside.''

''I will not go out with the slaves. The sun is too hot, and this is as much my place as it is yours. So stop that loud chewing!''

The smirk left Ephraim's face. ''No. You're not going to order me around. We are not children and I will no longer listen to you.''

''Order you around? I'm just asking you to exhibit common courtesy.''

''You've commanded me since the day of my birth. And now''—Ephraim gave Manasseh a look of jaunty superiority— ''I'm not going to listen. The fact that you are the elder—well, it doesn't mean anything. Not anymore.''

Manasseh blinked, as surprised as if Ephraim had slapped him. And even though his brother hadn't said the actual words, he knew what Ephraim was thinking: *Israel gave me the blessing of the right hand. I am the favored one. The fact that you are the firstborn counts for nothing.*

Manasseh took a deep breath and stifled the urge to choke his brother. He was twenty-five, no longer a child, and as brothers they ought to be able to behave as grown men. If only Ephraim were not so infuriatingly childish!

He brought his knees to his chest and looked away. Perhaps he ought to go outside, but the sight of the mortuary boat depressed him, reminding him again of that sore afternoon when Israel had looked at him with the same mild interest Joseph always displayed. Then the old man had *smiled* at Ephraim, those weak old eyes fairly twinkling as they alighted on Ephraim's twisted and supposedly charming grin.

The memory edged his teeth as he turned to his brother again. ''It is good that Father did not see the way you behaved during our banquet with the queen,'' he whispered, casting a surreptitious look at Joseph to make certain those lined eyelids remained closed.

''What do you mean?'' Ephraim frowned. ''The princess

thought I was captivating. And if I did go a little too far, at least my behavior was no worse than yours."

"I held my tongue, but you talked like running water, and only to the princess. The queen must think you a terrible fool."

"At least Sitamun likes me." Ephraim shrugged indifferently, then his heavy brows arched into triangles. "And therefore, I have more to be happy about than you, brother. The object of your undying affection does not know that you are alive."

"The object of—what?" Manasseh was glad of the shadows that hid the flush in his cheeks. "I don't know what you mean."

"Even the queen noticed it, or do you think I am as dense as a rock? You gazed like a cow at the little harpist the entire afternoon. Even Sitamun noticed it. She thought you were terribly funny."

Manasseh felt himself flush with humiliation and anger at himself. He had never meant to act like a fool, but apparently he had. He only saw Jendayi on rare occasions, so how was he supposed to sit in the room where she was and pretend she didn't exist? Should he glance only occasionally at the one treasure of his heart, turn only rarely to the most beautiful sight in all creation?

He lifted his chin defensively. "I don't care what Sitamun thinks." He lowered his voice in case a servant stood with an ear to the papyrus wall. "I think she is vapid, entirely foolish. She lives only for pleasure. I never know when to take her seriously. You may find her fascinating, but I—"

"You are no fun at all, Manasseh," Ephraim interrupted, grinning. "No wonder Sitamun finds you boring. Well, your loss is my benefit. I will marry a princess while you moon over a slave. And which of us will be happier five years from now?"

Unable to bear the taunts any longer, Manasseh stood to his feet. Baking under the hot sun would definitely be preferable to remaining in the same cabin with his brother.

———

Several cargo ships joined the convoy to Canaan a few miles past the palace at Malkata. Flocks of sheep, cattle, and goats filled the stalls of these ships, enough to feed the travelers until the journey had been completed. Manasseh marveled at the sheer number of animals until he realized that his father's generous estimations had included feeding not only a sizable host of Egyptians, but his own ever growing family in Goshen, too.

Standing at the rail of his father's ship, Manasseh focused his eyes upon the far-flung shore. The receding waters of the inundation, the reddish brown color of birth and blood, had littered the shore with uprooted tropical plants, washed from lands far to the south. Occasionally the water rippled as a crocodile or hippopotamus ducked beneath the surface, eager to flee from human companionship. To the east and west of the river, the life-giving floods had muddied innumerable small squares of land marked by stone pillars and clay walls. Soon Pharaoh's subjects would come forth to till the newly refreshed soil. God would again bless Egypt, and another round of bountiful crops would dim men's memories of the seven years when the annual flood had not come, when only the narrow ribbon of land bordering the river brought forth any crops at all. For those years, Joseph had told his sons, God brought him to the Black Land. Because God Shaddai knew the future, His voice could be trusted in all things.

A tiny vessel appeared on the southern horizon, cutting through the winter waters at such a rate as to decorate her bow with a white garland of foam. Squinting toward it, Manasseh recognized Pharaoh's standard on the ship. Had Amenhotep decided to travel with them? Or another member of the royal circle? Surely none of the king's family would travel in a ship so small.

Manasseh moved to Ani's side. "Who comes yonder?" He pointed toward the ship in the distance. "There, beyond the cattle boats. The felucca."

Shading his eyes with his hand, Ani studied the boat for a moment, then his lined face cracked into a smile. "By the life of Pharaoh, the king *did* remember to send them," he murmured. He turned to give Manasseh an affectionate smile. "Pharaoh promised to send his best musicians, but I was not sure he would remember. Akil and his instrumentalists are late, but at least they have arrived."

Akil and his instrumentalists—Manasseh's heart jumped in his chest. If Pharaoh had sent his best, including Akil, then Jendayi rode on that ship.

"Should they sail so far behind?" Manasseh clutched Ani's

arm and struggled to keep the eagerness from his voice. "They are Pharaoh's servants, after all, and should sail closer to us so that we may protect them. If they remain back there beyond the cattle, we would not know if they had trouble on the river. Signal them, Ani. Have their rowers increase their speed until they are directly behind us."

Ani turned to eye Manasseh with a lifted eyebrow, then a secretive smile softened his thin lips. "Yes, Master Manasseh, I think that is a good idea." He gestured for the slave who handled the signal flags on the mast. "I will see to it at once."

Manasseh turned away, his mood suddenly buoyant. If Jendayi traveled with them to Canaan, he would certainly have a chance to speak with her. Away from the strictures of Pharaoh's palace, she might feel free enough to open her heart. Anything could happen under a star-filled sky where the wild wind blew away the restraints and conventions that might inhibit love between a slave girl and a nobleman's son.

A trembling thrill raced through his soul as he turned again toward the water. Soon he would know if love and marriage would be a part of his future. For since seeing the little harpist at the queen's banquet, Manasseh had renewed his vow. Unless he could have Jendayi by his side, he would not take any wife at all.

The ancient river broke into seven tributaries as it entered the Delta, and the floating funereal procession anchored upon the easternmost branch, a short distance from the Hebrew settlement at Goshen. From this point they would journey by camel and donkey and chariot until they reached the burial place near Mamre.

Coming down the gangplank of his father's boat, Ephraim frowned at the disorderliness of the Hebrew camp. He had not noticed this confusion when he visited at his grandfather's death. Perhaps grief had tempered his vision. But now, fully aware that his Egyptian companions disdained herders of all sorts, Ephraim thought the Hebrew settlement seemed almost slovenly. Stray animals wandered through the tents, chased gleefully by dirt-streaked children, and the smells of dung fires, cooking food, cows, and goats mingled with the scent of dust and hot dry earth. Against the gleaming white of the Egyptians' linen kilts, the rough tunics of the Hebrews appeared untidy. The windblown hair and beards of the men seemed unkempt compared to the cleanly shaven faces of the Egyptians. The Hebrews' heavy tents smelled of animals and age, a distinct and unpleasant contrast to the airy, perfumed villas of the Egyptians. And while the Egyptians moved off the ships in precise, military order, each man knowing his place and responsibility, the Hebrews wandered in careless confusion, like sheep without a shepherd.

Seeing his father's people with new eyes, Ephraim pressed his lips together and folded his arms. No wonder God sent his father to the Black Land! From the ancient and civilized people of the Double Kingdom, these Hebrews could learn much. They could rise above these tawdry tents and build fine stone houses. They could use the mud that now splashed around their ankles to form bricks that would last for generations. Like the ancient pharaohs who built the pyramids and the Sphinx, the Hebrews could build cities and monuments and settle permanently in this fertile region. For despite their ineffective methods and crude habitations, they had thrived in Goshen. Many babies had been born, and soon the children of Israel would be a mighty and populous people.

Ephraim's thoughts filtered back to the day of Israel's death. He would never forget a single detail of the moment when Jacob focused his pale eyes on him and prophesied that Ephraim would be the mightier son. Ephraim would never have dared to contemplate such an idea prior to that utterance, but since that day he had been thinking long, deep thoughts.

As the Hebrew son of Egypt's vizier, he could lead both nations to greatness. Some of his uncles might resist Ephraim's ideas, for Israel had always insisted that God had promised them the land of Canaan, but wasn't Canaan part of Egypt now? Tuthmosis III had invaded the land as far north as Megiddo. He had conquered Kadesh and tramped over Mount Carmel. Egypt now extended from the Fifth Cataract of the Nile to the Euphrates River, so why couldn't the Promised Land of God include Egypt, too?

"Good morning, Ephraim. This is quite a company you have brought."

Brought back to reality by the sound of a Hebrew greeting, Ephraim turned toward the voice and saw Jokim, Judah's grandson, standing beside him. Managing a polite smile, he lifted his hand to acknowledge the comment. "Yes, it is a large group, but my efforts alone could not have brought them here." He shrugged even though he was pleased that Jokim seemed to think Ephraim had something to do with assembling the procession. "Pharaoh has been generous to us. His guards, his warriors, even his cooks are ours to enjoy on the journey."

Jokim's eyes widened. "How wonderful! I knew your father had influence with the king, but I never dreamed Pharaoh would care so much for Israel!"

"Perhaps Pharaoh knows the Spirit of God rested upon our grandfather as it rests upon my father." *As it will also rest upon me.* Ephraim gave the younger man a tentative smile. "Are you willing to help me? We will need to divide the people here into companies. The Egyptians will take care of themselves, but the Hebrews are scattered like feathers in the wind. If we are to make this journey in peace and security, we must be better organized."

"I would be honored to help you, cousin." Jokim straightened his shoulders and a pleased, proud, and slightly possessive look filled his expression. "But where is Manasseh? I expected him to be with you."

"My brother," Ephraim said, the corner of his mouth lifting in a dry, one-sided smile, "waits for the musicians to disembark. He has lost his heart to a slave and his good sense to love. Leave him, Jokim, to his own folly." He placed his arm across his cousin's shoulders and turned toward the Hebrew camp. "Never forget," he said, a teasing note in his voice, "who is the more favored brother. I am the leader, not Manasseh. If you want results, come to me."

The youth's square face rearranged itself into a grin. "I will remember, cousin," he answered.

———

Akil was not happy to answer Manasseh's impatient questions, but he grudgingly admitted that yes, Pharaoh had commanded that they journey all the way to Canaan and back, and yes, Jendayi the harpist was among the women aboard the felucca. After making certain that the musicians would be comfortable upon the ship for the rest of the evening, Manasseh left the river and strode toward the Hebrew camp. His personal concern for the musicians caused him to arrive later than his father and brother, and that, he sternly told himself, accounted for the fact that no one made a special point of greeting him outside the camp.

Joseph had chosen to pass the night aboard his ship in solitude, so Manasseh looked forward to an evening of renewing friendships with his relatives. But Reuben, Simeon, and Levi, the three eldest uncles with whom Manasseh had always enjoyed an easy camaraderie, scarcely glanced up when he entered Reuben's tent. Simeon did offer a distracted wave, but Ephraim was seated with the uncles and a handful of younger men around a dinner feast, and he easily controlled the conversation.

Manasseh halted in the doorway, surprised by the nonexistent welcome, and was only half-aware that a young slave girl knelt at his feet, tugging on the strings of his sandals in order to wash the dust from his feet. *You are being foolish*, he told himself, shaking his head at the maid. *These are the men who told you that the blessing of the right hand meant nothing, that it didn't matter. And it doesn't, for you are still responsible for your actions, as Ephraim is for his, and nothing can change the fact that you are Joseph's elder son.* But the men who had said farewell to him before with warm embraces now gestured for him to come near the fire as indifferently as if he were a servant, not a firstborn son.

On stiff and unwilling legs, Manasseh moved toward the circle and crouched in an empty space. Ephraim was regaling the relatives with a step-by-step recounting of Jacob's mummification. "I oversaw the entire process," Ephraim said, an expression of immeasurable satisfaction gleaming in his eyes. "I observed as they removed Israel's heart and wrapped it for the ages. I checked on the body for each of the forty days it lay under the covering of natron salts; for over twenty days I supervised the priests who wrapped our father Israel in fine linen."

Reuben threw a sly grin in Manasseh's direction. "And what

did our nephew Manasseh do while you supervised so diligently?''

Manasseh wanted to shout that he had been in Goshen mourning with them for much of the time of embalming, but that truth seemed to have slipped his uncles' minds.

Ephraim grinned. "Manasseh does what he wants to do," he said, his eyes brimming with smug delight as Manasseh stirred uncomfortably. "You, my uncles, have ruined him for Thebes. Ever since he came back from Goshen, he has been fascinated by goats and cows. When he is not examining the new goats in their pens, he walks in the fields and studies the cattle. I am afraid that I will awaken one morning and find that he has coaxed a bull into our father's reception hall."

As the uncles roared with laughter, Manasseh shot Ephraim a hostile glare. Their argument on the boat had apparently escalated into petty warfare, and Manasseh had no wish to continue the feud through the upcoming journey.

But this little skirmish was Ephraim's doing, and he should be the one to apologize. Manasseh had done nothing wrong.

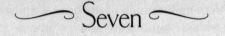

Seven

JENDAYI LIFTED HER FACE TO THE WARM FINGERS OF A caressing breeze, relishing the feel of it on her skin. She and her handmaid rode in a conveyance that Kesi had described as "a pair of huge baskets joined at the middle and slung over a camel's hump." After a short while, Jendayi decided that though the swinging motion so high in the air made her a little sick, she liked this form of transportation. Each girl rode in her own private compartment, granting them a rare measure of privacy. A canopy shaded them from the blistering sun, and the fibers of the woven basket remained blessedly cool to the touch. The rhythmic squeaking of the woven reeds and the camel's grumbling soothed Jendayi, helping her to forget that men of considerable importance and power—all of them her masters—rode in this caravan as well.

Secure in her perch, Jendayi breathed in the sounds and scents of the journey and realized that for some reason she had been pampered. Other slaves walked alongside the pack animals, and the other musicians rode in cargo wagons, but she and her maid had stowed upon a camel.

She sighed, understanding the undeniable truth. Undoubtedly her blindness had caused her to merit this distinctive treatment, but being singled out did not make her happy. She wanted to experience *life*, and yet once again she had been tucked away, literally hidden in a basket, protected by the watchful eye of a handmaid.

None of the other women of the orchestra had maids, but Kesi had been assigned to care for Jendayi shortly after the orchestra's arrival at Pharaoh's palace. Free of Jendayi's encumbering arm, Akil had been eager to enjoy his new mobility, and Jendayi had reluctantly come to depend upon Kesi's guiding hand.

But she did not want to need anyone. Sometimes when Kesi

was away, Jendayi practiced moving around her chamber with only her walking stick for a guide, and she usually managed quite well. But in her short life she had learned that another pair of eyes could be useful.

"Tell me, Kesi," Jendayi strengthened her voice to reach to the other side of the camel's hump, "what is this country like? Where do they say we are?"

"We are in the wilderness," Kesi answered, the basket creaking as she shifted her position. "The sky is blue from rim to rim; there are no clouds and no mountains to mar the horizon. They tell me there is water far to the north, but I cannot see it. The land is the color of a camel, brown and dusty. I see a few tamarind trees and occasionally an oak, but little else. This place is not like Egypt. I have not seen a flower in days."

"No flowers?" Jendayi adored flowers, their scent, their textures, their almost insubstantial weight upon her callused fingertips. Kesi kept a continual supply of flowers by Jendayi's bed in the servants' quarters, and Akil occasionally offered Jendayi bouquets when she played exceptionally well. One day, he told her, she would play a song so beautiful that Pharaoh himself would be impelled to stop and lay flowers at her feet. She could not imagine how to play a song more technically perfect than those she routinely performed now, but Akil seemed to think her best music still lay ahead.

At the thought of her future, she lifted her face again. "Tell me, Kesi, what you know about the people with whom we are traveling. I know they are Hebrews. I have heard them chattering for miles. I learned the sound of their language when I lived in the vizier's house, but I cannot understand them."

"Nor can I," Kesi admitted. The maid's basket creaked sharply. "From what I can see, most of them are traveling on donkeys. There are so many! Several women, older children, and men with long beards and hair that brushes the tops of their shoulders. They have dark hair like the Egyptians, but the Hebrews do not shave their faces or their bodies. Hair even gleams at the necklines of their tunics."

"The men wear full tunics?" Rarely did Egyptian men cover their chests. "Why?"

"I don't know," the maid answered. "Perhaps they do not feel the heat as we do. Most of them wear loosely woven tunics, belted at the waist. Of course, our vizier wears a similar tunic, for his ceremonial robe is long and flowing—"

"What do the vizier's sons wear?" Jendayi interrupted, trying to curb the curiosity in her voice. "Can you see them? Are they both present—the younger as well as the older?"

The basket creaked again. "My sly mistress," Kesi whispered, a hint of laughter in her voice, "if you wanted to know about the vizier's sons, why didn't you come right out and ask? I am your friend, Jendayi. Your secrets are safe with me."

"I don't have any secrets," Jendayi whispered, her face burning. *And I don't want any friends.* Unconsciously, she pressed her hands to her cheeks lest Kesi look over the camel's hump and see the flush upon her skin. "I used to live in the vizier's house. I am merely curious about the young men who once were my masters."

"Don't be coy. You can tell me the truth," Kesi insisted, her voice closer now. "Which son do you like, the older or the younger? I saw them the other day at the queen's banquet. They are both very handsome."

Jendayi paused, tempted to speak her heart, but Kesi might not understand. She would think her mistress possessed of some childish notion of romance, when all Jendayi wanted was to know that someone loved her. Her heart was asleep, but if someone cared enough to wake it, Jendayi would be able to stand in the Hall of the Two Truths and place a flesh-and-blood heart into Anubis' scale.

Perhaps Kesi could be of use after all. "I think I like the younger one," Jendayi whispered, taking pains to keep her voice steady. "When I lived in the vizier's palace, I once went to the garden to practice." She lifted her face sharply toward the younger girl. "Kesi, I will not tell you more unless you promise never to speak of this to anyone! If you are loyal at all, you will keep this secret!"

"My lips will be silent. Go on," Kesi urged. "What happened in the garden?"

Jendayi took a deep breath. "I was very young, you see. But I was sitting in the vizier's pavilion, playing my harp. The sun shone warm on my face, and in those days I could still see a faint glow of its light. I heard only the wind and the warbling of some water birds, but then a silent shadow passed over my eyes, and I knew that someone stood right in front of me."

"Who?"

Jendayi bit her lip. "He did not tell me his name. But he spoke and said my song was beautiful, and that . . . that I was beautiful, too. And before I could beg his forgiveness for making music without permission, I felt . . . his lips upon mine."

Kesi gasped. "He *kissed* you?"

Jendayi nodded, forgetting that her maid could not see into her confining basket. It was enough that Kesi had understood the significance of the story. No kiss between unrelated persons was ever given lightly. No man kissed a woman in public unless he was either very drunk, or they were betrothed. A drunkard who kissed a woman would undoubtedly suffer the rage of her husband or father, while a man who publicly kissed his betrothed would usually find himself the beneficiary of a quick wedding. Masters rarely even *spoke* directly to their slaves, so for a young lord to *kiss* a slave girl . . .

"Did he say nothing else?" Kesi asked.

"No." Jendayi sighed and propped her head on her bent knees. "Akil came into the garden and yelled as if *he* were the master and the vizier's son a mere slave. But the boy left me alone and never spoke to me again." She made a face, for in the retelling, the old story seemed more fiction than fact. "I don't know what he intended, but I am sure in that moment he must have loved me. Why else would he kiss me?"

"Noblemen do not marry their slaves," Kesi murmured, her voice a doubting drawl in the heat. "Never. If perchance a nobleman looks with favor upon a slave, he might make her his concubine. Men marry for position, power, and politics, not for pleasure. You should thank the gods that Akil came into the garden when he did. If the boy had remained alone with you—"

"Zaphenath-paneah and his sons are virtuous. They would not cruelly use me." Jendayi's heavy eyelids closed in the heat. "I did not fear that the vizier's son would harm me. In the days that followed, I feared only his indifference. . . ."

Her words drifted away, for not even in the privacy of this woven basket did she dare speak all the thoughts that filled her mind. Her mother had shown her nothing but disinterest. She had cast Jendayi aside as soon as it became apparent that the girl's eyes were weakening. If Jendayi ever had a father, she did not know him. She had not known the affection of brothers or sisters, cousins, aunts or uncles. Akil fulfilled a father's role more than anyone else in her life, yet she knew he saw her only as a responsibility. As long as she played well, Pharaoh continued to call for Akil, and Akil was pleased with Jendayi. But if she did not play up to the level of her master's expectation, or if for some reason Pharaoh did not call for Akil, the chironomist grew surly and uncommunicative. He would cast fierce taunts and threats at Jendayi, his words lacerating her heart until she wept. Only another invitation from the king would restore Akil's good humor.

No, Akil did not love her. He guarded her as a possession. He taught and disciplined her only to protect his place in the light of Pharaoh's divine approval.

"A secret kiss! What a wonderful story." Kesi clapped her hands. "Indeed, I am nearly crying! The romantic kiss given so long ago still lives in your memory! What if it lives in his, too?"

"I'm afraid it will always be only a story," Jendayi lifted her head, "unless by some miracle the son of Zaphenath-paneah gathers courage enough to speak to me. I confess I have hoped that his feelings have not changed. If I am not too bold before the gods and if he still finds favor in me, I thought he might approach me on this journey. We are away from Pharaoh's house. The gods could not have sent a more propitious opportunity. Unless," she nearly choked on the word, "he has forgotten all about me."

"Forgotten?" Kesi's voice rang with indignation. "How could he forget you? No, my friend. He will not! No doubt he remembers everything as clearly as you do, and he will know the time is right."

"But he is noble! And I am a slave. Nobles do not waste their breath conversing with slaves. He would surely be more willing to speak to a palm tree or to the dust beneath his feet than to me."

"Not the vizier's sons," Kesi retorted. "I've heard that all the vizier's servants are treated civilly. Some say the steward Ani is revered like a lord in that house, and even the kitchen slaves are well treated. If the vizier's son talked to you once, he will talk to you again."

"Then why," Jendayi forced the words over her insecurity, "hasn't he spoken to me before this? Both of the vizier's sons were at Malkata the other day. And there have been other times when he might have at least greeted me."

"Perhaps he is shy. Perhaps he is afraid to approach you."

"I am a slave. How could he be *afraid*?" Jendayi wailed.

"You are a royal slave, and you have a talent that no one can equal," Kesi answered. "He may be awed to the point of silence. He may think that you do not remember the day in the garden. You, mistress, must let him know you remember. You must tell him you want to speak with him."

A thrill of frightened anticipation touched Jendayi's spine. "*Me?* I cannot speak to him! I had thought to touch his heart with music. I have been working on a song—"

"Music is a universal language. It touches all who listen alike . . . unless a listener is forewarned." Determination flooded Kesi's voice. "I will speak to the vizier's son for you. Dictate what you would have me say, and I will relay your message in its fullness. Speak whatever is on your heart. If he is not willing to hear your words, he will call me a foolish slave and send me away. But if the words reach his heart, he will come to you. Out here in the desert there is nothing to prevent him."

Jendayi let her head fall back to the woven wall of the basket. "What message would I give him?" she wondered aloud. "I would tell him that I have waited years for him to explain that kiss in the garden. I would tell him that I have listened through the palace walls in hopes of hearing news of him. In Pharaoh's court I have listened to the vizier's voice and imagined it to be the son's instead. At night when I dream, I can still hear his quickened breath in my ear, his voice, and his admission that he thought my song and my paltry form beautiful. And if he loves me, if it is possible that I could serve him instead of Pharaoh, I would like to know."

"I can't remember all that," Kesi whispered, a smile in her voice. "Perhaps it would be better for you to speak to him yourself."

A wave of sheer black fright swept through Jendayi. "I

couldn't! I am nothing. I could not even approach him!''

Kesi remained silent for a moment, humming slightly as she sorted through her thoughts. "The solution is simple. I shall go to the vizier's younger son and tell him that you wish to inquire of his well-being. He will be polite. He will say he is well. If he is as well mannered as I've heard, he will ask about you. And I will say that you would like to dedicate a song to him in honor of the loyal service you once gave to his father the vizier.''

Jendayi frowned but did not interrupt.

"And tonight, after I have forewarned him, the men will gather around the fire as is their custom. They will call for music, and Akil will bring out the orchestra. And you will insist upon playing an original song, alone.''

"What if Akil objects? He has not been allowing me to play by myself.''

"You have power, Jendayi. You should learn to use it! Tell Akil you must play alone or you will never play for him again! And when he gives you a moment to play by yourself, open your mouth and sing one of the ancient love songs. If the vizier's son does not remember your time in the garden, he will think you are merely singing one of the old songs. But if the young man *does* remember, his heart will understand what your heart is saying! On the wings of Nut, goddess of the sky, compassion will rise from his heart and fly into yours!''

Jendayi pressed her hand over her lips, a little stunned by Kesi's bold plan. She could not imagine committing such an audacious act in Pharaoh's palace, but out here in the wilderness such a plan seemed amazingly reasonable. Kesi's idea was as safe as any course of action she might undertake. If the vizier's son was insulted or otherwise offended by a slave's approach, Kesi would bear the reprimand. And Jendayi *had* been practicing a song for Ephraim. What better time to sing it than tonight?

"Be it according to what you have said,'' Jendayi whispered. "Tonight, when we have made camp, find the younger son of Zaphenath-paneah. If he will speak with you privately, tell him the next time I am asked to play alone, I will sing and play for him. I do so in appreciation for the kind treatment I received while I lived in the vizier's house.''

"Wonderful!''

"Shh. Now be silent. I must practice until the fingerings are perfect!" Jendayi frowned and fumbled for the small practice harp in the basket with her. "I don't know why I listen to you, Kesi. Akil will surely disapprove and scold me. But I must know if the vizier's son remembers. I must know if he might be willing to take me from Pharaoh's house."

As her fingers closed around the neck of her harp, the dark memory of her recurring dream passed over her like a shadow, and she shivered. Her cold and stony heart had clattered into Anubis' golden scales on too many nights. She had glimpsed love only once in her life, and she would follow where it led her, no matter how perilous the journey.

───────

As the sun began to sink toward the western horizon, the caravan circled and made camp for the night. Kesi held tight to the rim of the basket as the moving mountain of camel flesh beneath her dipped to its knees and sank onto the ground, then she helped Jendayi out of the other basket so the herdsmen could water the animals.

"Are you still going to do it?" Jendayi whispered, clinging to Kesi's arm as the camel clambered to his feet and shuffled away.

"Later. After we have eaten," Kesi said, moving toward the huddled women who clustered around Akil. "But first I will see that you are sheltered and fed."

The first Amenhotep, a prudent pharaoh of the twelfth dynasty, had established the Wall of the Prince, a loose string of garrisons that guarded Egypt's frontier borders. The caravan had stopped outside one of those garrisons, Kesi realized. A handful of Bedouin border guards walked through the encampment with undisguised curiosity in their eyes.

Kesi left Jendayi in a hastily erected tent, brought her mistress a hunk of crusty brown bread and some dried goat's meat from a supply wagon, then wrapped a shawl around her head in the manner of the Hebrew women. As the unloading progressed, Kesi saw that the camp had split into two nearly perfect concentric circles: Egyptians in the forefront, Hebrews at the rear. Into which camp had Zaphenath-paneah and his sons settled?

Pensively, she looked out into the darkness, then spied the

white-and-gold vizier's tent rising like a phoenix at the confluence of the two groups. Kesi dropped the covering veil and moved boldly forward, relieved that she would not have to search among the Hebrews. An Egyptian slave woman dipped her head slightly in greeting as Kesi approached the outer periphery of the vizier's ornate tent. The sides of the canopy had not been unrolled, and the tent remained open for all to see the vizier inside. He sat upon a light wooden chair, a delicate, elegant piece of furniture that had appeared as if from out of nowhere in the midst of the wilderness.

Kesi lingered among a group of slaves outside, her eyes skimming over the tent's inhabitants. The Egyptian nomarchs had been invited to eat with the vizier; they lounged upon cushions and pillows, their postures relaxed, their eyes merry with wine. *It is obvious,* Kesi thought, glancing around the circle, *that this procession is not made to bury one of their fathers.*

The darkly compact captain of the guard stood at the vizier's side, his sharp eyes roaming over the crowd as his hand hovered near the hilt of the dagger in his belt. For an instant his eyes caught Kesi's, and a tiny tremor of fear shook her when he lifted an eyebrow as if to say, *You do not belong here.* She lowered her eyes and turned away, hoping to escape into the crowd, but before her guilty feet had carried her four steps, a hand abruptly caught her elbow. Another alert warrior escorted her to the muscled captain of the guard, who had moved outside the tent.

"You wear the garb of Pharaoh's slaves." The captain's eyes hardened with speculation. "Why do you take such an interest in the vizier's dinner? Have you no work to do?"

"I have work," Kesi stammered, keeping her gaze lowered. "I am on my mistress's bidding."

"And who is your mistress?" He dipped his head to better see her face. "I don't recognize you."

"My mistress is Jendayi, Pharaoh's harpist."

The guard lifted his chin as if satisfied with her answer, but a slight hesitation remained in his hawklike eyes. "What business does Pharaoh's harpist have in the vizier's tent?"

Kesi clasped her arms across her chest. "My mistress used to live in the vizier's house."

"I know. Go on."

"She asked me to find one of the vizier's sons. They are . . . friends."

"One of the vizier's sons has befriended a slave?" She expected anger, but amusement flickered in the guard's eyes, and his mouth quirked with humor. He shifted his weight and tapped his chin with one finger. "Let's see . . . who did I hear discussing the little harpist just this morning? One of my young masters, as I recall, praised her beauty to the skies."

"You jest!" Kesi clapped her hand over her lips as soon as the words escaped her.

"I do not make idle jokes." The captain lowered his voice. All signs of severity vanished from his face as he stepped closer and bent to whisper in Kesi's ear. "The vizier's son has often confided in me of his high regard for the little harpist. Only providence and propriety have kept him from declaring his feelings. I daresay the lad is bold enough to approach Pharaoh himself to beg for her release."

A thrill shivered through Kesi's senses. Surely the gods had arranged this meeting! "I have a message for the young man," she said, her heart hammering against her ribs. "I should deliver it personally, but I do not want to venture into that tent. No one knows me, and too many people would wonder what business I have there." Her eyes met the guard's. "Just as you did."

"You are wise to be discreet, for one does not speak openly of coveting one of Pharaoh's slaves," the captain answered, grinning at her. "This is a risky business, so I will give him your message myself. And you may tell your mistress that Tarik, captain of the vizier's guard, owes her a great debt, for years ago the beauty of her music inspired me to propose marriage to my own wife, Halima. We have married, and I am very happy in love."

Kesi smiled in pleased surprise. "Then my mistress bids me tell your master that on account of her fond memories in Zaphenath-paneah's house, the song she will play and sing tonight is only for him." Her eyes flitted over the gathering in the fire-lit tent. "She is planning to play for the vizier's entertainment."

"Then let us not keep love waiting," the guard replied, still smiling as he moved away.

Jendayi bit her lip in concentration, forcing her fingers to fly over the strings of her harp. Akil would cut out her tongue if he knew what she planned tonight, for one did not ordinarily sing of love during a funereal procession, no matter how long and protracted the excursion might be. But Kesi had bubbled with jubilation on her return; the message had been delivered.

More shocking than the delivery, however, was the news her maid had gathered from the captain of the vizier's guard. "Even now, the vizier's son thinks of you!" Kesi crowed, unsuccessfully struggling to keep her voice low. "The captain says the young man is bold enough even to beg Pharaoh for you!"

Jendayi's fingers trembled now, and they seemed unusually cold and stiff. Why? She couldn't remember the last time she had felt nervous. Playing was as natural to her as eating and sleeping. She thrived on creating intricate improvisations that would bewilder or exhaust other harpists. Akil had long stopped trying to direct her solo work. When given the signal to take the lead from the oboist or lutist, Jendayi played the melodies in her head, producing remarkable sensations of sound, rippling passages that often surprised herself and drew breathless admiration from all who heard. But tonight her words and voice would command center stage. The glissandos of the harp would be only the frame around the painting, a jewel to adorn the crown.

"Mistress, Akil waits outside. The vizier calls for music."

Jendayi stood and brushed her damp hands across the linen of her gown, then pulled the harp into the circle of her arms. Tonight, through her harp, she would offer her heart . . . and wait to see if it would be accepted.

While the musicians played a steady stream of dinner music, Manasseh struggled to keep his face composed in bland, pleasant lines. Since Tarik had brought him news of Jendayi's intention, his heart had alternately lurched in anticipation and twisted in the agonies of despair. The harpist intended to sing for *him* tonight, Tarik had reported, but what if she sang of the brutality of noblemen or the sufferings of life? What if she offered merely a song of sympathy to ease the passing of his grandfather, or, even worse, to console him for not receiving the most favored blessing? Perhaps the palace gossips had filled the girl's ears with news of Manasseh's humiliation, and she intended only to comfort him with sweet music.

She did not know how he adored her. How could she imagine a love as deep as the ocean? She was a royal slave. She dared not even dream of release. Unless Manasseh could reach her, she would live and die within the confines of Pharaoh's palace. Her talent, her virtue, her life were Pharaoh's to command. So it had always been, and so it would always be.

But she did not know how Manasseh loved her. *And my heart*, he thought, watching her lovely face across the tent, *understands hers. I know the despair of losing a mother. I know how it feels to reach out for a father and find only a substitute. But my father was once a slave and is now second only to Pharaoh himself. So I see you, little Jendayi, not as a slave, but as what you shall be: a great lady, my wife.*

Would Akil *never* tell the others to be quiet so she could play alone? Manasseh was tempted to stand and demand a harp solo, but Jendayi might think him spoiled and foolish if he behaved so impetuously. His father's important guests—the governors, priests, and counselors—had eaten their fill and slouched now in the quiet contentment of satiated men. Their eyes would not remain open another quarter hour. If Jendayi was going to play, she must play soon.

"Most honored Akil."

Manasseh flinched as his father's voice sliced through his thoughts and rose above the subdued murmurs of the group.

"I wonder if you might allow us to be dismissed tonight with something special. We have passed a long and tiring day in the wilderness where all seemed gray and bleak to my eyes. Surely your harpist has hidden a few emerald grasses and the rush of the river in her instrument?"

Akil bowed his head in a deep gesture of respect, then turned, a bit reluctantly, and extended his arm toward his harpist.

One of the other women nudged Jendayi. Manasseh leaned forward. Did his eyes deceive him or were her fingers trembling? As Akil folded his hands and stepped back, surrendering the attention of the audience, the girl ran her fingers lightly over the strings. Golden streams of sound splashed into the silence and then, wonder of wonders, she opened her mouth and began to sing.

"How weary is the nobleman," she sang, the sound as light as a flitting bird that wings the air. Manasseh blinked in astonished silence, caught off guard by the vibrancy of her voice.

> Good fate has become true.
> Verily, bodies have perished since the days of the god,
> Others taken their place.

Manasseh felt the squeeze of disappointment. This funereal song was not what he had hoped for. But she sang on:

> Spend a happy day, son of the nobleman,
> Follow your heart for as long as it is yours.
> Spend a happy day, ignore all evil and remember
>   happiness
> Until the day arrives when you moor in the land
>   that loves silence.
> Spend a happy day. Do whatever you praise.
> Let your heart be very, very happy.
> Spend a happy day, son of the nobleman,
> Follow your desire so long as you shall live.

By the time Jendayi had finished, Manasseh's own heart sang with delight. How terribly clever of her to mingle her encouragement for him with a sympathetic reminder that life was fleeting! And since nearly every man in the gathering considered himself the son of a nobleman, both the intended recipient and her message had been hidden in the most obvious of contexts.

The Egyptians applauded loudly, demanding to hear the song again, but Akil quickly stepped in and directed the oboist in another melody.

Glorying in the moment, Manasseh leaned toward his father. "Wasn't she wonderful?" he whispered, reaching his hand to his father's arm.

"What?" Joseph's eyes stirred with many thoughts. Manasseh's question was an obvious distraction.

"The song! Didn't you hear it?"

"Very nice, as always." Joseph smiled politely and turned to the Crown Prince, who sat in the chair nearest him. "Akil does a wonderful job with Pharaoh's musicians. It was most gracious of your father the king to send them on our journey."

He had not heard. He had no idea of the song's significance. Manasseh listened with rising dismay as Joseph continued a quiet conversation with the Crown Prince and one of the nomarchs. But his father's opinions did not matter. Jendayi had sung for Manasseh, sweetly urging him to follow his heart and its innermost desires. And he desired only one thing, one woman.

Turning away from his father and the prince, Manasseh settled upon his cushion and stretched his long legs before him. When they returned to Thebes, he would don his finest clothes, silver armbands, and cloak, then present himself to Pharaoh. Perhaps he could persuade his father to write a letter on his behalf. But through flattery, friendship, or finagling, Manasseh would convince Pharaoh to return Jendayi to the vizier's house. Tonight he had learned that she was willing to be his, and he would not rest until she was free to be his wife.

Manasseh lifted his hand and caught Tarik's attention. The captain casually strolled over, nodding at a few nobles as he walked. He wore a sly smile when he finally reached Manasseh's side. "So tell me, young master, has the evening's entertainment been . . . interesting?"

"Yes," Manasseh answered, his courage and determination like a rock inside him. "Most interesting, Tarik. The girl is willing! You heard her. Now I must go to Pharaoh for her. I will not be happy until she is my wife, and I will tell her so this very night, as soon as my father's guests have dispersed."

The captain held up a warning finger. "You must curb your eagerness, young lion! She is not just any slave. She is Pharaoh's property. And here," he lowered his voice while pointedly glancing right and left, "we are among Egyptians who would not hesitate to tell the king that the vizier's son has taken advantage of the royal favor. You must not speak of your intentions to anyone. You are setting out to climb an impossible mountain, and if you are to succeed, you must carefully plot your course."

Manasseh glanced up in dismay. "Impossible?"

"Perhaps." Tarik shrugged, then smiled. "But your father would say nothing is impossible for your God Shaddai."

Manasseh transferred his gaze back to Jendayi's pensive face. She was waiting for his response. She would want to know what he would do. "Tarik, I must speak with her!"

"You must not! Stay away from the girl and do nothing unusual. If anyone here later insinuates that you have done so much as touch her, the king will never grant your request. Pharaoh may even deem it necessary to punish you, or he might use her to set an example for other slaves. Tread cautiously, Manasseh. Love has quickened your heart, but you must not foolishly pursue it."

Manasseh grappled with his winged thoughts. Tarik was right. One did not trifle with Pharaoh's slaves, Pharaoh's children, even Pharaoh's counselors. He knew he ought to be silent and sly. He would have to put a tight rein around his eager heart. With one careless word or unthinking action he could destroy both his life and Jendayi's.

"All right," he said, looking up at the bantam guard who had often proved to be a wise and willing counselor. "I will be careful. I will guard my lips so that you alone know of this, Tarik. But I must let her know that I love her. Find the slave who brought Jendayi's message to you. Tell her I understand. As soon as my grandfather is buried, and we have returned to Thebes, I will approach Pharaoh on Jendayi's behalf. Though my own life be forfeit as penalty for my boldness, I will redeem her from Pharaoh's house. I will not fail her."

With a slow secret smile, Tarik nodded. "I will relay your message."

————

"He listened?" Jendayi's voice rose in surprise.

"Shh!" Kesi whispered, laughing. She lifted the thin blanket that covered Jendayi and slipped beneath it, snuggling close to her mistress. "Yes. I have just spoken to the captain of the vizier's guard, who brought a message directly from the vizier's son. The message is this: As soon as Israel is buried and we are returned to Thebes, he will approach Pharaoh and ask that you be returned to the vizier's house. Though the attempt cost him his life, he says he will not fail.''

Jendayi pressed her hands to her mouth, shock wedging words in her throat.

"There is more," Kesi went on, her breath warm in Jendayi's ear. "The guard says you must be discreet with this news. You must speak of this with no one but me, for you are Pharaoh's slave, and no man has any right to talk to you, much less desire you as his own. You must not seek out the young man so no one can suspect him of immodest behavior toward you. And you must guard your tongue, lest you slip and reveal this secret."

"I can guard my tongue," Jendayi whispered, still lost in incredulity. The vizier's son was an endless surprise. She had never dreamed that he might be truly serious in his concern for her. And he was right. This would have to be a solemn and secret enterprise, for she was not only a slave, but a prized one, certainly worth her weight in silver or gold.

"Can you believe it?" Kesi whispered, a tremor of excitement in her voice. She pressed her trembling hand to Jendayi's arm. "In all my days, I never imagined such a thing could be possible. You long to be reunited with the vizier's son, and he wishes to bring you back to his house! It is like a dream, a wish only the gods have power enough to accomplish."

"Yes," Jendayi whispered, certain now that her heart would learn to live and love. "The gods *will* bring it to pass. I would stake my life on it."

~⌐ Eight ⌐~

ANXIOUS TO AVOID ROGUE BANDS OF WARLIKE PHIL-
istines, the company journeyed through the desert to the Salt
Sea, then skirted that sea's eastern shore and moved north
toward the Jordan River. When they came to the threshing floor
of Goren ha-Atad, north of the Salt Sea and east of the Jordan,
the mixed company of Hebrews and Egyptians set up camp. Because his duties had kept him in Thebes while his brothers
mourned in Goshen, Joseph proclaimed that they would not
move farther until he had observed seven days of mourning for
Israel with his brothers. And they sorrowed there with a very
great and heavy lamentation.

At the close of the seventh day, the Hebrews and the Egyptians assembled in one circle around one fire. Ani, who had
grown as capable with the Canaanite tongue as he was with the
Egyptian, stood in the center of the clearing to interpret for those
who had not picked up the other nation's language.

As they had in Goshen, the Hebrews stood and told the story
of Israel's life. One by one, each of Jacob's sons recited a tale:
Israel's birth, his lineage from Abraham, his struggles with his
brother Esau, his experience at the gate of heaven, his marriages
to Rachel and Leah, the begetting of his twelve sons. Then the
Egyptians, beginning with the Crown Prince, continued the eu-
logy, praising Jacob's descent into Egypt, the glory of his son
Zaphenath-paneah, his decision to allow Ephraim and Manasseh, sons of Egypt, to be counted among his heirs.

Joseph stood last. "By faith," he said, his dark eyes raking
over the silent priests of Amon-Re who watched with undisguised curiosity, "we understand that the word of the invisible
God prepared the world. The things we see were not made by
visible hands, but invisible."

As Ani's translation rang out over the gathering, the Egyp-

tians and Hebrews alike nodded in assent. The Hebrews knew
the invisible God as El Shaddai; the Egyptians knew him as
Neter.

"Without faith in the invisible One, it is impossible to please
God Almighty," Manasseh heard his father continue, "for he who
comes to God must believe that He is, and that He answers those
who seek Him."

The Egyptian priests cast each other assuring smiles. Manasseh was certain they had heard rumors about Zaphenath-
paneah's strange and invisible god, but thus far they had not
heard anything they did not believe themselves.

"With assurance and reverence," Joseph continued, "Noah,
being warned by God Almighty about things yet to come, prepared a bark for the salvation of his household. By his obedience
he and his family were saved from the great flood, and the world
rose from the waters so that men again might fill it."

The priests' smiles trembled now. Manasseh knew they believed life came from the primeval waters, but the story of Noah
was as new to them as it was to him. Too busy with the affairs of
Pharaoh's kingdom to personally tutor his sons, like other Egyptian nobles Joseph had left the religious and social education of
his sons to Ani and others of his household. But Ani was an
Egyptian and had never spoken of this man called Noah.

With the graceful air of an individual at home in many
worlds, Joseph went on: "With trust in God Almighty, Abraham,
when he heard God's call, obeyed by going out to the place he
was to receive for an inheritance. He went out, not knowing
where he was going. By faith he lived as an alien in the land of
promise, a foreign country, dwelling in tents in order to advance
when the voice of God compelled him to rise and move on. Abraham's wife, Sarah, received the ability to conceive even beyond
the proper time of life because she considered God Shaddai
faithful and able to keep His word."

Joseph spoke slowly now, as if carefully measuring each word
before pronouncing it. "And so from Abraham came Isaac, and
from Isaac, Jacob, and from Jacob, twelve sons. And from the
twelve, as God has promised, will come descendants to rival the
stars of heaven in number, as innumerable as the sand of the sea-
shore."

Manasseh frowned. His father had never uttered these truths before. Was it wise to pronounce them before Egyptians who might feel threatened? Manasseh glanced toward the Crown Prince and the priests around him. The boy who would one day be king wore a perplexed expression. Lines of concentration had deepened even upon the priests' faces. They, too, were at a loss to explain their vizier's comments.

"By faith Abraham, when he was tested, offered up Isaac, a willing sacrifice. Though God had said, 'In Isaac your descendants shall be called,' Abraham believed that God was able to raise men, even from the dead."

A ripple of wonder echoed through the Egyptians, punctuated by at least one snort of disbelief. Though they were staunch believers in the afterlife, never had one of their gods restored a man to mortal life.

"It was by faith that Isaac blessed Jacob and Esau, even regarding things to come." Joseph's voice rumbled through the quiet of the night shadows. "And by faith my father Jacob, as he was dying, blessed each of his sons and included mine among his own. Like my forefathers, he died in full confidence that God Shaddai would fulfill his promises."

A servant threw a bundle of dry rushes onto the dying fire. The flames leaped up, throwing the darkness back, and Manasseh saw his father's form clearly in the fire-tinted darkness. He stood as tall and straight as one of Lebanon's towering cedars, and his eyes gleamed with the same certainty that had lit Jacob's dying gaze.

"As of this day," Joseph went on, "the Hebrews have no land to call their own. We are a growing clan, but we are still small in number, generations away from rivaling the starry host. But my fathers saw the covenants of God Shaddai and welcomed them from a distance, even as I do."

An indefinable feeling of contentment filled Manasseh's heart. He slid his gaze to the place where Ephraim sat beside Jokim and tried to catch his brother's eye. Could Ephraim not see how marvelously and uniquely God had blessed their people? God Shaddai, who was far more powerful and infinite than the gods of Egypt, had personally called the Hebrews out from Canaan and would yet return them to the land! This place, this vast, rimless wilderness of Canaan, belonged to *them*, as did the green valleys of the Jordan, the pleasant fields that were every bit as fertile as Goshen.

Ephraim was smiling absently, his eyes vacant and fixed on the fire, his thoughts miles away. How could he sit through the testimonies of Jacob and his forefathers and not feel the stirring of patriarchal passion in his blood? The sons of Israel were the *chosen ones*, destined to bless the world, elected by the holiest Spirit, the Creator of the world.

And yet Ephraim now studied his hands as if his only concern was for their next grooming.

Moving to the center of the circle, Joseph lifted his arm and gestured toward the Crown Prince and his priests. "Depart to your tents tonight in peace, my brothers and friends," he said, bowing deeply to the prince. "Take your rest in this place for a few days, for tomorrow the sons of Israel will go forth to bury their father. Honored priests, governors, and my prince, I ask you to remain here and enjoy the beauty of this fertile riverbank. I will leave my steward with you so that all your needs will be met. But I beg you to allow my brothers and me alone to take our father on his final journey."

The Egyptians looked automatically to their prince, and Manasseh knew the thoughts that skittered through their minds. This was a most unusual request. Why would the vizier take them all into the wilderness only to abandon them so close to the grave? The traditional Egyptian burial involved great ceremony at the site of the tomb, many prayers, incantations, rituals, anointings, weeping, wailing . . .

But Zaphenath-paneah could talk even a future pharaoh into anything. The prince's alert, weakly handsome face creased into a smile. He nodded at the vizier without speaking, granting Joseph's request, then stood and allowed his guards to escort him to his royal tents. Whether or not they agreed with their prince's decision, one by one the other Egyptians rose from their places and slipped through the shadows.

With a thickly beating heart, Manasseh wound his way carefully through the tangle of dispersing men to his brother's side. "Ephraim." He clutched the hardness of his brother's arm. "Do you not feel it?" He lifted his eyes to the sky, black and icy with a wash of brilliant stars, then lowered his eyelids and inhaled deeply. "Do you not sense it in this place?"

A look of annoyance shot across Ephraim's face. "Do I not feel *what*? I feel tired, if that's what you mean. And sorry for the old men. This desert journey will not be easy for them if we leave the chariots behind."

"I'm not talking about the burial." Manasseh shook his head impatiently and struggled for words. "I'm talking about our destiny! Could you not sense a feeling as Father spoke? We are the generation to come, the ones Israel intended to carry the blessing of God Shaddai. It is up to us!" He shifted uneasily and rubbed the stubble on his chin, not certain how to explain himself. He had seen everything so clearly while his father spoke. He had *felt* a mantle of responsibility fall onto his shoulders. He and Ephraim were the sons of Joseph, inheritors of the firstborn's blessing. They would naturally rise to lead the generation to come.

But Ephraim's dark eyes expressed more challenge than curiosity. "It is not up to *us*, brother," he said, his voice clipped. "If anything, it is up to *me*, for I will be greater than you, remember?"

For a moment Manasseh's mouth opened in dismay, then he dropped his eyelids quickly to hide his hurt. But Ephraim's dark eyebrows had arched in the mischievous look Manasseh knew well. "I'm only jesting, Manasseh, so wipe that affronted look off your face," he said, smiling. "You are tired. We all are. Go to sleep."

But his words had cut deep, spreading an infection of doubt. Were Manasseh's fervent feelings only the result of grief-induced exhaustion? Was this conviction that God intended them to lead the Hebrews only an offspring of his fevered imagination? Perhaps the desert had played tricks on him, inflating his hopes for the future with dreams of Jendayi and the false notion that he might prove to be as favored as his younger brother.

Abruptly nodding at Ephraim and Jokim, Manasseh wished them a good-night.

———

As soon as dawn lifted the horizon the next morning, the sons of Israel packed their donkeys and wagons and turned them toward the fertile Jordan River Valley. The Egyptians, remaining behind at Joseph's order, would wait for the children of Israel to rejoin them after the burial.

Still smarting from their encounter the previous night, Manasseh studiously avoided Ephraim's presence, preferring to walk with his uncles. Each of Jacob's sons seemed as strong and stable as the earth itself. Though stooped with age, Reuben could control the younger men with a simple flick of his gray brows. Levi displayed a quality of animal assurance Manasseh had never seen in an Egyptian. Simeon had been gifted with wit, directness, and intelligence. Judah possessed an unshakable spiritual force, a great presence born of certainty.

Manasseh supposed his uncles fascinated him because their lives had been so different from his. Born in a rough wilderness, they had learned to fend for themselves in an often cruel environment; he had been born in a polished chamber where slaves brought his food and would have hand-fed him had he commanded it. The Hebrews' livelihood as herders depended upon strength, quickness, and courage; he had spent his earliest years quietly learning how to read and write the hieroglyphs. Though he had later received military training from Tarik, Manasseh had never honestly feared for his life—indeed, he had ventured into duels knowing he would not be harmed. No one would dare wound the vizier's son. Only Ephraim had ever landed a blow upon him.

His uncles were monumentally self-confident, sensible, and practical. Their fierce, protective manner simultaneously amazed and encouraged Manasseh. The Egyptians he had known in his lifetime were easygoing and carefree, separated by class differences as cleanly as the Nile separated the cities of the living from the dead. And yet the Hebrews considered a cousin related by blood as close as a brother, regardless of his social standing or how far away he had sojourned in his life.

Simeon, the largest and loudest son of Jacob, invited Manasseh to travel with him and his wife. Manasseh accepted the honor, knowing the invitation had been prompted by Simeon's unique tie to Joseph's family. Years ago, before the brothers knew Zaphenath-paneah was their own long lost Joseph, Simeon had spent nearly a year as a prisoner in the vizier's house.

Simeon seemed especially eager to arrive at Mamre and the burial place. His long steps left gaping holes in the desert sand, and Manasseh grew breathless trying to keep pace with him.

"Once, many years ago, I went to the tomb alone," Simeon told Manasseh as they walked, his hand tightening around the staff in his grip. "Before we descended into Egypt. Before I married Mandisa."

Manasseh cast a quick glance at the woman who rode atop the donkey. Though protective veils covered her head and much of her face, Manasseh could see that her eyes shone with a rich, fawnlike beauty. He had heard that Mandisa had once been his mother's handmaid, but she left the vizier's house when his mother died. When Manasseh searched his memory for his mother, he found only a whisper of sweet lotus fragrance, the ghost of a cool hand upon his head, the melodious tones of a young woman's voice.

"I stood alone at the burial cave," Simeon's voice drew Manasseh back from the brink of memory, "and there I felt the presence of God. I left the cave a changed man, Manasseh. Though I was not yet the man I should have been, my soul burned with the knowledge that a man cannot trifle with God Shaddai."

He turned suddenly and his dark eyes searched Manasseh's face, reaching into his thoughts. "You have been distressed of late," he said smoothly, with no expression on his face as his powerful frame moved with easy grace through the sand. "Would you like to tell me what troubles you?"

Keeping up the pace, Manasseh thrust his hands behind his back and tried to organize his thoughts. Would his uncle understand his thoughts of Jendayi? Could he appreciate the love that would propel him to approach Pharaoh as soon as they returned to Egypt? Or perhaps Simeon had noticed Manasseh's longing to know his heritage, his fascination with the history he had only just discovered.

"I am not troubled"—Manasseh pulled his drifting thoughts together—"but in the past few days I have learned so many things. I had never heard such stories of Abraham, Isaac, and Jacob. My father occasionally mentioned the names of my forefathers, of course, but never did he share those stories—

undreamed-of treasures! I never imagined that God would stoop to make promises and covenants with men."

Simeon grunted in response but said nothing for a long while. They had left the fertile valley of the Jordan River and now climbed the foothills of a mountain range. Bawling winds scoured the ridges and mountain rims, whistling through skeletal trees and leafless brush as it blew dirt into their eyes and hair.

"I think there is more on your mind than what you are telling me," Simeon finally said, firing the words over his shoulder as he moved ahead to take the reins of his wife's plodding donkey. "For I have seen your eyes, and a young man's longing glance is easy to read. Love has taken root in your heart, has it not?"

Manasseh bit his lip and lowered his head against the wind. He wanted to cry *Yes! It has!* But Simeon would think him insane, totally mad. An iron core patriarch like his uncle would not understand or encourage the throes of love.

But the face Simeon turned to him displayed an uncanny awareness. "Remember this lesson." Simeon slowed his step as he lowered his gaze to Manasseh's. "If you love, you must be prepared to sacrifice all you have. If you are not willing to surrender even your life, you do not love at all."

In a gentle movement as unexpected as a clap of thunder on a clear day, Simeon reached up, took his wife's hand, and pressed it to his lips. The smile Mandisa gave him in return was as intimate as a kiss.

One day, Manasseh thought, the back of his neck burning as he turned his eyes from the tender scene, *Jendayi will smile at me that way.*

————————

Two days later the procession of Hebrews passed by Hebron, a prosperous walled city of homes with luxuriant vineyards and fig trees. Two miles outside Hebron, the company halted at the grove where Abraham had resided. While the women set about preparing a meal, the men watered the animals and made camp. "We will pass the night here after our father's burial," Joseph declared. "As soon as camp is established, let us fulfill our vow to Israel."

Manasseh was helping one of his cousins raise a tent when Simeon pulled him aside. "Come see this," Simeon said, gesturing toward the grove. He lifted his hand and pointed to a majestic terebinth tree whose massive trunk divided into four colossal branches and spread like wings toward heaven. "Our forefather Abraham sat under that tree," he said, his voice heavy with an almost reverent nostalgia. "He was sitting under that tree when the three mysterious visitors from God told him Isaac would be born." Simeon's dark eyes, set in valleys webbed and serried like the earth in drought, shone with kindness as he smiled at his nephew. "I thought you would like to know."

A stab of feeling, like a message hurtling through the years, caught Manasseh off guard. "Yes," he answered in a husky voice he scarcely recognized as his own. "Thank you for telling me." Leaving his uncle's side, he walked slowly toward the ancient tree and laid his hands upon the scabrous, pitted bark. Abraham, the one who bargained with God, had stood here. Perhaps his hands had touched this bark, his flesh had pressed against its rough ridges.

Manasseh turned, resting his back against the rugged surface of the tree, then slid slowly down, scarcely feeling the discomfort. What thoughts and dreams had filled the patriarch's head as he sat here? Abraham had believed God's covenant to create a nation from his seed, but had he known that a ruler of Egypt would rise from his lineage? And from that ruler, two sons? "Would he," Manasseh mused, lifting his gaze to the branches overhead, "have given my brother the blessing of the right hand? Or would he have seen in me something that Grandfather could not?"

He wasn't sure how long he remained there, lost in his thoughts, but the soft shooshing sound of the burial sledge distracted him from his reverie. He turned in time to see the ox-drawn sledge, topped by the elaborate sarcophagus and the chest of canopic jars, begin to move out of the camp. Jacob's sons, six on each side, walked beside the conveyance, their somber faces like stone masks of grief.

Ephraim walked at the end of one line, like a thirteenth son, and Manasseh grimaced slightly as he stood and brushed the dirt from his tunic. Jacob's dying gesture had proclaimed him and

Ephraim as sons in name and inheritance, and he realized he ought to be walking with them, across from Ephraim. Quickly he hurried into place behind Benjamin and hoped that none of the others had noticed his absence.

For twenty minutes they walked in silence, the only sounds the whisper of the sledge and the occasional jingle of the oxen's harness. An unseasonable heat covered the mountain slope like a blanket, drying the perspiration on Manasseh's skin before its dampness had a chance to cool his body. He wore a long tunic and cloak in the style of his uncles; now he sent a covetous glance toward Ephraim's elegant kilt. Every bit the Egyptian, Ephraim looked cool even under his heavy wig.

The procession came to a halt outside a large stone outcropping at a brown and barren ridge. A half-dozen rock hyraxes squealed and scurried away as Simeon's shadow fell across the rocky debris at the base of the cliff. Without comment, Reuben, Simeon, and Levi advanced and jammed a beam of wood beneath an immense boulder. Wedging a smaller rock beneath the beam for a fulcrum, they pressed downward with all their might. Within a moment the boulder scraped against the wall of stone and moved away.

A fetid breeze broomed the dust momentarily, and Manasseh peered toward the opening, half-afraid of what he would see. The Hebrews did not ordinarily mummify their dead, and Manasseh stirred uneasily at the thought of accidentally viewing an unpreserved corpse. Abraham and Sarah were buried here, along with Isaac and Rebekah and Leah. Had the dry air of the desert preserved them? Or had their mortal remains submitted to the slow decay of death?

He was relieved when he realized he would not discover the answer to his questions. Joseph and Benjamin, the sons of Rachel, pried open the sarcophagus and wooden coffin, then carefully lifted out Israel's mummified remains. While the others watched in silence, these two carried the body of their father into the tomb and laid him to rest for the ages. As an afterthought, Judah pried open the canopic chest and removed the jars. These he gave to Dan, Naphtali, Asher, and Zebulun, who deposited them inside the tomb.

The expensive granite sarcophagus and elaborate canopic

chest were left outside the burial place. They were too heavy to lower into the cave and of little significance to the Hebrews. No Egyptian would think of entering the otherworld without adequate protection for his remains and enough worldly goods to sustain life in the spiritual realm, but Manasseh knew that his father placed no faith in the Egyptian beliefs. He had allowed the priests to perform a ceremonial mummification in order to preserve the body, but Jacob would be buried according to Hebrew tradition.

When Joseph and Benjamin finally came out of the cave, their faces drawn with grief and weariness, Levi, Reuben, and Simeon maneuvered the guardian stone back into place. When it had settled back into its customary position, the brothers looked to Joseph, expectation on their faces.

He drew a ragged breath and broke the silence. "I love you, O God, my strength," he said, lifting his hands to heaven. His words echoed among the rocks like a voice from an empty tomb. "God Shaddai is my rock, my fortress, my deliverer. He is my God in whom I take refuge, my shield and the horn of my salvation, my stronghold. I call upon El Shaddai, who is worthy to be praised, and I am saved from my enemies. Though the cords of death encompass me and the torrents of ungodliness terrify me, though the cords of Sheol surround me and the snares of death confront me, in my distress I will call upon God Shaddai. He will hear my voice and my cry before I even speak it."

The uncles' somber faces seemed to relax at Joseph's reassuring words. They breathed more easily, for their responsibilities had been fulfilled and their father laid to rest. The day of Jacob had passed. They were the fathers now. And they were ready.

"God Shaddai sent help from on high," Joseph went on. "He drew me out of the pit. He delivered me from my strong enemy and from those who hated me. They confronted me in the day of my calamity, but God Shaddai was my stay. He rescued me because He delighted in me."

Manasseh's emotions bobbed and spun like pieces of jungle vine caught in the Nile flood as he stared past his father into his own thoughts.

God Shaddai ordained a covenant with one man, Abraham, in order to bless the nations of the world.

God Shaddai reached down to rescue his father from the prison pit in order to preserve Abraham's seed.

God Shaddai not only ruled the overarching affairs of nations, He reached down to offer help and solace to individual needy souls. The God of many was also the God of one.

"You have delivered me from the contentions of the people. You have placed me as head of the nations." Manasseh heard his father's voice as if it came from far away. "A people whom I have not known serve me. As soon as they hear, they obey me; foreigners submit to me."

A hush settled over the men congregated at the tomb. Manasseh could hear nothing but the distant drone of his father's voice and the pounding of his own heart. The muscles of his forearm hardened beneath the sleeve of his tunic as his hands clenched. His thoughts seemed to ride a current of air he had never breathed before, a higher level of understanding. He looked toward the sky, almost expecting to see the heavens open before his eyes.

New insights filled his head. The stories of his forefathers now fit seamlessly into a pattern he had been too close to see. The old ones buried in this place had heard the voice of El Shaddai and obeyed it. Forsaking all, ignoring those around them who worshiped the powers of nature, they sought and followed the Originator, the Creator of the world.

"God Shaddai lives," his father continued. "Blessed be my rock, and exalted be the God of my salvation, the God who subdues peoples under me and delivers me from my enemies. Therefore I will give thanks to you among the nations, God Shaddai, and I will offer praises to your name."

Suddenly, in a breathless instant of comprehension, Manasseh saw the panorama of history revealing the work of the Almighty's will. For the first time he understood the connection between the oft repeated story of his father's miraculous rise to power and the God his grandfather had worshiped. The God who had blessed Joseph in the Black Land also sent him away from Canaan! God Shaddai's divine will was the guiding force behind the jealous brothers who drove Joseph away from Jacob's camp. God Shaddai was infinitely more complicated than the single-minded Egyptian gods. He was the One who held things together, who connected the past and present, who fulfilled the longings of desperate human hearts and worked His will even in the direst of circumstances.

For generations El Shaddai had sought men who were willing to believe and follow him, and only a few had ever answered that divine call to total surrender. Abraham had. And Isaac. Jacob and Joseph. Simeon, certainly, judging by the look of reverent awe upon his face, and Judah. But many of the others had not, and Ephraim had not. And until that moment, Manasseh realized, he himself had not completely understood what God Shaddai expected of a man.

Obedience. Total, sacrificial, blind-and-yet-seeing obedience. His father had used another word for it at Goren ha-Atad: *faith.*

———

Leaving the funereal sledge at the tomb, the brothers unhooked the team of oxen, then turned and made their way to the camp they had erected near the grove. Ephraim frowned as he walked; the entire burial had been a frustrating and troubling experience for him. He was glad the Egyptians had not accompanied them to Mamre, for they would have severely criticized the sons of Israel for their shameful treatment of their father. No treasures, no supplies had accompanied the body into the grave. They had not even carried the majestic canopic chest, Pharaoh's gift, inside the humble cave. No wonder his father had asked Pharaoh's representatives to remain behind!

They might as well have dug a hole and tossed Jacob in, he thought, seething with quiet anger and humiliation. *The meanest nobles of Thebes are buried with professional mourners, weeping women, marvelous ceremony. But what did we do to honor Jacob, the father of twelve sons? We laid him in another man's tomb, with nothing but gravecloths to protect him. Canaanite grave robbers will roll away the stone when we have gone and will mock the little we have done for the father of Egypt's noble vizier!*

The mood of his uncles had lightened considerably. The sons of Israel now walked in companionable groups of three and four, but Ephraim found himself walking alone behind his father. He glared at the back of Joseph's head with burning, reproachful eyes. The Egyptians of Thebes, including Pharaoh, would be hurt and angered if they knew the boatloads of supplies had not followed Jacob into the tomb but had been used to provision the funereal procession. Though Ephraim knew his father did not believe material comforts were necessary to provide for an immortal soul, some traditions simply ought to be maintained! Those burial customs had strengthened Egypt, the greatest, most glorious kingdom in the world, and yet the Hebrews blindly refused to adapt. They lived and died with only the barest necessities, living like common shepherds in Goshen, still clinging to those smelly, dusty tents.

A wild ass, startled by the company's approach, looked up from his grazing. He stared at Ephraim for an instant, a shred of tough desert grass hanging from his mouth, before turning and trotting away.

Go, Ephraim silently urged him. *You are a creature of the desert, but my people are not.*

He would convince the others to change their ways. Only a lingering respect for Jacob had stilled Ephraim's tongue thus far, but now Israel rested with his ancestors. Ephraim would rise to leadership among the sons of Israel, and they would listen to him, for he was the favored son of the favored son. Though his father actually held the reins of authority, Joseph's duties to Pharaoh would leave him little time for the Hebrews in Goshen. So Ephraim would move to influence them. He would teach them about the glories of Egypt, about strength and power and how to maintain influence in Egyptian society.

He licked his lower lip, managing to quell his anger by anticipating the victory to come.

~ Nine ~

THE SONS OF ISRAEL CAMPED THAT NIGHT AT THE grove near Mamre. Insistent breezes blew down from the hills, pushing the suffocating heat toward the arid region to the west. Manasseh unrolled his cloak upon the ground at the base of the ancient terebinth tree, preferring to sleep under a canopy of branches and the endless plain of stars than in one of the dusty tents.

But sleep would not come. He lay for some time in silence, his fingers linked upon his chest, his head spinning with thoughts about the events of the day. Above him the moon bathed the area with dazzling light. His exhausted uncles and kinsmen slept around him; many snored irregularly through the silence of the night.

Leaning back on his elbows, Manasseh sat up and studied the Hebrews nearby. Ephraim slept not far away, quiet and still, and Jokim lay near the fire pit, his face reddish gold in the gleaming embers' light. Manasseh yearned to talk, to compare his profoundly moving experience at the tomb with someone else's, but all the others seemed to sleep as soundly as Jacob in his grave.

He glanced over at his father's tent. Tarik might understand if Manasseh chose to wake him, but Joseph would not appreciate being aroused in the dead of night. He was undoubtedly tired. For as long as Manasseh could remember, his father had smiled at him with exhausted eyes. Tonight, as Joseph slipped into his tent, Manasseh caught a glimpse of his father's haggard face. Fatigue had settled in deep pockets under Joseph's eyes, and he bid his brothers good-night in a pose of weary dignity.

No, his father would not want to hear Manasseh ramble on about the mysteries of God Shaddai. Not tonight.

He slouched out upon his mantle, bleary-eyed and restless, until his mind drifted into the fuzzy haze of sleep. After an immeasurable interval of time—it might have been a few moments or a few hours—he dreamt that he walked along the Nile with Jendayi by his side. The sky was a faultless wide curve of blue above him, and the river, bright with the verdigris color of summer, ran without a ripple in the windless calm. A choir of songbirds sang from a stand of trees on the shore, and Jendayi's deep gray eyes moved into his and shone with love.

He linked her hand through the crook of his arm and felt his heart turn over. In all his life he could never remember such a feeling of contentment, of bottomless peace and satisfaction. This was how life should be, how his life *would* be, if God Shaddai answered prayer. . . .

Manasseh's thoughts must have summoned the Almighty, for suddenly the sun brightened and descended with a terrific downward swoop. Manasseh threw up his hands to shield himself from the blinding light; sweat poured in rivulets down his back and arms.

The dreamy silence shattered, and over the roaring of blood in his ears, Manasseh knew he was hearing the voice of his father's God: "Cursed is the man who trusts in mankind and makes flesh his strength," the voice whispered, a surprisingly gentle softness in its tone, "and whose heart turns away from the Lord. For he will be like a bush in the desert. He will not see when prosperity comes, but will live in stony wastes in the wilderness, a land of salt without inhabitant."

Manasseh froze as if rooted to the riverbank. Would the Almighty God really speak to *him*? Or had this dream been conjured up by the day's momentous events?

"Blessed is the man whose trust is in God Shaddai," the voice continued. "For he will be like a tree planted by the water that extends its roots by a stream. He will not fear when the heat comes. But his leaves will be green. He will not be anxious in a year of drought, nor will he cease to yield fruit."

Above the blazing orb the wide blue sky darkened. The preternatural voice echoed now with entreaty. "Speak, son of Joseph, to the sons of Israel. Say to them, 'When you cross over the Jordan into the land of Canaan, then you shall drive out all the inhabitants of the land from before you. You shall destroy all their figured stones and molten images and demolish all their high places. And you shall take possession of the land and live in it, for I have given the land to you to possess it.''

''Canaan?'' Manasseh asked in a suffocated whisper. ''We are to possess Canaan now?''

He squinted to look at the hand before his eyes—it was solid, of substance, so this was no vision. When he lifted his gaze, the dream world went black around him. The blazing fireball and the river had disappeared. So had Jendayi. He lay on the packed earth of the grove. Above him loomed Abraham's ancient tree, backlighted by the endless starry plain of evening.

And yet the voice lingered. ''I have given you the land. Go possess it.''

Manasseh breathed in quick shallow gasps, silently waiting for his heart to settle to a more even beat. If he had been asleep, he was definitely awake now. And he had heard the voice in the darkness of the grove as clearly as in his dream of Jendayi.

When he was reasonably certain his own voice would not crack in terror, he sat up and crawled to Ephraim's side.

''Brother,'' he whispered, shaking Ephraim's shoulder. ''Did you hear something a moment ago?''

''What?'' Ephraim wiped his hand across his eyes, forcing himself to wake. His face tensed when he read the expression on Manasseh's face. ''Is there danger? Should we wake the guards?''

''No.'' A great exultation filled Manasseh's chest. He squatted on the ground and looked up at the sky. The silence of the night was broken only by the light applause of fluttering leaves from the tamarind and terebinth trees. ''I had a dream. But when I woke, I could still hear the voice in my dream. Did you''—he took a deep breath, forcing himself to calm down—''did you hear it?''

Ephraim frowned in exasperated fury. ''You woke me up on account of a *dream*?''

''It was not just a dream. I think it may have been like the vision in which Jacob saw the ladder to heaven.''

''A vision? You are insane, Manasseh. You have lost your mind!''

''Quiet.'' Manasseh glanced over his shoulder. Fortunately, the others did not stir.

Ephraim's expression darkened with unreadable emotions.

"You will go back to sleep and forget about this . . . *vision.*" A thread of warning laced his voice. "The uncles' tales have filled your mind with all sorts of fanciful stories. But if you say anything to the others, they will laugh at you."

"But El Shaddai spoke to me! I heard Him!"

"Why would God speak to you?"

"I don't know." Disconcerted, Manasseh crossed his arms and looked away from Ephraim's accusing glare. Why wouldn't his brother believe him? For though God Shaddai could have chosen Joseph, Judah, Reuben, Simeon, or any of the others, he had spoken to Manasseh.

Waking Ephraim had been unwise.

"I don't know why He would speak to me," Manasseh finally whispered, dismayed to hear a faint quaver in his voice. "But I *know* I heard Him."

"Fine." Ephraim shook his head as he sank back down upon his cloak. "Now you have a story to tell when the sons of Israel next gather around their campfire. That is all you wanted anyway."

Manasseh opened his mouth to protest, but Ephraim closed his eyes, a clear signal that he would not listen to anything else.

———

The next morning as the sons of Israel gathered their belongings and prepared to rejoin the Egyptians at Goren ha-Atad, Manasseh walked boldly into the center of the company and lifted his hands. "Sons of Israel, uncles and cousins," he called with quiet but desperate firmness. "Last night the voice of El Shaddai spoke to me in a dream."

The noise of the camp ceased. Waves of silence began from those nearest him and spread outward even to the servants who were loading the donkeys.

But no one interrupted, not even his father. Emboldened, Manasseh pulled back his shoulders and continued. "El Shaddai spoke to me and said—"

"God Almighty spoke to *you*?" Reuben interrupted. The aged man stepped from the cluster of his sons and took two steps toward Manasseh, an expression of pleasant curiosity on his face. "Why would El Shaddai speak to you?"

Reuben's implication was clear. If God had a message for them, why wouldn't He address one of the elders?

"I don't know why He chose me." Manasseh lifted his jaw. "But I am certain that He did."

"What is Joseph's son saying?" Dan, who had deafened over the years, called out through the silence. "What is the boy telling us?"

A cacophony of voices rose in response.

"What sort of madness is this?" Gad demanded.

"Joseph, what has happened to your son?" The question came from Issachar.

Ephraim stepped forward, his arms folded tight as a gate. "Brother, I warned you not to speak of this!"

Manasseh's breath quickened; his face grew warm. Crimson with confusion and humiliation, he crossed his arms and looked away.

The noise ceased when his father broke through the crowd, resplendent in his gleaming vizier's robe and the Gold of Pharaoh's Praise about his neck. Joseph's steps slowed as he drew near and lifted his gaze to Manasseh's face in an oddly keen swift look. "Tell me, son." Joseph's eyes flickered with interest. "What did El Shaddai say to you?"

Joseph's question silenced the doubters.

Surprised as much by his father's apparent support as by the stillness, Manasseh hesitated. "God Shaddai"—his breath caught in his lungs—"said that we should enter the land of Canaan and possess it."

A new and unexpected warmth surged through Manasseh as he proclaimed the message. He lifted his chin, amazed at the thrill that raced through his soul.

But the sons of Israel broke into laughter.

"Possess Canaan?" Simeon looked at Manasseh in amused wonder. "With what? We have no army."

"We have two squadrons of Egyptian chariots and a company of warriors waiting at Goren ha-Atad," Manasseh said, taking an abrupt step toward Simeon. "The Canaanites are afraid of us. All we would have to do is make a stand now. They would not resist us."

"What of our flocks and little ones in Egypt?" Shelah grimaced in good humor. "Would you have us leave them behind? My mother-in-law I would not mind leaving, but it would pain me to leave the wife and six young children who wait in Goshen."

"Not to mention your fine herd of cattle," Dan quipped. "Which would it pain you most to lose, Judah, your wife or your cows?"

"We can send the Egyptian troops to Goshen. They will return, escorting those we have left behind," Manasseh said, opening his hands. "The Crown Prince could act as our ambassador and explain our situation to Pharaoh. The king would understand if we tell him that our God has spoken."

"I do not think so." Joseph regarded Manasseh with open amusement. "You do not know Pharaoh like I do, son. One does not simply send a message to the king and expect him to understand."

Ephraim swaggered forward, a bold grin on his face. "You surprise me, brother." He lowered his voice so that only Manasseh could hear. "What of the little harpist you love so dearly? If you think you can keep her here in Canaan, you are sorely mistaken. She is Pharaoh's property." He shook his head. "You will not live long if you persist in this foolish notion."

Frowning, Manasseh fell silent. He had not thought about Jendayi's situation. Because she had been in his dream he imagined that she would remain with him always, but how could he win her freedom if he remained in Canaan? Did God expect him to send her back to Egypt? Surely a loving God would not demand his heart's desire!

His mind spun with bewilderment, confused beyond reasonable thought. Perhaps he had imagined the dream and the voice. Yesterday had been a long and trying day. His heart had been rent by grief, his body wracked with weariness. His longing for Jendayi might have somehow been transmuted into a longing for El Shaddai, his desire to return to the roots of his forefathers into a desire to return to the land of promise.

Undiluted laughter floated now from his relatives as the men returned to their packing. "Even so, He did say to possess the land," Manasseh murmured, mentally reviewing his experience. He turned and saw his father watching him. The vizier's brow was creased with worry, his mouth set in a careful half-smile.

"It's all right, Father," Ephraim called, suddenly stepping forward to deflect Joseph's attention. He cast their father a disarming grin. "Our Manasseh has often been troubled by nightmares—you can ask Ani or Tarik. On many a night he has awakened them with his screaming."

"Only when I was a child." Manasseh glared at his brother. "I no longer suffer from nightmares."

Ephraim ignored him. "Last night he woke me," he went on, waving his hand in a gesture of reassurance. "But he will be himself soon. There is no need to worry."

Joseph tilted his head to study Manasseh for another moment, then he nodded at Ephraim. "Grief weighs upon all our hearts," he said, swiveling his gaze to Manasseh. "But soon we will be home and back to life as we have always known it."

"We look forward to it, Father." Ephraim looked briefly over his shoulder at Manasseh. "We will all be better when we are home again."

Joseph smiled in relief and turned toward his chariot. Ephraim waited until Joseph had moved away, then he tossed his head at Manasseh and tugged irritably at his wig. A warning cloud settled on his features. "Do not speak of this again." His eyes widened in accusation. "They will not listen. They will only mock you and laugh at our father. Soon all of Egypt will be laughing. Do you want that? Do you want to bring shame to the household of Zaphenath-paneah?"

Manasseh's soul roiled with turmoil, but he dropped his eyes before his brother's steady gaze. "No," he finally answered, his voice curt and clipped.

"Then remain silent," Ephraim muttered, stalking away. "Say nothing else of this to anyone else. Forget what you think you heard, for you heard nothing."

———

Jokim ran his hand over the back of his neck and winced when his nails scraped his sunburned skin. Yesterday he had followed the burial sledge with his long hair tied back with a strip of leather, and now the flesh was tender. He jerked the leather out of his hair, reasoning that it was better to have heavy hair on the nape of his neck than to bear the pain of his rough tunic scraping seared flesh.

They had been traveling for half the day, and Jokim had purposely kept to himself. He had journeyed to Mamre with Ephraim, but Joseph's younger son now walked stiffly behind the vizier's chariot, a measured distance away from his brother. A pall of humiliation seemed to hang over both young men. Apparently Manasseh had not recovered from the storm of protest that met his bizarre pronouncement, and Ephraim seemed embarrassed for his brother. Not knowing them well enough to intervene in an uncomfortable situation, Jokim left them alone and walked with his own family.

Catching an intriguing scrap of conversation between his father and grandfather, he quickened his pace until he walked alongside their donkeys.

"But perhaps Manasseh's idea is valid," Shelah was saying. He shrugged. "Perhaps we should consider moving back to Canaan. After all, we came into the Black Land on account of the famine, and that starving time has long past."

"But Joseph is in Egypt." Judah frowned. "And after the wrong we committed against him—"

"That is another matter for concern," Shelah answered, his voice rough with anxiety. "While Israel lived, Joseph would not dare to lift a hand in vengeance against you or your brothers. But his beloved father is dead. What if he turns against you now? The grief in his heart could easily blaze into anger."

"At the tomb," Judah murmured, stroking his beard, "he did say something about God delivering him from those who hated him."

"He meant you and the others." Shelah ground the words between his teeth. "You were the ones who drove him to a day of calamity! He has not forgotten! Even at his father's grave he spoke of his time of trouble." Turning, he lowered his voice. "How do you know, Father, that he does not hate all of you? If we return to Egypt where he wields the full authority of Pharaoh, he may use that power against us. He brought you into the Black Land for Israel's sake, but now he may destroy you to satisfy his own thirst for vengeance."

Unconsciously Judah's brow furrowed. "And so you think we should run? Back to Canaan?"

"I'm only saying that we should consider returning to the land of our fathers," Shelah answered, his expression one of pained tolerance. "Don't allow a few of your brothers to make a decision for all of us. The sons of Israel are more than twelve now. We are more than three hundred. Your sons and grandsons should also be consulted, lest they and their little ones die for the evil you and the others committed long ago."

Judah's distinguished face drew downward in a frown. "We will see," he murmured, staring forward at the others in the caravan. "We will talk to the others, and we will see."

———

"How can you sit there and play that tune over and over? I am going crazy. I am bored, bored, bored!"

Back at the Egyptian camp, Jendayi stopped playing and turned toward the sound of Kesi's agitated voice. The maid had been pacing in the tent all morning, and only through deep concentration on her music had Jendayi been able to block the sounds of the girl's annoying shuffling.

"You might find something to do," Jendayi answered, stilling the strings of her harp.

"There is nothing to do. My only job is to serve you."

Jendayi bit the inside of her cheek, momentarily wishing that she did not require a maid. Sometimes Kesi rendered more aggravation than help, especially when the maid was restless. But Jendayi had already passed through the rebellious stage of denying her blindness and trying to pretend she was no different from anyone else. She *was* blind, she needed help, and nothing would ever change that truth.

She cast a suggestion over her shoulder. "You might help one of the other servants."

"Bah! I am not a kitchen slave."

"One of the other musicians, then. Surely Akil could find something for you to do."

"There is nothing to do but wait, Jendayi, and the Hebrews are taking forever to bury the old man." A teasing note sprang into Kesi's voice. "I had thought to wander among the Hebrew women and see if I could discover anything interesting about your friend, the vizier's son.''

Fear, like the quick hot bite of Ammit, shot through Jendayi. ''You didn't say anything to anyone, did you? They must not know, you cannot—''

''I said nothing,'' Kesi interrupted soothingly. ''Do not worry, Jendayi. I understand. I intended only to ask about the vizier's younger son while saying nothing about you, but the Hebrew women are all gone on the journey to the tomb. Only a few of their slaves remain.''

Jendayi took a deep breath as her heart slowed to its normal pace. She was as nervous and pent-up as Kesi. Perhaps a walk would do them both good. She put her harp aside and stood, carefully brushing the wrinkles from the stiff linen of her dress. ''Let us go outside. The air by the river will refresh us both.''

''Wonderful!'' Kesi's hand closed almost roughly around Jendayi's upper arm. ''Several handsome soldiers have been posted along the riverbank. I was hoping for a chance to see them at a closer range,'' she said, giggling.

Jendayi sighed and lifted the sheer veil on her shoulders to cover her head. If Kesi insisted on dragging her out in the hot sun, she would at least protect herself from it.

''Lead on,'' she called with a resigned air.

Eager to be on her way, Kesi led Jendayi from the tent and filled the silence with complaints about the boredom of the journey, the dreary aspect of the landscape, and the rude behavior of the warriors who would not pay her proper attention.

Jendayi blocked the girl's whining from her mind by concentrating fiercely upon the scents and sounds around her. The sun was warm on her face through the gossamer veil she wore, the atmosphere surprisingly mild and pleasant. It was the season of Proyet, the Emergence, and soon the heat and drought of summer would be upon them in earnest. But she might belong to a different master by the time summer came. If all went well, she would be a slave in Ephraim's household. If he loved her truly, she might even be his concubine.

Since the night she had learned that Zaphenath-paneah's son intended to ask Pharaoh for her, a thousand questions had pestered her brain. What sort of man was Ephraim? She had heard that he was handsome, but what did handsome look like? How had he matured? She was not even certain she would know his voice if she heard it, for though she had heard him in a group, he had not spoken directly to her since his adolescence. Was he still as bold as he had been that day in the garden? She hoped so, for it would take a man as bold as a lion to approach Pharaoh and ask for one of the royal slaves. She felt a blush color her cheeks as her thoughts progressed. Did he still think her beautiful?

"Mistress." Light liquid laughter filled Kesi's voice. "You are thinking of him! I see it in your face."

Jendayi opened her mouth to protest, then decided it was useless to lie. Kesi knew her too well. "Of course I was thinking about him." She lifted her shoulder in a shrug. "You are always talking about one man or another. Why shouldn't I think about the one who has vowed to ask Pharaoh for me?"

"I only hope he is as wise as he is courageous." Kesi's steps slowed. "I don't know how he can expect Pharaoh to grant his request. You were a gift to Pharaoh from the vizier. Only a fool would ask to have a gift restored after it has been given to the king!"

"Pharaoh and the vizier have a close relationship," Jendayi whispered, hoping that her words were true. "Ephraim would not promise to ask for me if he did not believe he would be successful. Perhaps he plans to find another harpist for Pharaoh. His father might wield his influence. But if Ephraim has promised me, it will be done."

Kesi did not answer but continued to lead Jendayi, the soft sand muting their footsteps. "There has been no news of the Hebrews since they left," the handmaid abruptly volunteered. "I knew you wouldn't ask, so I've been inquiring every day. The warriors at the river are to sound the trumpet when they see the sons of Israel approaching. The vizier's servants are to prepare a great feast in honor of his return, so they will need every moment of warning to make ready."

"The vizier's servants?" Jendayi's thoughts came to an abrupt halt. "The vizier's servants have remained here at the river?"

"Of course." Kesi halted. "They are not Hebrews. The vizier asked them to remain behind."

"Then someone here might know something of him." Jendayi's hand went to her throat as her thoughts fluttered in unexpected anticipation. "I have not dared to ask of him, but if we are discreet, the vizier's servants might put my mind at ease."

"A good idea!" Kesi laughed. "I was beginning to wonder if you were made of stone. A young man pledges to ask for you, and yet you say nothing. You ask no questions, and you accept his pledge as calmly as if I had just announced that dinner was being served—"

"Stop talking," Jendayi clutched tighter to her maid's hand, "and lead me to the vizier's tent!"

"With pleasure," Kesi answered, pulling Jendayi by her side.

They walked for a short distance, and Jendayi followed Kesi's cue, nodding vaguely in the direction of voices that called out greetings. She smiled until her cheeks felt stiff and lifted her sandals through the sand in dainty, mincing steps, all she could manage in her closely fitted gown.

"Here is the vizier's compound." Kesi turned so eagerly that Jendayi stumbled, her sandals filling with sand. "Nearly all his servants remained behind while the sons of Israel went to the tomb. Perhaps one of the slaves here will answer your questions. There are no men in the area, only a handful of serving women. Shall we go inside and speak to them?"

"Do they look trustworthy?" Jendayi whispered, hanging back. "I don't want them running to their master with gossip."

"One of the women inside is old but seems to be of a pleasant disposition," Kesi answered. "She is probably able to hold her tongue. But to put your mind at ease, we will say nothing of Ephraim's promise to you."

Still uncertain, Jendayi resisted and would have pulled away, but Kesi dragged her forward. The musical murmur of servants' voices stilled as the pair moved into the cool shade of a tent, and Jendayi felt herself being drawn through a silence that was the holding of expectant breaths. Oh, if only immortality were not so important! She had done well without love in this life. She could do without it in the life to come if only she would not be eaten by Ammit.

Feeling extremely self-conscious even beneath her veil, Jendayi stepped forward.

"Long life and peace to you," Kesi said, greeting someone. The old woman?

Jendayi lifted her face and blinked in surprise when the servant returned the greeting in smooth, well-modulated tones. She had been expecting the voice of a hag.

Kesi wasted no time in coming to the point. "My mistress, Pharaoh's harpist, used to belong to Zaphenath-paneah. Though she was only a child, she once had occasion to speak with the vizier's son—"

"Which son?" the servant interrupted, a spark of curiosity in her voice. "The master has two fine sons, both of whom are with their father on the burial journey."

Jendayi summoned her courage. "The younger one."

"Ephraim." The woman answered in a mild tone, but there was no mistaking the approving smile in her voice. "Ephraim is quite the charmer. A more smooth-talking persuader I have never seen."

"You speak as though you know him well," Jendayi offered.

"I do," the servant answered. "I have known Ephraim and Manasseh since they were children. I served as a kitchen slave in the vizier's house until Zaphenath-paneah allowed me to marry Tarik, the captain of his guard."

A faint bite slipped into the woman's dulcet voice. "But why would one of Pharaoh's slaves be interested in the vizier's younger son?"

Jendayi felt a sudden chill. How could she explain her interest without revealing her secret?

Kesi came to the rescue. "I wanted to know about him," the maid said, a confident and breezy tone in her voice. "I have lived in Pharaoh's house all my life and could not believe that a nobleman's son would actually speak to a slave. Yet Jendayi tells me that the situation is different in Zaphenath-paneah's house. She says masters and slaves often converse together."

"Yes." Jendayi could hear no trace of suspicion in the woman's voice now. "Things *are* different in the vizier's house."

"And this Ephraim, the one who spoke to Jendayi, is a man of his word?"

Kesi was being far too forward. Jendayi would have scolded

her but was too interested in the woman's response to rebuke her handmaid.

"Ephraim is very honorable and much like his father," the servant answered. "He is a natural leader and more at ease with people than his older brother. He possesses great zeal and attracts followers like honey draws bees. His name means 'doubly fruitful.' At times I wonder if he has not been doubly blessed, even more than Manasseh."

The woman lowered her voice, being purposefully mysterious. "They say Israel himself gave the blessing of his right hand to Ephraim, the second-born, instead of Manasseh. Many in the vizier's household see this as a sign from the gods, but Ephraim seems to think little of it. And what Manasseh thinks, who can know?" Jendayi heard the gentle rustle of the woman's gown as she shrugged. "He is a man of few words."

"Doubly blessed," Jendayi echoed, running the phrase through her mind. It was a good meaning and a good name. She reached out and smiled when the woman's hand slipped into hers. "Thank you for your help. May the gods of heaven and earth bless you!"

"I have already been blessed," the woman answered gently, "by the vizier's God Shaddai."

~ Ten ~

JOSEPH CLUNG TO THE SOFT DARKNESS OF SLEEP AS
hard as he could, refusing to open his eyes, but the hand that
rocked his shoulder was insistent. "Master, you must wake." The
voice, tremulous with age, belonged to Ani, Joseph's steward.
"Your brothers have assembled outside your tent, and they have
commanded me to bring a message to you."

Joseph reluctantly quit his sleep and opened his heavy eyes.
He and his brothers had rejoined the Egyptians on the previous
night. Exhausted beyond words after the ordeal of Jacob's burial,
Joseph had immediately retreated to his tent.

"They are outside now?" he whispered, his voice clotted
with sleep. "What is so important that it cannot wait?"

"They did not sleep last night," Ani murmured, fetching Joseph's robe and sandals. "I heard them talking through the
darkest hours. Sometimes they argued. Once or twice I heard
men weeping. And this morning they came to me before sunrise
and begged me to wake you at once."

"All right." Joseph slung his legs off the low bed and slipped
his feet into soft leather sandals. Covering his face with his
hands, he let out a long exhalation of breath, then lowered his
hands to his knees. "I hope you know what they want."

Ani bobbed nervously and twisted his hands. "Yes, my lord,
I did hear a word or two of their concerns. They are afraid. They
have suddenly realized that their father acted as their protector.
Now that he is dead, they fear you will take vengeance upon
them for the shameful way they treated you years ago."

The room around Joseph suddenly sharpened into focus.
"They fear me? They talk of vengeance?"

"Yes, master." Ani lifted his hands in a primitive gesture of
reassurance. "I know they are being unreasonable, and I tried to
tell them not to wake you, but they have come with an offer."

Listening in bewilderment, Joseph shook his head. An offer? What did they think of him, these sons of Israel, his own flesh and blood? For the past seventeen years he had tried to live with them as brothers. Even though the distance between Thebes and Goshen separated them physically, while the vast gulf between royalty and common folk separated them socially, he had striven to provide for them, lead them, do everything that an elder brother should. And now they quaked like mice before a cat, believing only Jacob's wrath had prevented Joseph from taking his revenge.

He swallowed hard, trying not to reveal his anger and hurt. "Summon them." He pointed toward the opening of his tent. "Assemble all the people of Israel, Jacob's sons and grandsons, their wives and servants. I will speak to them as soon as I have dressed."

"Don't you want to hear their offer?" Ani asked, ducking his head slightly.

"No. I will dictate the terms of our relationship from this day forward." Joseph closed his eyes against hot tears of disappointment. "Tell them to assemble, then come back in and help me dress. If they have not slept, they are tired. And I will not keep them waiting."

When he stepped out of his magnificent tent an hour later, Joseph approached his brothers as a representative of full Egyptian splendor. Ani had lined his eyes and painted his lids in the stern formal manner of an Egyptian nobleman, and the most elaborate wig in his possession now covered his head. The heavy Gold of Praise, representing Pharaoh's favor, hung about his neck. He wore his vizier's robe, as white as faultless ivory, and fine leather sandals graced his feet. A company of fully armed warriors fanned out from his tent at his approach, and a pair of fan-bearers stiffly took their places by his side as Joseph stepped up onto the dais and turned to face his brothers.

He intended for them to be impressed. If his brothers insisted upon fearing him even in light of his mercy and forgiveness, he would let them be afraid. Then, perhaps, when faced with the enormity of the punishment Joseph *could* choose to inflict, his grace would be appreciated.

Reuben, the apparent spokesman for the group, stepped forward and immediately prostrated himself on the ground. From behind his paint-lengthened eyes Joseph stared, amazed that the brother who had embraced and wept with him at Jacob's tomb could now grovel before him like a slave.

Perspiration streaked Reuben's furrowed face when he lifted his head. "My lord." His dark, deeply wrinkled eyes squinted toward Joseph. "Your father, Jacob, charged me before he died, saying, 'Thus you shall say to Joseph, "Please forgive, I beg you, the transgression of your brothers and their sin, for they did you wrong." ' "

Joseph took care that the lines of his face remained set. For an instant he experienced the unsettling sensation of precognition—on another day, much like this one, he had sat in judgment of his brothers and pretended to feel one emotion while his heart twisted in the throes of another.

"How odd," he said finally, gazing at Reuben. "I was with our father when he died. I heard all the blessings. I heard him charge me to bury him with Leah in Canaan. I closed his eyes after his last breath. But I do not recall him charging *you* with anything."

"He did so before you arrived from Thebes." Judah stepped forward to intervene. Like Reuben, he fell to the dusty ground and pressed his hands to the earth. "And now, please forgive the transgression of the servants of the God of your father."

As one, the other brothers fell to the ground, prostrating themselves in abject humility. "Accept us as your slaves, only do not look with anger upon us," they pleaded, just as they had when they first came to Thebes and did not recognize the brother they had sold into captivity.

The old feelings of abandonment surfaced in Joseph's consciousness and pulled at his heart, dragging him down into the deep well of memories and loss. Even after years of enjoying his protection and provision, did his brothers not know and trust his heart? Did they doubt the tears of joy he shed at their reunion? Were they blind to his tender and loving care of them?

He could no longer pretend to be angry, for he loved them too much. With a choking cry he tore his gaze away from the sight of their humility and pressed his hands over his face.

"Do not be afraid," he murmured behind his hands, struggling to compose himself. Their desperate pleas ceased, and he could feel their eyes upon him, waiting.

Slowly he lowered his hands and looked out at them, his gaze clouded with tears. "Am I in God's place that I should judge you? You planned evil against me, but God planned it for good so that this day might come to pass. You are alive, you and your little ones, by the hand of God Shaddai! So do not be afraid. I myself will sustain you and your children. You need not fear anything as long as you are in Egypt, for I will care for you."

An almost palpable sigh of relief swept through his brothers and their sons. A half-smile crossed Reuben's face, the countenances of Simeon and Levi brightened. One by one, the brothers rose and turned with open arms toward their families, where they were met with newly confident smiles of rejoicing. They had not slept last night, Ani said. They must have been worrying for days, each man confiding his fears to his wife, his sons, even his servants. Now they rejoiced at Joseph's reassurance of love and loyalty. They would fly back to Egypt on wings of contentment and release.

And as Joseph watched them go, each man to his own family's tent, he had never felt more alone.

"Are you saying I was wrong?" his father asked.

Manasseh turned from Joseph, frustrated as always by his father's logic and unflappability. "No, you weren't wrong to forgive your brothers. I just think you should not have promised them protection in Egypt," Manasseh answered, resisting the dynamic vitality his father radiated like the sun. "*This* is the land God promised, Father. Why didn't you encourage them to stay here in Canaan?"

"I belong to Egypt," Joseph said, looking at his hands. "By the will of God Shaddai they sold me to Egypt, and now I cannot leave. Pharaoh relies upon me. The king was gracious to allow me even to journey to Mamre."

"You speak as if Pharaoh truly controls you." Irked by his father's cool, aloof manner, Manasseh twisted his mouth in exasperation. "He does not. Amenhotep listens to you, but you could do anything, suggest any idea, and somehow make Pharaoh agree with you." *You could even ask for a royal slave to be your son's bride. . . .*

Joseph stiffened as if Manasseh had struck him. "You ought to be glad no one else heard that!" he snapped, his voice like steel wrapped in silk. "Those are words of treason!"

"I meant no treason."

"Still . . ." Joseph sighed loudly and locked his hands at his waist. "There was a time when Pharaoh listened to me, but those days have passed." A brooding quality echoed in his voice as he stared at the floor. "Now I am like the father of a grown child. Pharaoh needs me, but he will not admit it. Neither will my brothers. They have the forgiveness they sought. Now they will go back to Goshen and be happy. And they will forget all about me."

"They are not *you*, Father." To his dismay, Manasseh heard a note of sarcasm in his voice. "*They* do not have to go back to Egypt, for they do not belong to Pharaoh. They are the sons of Abraham, and Canaan is their Promised Land."

Joseph's lips thinned with irritation as he looked up. "I know who they are, Manasseh. And I know them far better than you do. In a way they are like children. They quarrel and bicker and would harm one another if left to themselves. If I allow them to remain in Canaan, within a year their sons will marry Canaanite women, and within two years they will be worshiping the idols we passed on our journey." He glared at the floor, frowning. "But I can watch over them in Egypt."

"If they are like children"—Manasseh moved toward his father—"then they must grow up. Please, Father, can't you see the time has come to push them out of the nest? We are in Canaan now, and possession gives us advantage. You are here, their leader, with two squadrons of chariots and a hundred warriors ready to do your bidding. You could move to Hebron under cover of darkness and seize that city. Build a fortification, leave a hundred men there to guard it, and return to Egypt if you must. You have the authority to arrange an escort for the women and children who remain at Goshen."

Caught up in his eagerness, he knelt on one knee at his father's feet. "I know you don't believe me," he said, his voice hoarse with frustration, "but God Shaddai *did* speak to me the other night. And He told me the land is ours. We are to take it, possess it, live in it."

For a moment Joseph studied him with a curious intensity, then his eyes clouded, and he waved his hand in a gesture of dismissal. "You do not know our people, son," he said, his voice heavy and final. "While I admire your spirit and your sincerity, you speak with the simplicity of youth. They are my people and my responsibility. Until I die, I will keep them in Goshen. They want protection. Didn't you hear them this morning? So I will be their protector. I have promised to take care of them, and I will keep my word."

Like an old wound that ached on a rainy day, Manasseh again felt the distance between himself and his father. Joseph was the vizier, the leader, the Bread of Life, and Sustainer of Egypt. Manasseh was an ill-favored son, an unfortunate dreamer. Nothing more.

———

When Manasseh had gone, Joseph leaned his head on his hand and closed his eyes as jagged and painful thoughts whirled inside his head. He had confidently rejected Manasseh's idea as absurd, but doubt reared its ugly head in the silence of his empty tent. How could he have spoken with such perfect confidence? He did not know what the will of God was. He had dreamed no dreams of late. He had not heard the still, inner voice he had come to recognize over the years. Either God Shaddai had fallen silent . . . or He was now speaking to someone else.

But would He speak to Manasseh? Joseph doubted it. Manasseh had fine qualities. In fact Joseph had always cast a particularly fond eye toward the boy, for Manasseh reminded him of a younger version of himself. But while Manasseh was bright and intuitive, Ephraim was more suited for a role of influence and leadership among men. Even Jacob had recognized the difference in Joseph's sons. Israel had revealed a unique depth of understanding when he crossed his hands during the blessing.

Perhaps you are no longer a fit vessel for service. The thought made his right temple pound, and Joseph rubbed the throbbing area as his right eye watered. Another headache, and this would be a severe one. Soon he'd be in bed, overcome by nausea and weakness, ashamed to allow anyone but Tarik or Ani into his presence.

The headaches had first begun to afflict him during the years of famine. Once his own family was safely ensconced in Goshen, Joseph had turned his attentions to consolidating Pharaoh's power. Amenhotep had been young and unsure of himself in those days, and Joseph secured the king's position by trading stored grain for silver, then cattle, then the land itself. When the people had nothing else to give, they surrendered themselves in total allegiance, swearing to align themselves with Pharaoh's purposes. Joseph wisely distributed Egypt's citizenry from one border to the other, uprooting age-old loyalties to cities and regions, until the land and its people were united in service to Pharaoh alone. Only the priests had remained outside Joseph's sweeping reforms, and he had been keenly aware that they despised him. He did not worship their gods. He might have even persuaded the king to worship El Shaddai, but the priests held one undeniable advantage: Pharaoh ruled as the divine son of Amon-Re. If Pharaoh denied that god, he denied both his own divinity and his right to rule.

Amenhotep was inexperienced, but he was no fool.

The pain pounded like a drum behind Joseph's eyeball, and he clenched his fists, trying to will it away. His physicians had tried every sort of ointment, chant, and massage, but nothing soothed the agony except darkness and quiet.

His thoughts whirred and lagged as he pressed his hand to his temple. Had he been wrong to work so diligently for Pharaoh? Had he been too acquisitive? Personally greedy? No. He did not confiscate the silver and cattle for his own benefit, but for Amenhotep's. And his estate surrendered a fifth of its produce to Pharaoh, just as did every other nobleman's manor.

Opening his eyes, Joseph came back to present reality. His estate, his work, waited in Thebes, and he longed to return to it. And just because God was silent did not mean He would not speak. Joseph had known times of silence before, long years of unjust imprisonment, other years of slavery. But even during those times of testing, Joseph had known God had His hand upon him. He had only to wait until God revealed His will.

And he would wait now. Until God spoke and indicated otherwise, Joseph would keep his people in Egypt, near his own protecting hand. And when the time came for them to move, Joseph would know it.

———

A light relaxed mood filled the entire camp that evening as the Hebrews and Egyptians finalized details for the journey home. Jacob had been mourned and buried. Joseph's forgiveness had been asked and received. As Manasseh glanced around at the cook fires and festive gatherings, he wondered why none of the others had considered that this might be the ideal time to discuss the possibility of remaining in Canaan.

A large ceremonial fire burned in the clearing before his father's tent, and around its welcoming flames a host of Egyptians and Hebrews had gathered to share stories. With Jokim on his left hand and the Crown Prince on his right, Ephraim served as the center of attention and interpreter for the convivial group. Joseph, Manasseh noted, had not come out to join in the revelry.

Glumly, Manasseh found a place in the company and pressed his sandals into the dirt, only half listening to the lively conversations around him. He did not want to talk. His own feelings were still too raw to discuss. His recent defeat at the opinions of his father was too fresh in his mind.

A servant threw a shovelful of dung onto the fire, and its impact sent a volcano of sparks into the night sky. As Manasseh stared at the glowing cinders, soft shuffling sounds broke his concentration. His heart leaped when he saw Akil enter the circle with the musicians.

"If it please you," the chironomist said, formally bowing to the Crown Prince, "I thought a little music might strengthen your heart for the journey home."

"Yes, please," the prince murmured, his young face wreathed in a smile.

"Excellent idea, Akil." Ephraim lifted his hand in salute. "Please play a happy song, a song of praise."

The men in the circle parted to make way for the musicians. The women came shyly forward, then took their places in the sand before their director. Manasseh felt his weary heart expand as Jendayi moved gracefully into the glow of firelight, her harp in her hands.

He lifted one knee and rested his arm upon it, contemplating her lovely face. Regardless of whatever happened between the Egyptians and the Hebrews, he would soon go to Pharaoh to ask for her. If by that time he had managed to convince his uncles to return to Canaan, perhaps he and Jendayi would make their home in Hebron. If not, they might live in Thebes—

He frowned, finding that idea distasteful. Jendayi needed to be free from Pharaoh and the people who had enslaved her. If he could not take her to Canaan, he would make a home for them in Goshen, where she could live and create her music at her own whims, not those of a master.

Would she care, he wondered, watching her, that he had just fought—and lost—one of the most personal battles of his life? He wished she could have been by his side as he confronted his father. Though she might not understand the significance of God's promise to Abraham, as a slave she certainly would understand his desire to be free from Egypt. Oh, what he would give in exchange for the right to freely talk to her! He yearned to spend time with her, to discover the secret joys and sorrows that filled her lovely frame. But until she was his, he had no right even to approach her.

Akil beat a soft rhythm on his knee, and the women began to play. The sharp, nasal tone of the oboe whined against the darkness; the soft strum of Jendayi's harp blended with the fire shadows dancing upon the faces of the jovial men. Ignoring the others and their feeble attempts to enjoin him in conversation, Manasseh studied Jendayi, impressing her enchanting image upon his aching heart as if it were a salve that could heal the wound he had received.

In time, he thought, marveling at the purity of her countenance, he would find a way to lead his people to God's Promised Land. Jendayi had certainly known loneliness, pain, and sorrow, but she had persevered with her gift, seeming to find fulfillment and joy in it even as a slave.

And he would rejoice in his holy call. His father might deny him; Ephraim might mock him. The others might not believe. But if God Shaddai had truly called him, God would equip him for whatever lay ahead.

As the music stopped, the men around Manasseh lifted their hands and voices in appreciation. Akil stood, bowed from the waist, then managed a small tentative smile. "I know what I am about to propose is unconventional." His eyes wandered over the men assembled by the fireside. "But Pharaoh's slave, the Harpist-Most-Blessed-by-the-gods, has asked permission to offer a song tonight."

"Bravo!" Ephraim called, the whiteness of his smile dazzling against the darkness. "Bring her forward, Akil!"

Others took up the chorus, urging Akil to allow the girl to sing, until the man finally lifted both hands in mock surrender, then gestured toward her. "Listen, then, to the Harpist-Most-Blessed."

Manasseh stirred in his place, searching for a plausible explanation. Did this unexpected gesture have anything to do with him? He did not dare hope that it did, but Jendayi now knew he cared for her. Perhaps this song, like the one she had offered in his father's tent, would contain a subtle message of encouragement.

A confusing rush of anticipation and dread whirled inside him as he leaned forward. He longed to announce his love and his intentions to the world, but only a fool would boast of loving one of Pharaoh's slaves. Men had been executed for comments far less brash. But Jendayi must be careful as well. Any message to Manasseh would have to be merely insinuated.

The semicircle of musicians parted; every eye focused upon the harpist's slim young figure as she slowly stepped forward and sank to the sand. Her wig, intricately braided with golden strings and tiny beads, fell past her shoulders in a soft dark tide. Her smile lighted her face from the inside, like a candle in translucent alabaster. She steadied the harp against her shoulder, then her long sensitive fingers caressed the strings and released the delicate trickling sounds of running water.

"My beloved master," she sang, and at her words several of the men smiled in anticipation. Manasseh shivered, half in fear, half in the hope that she would sing of him. But she was discreet, her "beloved master" could be Pharaoh, beloved to all his people, or Manasseh, the husband she hoped to have.

Her voice carried the melody while her hands provided soothing sounds of accompaniment.

> Of whom shall I sing today?
> Of my beloved master, who is a leader among men.
> My beloved master, who persuades others to do his
> bidding."

Manasseh felt heat steal into his face. If she intended the song for him, she had obviously not heard how he had failed to convince his Hebrew relatives to follow him.

> Of whom shall I sing today?
> Of my beloved master, born to the Great Provider,
> My beloved master, the favored one.
> Like a vineyard, he is generous to his people,
> Like fine wine, his kiss is sweet upon my lips.

Despite his embarrassment, Manasseh felt a warm glow flow through him. *He* was the son of the Great Provider, Zaphenath-paneah. One day the men who had mocked him would remember this night and know that Jendayi had sung of him, not Pharaoh. Then their cowardly hearts would shrivel with jealousy!

> Of whom shall I sing today?
> Of my beloved master, who will lead his people to
> greatness,
> My beloved master, the blessing of double fruit.

Manasseh blinked in stunned silence as the circle of men erupted into exclamations of raucous delight and surged toward Ephraim, eager to clap him on the back. Jendayi had apparently forgotten that many in the gathering spoke Hebrew; her meaning had been plain enough for half the company to understand. The Hebrew word for "double fruit" was *Ephraim.*

She had sung of a kiss Manasseh had never given her . . . and of *the favored one.*

One cold and lucid thought cut through the misty colored dreams that swirled in Manasseh's head. Ephraim was the favored one. Jacob had decreed it. Jendayi had sung of Ephraim, not Manasseh, from the first word of the song.

A suffocating sensation tightened Manasseh's throat. He had been foolish enough to misunderstand everything. She sang that her love had kissed her, and Manasseh had never dared to take such a liberty. He would not even dream of doing so until he had spoken to Pharaoh.

Had Ephraim? He lowered his head, cringing with humiliation. Of course! His bold and impudent brother had probably kissed a hundred women. He wouldn't care whether they were slave girls or princesses.

Manasseh's startled hurt flared into resentment. He rose from his place, unwilling to look upon his brother's smirking smile one moment longer.

This time Ephraim had gone too far! Manasseh knew his brother longed to marry Princess Sitamun. But Sitamun had remained in Thebes, while Jendayi was here, vulnerable and within reach.

Numb with increasing confusion and shock, Manasseh whirled away from the fire and retreated into the darkness, desperate to be alone with his thoughts.

————

An oddly primitive warning sounded in Jendayi's brain at the sound of the riotous clamor around Ephraim. She had been certain that he would grasp her hidden message, but she had not thought that anyone else would guess that she sang of any beloved master other than Pharaoh.

"By all the gods, Kesi, what are they doing?" she whispered, her hands reaching out through the darkness. "Why are they calling Ephraim's name?"

"Do not fear, Jendayi." From somewhere behind the other musicians, Kesi crept closer. "Ephraim smiles and laughs as the others tease him. Even the Crown Prince seems to be impressed at your wit. No one is angry, except perhaps—"

"What are you doing?" Akil's curt voice broke into the girls' conversation, and Jendayi flinched at its harsh tone. "You foolish, insolent girl! Sing again, and sing of Pharaoh this time, or you will find yourself working in some temple kitchen! You are as stupid as stone, as ugly as a baboon. If you value your life, you will play again!''

"I only meant . . ." Jendayi faltered, fumbling for her harp.

"Here." Kesi thrust the instrument into Jendayi's arms. "Play, and quickly. Akil is right. Oh, I didn't think, mistress, but this was a rash act!''

Why? Jendayi wanted to shout. She had spoken in the only way she could, for a slave could not approach a nobleman, especially the son of a mighty ruler like the vizier. And apparently her song had its desired effect, for Ephraim had smiled. . . .

"Play!" Akil's voice hardened ruthlessly. "Obey me, or I shall sell you to the temple priests myself! Sing about Pharaoh!"

Her fingers trembling, Jendayi began the song again.

⌒ Eleven ⌒

MANASSEH DID NOT SLEEP THAT NIGHT BUT WALKED for hours in the dark desert, not caring if a lion or bear or darting snake should catch him unaware. He thought about walking due west, toward the Great Sea, without stopping. Part of him wanted to walk into the water and feel it rise over his arms, his shoulders, his head, his life. He had spent his youth preparing to undertake a role as significant as his father's, and within the last month his heart had been moved to adopt two purposes: Canaan and Jendayi. But within the space of twenty-four hours, both dreams had been denied to him. For what, then, had he spent his life preparing?

His thoughts and feelings were a molten mass of confusion, one powerful yearning melding with another. He had dared to think that God Shaddai might speak to him, but his father had crushed that dream with a few well-chosen words. He had dared to think that Jendayi loved him, and the girl herself had dispelled that notion with a simple song. Her heart yearned for the favored one, glib Ephraim, who would as soon abuse her heart as cherish it, who collected the attentions of women as easily as other men collected weapons or horses.

"Will you give up so easily?"

Manasseh lifted his head, flinching before the stranger who had fallen into step beside him. The man wore a simple tunic like the Hebrews and carried a shepherd's staff. Thick tawny-gold hair fell to the top of his shoulders, and he moved with easy grace over the uneven terrain, as if he'd been walking in the moonlit desert forever. Light smoldered in his gold-flecked eyes when he turned to Manasseh.

The man's chiding tone aroused Manasseh's anger. "Who are you? And why do you think I've given up?"

A smile played briefly on the stranger's lips. "You're walking toward the sea, aren't you? Come, Manasseh, you have only begun your work. If God called you, God will provide all you need to obey."

More annoyed than frightened, Manasseh closed his eyes and doggedly kept walking. "I am resisting a Pharaoh and my father. Of all the men on earth, those are the two I could never defeat."

"With God, all things are possible."

"With God, all things are confusing." Manasseh kept walking, refusing to open his eyes. "If God Shaddai wants me to lead my people back, why doesn't He speak to them, too? They are like stubborn sheep, and I am only one herdsman. I can't move the entire flock, especially when the old ones will not budge."

"Manasseh." The stranger's silky voice held a challenge. "The men God honors are those who have a clear vision of what might lie before them—glory, danger, even defeat—and yet they still go out to obey. Obey the will of God, Manasseh. Regardless of what others may do, choose to obey."

Manasseh stiffened but kept stumbling forward with his eyes clenched shut, and after a while the sound of the stranger's footsteps faded. When Manasseh opened his eyes again, he walked alone in a sea of parched sand. From one edge of the moonlit horizon to the other, there was no sign of another living human.

His heart jolted within his breast. Without doubt, he had been visited by one of the angelic messengers. His uncles had spoken of them. In fact, Abraham had reportedly entertained three of them beneath the terebinth tree. But his father had never spoken to one, and neither had any of the uncles. Yet he had been visited, encouraged, and supported by one. God Shaddai had seen the hurts of his heart and had sent someone with balm from heaven.

Yet Manasseh had the sinking feeling that his family would find this encounter even less believable than the story of his dream.

He slowed his steps, considering the stranger's words and the import of this incredible visitation, then he turned toward the east ... and the Hebrew camp. When the time of half-light dawned upon the desert, Manasseh found himself facing a brightening sky. Jendayi and Canaan now lay before him, waiting. And neither of them would be won without a struggle.

"With God, all things are possible." Manasseh savored the feeling of confidence the angel had left with him.

So be it, God Shaddai. I don't know what lies ahead—glory, danger, or even defeat—but I will not abandon your calling to Canaan . . . and I beg you not to forget my love for Jendayi.

If Ephraim was the favored son, perhaps Manasseh could at least prove himself to be the more persistent. If his people were not willing to remain in Canaan now, they might be persuaded to return soon. If God truly wanted him to lead this effort, God would have to show him how.

When he arrived back in the camp shortly after sunrise, no one seemed to notice either his blood-shot eyes or his disheveled appearance. Slaves and servants scurried about, rolling canvas, coiling ropes, loading pack animals. The camp would collapse and disappear far more rapidly than it had risen. They would leave Canaan within the hour, and each step would take them farther away from where God wanted them to be.

Soon Manasseh would begin his work to bring them back. But first he must take care of another matter.

Ignoring the servants and guards working around his father's tent, Manasseh shouldered his way through the milling crowd until he spied his brother. He clapped Ephraim on the shoulder and firmly spun him around, catching the younger man by surprise.

"Manasseh! Where have you been?" As always, mischief gleamed in Ephraim's eyes. "You look terrible, brother. Did nightmares keep you awake again last night?"

Several of the nearby servants snickered, but they fell silent when Manasseh rebuked them with a stern glance. "Last night," Manasseh's eyes narrowed as his gaze returned to Ephraim, "Jendayi sang of you . . . and a kiss. What have *you* been doing, brother?"

The question seemed to amuse Ephraim. "Me? Surely you don't think that I have been toying with the little harpist?" He broadened his smile and winked at one of the guards. "I haven't time for such pleasantries." His dark eyes moved into Manasseh's, and he suddenly unsmiled. "Nor the inclination."

"She wouldn't lie. You have kissed her."

Ephraim's mouth twitched with amusement as he shrugged. "Maybe I did once. I can't remember."

"You will remember!" Scarcely before he knew what had happened, Manasseh crossed the space between them and pressed his hands to Ephraim's shoulders. He had wanted to confront his brother, to rebuke him for his distasteful behavior, and yet his fingers, as if possessed with a jealous fury all their own, yearned to slide upward to his brother's neck and choke the air of life from his throat.

A steel will kept Manasseh on the edge, one step away from irrational fury. . . .

In a blur of movement, Ephraim brought his hands up before his face, then spread his arms wide, effectively knocking Manasseh's arms away. The defensive maneuver was simple and familiar, for Tarik had taught it to both brothers, but the Hebrews had never seen anything like it. Jokim, who stood behind Ephraim, gasped in admiration.

Manasseh stepped back, unwilling to remain on the knife edge of danger. Jealousy had fueled an anger unlike any he had ever felt in his life, but he would not hurt his brother.

Barreling his chest, Ephraim stepped forward, close enough that Manasseh could smell the scented oil upon his skin. "I did kiss her once," Ephraim whispered, the glitter in his half-closed eyes both possessive and defiant. "And apparently I made quite an impression. But it was long ago, Manasseh. I have not touched her. I have not even spoken to her during this entire journey. So calm yourself and sheathe your anger. There is no reason for you to make us look foolish before the Hebrews *and* the Egyptians."

"If you do touch her"—Manasseh met Ephraim's hard gaze straight on—"you will be more than merely foolish."

Ephraim took a half-step back and strengthened his voice so the others could hear. "Pharaoh's slave is a pretty thing," he said, eyeing Manasseh with cold triumph. "And apparently she approves of me. Perhaps after Pharaoh allows me to wed Sitamun, he will present us with the little harpist as a wedding gift. She would make a sweet concubine."

The words unleashed something within Manasseh and he lunged, his treacherous hands again intent upon Ephraim's throat. Instantly the crowd around them boiled to life. Men who had been busy packing camels and donkeys dropped everything to rush forward and separate the brothers. Manasseh felt hands scraping his arms, his legs, even his chest, but he could only think of causing Ephraim pain equal to the hurt he had just inflicted.

JOURNEY

Strong arms held Manasseh, pulled him from the ground where Ephraim lay on his back, his face marred only by a mocking grin. "See, friends, what a fighting spirit my brother has," Ephraim joked, accepting the hands that offered to lift him up. "No wonder he wants us to remain in Canaan. No doubt he intends to defeat the Canaanites single-handedly."

The men around Ephraim laughed, then helped him brush sand from his cloak and kilt. Though he still seethed in silent resentment, Manasseh jerked his head in a tense nod and shook the restraining arms away, wordlessly agreeing that he would not attack his brother again.

For what possible reason had El Shaddai chosen him to receive the call of leadership? He turned and lowered his gaze, unable to look his relatives in the face. He was an angry, jealous, and resentful youth, unable to lead or command the others. He couldn't even command his own emotions! His spirit was willing to obey God and lead, but his heart was given to treachery, despair, and confusion.

When the intervening Hebrews and Egyptians had finally gone back to the business of packing, Ephraim turned to face Manasseh.

"It is a pity that Grandfather Israel did not see this stouthearted side of you," Ephraim said, lifting one brow as he folded his hands. "Perhaps he would have been more inclined not to cross his arms."

Resentment bubbled again in Manasseh's soul, but before he could react, Ephraim darted away, hurrying toward Tarik's chariot.

———

Far in the back of the caravan, Jendayi sat in her woven basket and rested her forehead on her knees. Her song had been a dismal failure, for though the men had applauded and howled their appreciation, Ephraim had not responded. Had he approved of it? Or had she embarrassed him beyond recourse? If he cared for her as he vowed he did, shouldn't he have made some response, and wouldn't she have heard of it by now?

Had he flushed, preened, or wept as the words poured from her heart? Clenching her fist, she silently cursed her blindness. If she had sight, she would have been able to look around the circle and judge the effect of her song upon its hearer. She might

• 147 •

have caught a warning glance and stilled her voice before going too far. Afterward, of course, she had heard Akil's dreadful outburst and hastily sought to repair the damage by offering a song of praise to Pharaoh, her true master. But perhaps she had unwittingly caused Ephraim irreparable harm.

If only she could freely approach him! But even if she were free from Pharaoh's ownership, she would have no right to speak to him. She did not know him. He had not spoken directly to her since that long-ago afternoon in the garden. Her memory could not recall his scent, and she had never taken the liberty of touching him. She knew only the sensation of his lips upon hers, but that caress had been enough to convince her that he cared.

She pressed her own fingertips to her lips, remembering. If he still cared, he would find her. She was a powerless slave. She could do nothing but offer prayers to the gods of Egypt . . . and wait.

———

Manasseh walked alone over the dun-colored sand, at least twenty feet to the side of the caravan, consciously setting himself apart from both the Hebrews and the Egyptians. Movement atop a hillside caught his eye, and as he looked up he saw a band of armed Canaanites scurry away from the ridge. He had felt their eyes upon the caravan all morning. They must now be preparing to offer sacrifices of gratitude to their gods. All over Canaan tonight, men and women would sigh in relief that they would not be called to defend the land that had been set apart for another nation. All because the sons of Israel, led by Zaphenath-paneah, the Hebrew with an Egyptian heart, did not have courage enough to claim what God had willed for them to possess.

And as Canaanites danced around their heathen idols and offered sacrifices to gods of wood and stone that had nothing to do with their supposed deliverance, the Hebrews would continue into the Black Land, choosing comfort and provision over a season of faith.

Somewhere, Manasseh thought, Jacob, Isaac, and Abraham were sorrowing.

JENDAYI

Now Joseph stayed in Egypt, he and his father's household . . .

Genesis 50:22

∽ Twelve ∽

"AGAIN! BY THE LIFE OF PHARAOH, I *AM* AS DUMB AS a post. Why can't I play this?"

In a flurry of frustration, Jendayi slapped her palms to the vibrating harp strings. She had been diligently attempting a particular melodic run that had rippled in her head all morning, but her fingers balked at the maneuvers required of them. It was as if her hands expected to play for Ephraim, not Pharaoh, and refused to cooperate until they had been returned to the vizier's house.

But Jendayi had heard nothing from Ephraim. They had been back at Malkata for ten days, and there had been no news from the young man who had promised to risk Pharaoh's disapproval for Jendayi's sake. Had he been teasing her? Or had Kesi invented those messages in an effort to bring hope to a life that had none . . . that would never have anything.

A hot tear rolled down her cheek, and Jendayi angrily dashed it away, then returned her hands to the harp. "As Merit lives, you *can* do this," she told herself, concentrating fiercely. She took a deep breath and began the passage again.

A soft footfall sounded on the tile behind her, but Jendayi smelled the particular oil of lilies that Kesi used and did not turn around. *It would be better*, Jendayi thought, ignoring her maid as she nodded to emphasize the tight rhythm of the melody, *if the maids bathed more often and used fewer unguents. . . .*

"Mistress, Akil bids me tell you that Pharaoh plans a banquet tomorrow."

"So?" Jendayi heard a note of impatience in her response. She kept her fingers moving. Such news need not interrupt her practice. "Pharaoh has a banquet nearly every day."

"But this one is special. He will most certainly request a new song from you. Akil suggests that you compose one—a proper hymn of praise."

Jendayi clenched her mouth tighter. "He is always asking for songs. I will give him one he likes." Her fingers moved over the strings as her head counted the demanding rhythm: *one-Or-sir-is, two-Or-sir-is, three-Or-sir-is . . .*

"There will be guests."

"There always are." *Four-Or-sir-is, no, no!* The rhythm was wrong. This was not what she had imagined.

Kesi continued, a coaxing note in her voice. "This banquet, mistress, is to honor the vizier. Pharaoh wants to hear the details of the burial journey. And since his sons will be present, I thought you might want to be forewarned—"

Jendayi slapped the strings in frustration. "What do I care about his sons?" Bristling with indignation, she lifted a brow and turned in Kesi's direction. "I was wrong to be hopeful, Kesi, so do not think my heart is broken. I am a slave and I will always be a slave. Apparently my last song was not to Ephraim's liking, and he has decided to find a more talented harpist. So I am content with my lot. Humiliated"—she felt herself flush—"but content."

"You are not humiliated." Kesi's hand fell lightly on Jendayi's shoulder. "No one knew anything about your hopes. You followed the song about Ephraim with a tribute to the Crown Prince. The Hebrews probably think you merely meant to sing a song to praise those noble sons. Such things are often done."

"No." Jendayi's anger rapidly dissolved to fear. "My song did not win his heart. Somehow it turned him against me. And last night I had the dream again."

Kesi moved closer and lowered herself to the floor. Her warm hands clasped one of Jendayi's. "Not the old nightmare."

"Yes." Jendayi blinked and turned away, annoyed that tears had risen in the sightless wells of her eyes. "Anubis again asked for my heart. I brought it forth and there was nothing in my hand but a stone! And the stone was not even smooth and beautiful this time, but hard, pitted, and ugly! I could not place it in the scale, knowing I would surely fail the test, so I clutched it to me and screamed and woke—"

"Hush now." Kesi's arms slipped around Jendayi's neck. "Do

not let these dreams trouble you. I know you haven't been eating, and there are dark circles around your eyes. Forget the dreams, Jendayi. Concentrate on pleasing Pharaoh.''

"Anubis says my heart is dead," Jendayi insisted, fear and anger knotting inside her. "But how can my heart live if it is not loved?''

"I love you," Kesi said, her voice artificially bright.

Jendayi gave the girl a weary smile, then shook her head. "You are my handmaid." She pulled out of the girl's embrace and leaned her forehead on the stem of her harp. "If Pharaoh gave you to one of his wives or his daughters tomorrow, you'd be happy to leave me.''

Kesi remained silent and Jendayi knew the maid would not dispute her. Friendships among slaves were shallow and brief, for a slave's ultimate bond was to her master. Any other attachments ran the risk of being broken.

"Sometimes you are as silly as a tipsy widow." Kesi tried a more playful approach. "Of course you are loved! Akil is devoted to you.''

Jendayi snorted softly. "If I refused to play the harp, Akil's devotion would disappear like a leaf in a windstorm.''

"Even so, you are loved. I am certain that people of your past adored you—your own mother, for instance! Every girl's mother loves her.''

"Did mine?" Jendayi stared into the deep dark well of her memory, back to the days when her diseased eyes had been able to discern fuzzy images and outlines. Perhaps there had been a woman who tended her, but any sense of protective and tender care had faded with Jendayi's sight. Over the years several women had moved through her life, many who played instruments of music and sacrificed to Merit, the goddess of song. These women, who combined in Jendayi's memory as a whirlwind of soft voices, sweet scents, and twirling music, had often admired, petted, and disciplined her. But had they *loved* her? She did not think so.

She could not recall a gentle hand combing her hair, a tender kiss at bedtime, or anyone gathering her into a sincere and warm embrace. She had no idea when she had been born, or where. She had no knowledge of father or mother, grandparents, aunts, uncles, brothers, sisters, cousins.

Sometimes she felt that she had dropped into the world like a raindrop, utterly without significance or meaning.

"Jendayi, you are ungrateful!" Kesi's outburst was sudden and raw and very angry. "Merit herself loves you. She has given you a talent far beyond any other woman's. Your fingers fly faster than anyone's. Sometimes I wish you could see Akil's eyes widen when you play one of your own songs. I have seen Pharaoh drop his cup in order to lean forward and watch you play! Even the queen approves of you!"

"If Merit loves me," Jendayi lifted her head as her fingers moved back to the strings of her instrument, "then she will save me from the fate I must suffer in the otherworld." Her mind replayed the troublesome passage she wished to master. *One-Or-sir-is, two-Or-sir-is, three-Or-sir-is, four—*

Another thought whipped into her consciousness: *I pray Merit's love is more steadfast than that of the vizier's son.*

———

Ephraim's mouth opened in wonder when he entered the king's banquet hall with his father and brother. Amenhotep had charged his chamberlain and steward with preparing a magnificent formal feast to honor the greatness of the vizier's father, and those officials had spared no extravagance. As he stared around the sumptuous hall, Ephraim could think of only one or two previous state occasions that would rival this one in splendor.

A company of the famed Medjay warriors, the king's elect Nubian guards, had greeted their boat at the small harbor outside Malkata and escorted them directly into the glorious banquet hall. Other warriors in resplendent white kilts, shining leather sword belts, and leopard-skin sashes stood like posts around the walls of the chamber, their arms hanging rigid, awaiting Pharaoh's command. Several nobles had already been seated in chairs scattered throughout the chamber, and a pygmy with jingles tied to his ankles danced his way through the assembled guests.

In the center of the vast hall an Egyptian drummer held his instrument at a jaunty angle and whacked out a steady beat. A line of trumpeters blew their instruments. One man lifted his horn toward the painted ceiling in a vain attempt to make the sound of his instrument heard above the others. A group of Libyans, recognizable by their ornate feathered headdresses, beat their clappers in a staccato rhythm, while in another corner a band of priestesses played their sacred sistra, the delicate thumping sounds pattering softly through the room. The chamber seemed alive with noise, the sound rising from the musicians and dancers and then spiraling down again from the tall ceiling.

The king's chamberlain led Zaphenath-paneah and his sons to seats of honor near the raised dais where Amenhotep and Tiy would sit. Ephraim sank back in his chair and steepled his hands as he looked around the room. Manasseh, who had said little since they landed on the western riverbank, sat next to him, his drooping eyes fixed upon a bas-relief painting of Pharaoh on the opposite wall.

Intuition and memory brought insight, and Ephraim leaned forward to whisper in his brother's ear. "Do not fret, Manasseh. Pharaoh would not give a feast without the little harpist. He will save the best for last."

Manasseh's lips thinned with anger, but his retort was cut off by a sudden blaring of the trumpets. A group of ladies, adorned in identical wigs with tall unguent cones of fat upon their heads, danced into the room. They waved acacia branches as they came, and the diaphanous material of their sheer gowns reinforced Ephraim's opinion that the king had a discerning and expert eye for feminine beauty.

After the women came a group of men, shaven and oiled, walking with dignified and erect postures as they carried gigantic vertical bouquets. Hundreds of fragrant lotus blossoms, poppies, and cornflowers had been tied to long river rushes and palm branches in tiers, the smaller flowers filling the space between the larger ones, so the slaves carried a profusion of blossoms on a single stalk. Ephraim could smell the flowers even from a distance, then the men spread throughout the chamber, infusing sweet fragrance to every corner.

After another blare of the trumpets the royal children entered. Ephraim smiled as he counted heads, realizing that Amenhotep intended for this to be a truly significant occasion if he had invited Tiy's children—even Joseph had once remarked that Tiy's offspring were as wild and unruly as unbroken horses. And yet here they came, on their best behavior, eyes downcast and their hands clasped in front of them: the princesses Ast, Hentmerheb, Hentaneb, Baketamun, and Sitamun. Behind the royal daughters, in a circle of glory all his own, strutted Neferkheprure' Wa'enre', the Crown Prince and future king.

Ephraim gave a polite nod of recognition and acknowledgment to the prince, then ran his hand over his chin and sought Sitamun's eye. She had been seated on the opposite side of the chamber, but with any luck, she'd soon be sitting beside him instead of dour Manasseh. Pharaoh's formal banquets tended to be drawn-out affairs, and diners frequently moved about during the meal.

When at last Sitamun did look up, Ephraim's eyes caught and held hers. Her gaze swept over his face approvingly and he grinned, making no attempt to hide the fact that he had been watching her.

Another trumpet blast, this one deafening, pulled him to his feet. Every man and woman in the chamber, including the royal offspring, prostrated themselves on the floor. Ephraim stared patiently at the painted tile beneath his nose, knowing it would take some time for the king and queen to walk to the dais where their chairs waited. Finally the chamberlain's voice broke the silence: "Rise, all of you, and be blessed by the presence of your god and king, the Son of the Sun, Son of Amon-Re, God of gods, Lord of lords, King of kings, King of the gods!"

The diners rose and stood by their chairs. Pharaoh stood before them, his arms crossed over his chest, the ceremonial crook and flail in his hands. Though he stood only five feet tall, far shorter than any of the Hebrews, his narrow handsome face suited his small frame and gave the impression of compact musculature. His almond-shaped eyes, topped by heavy lids, seemed almost elliptical under the heavy black lines that flew outward from his lids. Both the king and queen wore elaborate collars composed of blue glass beads and fresh lotus blossoms, the floral symbol of rebirth.

The royal couple stood with somber eyes, mournful faces, slightly sagging shoulders—the appropriate pose of sorrow. All to honor Israel.

"You must tell me, Zaphenath-paneah," the king's eyes moved toward his vizier, "of the burial of my friend, Israel, son of Isaac. Did you have a good journey? Does he now rest with his ancestors according to his wish?"

"Yes, my King." Joseph stepped forward. He pressed his hands to his breast in a humble gesture and bowed his head before Pharaoh. "And we offer our thanks to you. You generously supplied us with so much, including the presence of your beloved son. My family will be eternally grateful to you. The sons of Israel will forever speak of your kindness."

"And so I will be as immortal as Israel." A soft smile crinkled Amenhotep's lips. He took a sudden breath as if he would say something more but apparently changed his mind. He smiled at his wife, and together the royal couple took their seats. Cautiously, the guests slid into their chairs while Pharaoh inclined his head toward his steward. The slave clapped his hands, and within a moment the room flooded with servants bearing trays.

The delicacies were presented to the dancing beat of drums. First in the rich procession came a multitude of breads and sweet cakes, some baked in loaves as large as a man's head and others so small that five could fit on a man's palm. After the breads, slaves brought in baskets of roasted onions, followed by nine kinds of meat, including beef kidneys, goose, duck, teal, roast beef, dried and salted fish, and roasted pigeons. Two different cheeses filled a carved wooden bowl so big that two slave girls struggled beneath the weight of it. As was customary, the foods were presented first to Pharaoh, who waved the parade on with a subtle flick of his royal wrist. Only after a dish had been offered to the divine Pharaoh could it then be whisked away to fill the dinner trays of mere mortals.

Ephraim plucked a dainty shat cake from a passing platter, then raised his eyes to find Sitamun watching him from across the chamber. Her teeth, even and white, contrasted pleasingly with her olive skin and dark wig. Her smile shimmered toward him like sunbeams on the surface of the Nile, then she looked away and murmured a comment to her sister. Fully aware that Ephraim still watched, she leaned forward on the edge of her dainty chair and carefully brought a slice of the juicy melon called *sekhept* to her rosy lips.

A wave of warmth trilled along Ephraim's pulses. In his twenty-three years he had never given serious thought to what sort of woman he might take for a wife, but sparks of unwanted excitement shot through him as he watched her. She favored him. The eager affection radiating from her was as evident as the sun at noon. And she was a princess! Since he had grown up in the second most influential household in the world's most powerful kingdom, it was only natural that his heart should yearn upward toward Pharaoh's household. If he took a royal wife, he could possibly become a man even more powerful than his father. If Sitamun would not have him, he could marry Hentaneb, Baketamun, Ast, or Hentmerheb. Pharaoh was rich with daughters.

He was about to lean over and ask Manasseh which princess he thought the most beautiful, but Akil suddenly appeared between two painted pillars. Ephraim straightened and stuffed another piece of bread in his mouth, knowing Manasseh would be unfit for conversation from this time forward. Behind Akil, with one hand on her maid's arm and the other around her instrument, walked the little harpist.

"Grace and prosperity to you."

The throaty voice in his ear was familiar, and Ephraim turned, surprised that Sitamun had been able to sneak up without his notice. "Grace and peace to you," he answered, releasing a short laugh touched with embarrassment. "You must forgive my manners, but I didn't hear you, Princess."

"I didn't want you to hear me." She sank onto a low cushion by the side of his chair and tucked her legs under her. "Our fathers will talk of the burial for an hour to come, and—forgive me, please—I am not interested in a man who has passed into eternity." Her eyes danced as her mouth tipped in a faint smile. "I much prefer a man who is alive."

Flattered beyond all reason, Ephraim leaned forward and lowered his voice. "I am glad that you came to join me. I had considered venturing to your side of the hall, but I did not think my father would approve. He already thinks me too forward."

"Your father is a powerful man," her eyes boldly raked over him, "but my father is Pharaoh, and he will not care if I kneel at your feet. I was nearly able to persuade him to allow me to accompany you into the desert." She lifted one small bare shoulder in a shrug of disappointment. "But my mother convinced him that I should remain in Thebes."

Ephraim laughed and she smiled, and for a moment they simply stared at each other. From across the room Ephraim could hear his father telling Pharaoh about El Shaddai and the jealousy of the Almighty God, but his mind was rapidly filling with jealousy of a different sort.

By all the gods, was this love? His thoughts seemed to be drifting on a cloud; a strange tingling in the pit of his stomach overpowered his appetite. His gaze traveled over Sitamun's young body, then moved over her face, searching her eyes. Yes, if she were his wife, he could freely give himself and all he possessed to her. Even from across the room she drew him, the smoldering flame in her eyes intrigued him. And if they could be married, Pharaoh would be honor bound to place his daughter's husband in a position of high authority. He might even name Ephraim vizier of all Egypt, because Joseph *was* growing older. . . .

Without taking her eyes from his, Sitamun inclined her dark head toward the dais where Pharaoh and his vizier debated. "Your father is speaking of his god again." Her mercurial black eyes sharpened. "What think you of this Almighty God, Ephraim?" The tender way she spoke his name sent a shiver through his senses. "Your father says he has never worshiped any other god, and yet he is sworn to serve my father, the son of Amon-Re."

"El Shaddai is the God of the Hebrews." Half of Ephraim's brain struggled to weigh his words while the other half hummed with perilous, erratic energy. "But He welcomes anyone who comes to Him. I've heard it said that Queen Tuya worships God Shaddai. And Tuthmosis, your grandfather, sought knowledge and truth from my father's God."

"The Queen Mother is an old woman." A rush of pink stained Sitamun's cheek for no apparent reason. "And Tuthmosis has been dead for many years."

"Tuya is no older than my father." Ephraim tore his eyes away from Sitamun's delicate oval face and glanced over at his father. Joseph was moving his hands in tight, intense gestures, pouring out his heart to Amenhotep and Tiy. The queen looked bored while Pharaoh stared straight ahead, a patronizing quirk at the corner of his mouth.

Ephraim suspected that this king would never worship God Shaddai. Tragedy had driven Tuya and Tuthmosis to seek the Almighty God who could deliver them, but Amenhotep had known nothing but blessing in his life. Though from his childhood he had been presented with the Truth, he had let it slip from his grasp, choosing instead to placate the priests of Egypt and his enormous appetite for pleasure.

That thought had barely crossed Ephraim's mind before another followed. If Joseph would never persuade Pharaoh to accept God Shaddai, Zaphenath-paneah would not be the man God would use to implement an Hebrew-Egyptian alliance that would bless the entire world. God would have to use someone else.

"Ephraim." Sitamun placed her hand on his, and his flesh prickled at her touch. She smiled with satisfaction at the look in his eyes when he turned back to her. "Tell me what you are thinking. Sometimes I think you like to take your thoughts from me."

"Never," he loyally assured her, rewarding her with a larger smile of his own. "My thoughts would love to remain with you all the day long. They would play with you in your garden and sit with you at your dressing table as the maids apply malachite to your lovely eyes. . . ."

One corner of her mouth dipped low. "Stop, my friend, or your thoughts will be following me into chambers where they had best not go. Tell me instead what you were thinking when you looked at my father. Your countenance closed before me as if you are guarding a secret."

"I was thinking . . ." Ephraim paused. "They are unusual thoughts. You may not appreciate them."

"Go on," she urged, and for an instant wistfulness stole into her expression. "I want to know you better."

"If the truth can be told and your heart can be trusted"—he took her hand in his—"I was thinking that your father the king will never be the man my father expects him to be. Your father is a man of many gods, while my father worships only one."

Her eyes clouded as her face fell in disappointment. "That is no great revelation."

"But it is." He squeezed her hand. "For it demonstrates that God Shaddai will not conclude His work in this generation. Don't you see? God promised my forefather Abraham that He would bless the entire world through Abraham's descendants. He also promised to give us the land of Canaan as an eternal dwelling place."

Sitamun stared at him with a look of mingled ignorance and annoyance.

He would have to try another approach. "Consider this, pretty one." Ephraim bent closer to her. "Which is the greatest kingdom in the world?"

"Egypt." She tossed her head. "Of course."

Ephraim nodded in approval. "And through Egypt's bounty the entire world has already been blessed. Now, which kingdom has the greatest military power in the world?"

"Egypt," she answered again, her lips pursing in suspicion.

"You are bright as well as beautiful." Ephraim broke into a wide, open smile. "Now, which kingdom's past king conquered much of Canaan? And which kingdom could easily conquer the whole of Canaan if it desired?"

Her narrow brows rose in obvious pleasure. "Egypt again."

"Yes." Ephraim paused a moment to let the full import of his words sink into her brain. "God Shaddai has promised to bless the world through the Hebrews, and what could be a better channel for blessing than the power and glory of Egypt? God promised to give the sons of Israel a permanent home in Canaan, and what could be a better way to attain it than through the military might of Pharaoh's forces?"

He lowered his voice and leaned to whisper in her ear. "But these things will not come to pass in my father's lifetime, for he is content with the way things are. And so I suspect our destiny—yours and mine, Sitamun—must wait. When my father is no longer the vizier, perhaps your father may be persuaded to act."

The sound of clanging brass broke the stillness behind him, and Ephraim jerked around. The Crown Prince stood behind Ephraim's chair, his heavy eyelids wide open, a startled-fawn expression on his face. A slave scurried to pick up the goblet the prince had dropped, and for an instant icy fear twisted around Ephraim's heart. Had he said anything that could be considered subversive? But the prince's startled look melted into a look of mad happiness as he smiled at Ephraim.

"The gods have blessed you with wondrous thoughts," Neferkheprure' Wa'enre' whispered, bending close so that only Ephraim and Sitamun could hear. "But say nothing of this to anyone else. A man's destiny will come in its own time."

Across the room, Jendayi dutifully strummed her instrument and tried not to think about the pain in her heart. The soft sounds of laughter and conversation filled the empty spaces between the orchestra's songs. The gentle clap of Akil's hand upon his knee rooted her to reality. Her heart was breaking, but no one could see. The revelers in the banquet hall had scarcely noticed the musicians. There had been no requests for special songs, no offerings of praise to the gods. After an hour of eating and drinking, the funereal atmosphere lifted. Pharaoh seemed in rare spirits, his rhythmic laughter often broke from the sounds of the others, and the shrill timbre of the queen's voice drifted around the room like the sharp scent of medicinal herbs.

Yet through the dissonance of muted conversations, the whispers of slaves, and the percussive clatter of serving bowls, Jendayi recognized the vizier's resonant voice and knew that his sons must be in the room. The elder son was a cipher with no place in her memory. The younger one, she sternly told herself, was a charming jester whose foolish flirtations had raked her heart. She had spent hours pondering the myriad ways through which Ephraim might have been prevented from keeping a sincere promise to obtain her, but time after time she arrived at one truth: he was a free man and an influential one. If neither Kesi nor the vizier's captain had lied—and Jendayi was certain they had not—then by this time Ephraim should have spoken to Pharaoh about her. But he had not, so he did not hold her in any regard. He had merely toyed with her as a diverting amusement. He had listened to her music, the offerings of her innermost soul, and had considered them nothing but idle entertainment.

Plucking the notes of the root chord, Jendayi heard the other instruments blend into the cadence of completion. A smattering of light applause sounded across the banquet hall, but the constant thrum of conversation did not cease. Jendayi shifted on her feet, wishing Akil had allowed her to bring the small harp she could play while sitting down. Even though she could not see the diners in the chamber beyond, standing before them left her feeling exposed and vulnerable.

Was Ephraim looking at her now? Laughing behind his hand? Sharing the joke with his elder brother?

Leather sandals slapped the tiles nearby, then a slave buzzed loudly in Akil's ear. Jendayi lowered her eyes and vainly hoped that the slave had requested a dancing song. The princesses were fond of dancing. Perhaps they wished to impress the king with some new artistry—

"Jendayi." Akil's voice cut through her thoughts like the flick of a whip. "Pharaoh wishes you to sing an anthem of praise."

She felt as if a hand had closed around her throat. She couldn't sing, not while Ephraim watched. *Twice* she had sung for him alone, and twice he had ignored her. Not even for Pharaoh could she repeat that humiliation. She would die first.

"I can't." She refused in a hoarse whisper.

A soft gasp escaped the chironomist. "What?"

"I can't, Akil." She clung to the neck of her harp as though the instrument would protect her.

"You must, girl!" She stiffened before the jagged and sharp threat in his voice. "Only a stupid slave would dare refuse Pharaoh! If you would live to see Re sail across the sky tomorrow, you must do as the king commands!"

She lowered her head, wishing the floor would open and swallow her, and something in her posture must have given Akil pause. When he spoke again, his voice had gentled somewhat. "Listen, girl, and perhaps you will find your courage. We will perform the story of music. It is one of Pharaoh's favorites. I will begin for you. I will tell the story while you play the accompaniment, then you will sing."

Soft currents of air brushed past Jendayi as the other women silently picked up their instruments and moved away, leaving her alone with the chironomist. Torn between rebellion and obedience, she straightened and heard Akil clap his hands for attention.

In an instant black silence, she felt the touch of a hundred pairs of eyes. Her fingers trembled as she pressed them to the strings.

"Oh, Divine King, live forever," Akil began, confident she would not disappoint him. "Long ago, Thoth observed the orderly arrangement of the stars and the harmony of the musical sounds and their nature."

A river of apprehension coursed through Jendayi, but her hands remained on the harp, creating a gentle stream of sound beneath Akil's recitation.

"Thoth made a lyre and gave it three strings, imitating the seasons of the year: the Flood, the Emergence, the Drought. Then he adopted three tones, a high, a medium, and a low, and gave high to the summer, medium to the spring, and low to the winter."

Jendayi tried to keep her heart cold and still, but her pulse began to beat erratically. Ephraim was watching her, *now*.

"The genius of Thoth led him to build a bigger harp," Akil went on, "and to fashion mortals who had the gift of music. Then he created Merit, the personification of harmonic melody, and taught her to sing through the lips of mortal men and women. Merit has gifted this girl before you, divine Pharaoh, like no other woman before or since. Listen to her now, as she seeks to please your divine heart."

The pounding in Jendayi's ears drowned out Akil's voice. Suddenly her mutinous hands deserted the harp and fell to her side. The floor seemed to shift beneath her feet. Her head swam. The harp, no longer supported, crashed to the floor in a sickening clash of sounds.

The familiar darkness of her sightless eyes thickened, muffling all sounds and sensations from the banquet hall. She struggled to lift her leaden arms, then the blackness swarmed up like a cluster of buzzing bees and claimed her.

~ Thirteen ~

"LOOK AT THAT." EPHRAIM LEANED FORWARD IN SUD-
den interest. "The little harpist has fainted, and my brother has
forgotten himself." Manasseh had leapt from his chair in the first
moment the girl appeared to sway. Now he knelt at Jendayi's side
while the alarmed chironomist stood helplessly by, wringing his
hands.

"Let the servants take care of the slave." Sitamun's hand
gripped Ephraim's arm. "And pray my father shows mercy to
your brother."

Ephraim said nothing but sat back, momentarily speechless
with surprise. Manasseh's confident lunge toward the slave
flaunted all protocol, tradition, and even common sense. His
mindless dash to aid the girl had carried him directly in front of
Pharaoh's chair, therefore he had risked death itself to tend a
fallen slave. According to Egyptian religion and tradition, the cobra affixed in Pharaoh's headdress, a model of the serpent goddess Wadjet, had the power to deal out instant death by spitting
flames at any enemy who approached the king. Either Wadjet had
failed in her duty as Manasseh ran heedlessly across Pharaoh's
dais, or the goddess had known he was not an enemy. The in-
terpretation would depend upon Amenhotep.

Ephraim thought his father went a little pale as Pharaoh stiffened in his chair. The king blinked, as if he was not quite certain
that he had actually seen someone invade his private space, then
he fastened his eyes to the spectacle of the fallen slave and the
vizier's son hovering over her.

"It would seem, my king," Joseph said, his voice tremulous
and weak, "that my son has forgotten his manners in his hurry
to aid your harpist."

Pharaoh's dark brows slanted in a frown. "I must agree,
Zaphenath-paneah." He gazed at Manasseh with chilling intent-

ness for a long moment, and Ephraim held his breath, certain the royal anger was about to explode in reckless fury. Manasseh had not only intruded upon the king, but now knelt next to the slave as if he, not Amenhotep, owned the girl. If Manasseh was not careful, in another moment Pharaoh would see the light of love in his eyes.

Manasseh might be a romantic fool, but Ephraim still possessed his wits. Without pausing even to glance at Sitamun, he sprang to his feet. "Live forever, most glorious Pharaoh," he called, prostrating himself on the floor in the opposite direction of the place where Manasseh fretted over the fallen girl.

Distracted, Pharaoh turned toward him. "Who speaks now?"

Ephraim lifted his head and broke into an open friendly smile. "I am Ephraim, the younger son of Zaphenath-paneah. I would beg you, Divine King, for news of your new temple at Southern Opet. Since we have been away, I have not had an opportunity to visit the site."

Pharaoh tilted his head and smiled, warming to the subject of his beloved temple, and Ephraim knew the episode with Manasseh would soon be forgotten. Amenhotep's love for building came second only to his love for beautiful women. The temple he had dedicated to Amon-Re was one of his favorite projects.

Pharaoh cast an approving glance at his vizier. "You have a most astute son." His dark eyes were sparkling when he turned again to Ephraim. "I have recently commissioned artists to adorn the walls with reliefs depicting my birth and my royal parents," the king explained, shifting his weight in his chair and folding his arms. "Six statues, more colossal than any before built, will adorn the area leading to the second pylon. . . ."

The king continued, unmindful of his guests' drooping eyelids, and Ephraim remained on his knees, ignoring the pain of his bones grinding against the hard tile floor. But though he kept his eyes dutifully fastened to the king's face, with his peripheral vision he could see Manasseh lifting the harpist into his arms. Quietly guided by the chironomist, he carried her away, safely out of sight.

Ephraim smothered a smile and lifted an eyebrow as if vitally interested in the king's architectural plans. He had been rather hard on Manasseh that last night in Canaan. Perhaps his jests had been too brutal. But he had imagined his brother the victim of a foolish infatuation, not sacrificial love.

Perhaps he'd been wrong. And if his penance was enduring a pair of bruised knees, he would suffer them in silence.

———

A flurry of wild improbable dreams assailed Jendayi, then awareness hit like a punch in the stomach. She thrashed, feeling unfamiliar hands upon her arms, but a male voice thundered through her fear. "I won't hurt you," he said, and the pressure of his hands lifted.

Jendayi froze. Where—and with whom—was she? Panic like she'd never known before welled in her throat.

"You fainted." The man's voice was soft and eminently reasonable. "Akil has left me to take care of you." Jendayi shivered, slightly reassured. Akil would not leave her with a monster. This man had to be one of the servants, or perhaps one of Pharaoh's bodyguards.

Her memory returned with a rush, and she cringed, imagining the scene she had just caused. "Is Pharaoh very angry?" she asked, pressing her hand to her forehead.

"Pharaoh is *busy* at the moment. Ephraim thought to distract him by asking about the work at the temple of Opet. By now Pharaoh has forgotten all about your unfortunate tumble." She heard a smile in the slightly familiar voice.

Ephraim had come to her aid! She slid her hand down over her eyes, afraid that a sentimental tear might slip out and wend its way down her cheek. And she had thought Ephraim cruel and flirtatious! He *did* care, or he would have gawked at her like the others. He had boldly risen to divert Pharaoh's mind from her folly. Out of concern for her he had risked attracting Pharaoh's displeasure!

"Are you all right?"

Her guardian's voice now seemed husky and golden and warm as the sun. He spoke with the clear accent of an educated nobleman, therefore he must have been raised in an important household.

"I am fine." She turned and pressed her hands to the floor to push herself up. "It's just that—" She paused, her head swim-

LEGACIES OF THE ANCIENT RIVER

ming with dizziness, and felt the warmth of his touch on her shoulders.

"Should I call the physicians?"

Despite her pain, she couldn't control a burst of laughter. What a jokester this one was! As if the royal physicians would attend to a slave!

"Though I have heard your voice before, I don't believe I know you," she said, allowing him to help her upright. "But you are very kind to sit with me. I'm surprised Akil did not have me carted to the slaves' quarters and dumped on a mattress." She turned her face in his direction. "Do you work in Pharaoh's apartments? Queen Tiy's, perhaps?"

He remained silent for a moment, then his gentle laugh rippled through the air. "I do not serve Pharaoh." His tone was slightly apologetic.

She paused. "The vizier, then. Are you of his household?"

"Yes." His words were clipped, exact. "I serve the vizier."

She caught her breath and forced her heart to remain calm. This man lived and worked in Zaphenath-paneah's household, so he might know the reasons behind Ephraim's reluctance to speak to Pharaoh. He might even be willing to carry a message for her.

"Will you tell me your name?" She tilted her head as if her sightless eyes could study his face. "I could use a friend at the vizier's house."

"You want me to be your friend?" Something caught in his voice.

"You seem to be the only one around." She gave him a dry smile. "Look about. Do you see others here to help me? Even my maid has fled away, for they all think Pharaoh's wrath will descend any moment. As it would, if not for Ephraim—"

The words caught in her throat, and she pressed her fingers to her chin in a vain effort to stop it from trembling. The gods had spoken tonight. They had shown her that Ephraim did care. He was doubtless biding his time, weighing his options, trying to design a faultless plan with which he could bring her back to Zaphenath-paneah's house. Men had been killed for far less temerity than asking for one of Pharaoh's possessions. Ephraim had not yet acted because Zaphenath-paneah had warned him against such foolhardiness, or he was trying to discover another way to earn her freedom.

"I would be happy to be your friend, Jendayi." The stranger's voice was like a warm embrace in the vestibule's chilly air. "You seem to need one."

She turned her thoughts to him. Something in his deep voice assured her he could be trusted. "Then, friend, since you know my name"—she smiled through the tears that stung her eyes—"tell me yours."

A long careful silence followed. "The vizier's people know me by a Hebrew name, but you may call me Chenzira." She stiffened in surprise when his strong hand lifted hers and held it gently. "It's an Egyptian name meaning 'born on a journey.' But you probably knew that."

"I didn't." She closed her eyes and wished for a moment that the warmth against her palm had been provided by Ephraim's hand. "Were you born on a journey?"

"Yes," he answered, his voice as soft as a caress. "I think I was."

"Then, Chenzira, if you are my true friend," she whispered, desperately hoping that one day Ephraim would sit by her side and listen to her heart, "take this secret with you to the house of Zaphenath-paneah. If you have an opportunity, speak to Ephraim, the vizier's younger son, and offer him my life. Tell him I will serve him in any way I can, but I am waiting for him to take me from Pharaoh's house."

"Is life so hard in the palace?" His voice rang with doubt and something else—jealousy?

"Chenzira," she chided gently. "Pharaoh is no better or worse than any other master. But in the vizier's house I hope to find love."

His hand fell away from hers, and for a long moment she heard nothing, not even the sound of his breathing. Had she asked too much? Did he fear to carry such a personal message? A whisper of terror ran through her. Was she still dreaming? Would she awaken in a moment and find that she had just confessed her innermost secrets to a spirit?

Abruptly thrusting out her hand, she felt the smooth bare skin of a man's chest beneath her fingertips.

"I am still here." He spoke in a strained, yet gentle tone. "And you ask a lot of a man."

"I know." She guiltily lowered her eyes. "I know a slave should not be so forward with his master. But if you will speak to Ephraim for me, I am certain he will not be displeased. He and I are . . . friends." The memory of Ammit's gleaming eyes propelled her further. "I must keep his friendship or die forever."

Chenzira's hand squeezed hers, then let her go. "I will do anything I can to help you, Jendayi."

———

Restless and irritable the next morning, Manasseh paced in his small chamber and considered his options. Last night had been both a dream and a nightmare, agony and ecstasy. He had never felt anything like the dizzying current that raced through him when he lifted Jendayi into his arms, nor had he ever been as stunned and sickened as in the moment when she confessed that she would give her life to serve Ephraim.

Once again, without even trying, Ephraim had wrested away something that rightfully belonged to Manasseh.

Assailed by a bitter sense of injustice, Manasseh sank onto his low bed and knocked a fist against his forehead. Had some evil priest put a curse on him? He could not think of anyone who hated him enough to invoke the forces of evil against him, but there had to be some reason for the incredible events of the past few months. Throughout his entire life he had been well liked, even spoiled, by his father's servants and Pharaoh's household. He was quick and capable, a little too sure, perhaps, of his position as the vizier's elder son, but never had he done anything to warrant the torment that now ripped at his heart.

He lifted his eyes to the high, narrow window that directed a sliver of sunlight into his small chamber. Even God Shaddai had worked against him. The God of Israel had spoken to him in a dream and then had hardened the hearts of Jacob's people. And the angelic messenger, if that was truly what Manasseh had seen, had assured that God would equip him for leadership. But all God had done was break his heart!

The sorrow of frustration knotted inside him, and Manasseh ran his hands through his hair, suddenly weary of his confusing thoughts. Why should he concern himself with thoughts of Canaan and God Shaddai? He had obviously been mistaken. He had experienced a strange dream and a hallucination, both invoked, no doubt, by the spirited stories of his uncles. What he took for inspiration was nothing more than the product of a vivid imagination. If God wanted to impart a message to the sons of Israel, He should have spoken to Joseph or one of the uncles, not to a dishonored elder son who knew less than any of the others about Abraham's Almighty God.

And Jendayi—Manasseh covered his face with his hands. God's cruelest joke was that a slave girl who knew neither of Zaphenath-paneah's sons very well had chosen to love the one least likely to return her devotion. Though last night she had been too shy and discreet to say the word "love," he now knew her attachment to Ephraim went deeper than mere infatuation. She was obviously unhappy at the palace and desperate to return to the vizier's villa.

And he had promised to help her. Manasseh supposed he could still attempt to speak to his father to see if Pharaoh might trade another harpist for Jendayi, but wouldn't she be more deeply hurt by Ephraim's indifference if she had to encounter it every day? If she returned to the vizier's house and learned that Ephraim had never loved her, she would bear the grief of a broken heart even as Manasseh did now.

He laughed bitterly. Perhaps then, as the slave Chenzira, he would comfort her. And if God was good—

But God was not good. God was a cruel trickster, a force beyond the strength of mortal men. Who would hope to win the struggle against Him?

"If you had only moved one of them to support me," he whispered, resting his heavy head in his hands. "Ephraim. Or my father. Anyone. But you have left me alone, and I cannot do what you asked of me."

———

The sun stood like a bright baleful eye over the courtyard as Ephraim wiped a faint trickle of perspiration from his temple. Under Tarik's watchful eye, he lowered a shining blue gray sword to the level of Manasseh's chest and squinted down its length. "It is a good blade," he said, taking a practice thrust as Manasseh leapt nimbly away. "But this iron is heavy. It will weary a man's arm faster than a copper sword."

"Heavier, yes, but the metal is strong enough to break a blade of copper." Tarik thrust his own copper blade between the restless points of the brothers' weapons. "And iron is more valuable than silver. It is a precious rarity. I've heard that Pharaoh keeps an iron dagger by his bedside."

With graceful determination, Ephraim parried Tarik's blade and feinted to the right, then lunged to Manasseh's left, lightly kissing the skin of his brother's rib cage with the sharpened point of the blade. Glancing down, Manasseh let out an oath.

Ephraim grinned. "Do not drop your guard, brother, when I am armed." He tossed the sword to a servant who waited nearby. Sweat and blood from an earlier mishap soaked the hair of his own chest, and another slave handed him a square of linen to clean himself. "Tell me, Tarik," he glanced at the captain as he dried himself, "which of us is the best swordsman?"

The guard pasted on a diplomatic smile. "You are equally good and equally headstrong," he said, reaching out to take the sword from Manasseh's hand. "But you have not been truly tried. What a man does in the practice ring, Master Ephraim, is not always what he will do on the field of battle."

The captain's wry remarks weren't enough to dispel Ephraim's good humor, and he grinned at Manasseh. He was about to taunt his disgruntled brother again when a slave from the gatekeeper's lodge sprinted toward them.

"Life, health, and prosperity to you, my masters," the slave called, bowing from the waist. The man wore a grim expression, and when Ephraim glanced toward the parchment scroll in the slave's hand, he realized why—the scroll had been sealed with the imprint of the royal house. "The message," the slave bowed again, "is for Master Ephraim, son of Zaphenath-paneah."

Tarik studied the outside of the scroll for a moment, then took it and gave it to Ephraim. "For you." His expression stilled and grew serious. "I hope no trouble is stirring."

With an easiness Ephraim did not feel, he took the scroll and weighed it in his hand for a moment, considering what message it might contain. His father had just returned from the palace at

Malkata, and he had not sent word of any matter that would concern Ephraim. So why had a message come from the palace?

No answer came to him, and despite his seeming indifference, his hand trembled as he broke open the seal. He was well aware that both Tarik and Manasseh watched as he read the carefully penned hieroglyphs.

"My father and I"—he snatched a quick breath of relief as he looked up at Tarik—"are invited to the palace at Thebes tonight for a banquet given by Queen Tiy and Sitamun."

The captain lifted a brow. "Just the two of you?"

"Just two," Ephraim answered, suddenly realizing the significance of Tarik's question. He shot a glance at Manasseh, whose expression had hardened to stony indifference. It was odd that the queen should not have invited both of them, but perhaps this banquet had been Sitamun's idea. If so, she certainly would not choose to invite dour and disapproving Manasseh.

But Manasseh would not understand. "If you, brother, had not begun to grow that filthy beard," Ephraim joked in an attempt to ease his brother's embarrassment, "perhaps the queen would look with more favor upon you. I don't know why you insist upon being as hairy as a common sheepherder—"

"I look like what we are," Manasseh interrupted, one corner of his mouth twisting upward. "We are descended from sheepherders, Ephraim. There is nothing shameful in it. Abraham, Isaac, and Jacob all kept sheep—"

"Enough, please." Ephraim turned away and tossed the dirty linen to a waiting slave, then snapped his fingers at a young girl who waited with a pitcher of water. "You may be a shepherd if you want to"—he stooped slightly as the silent girl poured water over his bare shoulders—"but I am the son of a vizier, and tonight I shall dine with a queen and a princess." He paused as another slave handed him a fresh cloth. "And there shall not be a sheep in sight."

Tiy sat in practiced repose, her hands steepled at her waist and her ankles crossed, while her thoughts raced like the wind. Her intimate dinner, quietly arranged in her own private chambers at the Theban palace, appeared to be a success. At the banquet to welcome the Hebrews from Canaan she had watched to see which foods Zaphenath-paneah particularly enjoyed, and those dishes were spread before him now: honey-basted quail, sweet pomegranates, ethereally light shat cakes, melt-in-the-mouth lotus bread. The vizier, devastatingly handsome as always, sat at Tiy's right hand. Ephraim and Sitamun sat slightly removed at her left.

The dinner conversation was light and inconsequential. If either the vizier or his son wondered at the reason for this banquet, neither of them had expressed his curiosity. They spoke of Pharaoh's construction at Opet, the recent trip to Canaan, and the remarkable beauty of the Nile at sunset. Though Tiy attempted to guide the conversation into more personal channels, the vizier remained annoyingly aloof. He deflected her praise for his thoroughness, attributing his success to Pharaoh's insight. He murmured that his abilities were not his at all, but blessings from his god. And always, no matter how closely she leaned toward him or how intently she tried to breach the wall behind those dark eyes, an air of isolation clung to his tall majestic figure.

Sitamun, Tiy observed, was having far more success with her suitor. Ephraim's nature seemed as full of sunshine as his looks. His was a sparkling, self-confident personality. Sitamun, who was too frequently given to pouts and temper tantrums, laughed freely in the young man's presence. She seemed a bit in awe of him and was perhaps a little confused by his easy charm. But all was well; the girl had been ruthlessly spoiled. She needed someone who could inspire her to admiration. When Tiy noticed Ephraim's gaze focusing on Sitamun's lips, she leaned toward her daughter and suggested that Ephraim might be interested in a tour of the royal gardens.

Sitamun lifted a brow, the idea pleasing her. Without hesitation, Ephraim pushed himself to a standing position and offered his hand. The gallant gesture touched Tiy. Amenhotep had once behaved in such a way . . . a long time ago.

"Are you certain, my Queen, that they should venture out alone?" Zaphenath-paneah asked, swiveling his head to keep the young couple in view.

"No one is alone here in the palace." Tiy shifted in her chair to face him. "There are too many guards and slaves, priests and royal relatives. It is impossible to be truly alone here, and yet it is quite possible to be lonely."

As the two young people moved away through the open doors, Tiy clapped her hands. Slaves materialized from several doorways, and with a languid gesture she indicated the bowls and dishes of steaming food remaining on trays scattered around the room. "Away, all of it," she commanded. The slaves sprang into action.

"You have been very gracious, my Queen." Zaphenath-paneah bowed his head toward her in respect. He folded his hands and looked at her with polite and tactfully incurious eyes. "The dinner invitation was most kind. Of course, I imagine that Sitamun prompted you to issue it."

Tiy smiled, waiting until the last servant had exited the chamber. When the drapery had fallen behind the departing slave's form, she lifted her chin and allowed the heavy weight of her beaded wig to pull her head back. "Sitamun did no prompting at all." She studied his face unhurriedly, feature by feature. His eyes fell beneath the power of her gaze, and she smiled. "Have you wondered, our noble vizier, what compelled me to bring you here tonight?"

He looked away with a smile that seemed almost boyish in its shyness. Did she detect a grain of softness in that granite strength? Had he suspected her secret motivations?

"I did not want to be presumptuous." A look of eager tenderness crossed his exquisite face as he glanced back at her. "But I wondered if you were attempting a bit of matchmaking."

She laughed softly. Perhaps he had begun to understand.

"Would the idea displease you?" She shifted so the length of her leg showed within the split in her fitted skirt.

Zaphenath-paneah did not seem to notice. His gaze did not leave her face. "I would be pleased if our houses were joined." His expression softened into one of fond reminiscence. "Since I tutored Amenhotep, I have often felt like his father. So of course I am honored to think that his daughter, whom I hold in great affection, might possibly consider my son for a husband."

Tiy took a quick breath and looked away so that he would not read the depth of her true feelings. He had grasped only the obvious. He was not as perceptive as she had hoped. What had happened to the vizier's vaunted powers of intuition and observation? Could he not see that she wanted to offer him much more than a royal daughter-in-law?

Perhaps this conversation was premature. He had grasped the obvious, and that was enough for now. She could use the growing relationship between Sitamun and Ephraim as a foundation and build atop it. With a little cunning and adroit handling, Zaphenath-paneah could be won over. And as the steward Senenmut enabled the queen Hatshepsut to rule as Pharaoh, Zaphenath-paneah would aid her. She would promise him anything, even herself, but one day he would see that Amenhotep was unfit for kingship, that *she* was the real power behind the throne.

"You are wise, as always, Zaphenath-paneah." She looked down at the floor and sighed heavily. "And I am grateful for your influence upon my husband's past. Yet Pharaoh is not the man you knew as a boy—but of course I do not have to tell you what you already know." She paused and looked away, allowing her eyes to dwell on the family paintings that lined the walls of her chamber—idealistic images that portrayed her and Amenhotep blissfully offering sacrifices to the gods. "Pharaoh cares for little these days but his harem and his building projects. Once he considered me the flower and joy of his youth, but—"

"He still cares deeply for you, my Queen," Zaphenath-paneah dared to interrupt. She lifted a brow and stared at him in disbelief, but he continued. "He places more trust in you than he does most of his counselors. In fact," he chuckled softly, "I daresay he trusts you almost as much as he trusts me."

"It is true that he allows me to handle a few ceremonial affairs," she admitted. "That is why I live here at Thebes. I am honored that he encourages me to meet with the governors and counselors who come to bring him tribute."

"So you see how much Pharaoh needs you." The vizier spread his hands. "He depends upon you. So do not doubt his devotion, my Queen."

"It is not his devotion that I doubt." She lowered her voice. "It is his wisdom."

If this slender, delicate thread between them were to strengthen, she must not move too hastily. Zaphenath-paneah was doggedly loyal; he would resist any outright proposition in which he sensed the seeds of betrayal. But despite his closed, aloof expression, she felt his vulnerability. He had no wife. He had not known the comfort of a woman's arms for a lifetime of years, yet he was still an attractive, compelling presence. The pull of his personality grew stronger every time she saw him, but she was another man's wife. She would have to tread carefully, for only by conclusively demonstrating Amenhotep's incompetence could she hope to win Zaphenath-paneah's support.

"I suppose a queen should not expect to be more involved in the government of the kingdom," she murmured. "After all, Amenhotep has you to guide his decisions. But wisdom is acquired by capacity, not by gender. And like Hatshepsut, who ruled for Tuthmosis III when he was a child, I have a great capacity for learning."

Zaphenath-paneah shook his head. "I don't know that Hatshepsut actually *governed*—"

"Then you don't know our kingdom's history as you ought to," she retorted, suddenly annoyed with the vizier's impenetrable equanimity. "I am sure you have heard that Hatshepsut was Tuthmosis' regent only, but she had herself declared Pharaoh. She assumed the royal beard of kingship and wore the full royal headdress. The high priest of Amon-Re supported her, as did others of the royal court."

"Then where," Zaphenath-paneah softly interrupted, "is her royal tomb? If she was so beloved, where are the shrines to perpetuate her name and memory?"

Tiy stared at him across a sudden ringing silence. "Hidden, mutilated, or destroyed." She clipped her words. "Though she was a powerful pharaoh, she was not without enemies."

"No one is." The vizier gave her a smile that seemed more an automatic civility than an expression of pleasure.

"Thank you for listening to my concerns." She cut him off with a smile of gratitude, which he acknowledged with just the smallest softening of his eyes. At that moment, the happy voices of Sitamun and Ephraim danced into the room, and Zaphenath-paneah's formal posture relaxed.

Another time, Tiy thought, studying the vizier's handsome profile as he greeted the two young ones. *I will make you realize that Amenhotep cares nothing for Egypt. I would make a better ruler. You and I an invincible team. Like Hatshepsut and Senenmut, we could grasp and hold the reins of power.*

Satisfied with the seeds she had planted, she rose to her feet and abruptly wished her guests a safe and happy farewell.

————

Joseph sat alone under the small oxhide canopy of the bark as it slipped along the dark Nile toward his own house. The evening with Queen Tiy and Princess Sitamun had left him feeling strangely out of sorts, and he could not understand why events had unfolded as they did. He had not been exactly surprised by the invitation to dine with the queen, for the attraction between Sitamun and Ephraim was obvious to anyone who watched them. The dinner itself had passed without any remarkable developments, and Ephraim had been at his charming best. But after dinner, when Tiy had dismissed the young ones to the garden, the gleaming light of hunger in her eye had unnerved him. Her breath had quickened as she leaned toward him and spoke of her unhappiness with Amenhotep. What was he to make of that? He had faced an aggressive woman in Potiphar's house, and that situation had nearly cost him his life. But he was no longer a handsome youth, and Tiy was no affection-starved maiden. She could not want an evening of love from him. She often denounced Amenhotep for spending too much time in such sensual pleasures.

So what drove her toward him tonight? What had inspired the glitter in her jet black eyes?

His gaze fell upon the river. The water running alongside the boat was the color of tarnished silver, smooth and glassy in the moonlight. Sensing that Joseph wished to be left alone, Ephraim stood at the curved bow, his hands tucked into the waistband of his kilt in a relaxed, familiar pose. When he lifted his face to study the eastern moon, his profile was so similar to his mother's that Joseph caught his breath. Asenath had been in her tomb for eighteen years, but when that particular wistful expression crossed Ephraim's face, Joseph almost expected the boy to turn and speak with his mother's soothing voice. Asenath's sweet love had lightened Joseph's heavy load and helped him endure those first turbulent and trying years as vizier.

An odd twinge of jealousy and pain stirred in his heart when Joseph recognized the expression in Ephraim's eyes. Love, youthful and idealistic, filled Ephraim's gaze just as it had Asenath's, and Joseph felt an instant's squeezing hurt at the memory of how love had evolved into grief during his wife's lifetime. For him, Pharaoh's welfare had always come first. Joseph had guarded his heart even during his marriage. Not since his encounter with Tuya had he completely abandoned himself to love, that most fickle and passionate of human emotions.

Tuya. Even now, her name brought a smile to his lips. He had not spoken to her in years, though he knew she still lived in the immense palace at Thebes. She was, after all, Pharaoh's mother, and therefore a national treasure. At one point, years ago, Joseph had asked her to become his second wife, but she had wisely refused. After that, he had taken pains to avoid her, to keep old memories and powerful passions safely tucked away. For Asenath's sake, he had never invited Tuya to his house. For his own sake, he had never sought Tuya out at the palace. And after Asenath died, he waited, half hoping that Tuya would send a message, but she did not. Apparently she was happy, so Joseph left her alone.

After the dark days, he delved into his work for Pharaoh, avoiding his empty house where Asenath's laughter still echoed in the halls, and her scent lingered upon the bed linens. Ephraim and Manasseh, the fruits of her womb, were content to follow Ani and Tarik through the villa, and the women servants were eager to spoil and tend to them. Joseph's days brimmed with Pharaoh's work: dispensing judgments in the great hall, receiving and recording reports from the far-flung nomes and outlying defense posts. Among other duties, Joseph was responsible for managing the royal residences, supervising the public works, directing the military forces and Pharaoh's elite Medjay troops, commissioning the royal artisans, overseeing the royal farms and granaries, monitoring the distribution of food to the king's laborers and officials, and collecting the taxes. Except for the priests, every individual in Egypt was directly or indirectly responsible to the king's vizier, and there were days when Joseph felt that he had talked to or heard from practically every soul in the kingdom.

The work was all-consuming, but it had its rewards, and chief among them was the salvation of his father's people. When Israel and his children entered Canaan, Joseph began to understand the reason for his personal suffering, his pain and desolation. God Shaddai allowed it all to strengthen him, to defeat his pride, to bring him to a place where he could lead. He had learned how to guide men . . . and how to forgive.

Now Israel was dead and the past forgiven. What work remained? For the first time in his life, Joseph felt drained, hollow, and lifeless. The God who had guided through dreams and whispered in a still, small voice had not spoken in years. What if He did not speak again?

The bow dipped and rose again in a sudden gust of wind, sending a cool splash of spray into the air. Joseph felt droplets touch his face as he closed his eyes and wearily considered his existence.

~ Fourteen ~

IF HE WERE TO WIN SITAMUN, EPHRAIM REALIZED that he might need more than the support of his father and Queen Tiy. The opinions of many counselors were considered in view of a royal marriage, and Sitamun's would be no different. Ephraim would have to prove to all of Egypt that a son of Israel could move confidently in Egyptian society.

And so, during the weeks following Tiy's banquet, Ephraim wrangled invitations to nearly every gathering and social occasion in Thebes. The citizens of that city, who were naturally fond of entertainment, music, and gaiety, opened their doors to him in surprised gratitude, allowing him to grace their gatherings with the aura of his father's illustrious name. Diligently courting noblemen and their wives, he reciprocated their hospitality by hosting a few festive banquets in his own quarters at his father's villa.

As part of his grand scheme, Ephraim sent gifts to the governors of Egypt's nomes and to the king's most trusted counselors. Knowing that no marriage would be possible without the approval of the priests, he even culled a dozen of his father's finest cattle from the herd and ordered them to be delivered to the temple of Amon-Re. These things he did without his father's consent, but in full certainty that Joseph would delight in the result to come.

And so each morning Ephraim rose and anointed himself and painted his eyes, then donned his wig, a finely pleated kilt, and a voluminous cloak. In the finest homes of the highest nobles, he danced and drank and discussed life, love, and politics with great sagacity and wit. He wrote sweet missives to Sitamun and ordered slaves to deliver them straightway to the palace. And while he attacked his work with steadfast determination, he noticed that his brother Manasseh grew more melancholy day by day.

————

More than happy to let his queen attend to the meaningless ceremonies of state, Pharaoh remained at Malkata with his harem while Tiy placated his counselors and officials. Zaphenath-paneah was forced to divide his precious store of time between Malkata and Thebes, spending half his day listening to the plans of the impetuous pharaoh and the other half tending to vital matters of taxation, productivity, and foreign affairs.

Every third day he reported to Tiy at the Theban palace, more out of courtesy, Tiy supposed, than out of any conviction that she would be able to offer real help or insight. The vizier was yet a long way from where he must be, and yet she never failed to feel her heart flutter when his tall, beautifully proportioned body moved into the throne room. She took great care not to open her countenance before the prying eyes of those who waited before her, but spoke with Zaphenath-paneah in tones of dignity and resolve. On the pretext of asking for his help, she dictated letters to kings of other lands and arranged for the giving and receiving of tribute between Pharaoh and several fledgling city-states bordering the Great Sea.

She felt her mouth curve into a smile when the vizier informed her that she was the first queen whose name had ever been inscribed upon official acts. So he had finally noticed her ability! The letter in his hand, to which he had just penned her name, was an announcement of the king's marriage to yet another foreign princess.

"Send that papyrus to Malkata with the others," she told Zaphenath-paneah. A group of six scribes sat cross-legged on the floor at her feet, recording every word she uttered. "And thank the Mitanni king for the offering of his daughter. Assure him that Pharaoh will be pleased to receive her as a bride, that she will be treated with every kindness, and so forth."

She waved her hand, and Zaphenath-paneah nodded in approval. With that matter out of the way, she rested her elbows on the arms of her gilded chair and laced her fingers together, eager to be done with the business that had filled the hall with scribes and counselors. "If there is nothing else, you may all go." She clapped twice. "Except the king's vizier. I need a private word with you, noble Zaphenath-paneah."

The eyes of more than one curious counselor flitted in her direction as her coterie rose and slowly filed out of the room. She kept a tight rein on her emotions and her expression until only the vizier remained before her. Then Tiy inhaled slowly, deepened her smile, and tried to contain the eagerness in her voice.

"I have wanted, honest vizier, to discuss a certain matter with you."

He bowed his head, keeping his gaze from her. "I am your servant, my Queen."

"This matter concerns your title." She brought her hand up to her cheek and rested her head upon it, hoping he would lift his eyes. "The title of vizier has always been conferred by the king. But I have been thinking—with the situation developing between our children, might the vizier's title become an inherited one?"

He looked up then, honest surprise in his eyes. "Inherited?" His mouth curved into an unconscious smile.

"Yes." She smiled, pleased that she had managed to discover the flinty edge of ambition within the man's soul. She might yet spark his interest.

"Your son Ephraim is a worthy young man, is he not? I have been hearing good things about his generosity and insight. And I imagine that he has been trained by the best tutors Egypt can offer."

"He has, my Queen." A naked flush of ambition colored the vizier's cheek as he bowed his head before her again. "But my elder son, Manasseh, stands to inherit—"

He broke off, then lifted his eyes as if confused. "My father knew," he murmured inexplicably.

"Your father?" She lifted her brows. "Your father knew what?"

"He crossed his arms." A spark of some indefinable emotion lit the vizier's eyes. "He placed his right hand upon Ephraim's head and said that the younger son would be greater than the elder."

Tiy forced remote dignity into her voice. "What your father did does not matter here. But I wanted you to know what I am considering. And, of course, to consult you and gather your opinions." She paused, and for a moment her eyes froze on his long lean form. "Is this, Zaphenath-paneah," she asked, suddenly breathless, "something that would please you?"

"Yes." He answered a little too eagerly and bowed again as if aware that he had somehow stumbled. "If it is for Pharaoh's good, of course. I want only to serve him."

"Do you desire to serve Pharaoh foremost, or his kingdom?" She felt blood coursing through her veins like the Nile in flood. She looked at him and made no effort to hide the longing in her eyes.

He stiffened but did not look away. "I have never considered the difference. Pharaoh is Egypt, is he not?"

"Is he?" Her brows lifted the question. "You have today signed my name to Pharaoh's documents. You have allowed me to use Pharaoh's seal because Pharaoh has given me his authority. If I am then equal to Pharaoh, and Pharaoh is equal to Egypt, then it follows that I, too, must be equal to Egypt."

His eyes gleamed toward her like glassy volcanic rock. "Your logic is apparently sound."

Tiy paused a moment, then closed her eyes. "I am glad to hear you say it." The fullness of time had not yet come, but it was near. "Thank you for your counsel, Zaphenath-paneah. You may go."

Joseph shifted uneasily in the litter that carried him through the streets of Thebes. The gauzy curtains did little to block the thin layer of gray dust that rose up from the pattering feet of the litter bearers, and the oppressive heat of the day weighed heavily upon his linen tunic.

More burdensome than the heat, however, was the queen's offer. Every father yearned for his son to follow in the path he had forged, and today Tiy had practically promised that Ephraim would marry a princess and be the king's next vizier. But at what price? He had been watching Tiy long enough to know that she was a negotiator. She did not bestow benefits without expecting something in return. She did not even make offerings to her gods unless they had met her expectations of them.

Still, Joseph found it interesting that she had suggested Ephraim, not Manasseh, to be the next vizier. Her offer harmonized nicely with Israel's blessing, so perhaps God Shaddai had revealed the future as Jacob lay so close to death. God could certainly raise Ephraim to power in Egypt. The Almighty worked a far greater miracle when He transferred Joseph from a prison to a throne. Joseph's experience had proved that nothing was too difficult for God Shaddai.

But still, the hungry look in Tiy's eye troubled him. This proposal could not be from God if it depended upon an unholy alliance between Joseph and the king's wife.

∼ Fifteen ∼

THE ORANGE RED SUN HAD NOT RISEN FAR THROUGH the cloud-studded sky when Jokim, his father, and Grandfather Judah disembarked at a dock outside Thebes. They had spent most of the night upon the river, and Jokim walked unsteadily for several minutes, unused to the feel of solid earth beneath his feet. The hard-packed paths of Thebes did not heave and yield like the deck of the felucca they had boarded for the journey, and as he thumped over the ground he thought again that he would never become accustomed to the Egyptians' seagoing ways.

"Shall you visit Ephraim now?" his father, Shelah, asked, pausing by a merchant stall.

"Yes," Jokim answered, unable to tear his eyes from the brilliant wares lined up like gaudy treasures. "I will find you tomorrow at the docks. I hope you have a profitable day of trading, Father."

He walked away with a quick step that implied more confidence than he felt, for he still spoke little of the Egyptian language and understood even less. The Hebrews in Goshen spoke the Canaanite tongue, and despite the sudden influx of Egyptian brickmakers, who were helping his relatives erect permanent housing, Jokim had not had many opportunities to practice the foreign language.

An obese, sloppy merchant directed Jokim to the vizier's villa, a sprawling, pink-washed estate south of the city. As Jokim followed a winding path along the river's edge, he noticed that the carefully cultivated acres outside the tall walls were lush with grain ready for harvest. The vizier's vast herds dotted other fields, a testimony to Joseph's wealth and power.

But the villa held Jokim's attention most. He had spent his life in tents of canvas and leather, so the marble and stone beauty of the elegant home rising from within the painted walls left him breathless with admiration. Nervous flutterings pricked his chest as he approached the gatekeeper's lodge, and he hoped that Ephraim would be willing to render hospitality to a long lost cousin.

For not only did he seek hospitality, but Jokim had been entrusted with a solemn responsibility, and he prayed that Ephraim would prove willing to help him bear it.

———

After greeting Jokim with an affectionate embrace, Manasseh explained that Ephraim was away. Jokim stuttered in embarrassment as Joseph's elder son ordered a slave to wash his guest's feet and bring him a clean tunic, then commanded that fruit and fresh bread be brought. When they were finally settled in the privacy of Manasseh's comfortable chamber, Jokim breakfasted on lotus bread, dates, and wild honey while his cousin asked about the family in Goshen—what were the uncles doing now that Jacob no longer lived? After a few moments of trivial talk, Manasseh blushed and asked if anyone had spoken of returning to Canaan.

As tactfully as possible Jokim changed the subject, but frustration filled Manasseh's eyes when Jokim mentioned the brickmakers, masons, and builders who had poured into Goshen since the clan's return from the burial journey. "The older people are tired of living in tents. They want something stable. Something better. And while none of them will build a home as grand as this one"—he gestured to the elegant house surrounding them—"would you begrudge them the right to have a proper roof over their heads?"

"I don't begrudge them anything." Manasseh leaned forward with his elbows on his knees. "But I don't like to see them put roots into the soil of Goshen. It is not the land of promise, cousin. It is not where God wants us. But no one wants to obey God Shaddai."

Jokim swallowed a stubborn lump of bread that had lodged in his dry throat. "So you have said." While acknowledging his cousin's remark, part of him hoped Manasseh would drop the subject. Jokim did not want to have to tell him that the uncles joked about Manasseh's speech in the wilderness, mocking him as a foolish youngster with hot blood, the one who would rush in and claim land more fit for desert animals than for men, women, and children.

"Perhaps you should try to understand them," Jokim said, reaching for a cup on a nearby tray. "You have lived in splendor all your life while they have lived in dust and dirt. Now they want the feel of stone under their feet. And many of them, my father included, say that if God wants us to dwell in Canaan, nothing will stop us from dwelling there."

"Do they expect God to pluck us up and miraculously drop us back into our homeland?" Manasseh's face darkened. "God has told us what He wants. He gave the message to Abraham, Isaac, Jacob, and me! But our people do not want what God wants. They want an easy life in the Black Land, where food is plentiful and comforts abound. They want brick houses and marble floors."

Jokim took another bite of the delicious bread and told himself to be quiet. He had been warned that Manasseh was like a young lion roaring after his prey. Though he yearned for the glory of the hunt, he would not be prepared for the pain of the kill.

He would say nothing else until later, after he'd had a chance to talk to Ephraim. If Ephraim truly was the greater of the two brothers, he would be more suitable for the task ahead.

———

"Jokim!" Perfumed and staggering slightly, Ephraim entered the room and held out his arms. "What a wonderful surprise!"

Manasseh felt his stomach churn as the cousins embraced. Ephraim was drunk again. In the past few weeks he had greatly changed. Though Manasseh was not certain what motivated his brother's newly hedonistic lifestyle, he could guess at a reason or two.

"We must celebrate your arrival." Ephraim fell into a chair near Jokim, hooked one leg over the armrest, and grinned at his guest. "We will show you the city and take you to a few entertainments. Thebes is a magnificent place. The temples alone will make your eyeballs bulge from your head. And the women—beautiful beyond imagining!"

"I'd like to see a few things." Jokim smiled pleasantly, then turned toward Manasseh. "Won't you come with us?"

Manasseh shook his head. The last thing he wanted was to accompany Ephraim on a jolly jaunt around the city.

"Manasseh will hamper our sport." A mischievous look gleamed in Ephraim's eyes. "We'll have more fun if we leave him behind."

"Please come, Manasseh."

Jokim obviously did not want to venture forth with a drunken kinsman.

Manasseh sighed. "I'll come." His hands gripped the armrests of his chair as he stood. "But we will not stay out long. And we will not go to any of your friends' parties."

"Not with you we won't." Ephraim closed his eyes, then lifted a hand and shook it slightly as if waving farewell to a host of people he would not be seeing. "We won't take the cousin to the parties. I promise."

Biting his lip, Manasseh looked at Jokim, then jerked his head toward the doorway. "Let's go."

———

The pharaohs of the eighteenth dynasty had lavished considerable care and wealth upon Thebes. The shrines, temples, and buildings erected during this dynasty alone had brought the city a reputation for splendor and beauty that would last for centuries. Flanked on the west by a two-mile-long prominence of cliffs that formed a backdrop for the small valleys and plains sprinkled with the tombs of the dead, the living city lay to the east of the river and pulsed with life even in the heat of the afternoon.

Ephraim and Manasseh led their disconcerted kinsman through the maze of winding paths in the heart of the capital, occasionally stopping to point out a particularly spectacular statue, temple, or a favorite merchant's stall. Ephraim, Manasseh noticed, seemed to walk more steadily than he had at the villa, and Manasseh hoped that the morning's beer had finally left his brother's system. The Egyptians drank only water, beer, or wine, and Ephraim's unruly friends had a pronounced taste for the strong black beer that flowed like water at social occasions, regardless of the hour of the day. The Egyptians not only tolerated drunkenness, but actually regarded it as pleasant. An oft-quoted poem from the twelfth dynasty commonly made the rounds at parties. Servants would offer cups of wine with the admonition, "Drink this and get drunk." The expected answer was, "I shall love to be drunk."

They wandered through the city for more than three hours, Manasseh dutifully following his brother and cousin while Jokim listened to Ephraim point out one architectural wonder after another.

"There are hundreds of temples at Thebes," Ephraim boasted, gesturing around him. "Probably more than any place on earth. The temple of Amon-Re is the largest in the world."

"And yet there are no temples to El Shaddai," Jokim observed.

Manasseh thought the remark would offend Ephraim's proud sensibilities, but his brother only grinned. "Why does an invisible god need a temple?" He lifted his shoulders in a shrug. "What are you going to put in it? Nothing! Why does nothing need a temple?"

"God Shaddai is not a nothing," Manasseh muttered under his breath. Though he'd had his own doubts lately about God Shaddai's wisdom and purpose, Ephraim's flippancy galled him.

"I didn't say *He* was nothing." Ephraim pressed his hand to his chest and smiled as though out of pity for Manasseh. "I said His temple would *hold* nothing."

The sun had begun to sink in the west when Manasseh gestured toward the river, hoping to lead his brother and cousin home. Jokim's tongue had loosened in the last hour. His previous awe and astonishment had evolved into open admiration of the confident way his cousins moved about the city. Jokim was in the midst of explaining his father's reluctance to enter the foreign Theban marketplace when a shadow fell across their path.

Manasseh looked up, annoyed that someone else had entered the conspiracy to ruin his day. His frown faded, however, when he saw the hulking brute who had blocked the sun. The interloper, a man who carried himself with a commanding air of self-confidence even when drunk, wore the distinctive kilt and leopard skin belt of one of Pharaoh's elite guards. He had probably come to Thebes from Malkata on a pass of some sort, but by the sour look on the man's face, Manasseh knew his holiday had not been pleasant.

"Ho! You river rats!" The man swayed drunkenly as he pulled a gleaming sword from its scabbard. His sour breath blew over them like a fetid breeze. "You'll not pass by me until you swear allegiance to my patron goddess. Nut's her name!"

With his free hand the barbarian pointed to a small stone statue by the doorway to the tavern. Manasseh frowned. The statue depicted a woman wearing a sun disk and cow horns. It was the image of Hathor, not Nut. But this inebriated ruffian was in no condition to know the difference.

Jokim paled immediately and withdrew, seeming to cower behind Ephraim's shoulder. Manasseh realized that his Hebrew kinsman was at a distinct disadvantage, since he couldn't understand the slurred words of the drunk Egyptian.

"Let us pass, friend." Keeping his voice calm and steady, Manasseh placed his hands on his hips. "We will not give you trouble, but neither will we bow to an idol."

"You will bow!" A vein in his forehead swelled like a thick black snake. "Nut demands it!"

"We will not," Manasseh answered calmly. For an instant he took his eyes from their adversary and glanced around for a weapon of some sort. He had no dagger in his belt, no club in his hand. Even Jokim's shepherd's staff would have been useful, but he had left it at the villa, not expecting this sort of harassment.

"Can I help?" Jokim asked in a low murmur. "I know trouble when I see it, and I have fought before. If he is determined to confront us—"

"He will let us pass," Manasseh answered in Egyptian, raising his voice so the soldier could hear. "As Pharaoh lives, this man has no reason to detain us."

"A pox on the life of Pharaoh!" the warrior roared, waving his sword. Manasseh cast a quick glance at Ephraim. The man was either out of his mind or senselessly drunk, for no one, especially a guard in Pharaoh's service, could curse the king and expect to live. If anyone else chanced to hear him—

"I can settle this." Ephraim advanced with a casual smile and spread his open hands before the man's mottled crimson face. "I would be happy to bow before Hathor—or Nut. Just clear me a space, will you?"

"Ephraim!" Manasseh barked, disbelieving.

"Hush, Manasseh. I'm going to bow." Ephraim kicked a pebble out of his way, then fell to his knees on the path. Mindless of the white kilt he wore, he sprawled out in the road, extending his arms toward the stone statue and pressing his face to the dirt.

Manasseh gaped in total incredulity for a moment, then realized that the warrior was staring as well. Without stopping to pause or rebuke his brother again, Manasseh stepped forward, reached up and twined his hand in the savage's hair, then brought the man's granite head down to his own uplifted knee. The sudden, surprising blow knocked the last vestige of understanding from the savage's clouded brain. He staggered back, then collapsed unconscious in the pathway.

"Come!" Manasseh grabbed Jokim's elbow and pulled his cousin toward home. Ephraim rose from his place in the dirt and ran to catch up with them, laughing as he came.

———

That night, after dinner with the vizier and the chief servants of his household, Manasseh said good-night to his cousin, brother, and father. He had scarcely lain in bed five minutes when a soft rap sounded on his door.

He sat up, instantly alarmed. "Yes?"

"May I speak with you?" The words were Hebrew, the voice soft and conspiratorial. Manasseh tossed off his linen sheet and padded to the door. Jokim stood there, his eyes glowing with a sheen of purpose. Surprised, Manasseh invited him in and directed him to a chair while he lit a lamp.

"What brings you here now?" he asked, taking a chair opposite Jokim. "What is so important we could not discuss it this afternoon?"

A flush ran like a shadow over Jokim's tanned face. "This afternoon," he said simply, his dark earnest eyes seeking Manasseh's, "I saw something I never expected to see."

"A drunken fool?" Manasseh laughed. "There is one on every street corner in Thebes. I am used to them."

"No." Jokim used his finger to dash small sparkles of sweat from his forehead, then folded his hands and leaned forward in the chair. "Today I saw a son of Abraham bow down to a stone idol. *That* I never expected to see."

"Ah," Manasseh answered, understanding. He slid down in his chair and rubbed the back of his neck. "Don't judge Ephraim too severely, Jokim. His action was part of a ruse to help us escape. And his plan worked! We did catch the drunken fool off guard, and no one was seriously hurt. The afternoon could have ended quite differently."

"But you wouldn't have done what he did." Jokim's eyes were sharp and assessing. "I would not have done it. And neither would I have called God Shaddai nothing."

Manasseh rested his head on his hand, considering. "All right. Maybe I wouldn't have bowed. But Ephraim doesn't worship idols. And he wasn't thinking clearly today, so his words were not what they should have been. I can assure you that he is not always so frivolous."

"He doesn't worship idols *now*. But we have heard things. Last week a trader told us that a dozen cattle branded with the vizier's mark had been offered to the priests of Amon-Re. My grandfather Judah protested and said the man had to be mistaken, but the trader insisted he spoke the truth. My father was certain your father had been robbed—either that, or someone from the villa pulled the cattle from Joseph's herds."

"Why would anyone here do that?" Manasseh shot Jokim a penetrating look, then rose from his chair and began to pace in the room. "That makes no sense. My father, Ephraim, and I worship El Shaddai and Him alone. We have never sent offerings to any of the temples. But these things are easy to check. If the cattle were taken to the temple, the steward will have a record of it."

Jokim nodded, but an almost imperceptible note of pleading remained on his face.

"There is something else?" Manasseh lifted a brow.

"Yes." For a moment Jokim studied Manasseh intently, then he continued. "I was not completely honest with you this morning when we spoke. I told you that the old ones are content to remain in Goshen, and that much was true." A strange, faintly eager look flashed in his eyes. "But there are many of us, mostly young men, who listened to you. We are ready to return to Canaan."

Manasseh let out a snort of disbelief. "No one listened to me in the wilderness. Why should you heed my words now?"

Jokim held up his hands. "You caught us by surprise, and we were silenced by the elders. But since we have returned to Egypt, we have seen our fathers cast off our way of life as easily as they disposed of their worn-out tents. They are old and tired, and they are resting on your father's promise to take care of them. They are depending upon Joseph, the almighty vizier, instead of the Almighty God. And so we, their sons and grandsons, find that it is up to us to lead the return to Canaan."

Manasseh felt his knees weaken. Was this another cruel jest, or had God finally decided to equip him for the task ahead?

The memory of his own words passed through him like an unwelcome chill. *"If you had only moved one of them to support me,"* he had prayed, tossing blame upon a just and holy God. He had imagined himself alone and helpless, yet all the while God Shaddai had been working in hearts unknown to Manasseh. . . .

He sank into his chair again and fixed Jokim with a steady gaze. "You are ready to go back? But we have nothing now. Before we had chariots, horses, warriors—"

"We can get those things." Jokim's eyes darkened dangerously. "We can get horses and camels, and already we have begun to talk to some of the border guards. For a price, they will join our company and fight with us."

"But we have nothing with which to pay them."

"We will have the spoils of Gerar, Gaza, and Ashkelon. They will fight for the promise of riches."

The promise of riches. The words rang in Manasseh's head like a clanging brass gong. He would win spoils in the battle— riches he could use to buy another harpist, some man or woman he could present to Pharaoh in exchange for Jendayi. He wouldn't need to trade upon his father's influence, nor would he have to bring her back to live in his father's house. He would take her to Canaan. They could be married there. . . .

God Shaddai had not left him hopeless!

"We will have to train in a safe place," Manasseh murmured, his thoughts racing along the track he had abandoned weeks before. "On the edge of the wilderness near Tura Quarry, my father has a house we can use as a base while we organize. It is isolated. He has not visited it in years."

"I had hoped we could count on you." A faint light twinkled

in the depths of Jokim's black eyes. "The others thought Ephraim would be the one to lead us, but this afternoon I saw that you are the one God has prepared. You know the Egyptians and the Hebrews. You can give us straight talk and simple answers. You, Manasseh, are the one we need. Say you will come and help us, and we will follow you back to Canaan."

In that instant Manasseh's resolve to forget the past shattered. A sense of fulfillment flooded his soul as his doubts vanished. God Shaddai *had* called him! Here was another proof of that call!

Feeling aggressive and alive for the first time in weeks, Manasseh stood and extended his hand to Jokim. "On his deathbed, Israel proclaimed that we would return to the land of our fathers. I will come to you soon, so prepare the others. And may God lead us back home!"

"He will." Jokim stood and clasped Manasseh's arm. His voice rang with the jubilation of supreme confidence. "Let the others do what they will, but we shall obey the will of God Shaddai!"

ZAPHENATH-PANEAH

"How long will you put off entering to take possession of the land which the Lord, the God of your fathers, has given you?"

Joshua 18:3

~ Sixteen ~

NO ELEMENT DISTINGUISHED PHARAOH FROM THE common man more than stone. Like other pharaohs before him, Amenhotep knew that through the magic of enduring stone, he and his name would live forever. To that end he secured the quarries that provided raw materials for his monuments: statues, temples, and pillars that would bear his name through generations to come.

Tura Quarry stood behind the green belt of the Nile like an aloof, august presence. The ancient Egyptians had dug limestone for the casing of Cheops' pyramid from these hills, and Manasseh paused on the trail that led from the river to the quarry and gazed upward at the chiseled cliffs. A score of slaves moved like ants over the cinnabar-colored walls, working diligently to cut stone for Pharaoh's latest project. A wagon loaded with meat, bread, and drink tottered along the stony path leading into the quarry itself, and under a faded canopy a group of scribes sat cross-legged in a shady spot, each man's parchments resting on the taut spread of his kilt across his legs as he recorded his share of the daily business. The air vibrated softly with the incessant *tap tap tap* of the workers' hammers keeping time with the heightened pounding of Manasseh's heart.

In the distance, directly south of the quarry but separated from the river by a rocky ridge, a white-washed, pillared building gleamed in silence, standing out like a beacon in the midst of the crimson hills. Manasseh lifted his hand and pointed to it.

"You are right, cousin." Jokim's eyes narrowed as he searched the spot. "It is perfect. Isolated and quiet."

"My father used to stay here when he was required to supervise projects at the quarry." Manasseh lowered his arm. "No one will think it strange that I am here or that a few of my friends and relatives have come to join me."

"But not your brother," Jokim murmured satirically.

"No. Not Ephraim." Manasseh heard the barely checked emotion in his voice. Before leaving his father's villa, he and Jokim had asked Ani about the rumor that the vizier's cattle had been accepted at Egyptian temples. To Manasseh's horror, Ani reported that Ephraim had ordered that two dozen of the finest cattle be offered to the leading temples at Thebes and Heliopolis.

A tumble of confused thoughts and feelings assailed Manasseh at the thought of Ephraim's disloyalty. Had he no faith in El Shaddai? Was he so determined to remain in Egypt that he wished to placate even a host of false priests?

Sick with the struggle churning within him, Manasseh turned his thoughts from Ephraim and gave his cousin a troubled smile. "It is good there are many who will join us. Ephraim must make his own decisions."

Behind Manasseh, Tarik broke into the conversation with a discreet servant's cough. "May I ask, Master Manasseh," he asked when Manasseh turned, "how long you intend to stay here? Your father will want to know."

Manasseh looked back to the rocky hills, feeling the power of the secluded spot. "You need not say anything to my father," he called over his shoulder, closing his eyes against the sun's brightness on the gleaming cliffs. "I doubt he will notice I am gone."

Even with his eyes closed, Manasseh could sense Tarik's hesitation. If the stalwart captain had a fault, it was that he still tended to think of Manasseh as an untried youth, unable to spend a night unguarded and away from home.

"You will be quite alone in this place," Tarik said, confirming Manasseh's thoughts. "If you are only planning to stay one night, why don't I remain with you? We can take the felucca back in the morning—"

"No, Tarik, I would not keep you from your duties." Manasseh opened his eyes and turned, easing into a smile. "And besides, you taught me how to defend myself. Didn't Ephraim and I have the best teacher in the Two Kingdoms? Do not worry. No harm will befall us here."

Tarik inclined his head in reply, but apprehension still flickered in his dark eyes. "Manasseh"—he lowered his gaze to the sand—"can you not tell me what you intend to do out here? It has been my duty and privilege to protect you since the day you came into this world—"

"And it has been my privilege to have you as my guardian." Manasseh stepped toward the captain and lowered his hand to the man's shoulder. Tenderly, he stooped a little to look into the older man's face. "But you, Tarik, are sworn first and foremost to serve my father, and I am not certain he will understand what Jokim and I intend to do. So if you do not know what we intend, your loyalties cannot be divided."

"Perhaps they already are." Tarik's jaw tensed, betraying his deep frustration, but he did not argue further. Instead he gestured toward a pair of servants who lingered behind him on the trail. "Come," he called over his shoulder, not taking his eyes from Manasseh's. "Bring the supplies into the house. Then we must return to Thebes."

"Thank you, Tarik." Manasseh shifted his hands to his hips as the servants began to carry baskets of food and jugs of water toward the house. "I shall not forget your help."

"Grant me one request," the captain said, stopping in midstride. His brow furrowed as he hesitated for a moment, then a rush of words poured forth. "I don't know what you are planning—and I shall not ask, since you won't tell me—but if you should need help, there is a warrior at Malkata who might be willing to assist you. His name is Abnu, and he is a friend of mine from long ago. He owes me a debt, and I give you permission to claim it."

Manasseh grinned. "What is he? A guard of the royal harem?"

Tarik's mouth twisted in a wry smile. "He is a giant. A Medjay warrior. Sometimes he fights for Pharaoh's entertainment, yet I heard he was tiring of the sport, for he always wins. But he enjoys an adventure, so remember his name. He would enjoy this one, I think."

"A giant?" Manasseh squinted toward the captain in disbelief. "Tarik, are you certain you are not drunk? When did you keep company with a giant?"

"My life did not begin with you, young master." The captain's brittle smile softened slightly. "But the past is only important if it can be of use to your future. Call upon Abnu if you need a strong arm. And may your father's God give you wisdom in the days ahead."

"Amen," Jokim echoed.

———

Tura lay a full day's boat journey north of Thebes but was only an hour's camel ride from Goshen and the Hebrew camp. After depositing their goods in the deserted house, Manasseh and Jokim bid Tarik farewell, then went to the quarry to bargain with the overseer. The old man in charge of the stonecutters fell to the dust as soon as he recognized Manasseh as the vizier's son, and Manasseh felt his face color as the man groveled in the dirt. Though he was accustomed to outward displays of reverence from common folk, in Jokim's presence the man's obsequiousness embarrassed him.

"Rise, friend." Manasseh bent down and extended a hand. "You should bow to the vizier, but I am only his son. If you are willing to be of service, however, my kinsman and I are in need of a camel—two, if you can spare them."

"For you, son of Zaphenath-paneah, we can spare anything," the man said, his grin toothless and stained in the midst of a ruddy face. He rose and squinted suspiciously for a moment at Jokim, then his head bobbed like a cork on the Nile. "Two camels, yes. You may take my own. They are worthy beasts and should serve you quite well."

"We'll only need them for a day or two." Manasseh rested his hands on his hips. "I do not want to inconvenience you."

"Two days, two weeks, it is all the same to me." The old man bobbed again. "Where am I going? Nowhere. Take them, with any of my slaves you might require. I have a daughter, too, if you're interested—"

"No, thank you," Manasseh interrupted, starting toward the small house where the overseer lived. "We need the camels only."

Later, perched atop a gurgling, growling camel that moved with long strides across the silent sands, Manasseh dropped the reins on his thoughts and let them wander freely. Solitude was a rare commodity in crowded Thebes and especially precious to one who had come from the bustling vizier's household. Here in the wide wilderness Manasseh found it almost possible to forget who and what he was. In Egypt men bowed and scraped before him because they knew him to be the vizier's elder son. What a joke! Israel, the one whose opinion mattered most, had seen Manasseh as subtly inferior. And Joseph, who could have rebuilt the foundation of Manasseh's self-confidence with a blessing of his own, seemed content to continue about Pharaoh's business. He spent the bulk of his time and energy upon Amenhotep, apparently satisfied to ignore his son and allow his brothers to remain in a land to which they could never belong.

A fierce steady wind shrilled southward, blowing up small clouds of sand that scraped Manasseh's arms and legs. He lowered his head, delighted to let his cousin lead the way back to Goshen. Jokim, like the other Hebrews, was accustomed to the desert. Manasseh knew he had much to learn, including how to dress. Like most other Egyptian nobles, he now wore only a kilt, a cloak, and a wide collar, and he found himself wishing he had donned a long tunic and head covering like the one Jokim wore. The scraggly beard he had begun to grow as a symbol of identification with his Hebrew brethren was not yet full enough to prevent the sand from scouring his neck.

If he were to lead his people back to Canaan, he would have to dress, talk, and think the way they did. They would follow a son of Joseph, but only if he behaved as a Hebrew and not an Egyptian.

After arriving in Goshen, Jokim led Manasseh to his father's tent, then went in search of the men who had sent him to Thebes. Shelah's tent stood empty when Manasseh entered, and he sank wearily onto a stool, then ran his hand over his face and tasted sand on his lips. Was there an inch of his body not covered with grit?

A flapping noise startled him, and he looked up to see a young girl standing in the tent's opening. She carried a pitcher of water in her arms.

"Jokim said you would want to wash your hands and face," she said, speaking Hebrew in a delicate whisper. She was a willowy creature, more child than woman, but the potential for feminine loveliness was evident in her form and the elegant curve of her cheek. Her thick dark hair hung in long graceful curves over her shoulders, and the hands that held the pitcher were delicate and long fingered.

She has Jendayi's hands, Manasseh thought, his intended greeting sticking in his throat.

Seeing him hesitate, the girl lifted a brow. Manasseh flushed with self-consciousness as he cleared his throat. "Yes, I would like to wash," he said, standing.

"No, you sit." She nodded toward the stool, and he sat again and held his hands out. With the glee of a small child she tipped the unwieldy pitcher over, allowing a stream of water to splatter upon his hot dusty hands. The liquid felt wonderfully cool and cleansing. He looked up to smile his thanks.

"There." She lowered the pitcher to the ground and wiped her own hands on her tunic, at once awkward and shy. Staring at him in a gentle, inquiring fashion, she leaned against a tent pole and thrust her hands behind her back. "Jokim says you are here to talk to his friends."

"That's right."

"He says I am not allowed to listen."

Manasseh ran his hand over his mouth, hiding a smile. "Does the conversation of men interest you?"

She pulled her lips into a round rosette. "Not always. But it is not every day that *you* come to Goshen."

Manasseh shriveled a little at her words. Was he the esteemed "vizier's son" even here?

His good humor evaporated. "I am afraid you might be disappointed if you listened to us. We will not be discussing topics to entertain a young girl. And if you want to meet the vizier's son, go to Thebes. The better one is there."

"I'm not a little girl. I'm fifteen." Her dark eyes defiantly met his. "You are as bad as Jokim, always thinking of me as a child." She flashed him a look of disdain. "And I care not that you are the vizier's son. What is the Egyptian vizier to me? Nothing. We are the children of Israel, a nation apart. Jokim says we are going back to Canaan. I just wanted to meet the man who will help us go."

With a springy bounce she lunged toward the doorway, but

Manasseh reached up and caught her arm. "Wait." His mind bulged with questions. "You know about our plan? And you want to go back?"

"Jokim tells me everything." Anger edged her voice as she jerked from his grasp. "And I know enough to keep quiet. Father does not want to talk about leaving Goshen, and neither does Grandfather. They are out surveying land right now, deciding where they should build their houses and pen their animals. My mother is with them, her head spinning with grand thoughts of the jewels she will buy and the garments she will make. They want to stay here, but I do not. I am ready to go back to Canaan."

"But why? You have no memories of it." Manasseh marveled that so small a frame could contain so fierce a spirit. "You are young. You were born here. How do you know you will like Canaan?"

A rosy flush rose on her cheekbones. "How does the eagle know to fly?" she whispered, leaning closer. She lifted her chin and stood on tiptoe, bringing her lips to within inches of his ear. "He hears the voice of God Shaddai."

Before Manasseh could react, she whirled and raced through the tent opening. He started forward, intent upon catching her, but Jokim lifted the tent flap and blocked Manasseh's path. Jokim watched the girl go, and a wry grin split his face as he turned back to Manasseh.

"I see you've met Atara." He sighed in mock heaviness. "It was all I could do to keep her at home when I left for Thebes. She wants very much to be a part of all this."

"She is your betrothed?" Manasseh asked, staring after the girl's willowy form as she threaded her way through a huddle of women around a cooking fire.

"By heaven, no, and I pity the man who marries her. She is my sister—my curious, mischievous little sister." He clapped a hand on Manasseh's shoulder, and when he spoke again his voice was lower and more intense. "The others are waiting outside the camp in a wadi a short distance away. We cannot meet here. Too many of those who disapprove would notice. We are trying to keep peace with our fathers, so we do not speak openly of our plans."

Shaking all thoughts of the girl from his mind, Manasseh followed Jokim from the tent.

———

Nearly forty men had gathered down in the dry stream bed where Jokim led him. They were seated on stones and various outcroppings of rock, and Manasseh was pleased to see that most of them wore a look of set determination. They were the new generation. Most were his age or a few years older. These were the grandchildren and great-grandchildren of Jacob, and they were eager to find their places in the land God had promised to His people.

Jokim led Manasseh through the waiting Hebrews, then gave a swift and sure introduction. "Brothers and kinsmen, I am certain you remember Manasseh, son of Joseph. When I went to Thebes I was certain God had sent me to bring Ephraim back to you, but God showed me *this* is the man to lead us. Listen to him, my brothers, as you once listened to his father and his father's father. For I am convinced God would have us journey back to Canaan. Manasseh heard the voice of God Shaddai. He is the man to take us home."

Without further ceremony Jokim sank to a rock and looked to Manasseh, his eyes alight with vivid excitement. Manasseh felt his mouth go dry as he looked at the crowd of bearded faces, remembering the last time he stood before his Hebrew relatives. On that morning he had proclaimed his dream and God's message, and they had mocked him. He thought they all disbelieved him, but these few, at least, had carried his thoughts and words with them.

He searched for words and found none, but God had promised to provide all he would need to obey. *What I need now, God Shaddai, is words.*

"Kinsmen," he began, spreading his hands. "I stand before you dressed like an Egyptian because this is the land that gave me birth. But unless we leave this place, all men of Israel will look as I do within a few years. Our people will forget the promises of God. We will forget God himself. And the land that now binds us with goodness and generosity will bind us with chains and whips."

"No!" One man lifted his fist in protest.

"Never!" echoed another voice.

"Yes, it could happen," Manasseh said with a cautionary lift of his hand. "My father and my brother and I live according to the truth of God Shaddai. There are no idols in our house, but anything we serve more than God—whether it is a habit, an idol, or a kingdom—will soon enslave us. If our people begin to love and serve Egypt, they will be imprisoned. Hear me, for I speak God's truth."

"How could such a thing happen?" one young man shouted, his face reddening in anger. He leapt to his feet and threw his hands up, fists balled. "The sons of Israel are not idol worshipers!"

Jokim stood and moved to the empty space between Manasseh and the young man. "This is Hezron, son of Perez, son of Judah." Deflecting Hezron's anger, Jokim turned to the audience and spread his arms in an expansive gesture. "We think we will never change, that we would never forget the God of our fathers," he called, his jaw tightening. "But though we love God Shaddai and our fathers have taught us truth, we cannot be sure our children will not be affected by the evil in Egypt. Just yesterday I watched Ephraim, who was elected to stand with Jacob's own sons in the inheritance, bow down to an idol. He committed the act in jest, I admit, but how do we know the acts of jest today will not be done in seriousness tomorrow?"

Manasseh felt his cheeks burn for his brother's sake, but a hushed silence fell over the group. Hezron sat down. Jokim had made his point.

"Manasseh is true to us and to our God," Jokim said, hitching his thumbs in the woven belt at his waist. "And he knows the Egyptians. He has sympathetic friends in high places. With his help we can gather horses, chariots, weapons—all we will need to retake our land."

"But look at us," another voice called. A gangly youth with a blotchy face stood and spread his thin arms. "Do we look like an army? There are scarcely forty of us, and there are thousands of Canaanites between Goshen and Hebron. Even if we had control of Pharaoh's army—"

"We might have an army, or at least part of it," Manasseh interrupted. "The border guards are skilled warriors paid by Pharaoh to protect his boundaries. They will fight for any cause so long as they are compensated. They will join us if we guarantee them a part of the spoils."

"But we are not trained for battle." Another young man looked at Manasseh with something very fragile in his eyes. "I am Zimri, son of Zerah, son of Judah. And I know nothing about fighting. I am a goatherd, but the goats stay close to the camp. I have never even fought a wild animal."

Manasseh felt his heart swell in pity. The youth had the mild eyes of a man who should grow old sitting quietly and humbly in his own house, but if God could use Jacob, the trickster, He could use anyone willing to obey.

"Zimri," Manasseh consciously gentled his voice, "I will teach you all you need to know. My father's captain taught me swordplay and charioteering. I can hurl a spear with deadly accuracy, and I can teach you to do the same. Have no fear, cousin. If God is on our side, who can stand against us? And we may not have to kill." Manasseh folded his arms across his chest. "If we are bold, we will march first on the small settlement of Gerar. Those men will flee rather than fight. But we will take the city, and the inhabitants of Gaza will hear of it. When we move northward, the men of Gaza will flee to Ashkelon, and the word of our force will grow. We will tell any who listen that we come in peace, that we seek only to return to our homeland."

Silence. They sat and stared at him, thinking.

"How many warriors might we enlist?" Hezron finally called out.

"One hundred, perhaps two hundred." Manasseh unfolded his arms. "And they are skilled in combat."

Another moment of silence passed, then Manasseh clapped in satisfaction. "I have secured a place." He swept his audience with a piercing glance. "A house outside the quarry at Tura. No one will notice us there, and we will have the entire desert in which to train. The overseer of the quarry will provide all we need, for he wants to remain in my father's good graces. As soon as we are settled, I will send word to the captain of the border guards. We should have his answer within a few days."

"One more thing!"

Manasseh lifted his head. Hezron had stood again, an implacable expression on his face.

"How can we know for certain"—Hezron turned to face the others—"that God Shaddai is on our side? That we are following His will? We have only this man's word to say that God wants us to do this!"

Forty pairs of questioning eyes shifted to Manasseh, arousing the old fears and uncertainties that slumbered within his breast. But God *had* spoken directly to him. The angelic messenger had reinforced the message, and Jokim's appearance in Thebes had confirmed it.

"Did God not tell our father Abraham that Canaan was the Promised Land?" Manasseh asked, his voice calm, his gaze steady. "Did God not tell Jacob to fear not to descend into Egypt, for He would preserve us and make us a great nation here?"

"Yes," came the murmured reply from a dozen throats.

"God has preserved us," Manasseh continued. "He has made us a great nation. And now it is not a question of whether or not God wills for us to reenter Canaan, but whether or not we are willing to obey Him. Are we willing to be obedient, disciplined, and holy? Are we willing to march into the land He has promised?"

"Yes!"

"I am!"

"I am ready!"

"Hear him!" Jokim lifted a fist into the air. "Now, kinsmen, go home to your families and take your leave. Bid your fathers and mothers good-bye; kiss your sisters farewell. But tell no man where we are going or what we are doing. The old ones will disapprove, and the women will weep and wail. But we will not be deterred."

As one, the group lifted their voices in a determined roar.

———

Manasseh smiled grimly as the hired warrior fell to the dirt, a trickle of blood streaking across his cheek. Hezron had managed the battle-ax very well, especially when Manasseh considered that he had only been introduced to the weapon two weeks before.

"Very good, Hezron." Manasseh thrust his hands behind his back as he nodded in approval. The burly shepherd extended his hand to help the border warrior to his feet. "You have caught the idea."

"You should not be surprised," Hezron answered, chuckling with a dry and cynical sound as he pulled his opponent up. "A battle-ax is nothing but a shepherd's staff with a blade attached. My brothers and I have battled far worse than this Nubian out in the fields. A bear once attacked me when I had nothing but a staff to defend myself, and Hamul over there once used the sharpened point of his staff to kill a pair of Philistines who came upon him in the night."

Manasseh bit down hard on his lower lip, determined not to defend himself in front of these men. He had never intended to imply that they were inferior or less skilled than he, but belligerent animosity had flared toward him several times. Peace was not easily kept among men who routinely and purposely worked themselves into the deadly frenzy of combat, and not all the Hebrews were ready to accept a leader so . . . Egyptian.

He turned swiftly and walked to the circle where Zimri and Shallum were involved in a wrestling match. Several of the others had gathered in the shade to watch, and Manasseh located Jokim amongst them and merged into the group at his cousin's side. Someone had heeled a slightly lopsided circle into the sand, and within it Zimri and Shallum hunched like prowling bears, each intent upon the eyes of the other.

Manasseh watched the circling men for a moment, then gave Jokim a slight nudge in the ribs. "There are new faces here." He frowned as he searched the gathering. "Who are these strangers?"

Distracted, Jokim tore his gaze from the wrestlers and looked around, then gave Manasseh a one-sided smile. "They are quarry slaves. The overseer gave them permission to train with us."

"What?" Manasseh's mind flooded with objections. "But—he can't! What if Pharaoh learns of this? Or my father? We don't need these men."

"We need every pair of hands willing to join us." Jokim looked back at Manasseh with a level gaze. "And if God chooses to help us by the hands of these Egyptians, who are we to say He should not?"

"We don't need the Egyptians!"

"We needed warriors."

"They are different. When the fight is done, they will return to their posts."

Jokim shrugged. "When the fight is done, these men will return to the quarry. They are slaves. They have no choice. But the overseer thinks he will please your father by allowing them to help us, so he volunteered their labor. He has no great need of them—Pharaoh has not called for blocks of limestone in months. The overseer said these days Pharaoh favors black granite from a place called Ibhet."

Alarm and anger rippled along Manasseh's spine. Once again, a younger kinsman had stepped into his rightful place and usurped it without even thinking! Without asking! Without considering the price that might have to be paid.

"What will happen when one of these slaves slips away?" Manasseh asked, his voice taut with anger. "When he takes a boat—or steals one—and goes up the Nile to tell everyone he meets about our work here? What will happen when my father finds out? I am still the vizier's son, Jokim. My father still has the power to—"

"To do what?" Jokim asked, his eyes bemused and opaque. "To punish you? To send you to your chamber? You are a grown man. Your father can offer you nothing but his blessing." He turned back to the wrestling match, oblivious to the effect of his poisonous words while something snapped in Manasseh's mind.

He looked away, not trusting himself to answer. A tumult raged in his soul. Despair, anger, denial, and aggression warred in his spirit. Jokim could speak so lightly of a father's blessing only because he was certain to receive one. He had never been denied. He did not know the searing pain of being passed over, while Manasseh felt a rock fall through his heart every time he thought of Israel and Ephraim. . . .

"I am not unaware, Manasseh, of what you are feeling," Jokim went on, speaking with light bitterness as he watched the wrestlers. "But I am not the firstborn. I do not expect that blessing and will not be disappointed when I do not receive it."

"You cannot know," Manasseh answered, the words tasting like gall, "what I am feeling."

"Perhaps not." Jokim turned to face him. "But I am not your adversary. I am not trying to take your place. I must answer to my own conscience and to what I know as truth, and so must you. The truth is that we need every man who will join us. I and the others are grateful for any man, Egyptian or Hebrew, who will risk his life to help our cause."

"Still, if I am to lead, I should be consulted."

"I had planned to speak with you tonight." Jokim turned his gaze back to the contest. "When we could talk in private. The overseer just left an hour ago, and there has not been time to approach you."

Manasseh gripped his arms. Jokim was right. The decision to accept the slaves was logical, sensible, and smart. And if Manasseh had not been so intent on thinking that only *he* could make decisions, he would have seen the merit in Jokim's reasoning. By heaven above, would his treacherous heart be as jealous of Jokim as it was of Ephraim?

He leaned on Jokim's shoulder for support as he pushed himself up, then turned away from the circle of cheering men. "I'll be in the house if anyone needs me," he said, moving away. "But perhaps it is good no one does."

~ Seventeen ~

"CAPTAIN TARIK!" A CHUBBY LITTLE SLAVE BOY, clothed in a smudged and wrinkled kilt, lifted the tapestry covering the doorway of the captain's small house. "Captain! The vizier calls for you!"

Tarik threw an apologetic glance at his wife, then rose from his chair and tied his sword belt over his kilt.

"Is there trouble, do you think?" Halima asked, a frown settling across her pretty features. "Zaphenath-paneah does not often call for you so late."

"Nothing out of the ordinary, I'm sure." Tarik's mouth curved with tenderness as he looked back at his wife. "Keep the roasted pigeon over the fire. I'll be back before you go to sleep."

He pulled his spear from the wall, then walked through pools of torchlight up the wide marble steps of the portico, through the vestibule, and into the vizier's grand reception chamber. Zaphenath-paneah sat in his gilded chair, still every inch an official, still intent upon his work, though the sun had set hours before.

Before him, in widely spaced seats, sat Ephraim and a heavily bearded man Tarik recognized as one of his master's elder brothers. He mentally stumbled through the list of Hebrew names to place the man's face.

"Tarik, you remember my brother Judah."

Tarik bowed formally. "Yes. Life, prosperity, and health to you, my friend!"

They exchanged polite, simultaneous smiles.

"Judah has come to Thebes to inquire about his grandson," Zaphenath-paneah went on, a watchful fixity in his face as his eyes bored into Tarik's. "Jokim is his name, as I'm sure you'll remember. He came to visit Manasseh and Ephraim nearly a month ago."

"Of course, master." Tarik nodded. Actually, Jokim had visited only fifteen days before, but Zaphenath-paneah was not always well informed about the goings and comings in his household. Tarik thought it best not to correct him.

"We have passed a pleasant evening in conversation, but a few moments ago Judah asked to see Jokim." The vizier paused, and a quick and disturbing thought struck Tarik. By Seth's diseased toenail, did Judah think Jokim was *here*?

Zaphenath-paneah, as discerning as always, read the thought in Tarik's eyes. "Yes, Captain, my brother has been led to believe that Jokim is visiting Manasseh and Ephraim. And I, of course, believed until this moment that Manasseh was in Goshen with his kinsmen."

Tarik lowered his eyes to the floor, dreading the question that would follow. He had never lied to his master, had never been anything but totally faithful. He would die for Zaphenath-paneah or his sons, and that love that had driven him to help Manasseh—

"Where are they, Captain?"

Tarik lifted his gaze. From the corner of his eye he saw Ephraim press his hand over his mouth, probably hiding a smile.

The day of reckoning could not be postponed forever. "I believe, master, that Manasseh and Jokim are at Tura."

Ephraim dropped his hand, his smirk wiped away by astonishment.

"What are they doing at Tura?"

Tarik took a deep breath; this would not be easy. He had promised to keep a secret for Manasseh, but he had sworn loyalty to his master. "It is my belief," he began, choosing his words carefully, "that he is . . . training."

"For what?" This from the old man, Judah.

Tarik wished he had been away at the stables when the vizier's summons came. "For possible battle, sir. In Canaan."

He could say no more, but he'd said enough. For a moment Zaphenath-paneah and Judah looked at each other, and Tarik knew they understood. Even he, an Egyptian, had felt the power of Manasseh's burning conviction that the Hebrews should return to the land of their fathers. Manasseh had insisted that his summons came directly from God Shaddai, and though Tarik could not imagine life away from Zaphenath-paneah or Thebes, he would have gone to the underworld and back if *his* master commanded it. Manasseh could do no less.

"This is ridiculous." The old man's bony hand knocked against the arm of the chair in some sort of frantic palsy. "They are nothing but youths—"

"They are men, sir," Tarik interrupted, knowing he could be punished for the insolence of speaking without first being addressed. "Do not fault him for the crime of being a young man. My master's son is mature and responsible. Manasseh possesses courage and grace in full measure. Time would only weaken, not improve, his strength."

Judah scowled. "Time would improve his character," he snapped, leaning forward. "And his wisdom!"

Tarik looked away. In the other chair Ephraim wore an expression of stunned surprise. "Jokim is my age, Uncle," he whispered, a slight hesitancy in his tone. "He *is* a man full grown."

"No man has the right to engage in war on a whim." Zaphenath-paneah's tense clipped voice forbade any further discussion. "War is for kings and princes, not starry-eyed, unrealistic young men. They must be brought home. They and whoever is with them must return to their people."

Zaphenath-paneah brought his hands together in an explosive clap, and two slaves appeared in the doorway as if they had materialized from out of the wall. "Fetch my scribe and a runner," the vizier commanded. "I will write a letter that must be taken downriver tonight." His eyes flashed imperiously toward his captain of the guard. "Tarik, summon the boatman. The letter must be safely delivered to Manasseh at Tura, and when that boat returns, Manasseh must be on it. Take two of your best guards to make it so."

Cold dignity had created a stony mask of Zaphenath-paneah's face. Never had his eyes seemed so hard. "Captain, can I trust you to see that my orders are followed?"

"Yes, my lord." Tarik's voice, like his nerves, was in tatters.

———

Down at the docks, Tarik paused before dismissing the boatman. Judah had already spread out his cloak to sleep beneath the canopy, and the usual contingent of rowers and seamen lined the railing. There was no need for additional men, even though Zaphenath-paneah had expressly commanded that a pair of guards be dispatched to bring his son home.

Tarik's promise to obey weighed upon him. Could the vizier truly know so little about his son? A pair of guards on the fel-ucca's deck would only arouse Manasseh's defensiveness. He would see their weapons and refuse even to show himself. He would be hurt, angered, driven to disobey his father's summons.

Tarik lowered his gaze, trying to hide his inner misery from the boatman's probing stare.

"Is that all, Captain Tarik?" the man asked, wiping his face with the back of his hand. "We'll be off unless there's anyone else—"

"There is no one else." Tarik lifted his gaze and looked the man squarely in the eye. "Just your seamen, the messenger, and the Hebrew."

The boatman ducked his head in reply, then moved out to the gangplank, his bare feet sliding over the weathered wood without a sound.

A wizened seaman pulled the gangplank into the boat, and Tarik caught his breath, the knowledge that he had disobeyed his master twisting and turning like a whirlwind inside him.

———

The rising sun swallowed up the wind that had howled around the secluded villa all night, and Manasseh stepped out onto the wide portico and lifted his arms to stretch. The house had begun to look like a barracks, for men slept everywhere they could find room to lie down. The slaves from the quarries deemed it an honor to sleep in the vizier's villa, and the Hebrews cared nothing about where they slept, for they dreamed of the green hills and dense groves of the Jordan River valley.

Manasseh himself had dreamed of Jendayi. Despite her attraction to Ephraim, his heart still yearned for her. Perhaps, once he had proven himself a warrior, she might come to love him. But whether she did or not, he was determined to keep his promise and win her freedom. As soon as they had cleared the way back to Canaan, he would return to Egypt, make things right with his father, and enter Pharaoh's palace. Before the gilded throne and the gleaming Wadjet eye on Pharaoh's headdress, he would offer sheep, oxen, all that he had gathered in the spoils of war. But he suspected that Amenhotep would be more swayed by the proffering of praise than possessions. Pharaoh had more than his share of the world's treasures. He lacked something entirely different.

Manasseh wasn't sure when the truth had come to him, but one afternoon as he sifted through his thoughts, he had been struck by the realization that he and Pharaoh shared a father figure, Zaphenath-paneah. To both Manasseh and Amenhotep, Joseph was a daunting example, but did Pharaoh feel smothered to the same degree Manasseh felt alienated? The common people joked that Pharaoh had built Malkata in an attempt to live with his harem apart from Queen Tiy, but perhaps he had built it to put distance between himself and his vizier. Though Zaphenath-paneah still spent a few hours each morning in ceremonial attendance upon the king, he spent most of his day in Thebes. Doing Pharaoh's work. Receiving Pharaoh's praise. And the people's. Everyone adored Zaphenath-paneah except the priests of Amon-Re—

No wonder Amenhotep had never converted to the worship of God Shaddai! In his theology, at least, Amenhotep could stand free from the clouding shadow of Zaphenath-paneah's powerful influence.

Alone in the desert with his thoughts, Manasseh had come to understand the frightened god-king on the throne. Amenhotep was as easily intimidated as any man. He found it easier to withdraw to Malkata than to see his glory dimmed in the presence of one who shone brighter. So when the battle for Canaan was done, Manasseh would approach Pharaoh, massage the royal ego with sincere praise, and offer whatever Pharaoh required in exchange for Jendayi's freedom.

Dawn was spreading a gray light over the quarry, draping misty veils over the sleeping stones and the little village where the quarry slaves and overseer lived. Manasseh squinted northward toward the stocky brick structures. Already one of the slaves stirred along the small path that wound among the huts—probably an ardent worshiper of Amon-Re out to catch a glimpse of the god as he began his morning ride across the sky. Either that, Manasseh thought with a wry grin, or the man was up early to answer nature's call.

Manasseh yawned contentedly, stretched again, and was about to turn back into the house when another movement caught his eye. Far in the distance, down near the western riverfront, the small triangular tip of a sail peeked from behind an outcropping of rock. Visitors! But from where? And who would risk traveling through the night to arrive at sunrise?

A wave of apprehension swept through him as he darted toward the face of the rocky wall that bordered the path and partially hid the vizier's house. Reaching for foot-holds and hand-holds he had known since his childhood, he lifted himself up and over the edge of the sheer wall. Lying flat on the rock's broad back, he inched forward, pushing himself with his toes until his eyes peered over the rim of stone.

For an instant his heart expanded in relief. The felucca was his father's, for the vizier's crimson and white standard flapped madly from the single mast. But if his father's felucca had appeared at Tura, either Tarik had sent word of some emergency or his father knew—*everything*.

His stomach heaved with anxiety and frustration. Without a doubt his father knew. Zaphenath-paneah always knew everything eventually. Manasseh should have known the confrontation could not be forestalled, that a showdown was inevitable. But he would not be reprimanded in front of his men.

Sliding backward off the rock, he slid down the cliff as quickly as he dared, then scrambled over the scree and hurried toward the river trail, determined to intercept his father's emissaries before they reached the house.

———

An hour later, Manasseh sat alone on a mounded levee at the river's edge, a papyrus scroll in his hand. The messenger had been happy to leave the scroll with Manasseh and depart immediately for Goshen, but before the felucca moved on, Manasseh caught sight of Judah's set face, clamped mouth, and flashing eyes beneath the canopy of the boat. It was good, he thought, that Jokim had not followed him down the river path.

Now Manasseh's eyes focused on the distant western horizon while his heart struggled with the knowledge that this time his father could not be obeyed, must not be trusted. God had spoken, and Joseph had not been willing to listen, nor had Judah. What was it about old men that made them unwilling to hear and obey the moving Spirit of God?

"Who was it, Manasseh?"

Jokim's voice startled him, but he did not turn around. Someone else stood behind him too, and Manasseh suspected by the light sound of the man's footfalls that timid Zimri had come down the mountain trail with Jokim.

"The boat brought a message from my father." Manasseh bent his legs and rested his elbows on top of his knees, wearily considering the eternal river before him. "We have been discovered. And our fathers—mine and yours, Jokim—demand that we return to our homes. It is not the right time to indulge in battle, my father says, and only Pharaoh can declare an invasion. So when the felucca returns from Goshen later today, I am to board her and join my father in Thebes."

Grunting, Jokim sank onto the levee beside Manasseh. Zimri sat beside Jokim like a well-trained puppy. "Since the felucca is only going back to Thebes, apparently your father doesn't expect me to board her," Jokim pointed out. "So I will stay, as will the others. Our fathers are not the vizier, and they haven't the authority to command us home."

"You know what the elders will say." Manasseh turned to Jokim with a critical squint. "They will say you are living in rebellion. And no good son rebels against his father."

"Unless a father rebels against God," Jokim answered with quiet emphasis. "In that case, we ought to obey God first. I will not disrespect my father. I will not argue with him, insult him, or dishonor him. But I believe God has called us out, Manasseh. And I will not abandon the cause, no matter who summons me."

Manasseh flinched at the subtle accusation in Jokim's voice.

"You do what you must do," Jokim finished, staring out at the river. "But now that your father knows our location and intent, it is too dangerous for us to remain here. We will move our camp into the wilderness, and we will relocate every night in order to escape detection. If you come back—"

"When I come back," Manasseh interrupted. "I *will* return. I will go home, make peace with my father, do my part to keep things quiet. And then I will return. I would be a worthless warrior if I put my hand to the sword and then proved unwilling to finish the battle."

Jokim smiled in quiet understanding. "When you come back, stop at the quarry and ask the overseer where we have gone. We will leave word with him so you will be able to find us."

Manasseh inclined his head in a nod, not looking at his kinsman, and after a moment Jokim and Zimri stood and walked away, their footsteps softly puffing over the sand as they climbed the trail back to the marble mansion. Manasseh closed his eyes to the sight of the shining river, suddenly hating it with every fiber of his being. The low river of the Drought was the bright color of the verdigris that grew on copper urns. Lying there, green and shining, it reminded him of a jungle python, sometimes thin and lazy, other times engorged and restless, but always moving, always pulling, always alive. You couldn't kill it or escape from it. It hypnotized, it mesmerized, it drew people from the mountains and deserts until they lived in a thin verdant ribbon along its banks. And, like the others who had come from the forests and the deserts and the stony mountains, his father and Abraham's people had come from the holy Promised Land to live alongside the glowing water. The river had saved them according to God's plan, but now they were loathe to leave it, still hypnotized by its beauty, caught up in its shallow pleasures, drowned in its promises of prosperity.

He rose to his feet, tall and angry, and crumpled the papyrus scroll in his hand. With all his might he flung it toward the controlling and treacherous Nile, then turned and stalked up the trail to fetch his cloak.

If he did not obey his father's order, Zaphenath-paneah would send others to search for him and his men. So he would leave on the felucca. He owed that much to the ones who had toiled with and for him under the blazing sun. He would meet the boat at the river, away from his men, so as not to reveal their faces or their number. He would reenter his father's house and pretend to be a properly obedient and chastised son.

But he would return to the fight as soon as possible.

———

The oarsmen rowed to the steady beat of the drum throughout the night. As the felucca raced over the crushed diamond water, Manasseh leaned against the railing and crossed his arms, grateful that his father hadn't sent an armed guard to escort him home. That would have been the ultimate insult, a subtle statement that the vizier's elder son could be trusted no more than a slave or condemned criminal. Manasseh mentally thanked his father for the gesture of confidence, even though he fully planned to abuse it.

The sun had begun to rim the housetops with the first gray-pink tatters of dawn as the boat neared Thebes. Manasseh gave a slight nod of thanks to the boatman who lowered the gangplank so he could disembark, then he stepped smartly down the ramp and darted toward a huddle of fishermen who were gathering their nets for the day's fishing.

Carefully he scanned the crowd at the docks. Manasseh thought it likely that his father would send a messenger to the river, a friend, perhaps, to escort Manasseh home, to sound out his feelings about this ignominious return. Manasseh concealed himself among the fishermen, stooping slightly to disguise his height until he spied a familiar face hurrying toward the waterfront.

Ani. Of course. His father had sent the villa's resident wise man, the beloved tutor to whom Manasseh had taken his questions about the earth, the sky, his body, his brain, even his heart. Joseph had been wise to send Ani, for Manasseh might have shared his plans with him, but Ani's aging eyes would fail him this morning. As the old steward peered across the crowds of fishermen and other travelers who hurried forth to greet the day, Manasseh slunk away, moving northward through the crowd.

He would face Joseph soon enough, but not now. His eyes burned from sleeplessness, and the malaise in him would choke off any words he might want to say to his father. He needed rest. He wanted the company of a friend, not an adversary.

His tired eyes spied an abandoned papyrus skiff near the reedy bank, one of the ubiquitous rafts that children often used to slide from one shore to the other. Without a sound, Manasseh stepped onto the skiff and by momentum alone sent it winging westward across the river. With any luck, the encroaching fishing ships would surround him within a few moments, and in the river traffic he could move unnoticed toward Malkata.

If he needed help, Tarik had promised, a giant called Abnu might be willing to give it.

But another, more pressing reason lay behind his urge to visit the king's palace. Jendayi waited there, and nearly two months had passed since he had last seen her sweet face.

Amenhotep had built his palace for living on a shore previously reserved for the dead. Malkata lay just north of Thebes on the Nile's western bank. Manasseh knew it might be difficult to enter the harbor without arousing suspicion, but in the last few days he had been surprised at how many things were possible if one had the temerity to attempt them.

When the towering granite pillars of Malkata rose from the emerald ribbon of foliage bordering the riverfront, Manasseh left the bustling, noisy river and floated into the harbor, crouching low on the skiff and paddling through the water with his hands. High reeds edged the king's harbor like a fur lining, and he remained in the rushes until he had passed the royal docks without raising an alarm. Moving slowly so he would not attract attention, he pawed through the reeds until he caught a glimpse of green water behind them—the secret canal! His father had mentioned it when they last visited Malkata, but Manasseh had been too engrossed in his dreams of Jendayi to look for the hidden entrance.

Pointing the nose of the skiff into the reeds, he threaded the boat through the thick growth, using the willowy stems to pull his way through the concealed opening. Finally the tiny boat broke free and slid into the waterway beyond.

For a moment Manasseh wondered if he had entered a different world. A pink granite wall rose at his left hand, tall and forbidding. The muddy banks had been kept clear of reeds and plant growth so any approaching enemy would be exposed. The raucous sounds of the Nile's sailors and fishermen were muffled by the wall of reeds. Manasseh heard only the steady slush and suck of the water beneath his small boat and, from somewhere behind the wall, a broom hissing over wet tiles. At his right, shimmering mirages made the western cliffs dance in the distance. The air vibrated softly with the swishing wings of swifts that flew low to catch insects hovering between the shifting line of sun and shade.

He crouched silently, his hands dripping upon the reed boat as the muddy banks slid slowly by. Finally he spied a gate in the granite wall. Two guards stood there, their backs to him, and Manasseh ducked down and lowered his hands into the water, turning the skiff into the bank. He beached the vessel out of the guards' sight, then paused to wet the edge of his cloak and wipe the previous day's accumulated grime from his hands and face. He moved cautiously, for even in the silent peace of this desolate spot, danger lurked beneath the blinding dazzle of the sun's path on the quiet canal.

But crocodiles and vipers were the least of his worries. Throughout the night he had considered ways he might slip into the palace, knowing that even noblemen did not enter Malkata without a proper invitation. Unless he could convince the gate guards that he had been summoned by someone inside the fortress, he would pay dearly for this adventure. He had enough confidence in his physical training to think he might overpower these two warriors, but a noisy disturbance would force a general alarm. He considered sneaking in through the servants' quarters and skulking around like a drudge, but a lifetime on the fringes of the royal circle had taught him that a man could rise to success in Pharaoh's court only as long as he did not show his insecurity.

He would walk into the palace as if he were an invited guest. If apprehended, he could always throw himself upon the mercy of Pharaoh, Queen Tiy, or even his father the vizier.

I will behave as if I have a perfect right to be here. Manasseh tugged on the kilt he wore and ran his wet fingers through his close-cropped hair. If he had known he would find himself at Malkata, he would have brought his wig and a blade to shave his straggly beard. In this unconventional guise he would stand out more than most men, but he had no other choice.

His appearance would have to do. He had come too far to turn back. Lifting his chin, he climbed up the bank. The guards were

Nubians, two of the famed Medjay warriors. He did not recognize them but thought it safe to assume that at one time or another they had manned the guard post at the front gate. They certainly would know his father, and perhaps they had even seen Manasseh enter with the renowned Zaphenath-paneah.

The warriors stood at the gate, laughing at some private joke, and Manasseh boldly positioned himself before them, spreading his legs in a strong stance and resting his hands lightly on his hips. *Be confident. Speak the truth, and they cannot suspect you of lying.*

Softly, he cleared his throat. The men looked up, and the tallest blinked in consternation.

"Life and peace to you, my friends." Manasseh thrust his hands behind his back. "By the life of Pharaoh, I pray you are well." He smiled and nodded at the larger man, who looked every inch an African warrior: tough, lean, and sinewy. "Is that a new collar you are wearing, Captain? I do not recall seeing it when my father, the vizier, and I dined here several weeks ago."

The guard's gaze traveled up and down Manasseh, taking in the fine linen kilt, the soft sandals, the gold wristbands . . . and the beard. He transferred his inscrutable gaze to his companion.

"I know I look a little disheveled"—Manasseh exchanged a smile with the second man—"but I have been out in the desert training." He looked pointedly at an angry-looking slash across his chest, then shrugged. "But this little scratch must seem like nothing to a pair of Medjay warriors. Tarik, the captain of my father's guard, has often told me of your bravery in battle. He says there are none in the world as skilled as the Medjays."

The big guard lifted his chin and stiffened his massive weight. "Life and peace to you, son of the noble vizier." He inclined his dark head in a deep bow. "We had not heard that you were expected."

"I am not here to disturb Pharaoh"—Manasseh held up a disarming hand—"but to speak with a warrior. The captain of my father's guard recommended that I find him." Pausing, he imitated Ephraim's most appealing smile. "Will you tell me where I can find the one known as Abnu?"

At the mention of the giant's name, the smaller guard cast a quick apprehensive glance toward his companion.

"I know Abnu." The taller guard lowered his voice. "I have sparred with him myself. Only the grace of Pharaoh saved my miserable hide. The giant would have run me through with a pike had the king not spoken." He said this easily, as if there were some merit in living to tell of a bout with Abnu.

"Pharaoh must think highly of you," Manasseh murmured.

The guard lifted one brawny shoulder in a shrug. "Indeed, I believe he does. You will find Abnu in the warriors' barracks, unless he is fighting in the courtyard. When you find him, tell him Nebu sends his greetings."

"And where are these barracks?" Manasseh gave the man an apologetic smile. "I have only visited the gardens and the royal house."

The guard stooped to etch a drawing in the sand. "Here is Pharaoh's palace," he said, completing a rectangle with his index finger, "and here are the chambers of the queen, prince, and princesses. Behind them is the royal harem. And behind the harem, in a building of whitewashed brick, are the quarters for Pharaoh's warriors."

Manasseh studied the drawing for a moment, imprinting it upon his mind. "Behind the harem?"

"Pharaoh wanted his guards between his treasures and his slaves." The second guard's dark face split into a broad grin. "The servants are housed behind the warriors."

Manasseh felt his heart skip a beat. God be praised! Jendayi would surely be found in the servants' quarters. If all went well he would speak to both Jendayi and Abnu today.

"Many thanks, my friends." He rose to his feet and walked between their sharpened spears as easily as if he were taking an afternoon stroll. "Nebu, I will not forget to give your regards to the giant."

~ Eighteen ~

A WIDE COURTYARD SEPARATED THE MAIN WALL OF the palace complex from the smaller residences within it, and Manasseh walked swiftly over the sand until he had passed the magnificent pavilions that housed the royal family. The shadows of the morning had shortened, fleeing from the spaces between the more humble buildings and the glorious villas, and Manasseh knew the day was already half-spent.

The warrior's rough map was accurate. Three rectangular structures of humble brick stood between the royal residences and the vast complex of Pharaoh's celebrated stables. The building closest to the palace was dedicated to Pharaoh's vast harem, the next to his warriors, and the final one to his slaves and servants. As much as his heart longed to explore the servants' chambers, Manasseh knew he should find Abnu first. The men who waited for him in the desert would need reassurance when he returned, and a Medjay warrior would cheer their hearts immeasurably. And if he spoke to the warrior soon, he might have the rest of the day to spend with Jendayi. These thoughts spurred his footsteps to the very doorway of the warriors' barracks.

Two guards sat just inside the doorway, a game of Hounds and Jackals spread on a tray between them. They looked up without a word as Manasseh entered the room, then returned their eyes to the board, each man intent on the game. Manasseh silently sighed in relief when they paid him no attention.

"Prosperity and peace to you," he remarked boldly to one of the players as his eyes swept through the room. The interior of the hall was cut down the center by a single aisle. At least fifty low wooden beds were lined up in rows as straight as the runnels irrigating Egypt's fields. Above the beds, a profusion of spears, shields, swords, bows, and daggers hung from pegs in the wall. Sleeping men occupied several beds at the back of the room, probably the guards of the midnight watch, and at least a dozen warriors clustered in small conversational groups toward the front, their hands busily employed with awls and leather strips as they mended the tough leather of their shields.

Manasseh crinkled his nose in disgust. The air smelled as if it had been breathed too many times, and someone had definitely forgotten to empty the chamber pots. The hall was drab and ordinary, not at all befitting Pharaoh's celebrated Medjay warriors.

"What do you want?" one of the gamers asked, not lifting his eyes from the board.

"I am looking for Abnu." Manasseh narrowed his gaze as he searched among the Nubians for one who might be considered a giant. "Tarik, who serves Zaphenath-paneah, recommended that I find him."

The hall fell silent, as if every ear had suddenly decided to eavesdrop. There was no movement, not even the whisper of a sound, then one of the groups near the doorway broke apart. A man who had been seated on the floor unfolded his tree-trunk legs and came toward Manasseh, a stalking, purposeful intent in his walk.

He *was* a giant. The shining skin atop his shaved head nearly brushed the nine-foot ceiling, and his wondrously muscled, built-for-action body moved with an air of authority. His face bore the expression of a man who demanded instant obedience.

Manasseh was suddenly sorry he'd come. He wanted a man to *serve* in his army, not command it.

"Who seeks Abnu?" The man's rumbling voice shattered the silence.

Manasseh floundered before the brilliance of the man's gaze. With great difficulty he coughed out an answer. "Manasseh, elder son of Zaphenath-paneah."

The warrior frowned and placed his hands on his slim hips. "Why do you seek me? I have nothing to do with the king's vizier. I fight for Pharaoh!"

God Shaddai, please get me out of here. This was a mistake. This man will never agree to help us, though he might enjoy removing my head from my shoulders.

Manasseh took a hasty half-step back. "This visit is nothing but a bad idea. Pray excuse me. I did not mean to disturb you. I came to bring you greetings from Tarik, captain of the vizier's guard—"

"Tarik!" As swiftly as a chameleon changing colors, the man's stony face broke into an inexplicable lazy smile. "That old son of Nut! How is he faring?"

"He fares well," Manasseh answered, halting. Perhaps the giant had gentle qualities. Perhaps he could even be manipulated. Manasseh looked up with renewed interest. "Tarik and his wife are happy."

The giant scratched a faint growth of hair on his chin, digesting this scrap of information, then pinned Manasseh with a long silent scrutiny. "Tarik was your teacher?"

"Yes." Manasseh gave him an abashed smile and cleared his throat. "Years ago he taught my brother and me how to fight. We learned to wrestle and to throw a spear, to manage a bow and sword, of course."

The giant leaned forward in the vaguest of movements, a shifting of shadows. He smiled again but his expression held only a ghost of its former warmth. "Did Tarik teach you well?"

"Very well. He is an excellent teacher."

Without warning, the giant turned and yanked a copper sword from the wall. Manasseh winced, torn between running and remaining to face whatever the man had in mind. For a moment Abnu hefted the sword in his broad palm as if weighing it, then he tossed it toward Manasseh. Too late Manasseh thrust his hands into empty air, and the blade clanged on the tile floor at his feet.

"I hope you are more skilled than you are alert." Abnu pulled a heavier sword of iron from a peg. He wound his thick fingers around the grip, then shot Manasseh an impenitent grin. "We will see just how good a teacher my friend Tarik is. If he did not teach you well, I shall visit the vizier's house and scold him thoroughly. After, of course, I convey my condolences about your demise."

"I assure you," Manasseh said, his heart in his throat as he bent to pick up the copper blade, "Tarik taught me ably. But I am not a warrior by trade. My skills are certainly not as finely honed as yours." His stomach churned and tightened as he faced the man, the sword dangling at his side. "I have no wish to fight you."

"No wish to fight?" In three tremendous steps the giant was close enough for Manasseh to appreciate the finely layered muscles rippling beneath the skin of his abdomen. "Listen to me well, son of the vizier, for I shall not repeat myself." The warrior's voice echoed from some place far above Manasseh's head. "You have, I fear, already made the crucial mistake of believing that strong men are stupid. If I were not in a generous mood, that mistake would have already cost you your life. But because I am not stupid, I know this: If Tarik sent you to see me, he wants me to help you, and that can only mean that you are somehow involved in a fight. Whether you want me to battle one man or twenty remains to be seen, but if a man expects me to pick up a sword on his behalf, he had better be ready to pick up one on mine. If *you* have no heart to fight, you are doomed already."

Manasseh swallowed hard and squared his shoulders. Though panic rioted within him, he could not help feeling exhilarated by the ferocity of the giant's passion. What a force he would be against the Canaanites! His size alone would intimidate any who came against them, and with God's power behind his weapon, the land would be quickly restored to Jacob's sons.

If God has ordained this meeting, God will give me the courage to see it through. . . .

Clinging to the cold copper in his hand, Manasseh slowly lifted his eyes to the giant's strong and rigid face. "If I go a round with you"—he swiveled his blade until it pointed upward toward the warrior's jugular—"will you consider my request?"

Abnu's eyes flicked at the sword, then glared back at Manasseh. "I will listen to you," he answered, a slight trace of cynical humor in his tone, "if you draw first blood. But if at any time you retreat or flinch, I will kill you, for a coward is a shame to his teacher."

"I am not a coward." Manasseh kept his gaze locked with the giant's. "And I will prove it."

As if a signal had been given, the loitering warriors stood from their places, eager to watch what would surely be more entertaining than a game of Hounds and Jackals.

"You must fight outside," one of the men called. "And be

quick about it! The captain does not tolerate disorder within our company."

"Don't worry," Abnu snarled, his rapier glance passing over Manasseh again. "This will not take long."

Afraid to take his eyes off his adversary, Manasseh turned slightly and allowed the giant to pass by him and stoop through the doorway. Outside, the sun had vanished behind a sudsy cloud bank that left the courtyard in shade. As he slowly advanced, he wrapped his hand around the sword. The ill-fitting copper blade in his grip felt slippery and cold, an alien weapon designed to gnaw away at his tenuous confidence.

A dozen impatient hands shoved Manasseh toward the empty space where Abnu shifted indignantly from foot to foot, his long arms hanging empty below his belt, the iron sword wavering slightly in the sand a few feet in front of him. Manasseh thrust his blade into the sand, too, then stepped back as the circle around them thickened and grew.

Even over the uncontrolled sounds of the zealous crowd he could hear his heart battering against his ears. Never in his most farfetched imaginings had he anticipated that he would have to fight in order to win an audience with this man. He was accustomed to people who obeyed his wishes, bowed before his name, or at least before his father's title, and laughed at his humor, no matter how dry the joke. He had expected help, even affection, from an old friend of Tarik's.

But lately all his expectations had vanished like pebbles dropped into the Nile.

Through the roaring din, he breathed a prayer. "God Shaddai, help your servant now!"

Then, as the challenger seized his sword and lunged forward with an earsplitting cry, Manasseh dove for his blade and rushed in lunatic flight toward destruction.

———

Hearing the uproar, Jendayi paused on her walk back from the palace kitchens. Warriors' cries gushed from the courtyard, battering her delicate senses with their animal coarseness. Taking a deep breath, she plunged toward the safety of the wall that would lead her to her own quarters and away from the loud and rowdy circle of warriors.

Pharaoh's men were at it again. She hated the soldiers' rough-housing. Their grunts and cries and curses echoed through her dreams long into the night. But this fight seemed different, for a tremulous ring of clashing metals punctuated the crowd's cries in a steady recurring beat. This was neither a wrestling match nor a drunken brawl. This was a duel.

Her fingers found the wall that would lead her home, but she halted beside it, paralyzed by her aversion to violence. She heard a low growl, a hoarse taunt, then the crowd gasped in unison, surprised by some action within the ring. A deep thudding sound echoed through the courtyard and vibrated under her feet, as though a heavy object had fallen.

Her blood rose in a jet when a familiar voice touched her ear. "Lie still, giant, and let me mark your cheek with my sword," a man demanded, his words broken by deep gasps. "God Shaddai has delivered you into my hand. You will grant me what you have promised."

Jendayi's mind swirled in a crazy mixture of hope and fear. That was Chenzira's voice! But why would he be fighting in Pharaoh's courtyard? Unless he had begun a brawl while his master met with the king. . . . Her breath caught in her throat. Was Ephraim at the palace?

She whirled toward the sounds of the gathering and lifted her sightless eyes toward whatever confrontation had taken place. The crowd moaned now in sympathy for the displaced champion, and one or two observers muttered soft curses as golden bracelets and silver armbands clinked and changed hands. Jendayi timidly stepped forward, knowing that in the midst of this confusion she might find someone who could tell her about Ephraim.

"All right, you slippery fish," a deep voice growled from the midst of the commotion. "I am yours to command . . . for a time."

"But you serve Pharaoh."

Jendayi felt a thrill of hope run through her as she confirmed Chenzira's voice. Her ears had not deceived her.

"I am a free man. I can serve whatever master I please," the defeated man answered, the depth of his voice lifting the hair at the back of Jendayi's neck. "And by trickery you have hired me. Where and when shall I report?"

"Meet me two days from today, at sunset, outside the vizier's villa. Do not approach the gate. Do not announce your presence." There was a short silence, then Jendayi heard the sound of two hands slapping in agreement. "And I will thank Tarik for teaching me that escape move. Only with his help could I have outrun your blade."

"Tarik is a better teacher than I thought." Jendayi heard the sound of a smile in the older man's voice as he moved away. "Give him my regards, and tell him I will see him soon."

Jendayi put out a hand to make certain no one blocked her way, then edged closer to Chenzira. She was about to whisper a greeting but heard him catch his breath in surprise. "Jendayi!"

"Yes." She couldn't stop a smile. "I recognized your voice and could not believe I heard correctly. What are you doing in the midst of a fight? And why are you here at all?"

"I—" He paused, then his fingers grasped hers gently. "Let us go someplace where we can talk freely."

"I know a place." She kept a tight grip on his hand as she turned. "Stay close behind me."

"I would not lose you for the world."

From the eager sound of his breathing, she believed he spoke the truth.

———

She led him to a small and private garden, hidden from the rest of Pharaoh's palace by high walls. By the way her sandals moved confidently over the path, Manasseh suspected that she came here often. She did not hesitate but moved with catlike grace, not in the least impeded by her blindness. His heart swelled with compassion as he followed. He closed his eyes, trying to imagine himself in her situation, but his feet immediately grew heavy and unsure of themselves.

"What has happened to you?" she asked, a mischievous note in her voice as she chided him for lagging behind. "Hurry. I want to show you a special place. But you must tell no one of it—except perhaps Ephraim."

"I will tell no one," he answered, opening his eyes. Golden

sunbeams laced the branches of the flowering acacia trees. The foliage around them vibrated softly with insect life. The narrow pebbled path pointed a curving finger through beds of massed flowers, but Jendayi suddenly plunged off the trail and moved through the plants toward the furthermost garden wall.

"No, Jendayi." Manasseh gently resisted the pull of her fingers. "You have left the path, this is not the right way."

"That all depends," Jendayi whispered, tossing a smile over her shoulder as she led him onward, "upon where you want to go." She stopped in a small clearing near the wall and released his hand. "Look around, will you? It is somewhere near."

Manasseh stepped back, baffled. She pressed forward, insinuating her way through the lush greenery growing against the wall, then she crouched down and ducked behind a stand of flowering trees. He lost sight of her for a moment, then heard her urgent whisper.

"Here! Come closer, Chenzira!"

Plunging clumsily through the plants, he reached the wall and found her kneeling before a door not more than three feet tall. "It is the door of escape," she said, her eyes squinting with amusement. "Akil showed it to me soon after we were brought here. If ever the palace comes under attack, we are to slip down to the canal through this little gate."

A brass ring had been set into the door. Her fingers found it and tugged the door open. Without even signaling her intent, she slipped through the rectangular hole and disappeared. Manasseh crouched for a moment in front of the opening, then crawled after her on his hands and knees. He scrambled for the space of four or five feet through the thickness of the wall, then climbed out onto a rocky bank. The canal flowed twenty feet away, gleaming like fluid copper as the blood red sun streamed across the still waters.

Jendayi was sitting on a stone, her face to the sun, her elbows tucked at her sides in a childlike posture of wonder. "Is it as lovely here as I imagine it to be? I know the sun is there"—she lifted her hand toward the blazing orb—"and the canal is before me. I come here nearly every night as the sun sets, for it is quiet and peaceful. And though sometimes odd wind-borne sounds reach my ear, I have the feeling that I am quite alone. Except now, of course."

"Why do you come here?" Manasseh asked, sinking to the rock beside her. "It is a lonely place. The life of the palace is inside the walls behind us."

"My life does not lie within those walls. It lies here"—she lightly pressed her fingers over her heart, then lifted them to her forehead—"and here. I live only in my imagination, Chenzira. For there I can make music so fleet that my human fingers cannot play it . . . and I there can visit Ephraim."

Manasseh resisted the urge to spit as she fell silent. Ephraim again! What had Ephraim ever done to deserve this beautiful creature's affection?

Her cool voice broke into his thoughts. "Are you going to tell me what brings you here? I was surprised to hear your voice and amazed that you escaped the warrior you fought. Does your master know that you have foolishly risked life and limb this afternoon?"

"No," he answered, managing no more than a hoarse whisper. He paused, desperate to confess the entire truth but doubted that she would be as willing to open her heart to a nobleman as a supposed servant.

"I am here because the vizier is unhappy with me," he said finally. That much was true. He bent one knee and rested his elbow upon it, suddenly grateful for the opportunity to unburden his soul before a compassionate heart. "And I escaped the blade of Pharaoh's giant because God Shaddai brought an ancient wrestling move to my mind. Abnu was not expecting it, so I managed to trip him."

"Then you worship this God Shaddai just as Ephraim does," she said, hugging her knees to her chest. Resting her head on her knees, she turned her face toward him. She was a picture of gentle innocence. "When I lived in the vizier's house, I heard much talk of the invisible God. Of course"—she shrugged slightly—"all gods are invisible to me, for I can see none of them. But I can *feel* them. In the temples the priests allow me to run my hands over the gods' carved faces. And I can smell the sweet scent of their incense and hear the hymns of praise."

"I can feel El Shaddai," Manasseh answered, staring at an ibis that waded in the canal, prodding the shallows with his curved beak. "Not with my hands, but with my heart. I can see His design in the way of an eagle in the sky and His goodness in the bounty of a loaded fishing boat on the river." He turned and fastened his gaze to Jendayi's lovely face. "And I see His passion in the way a man looks at the woman he loves."

A shy smile played at the corners of her mouth. "I suppose you are right, my friend. I have yet to discover that feeling. But soon I will." Her tone hardened. "I must."

"Why Ephraim?" Manasseh couldn't keep a note of impatience from his voice. "Why have you set your heart upon *him*? He is cocky and arrogant. He gives too much attention to too many different women—"

"You do not speak very respectfully of your master." Her tone had chilled.

With difficulty, Manasseh swallowed an angry retort and took pains to keep his voice steady. "Ephraim is not my master. The vizier is. But I know Ephraim well, and I must tell you, Jendayi, you are foolish to waste your feelings on him. He is not worthy of you."

Across her pale and beautiful face a dim flush raced like a fever. "Not worthy of me? No, I am not worthy of *him*! Do you think I hope to marry . . . that I want . . . oh, how *could* you? I am not in a position to choose. I would never be so presumptuous! I am a slave. I hope only to enjoy the smile of a caring master once again. Pharaoh is indifferent to all. I am one of thousands who answer to his command. But Ephraim cares for me, and if I can return to his house—"

"How do you know he cares for you?" Manasseh pressed his hand to her arm.

"Because I have received a message from him." The fire left her voice as a gentle blush colored her cheek. "And years ago in the garden of the vizier's house, Ephraim kissed me. Though he is a nobleman, and though I will never be more than a slave, he is the only person in the world to ever show that kind of . . . affection for me."

"What sort of message?" Manasseh choked on the words.

"I received it from my handmaid while we journeyed to Canaan. Ephraim promised to approach Pharaoh and ask that I be returned to the vizier's house." She lifted one delicate shoulder in a shrug. "He has not yet done so, but I am certain he is waiting for the right time. Perhaps he will take me with him when he establishes his own house."

Manasseh sat back, numb with astonishment. The message she referred to was obviously his, and somehow she had misunderstood. But Ephraim *had* kissed her. Jendayi had staked her hope and future upon one brazen act of an impetuous, vain, spoiled boy.

Ephraim ought to be flogged for his impulsiveness. He had not been sheltered like Jendayi. He thought no more highly of a single kiss than he did of an individual grape in the bunch he ate at dinner.

Manasseh clenched his fist as the bitter gall of jealousy burned the back of his throat. Ephraim had Jendayi's love, which he had not sought, and the right hand of blessing from Jacob, which he had not deserved. Manasseh had striven hard to please his father, his tutors, and his God, all for nothing, while charming Ephraim had smiled at Jacob and kissed Jendayi. And both of them had fallen in love with him.

So kiss her now. The thought came from out of nowhere, careening through his mind like an out-of-control chariot. If a kiss had given Ephraim the right to Jendayi's heart, might not another one, filled with tenderness and sincere affection, usurp that claim? They were alone. Manasseh could easily claim her lips now. He could crush her to him and make her hear the thudding, insistent drum of his heart. He could tear Ephraim's memory from her mind and overwhelm her childish devotion to an undeserving scamp. . . .

But if a kiss alone could win her, she was not truly won. Manasseh had not seen many examples of dedicated selflessness in his life, but he knew love involved far more than physical attraction. His uncle Simeon and Mandisa exhibited an almost wordless understanding of each other's moods. Tarik and Halima would have neglected the entire world rather than each other. Physical affection, it seemed to Manasseh, was pleasant and attractive, like the smooth limestone casing on a pyramid, but it had little to do with the solid blocks that formed the building's foundation and structure.

No. He would not attempt to win her the shallow way Ephraim apparently had. He would demonstrate his love. He would win her heart and mind and soul by proving his dedication. And he would wait for her to choose him, to come willingly into his arms.

"Jendayi—" He paused, struggling to interpret the turbulent emotions that buffeted his heart.

"I understand, Chenzira. You don't have to tell me. I can sense that you are troubled." She turned her face toward the flowing water. "I asked you to talk to Ephraim for me, and you weren't able to do it."

"No, I wasn't." He lifted his eyes toward the heavens. Sunset was beginning to stretch glowing fingers across the sky, but darkness imprisoned Jendayi. She could not enjoy the sight or experience the sense of exhilaration it elicited. She dreamed of slavery in a more pleasant house, while he yearned to release her from bondage, to shower her with love, and to elevate her to a position of authority in his own household. How could he teach her to dream of higher things? How could he show one who had never seen love that it encompassed far more than a token kiss?

"Jendayi"—his words poured forth in a rush—"you should forget about Ephraim."

"Forget him?" She turned on him with the fury of a determined tigress. "How can I forget the only kindness I have ever known? He alone has shown mercy to me. I ought to serve him the rest of my life in gratitude for that alone! If you are my friend, Chenzira, you will talk to him for me! Remind him of his promise. Tell him I am waiting."

"I cannot." He gritted his teeth, straining against the choice he had to make. The truth would wound her, but she would never open her heart to all he offered if she were bound by a misguided duty to counterfeit affection. "Jendayi, Ephraim does not love you."

She halted, shocked. Her mouth opened slightly as she drew in an audible breath. "How would you know?"

Manasseh closed his eyes, unwilling to see the hurt that would soon cross her face. "He plans to marry Princess Sitamun. Apparently the Queen, Pharaoh, and the vizier approve. I suspect the marriage will take place within the year."

She took a wincing little breath, then turned her face away. For a moment woven of eternity she said nothing. Then he heard her voice, flat and final: "It does not matter. He could still take me into his house. As long as he cares a little . . . it is enough. I am a slave. I have never hoped to be more than that."

Manasseh released a choked, desperate laugh. "By heaven above, Jendayi, do you love him so much? Would you be happy settling for crumbs from his table? If you will forget Ephraim, someone else might come into your life—"

"Love him?" She pressed her hand over her face. Her voice was muffled as she spoke through her fingers. "Ah, Chenzira, if you only knew."

Swallowing the sob that rose in his throat, Manasseh locked his hands and studied the sand at his feet. If she cared for Ephraim so deeply, what right had he to persuade her not to love his brother? He wanted her to be free. He could not deny her the freedom to choose the man she would love.

"I should be going." He pushed himself up from the rock where they sat. His private anguish almost overcame his control of his voice. "I shouldn't be here."

"You said the vizier was unhappy with you." As she lowered her hand from her face, Manasseh could see the silvery tracks of tears upon her cheeks. But she looked up and offered him a sweet smile of concern. "Why is your master unhappy? Are you in terrible trouble?"

"I suppose so," he answered, relieved that the conversation had turned to less emotional matters. "I have been in the wilderness with a group of Hebrews who are preparing to launch an invasion into Canaan. God Shaddai promised that land to Israel's descendants. Now that Jacob is dead, there is no need for the sons of Israel to remain in Egypt."

"An invasion?" She shivered slightly. "But why must *you* go to war?"

"God called me," he answered simply, "and I must obey. But since the vizier does not understand or approve, I have left his house."

Her hand flew to her throat. "These Hebrews—is Ephraim with you? Is he in danger?"

"No," Manasseh answered, his voice dry. "Ephraim is in no

danger. He is content to remain where he is, in the center of Thebes."

A shadow of satisfaction crossed her face, then her countenance settled back into delicately composed lines. "All the same, troublesome slaves are beaten, my friend. I would not like to think of you hurt."

Her hand fell upon his, burning his skin with her touch, and for a moment emotion clotted his throat so he could not speak. "I would be honored if you would just think of me, Jendayi," he finally answered, extending both hands to help her up. Still holding her hands, he stepped back to regard her in the golden light of sunset. Ethereal and fragile, she would be a welcome addition to Ephraim's household if Pharaoh chose to make her a gift to his prospective son-in-law. But she would not be happy as Ephraim's slave, for he would give her no more attention than he gave the prowling house cats that rid the villa of vermin and yet occasionally demanded an affectionate stroke.

What should love do? Work toward what she wanted or toward what was best for her? The question hammered at him.

"Jendayi, I must return to the vizier's house for a few days, and I will do what I can to help you," Manasseh promised, his voice breaking miserably. "But while I am gone, accept my farewells and know this—the path toward Ephraim is not the best one for you."

"Oh?" One delicate brow lifted. "And have you knowledge of another secret garden door?"

"That all depends"—he dropped her hands—"upon where you want to go." He turned and made his way down the bank of the canal. When he turned for a last look, she had vanished into the wall surrounding Pharaoh's palace.

———

Jendayi turned slowly and slipped back through the wall, stunned by the extraordinary void she felt when Chenzira pulled away and left her alone. *But you are foolish*, she chided herself. *You feel empty only because Chenzira is your link to Ephraim. Like a child who shivers when a cloud blocks the sun, you were growing used to the hope of Ephraim, and now you are alone again, with only a slave's promise of help. You are a slave, Jen-*

dayi. You are alone. Become accustomed to your lot in life, for it will not change unless the gods smile upon you with favor.

But one of Chenzira's questions kept slipping through her thoughts: *By heaven above, Jendayi, do you love Ephraim so much?*

"If you only knew, my friend," she whispered, feeling the cool breath of the garden upon her face. "I don't know how to love anyone, but I know I must love or die forever. And Ephraim is the one who can best show me how."

She thrust her head out of the tunnel and stood, brushing a few lingering leaves from her gown.

~ Nineteen ~

AKIL SCARCELY HAD TIME TO HIDE HIMSELF BEHIND A sycamore tree before Jendayi slipped back through the little door and brushed herself off. The chironomist stood very still, keenly aware of the girl's heightened sense of hearing, and only dared breathe again when she began to make her way back over the garden path.

Leaning on the gnarled tree trunk with one hand, he shook his head, amazed that she had managed to attract trouble even while safe behind the guardian walls of the king's palace. She had always given him more cause for concern than the others. Kissa, the lutist, was as lovely as the harpist, and the oboist, Sakmet, flirted constantly with the guards, but trouble focused on Jendayi with the unblinking eye of a god. When she was but a child, another slave trader had recognized her gift and tried to abduct her from Akil's tent. A hundred jealousy-spurred rumors had attempted to sully her name, and even in the vizier's house the younger son had taken her lovely face in his hands.

Thoughts of the vizier's sons lit a clenched ball of anger at Akil's center. They were always appearing when he least expected them, upsetting his tidily ordered and precise palatial world. Today Sakmet had come running to report that Jendayi was leading a man into the private garden, so Akil hurried out to safeguard his treasure. His annoyance turned to speechless shock when he recognized Manasseh, the vizier's elder son, and shock became panic when the pair disappeared through the secret escape door. If Manasseh was helping Jendayi escape, Akil knew his head would be in a basket before sunset. And so he followed, sneaking like a viper up into the branches of a sycamore where he saw and overheard enough of the riverside conversation to know that Jendayi did not plan to escape. Manasseh had come only to say good-bye before departing to join a military corps intent upon an invasion of Canaan.

The chironomist rubbed his expressive hands together, considering the information he had just gleaned. Pharaoh would not approve of this armed force. Any action not sanctioned by the king would be construed as a direct slap against his authority. A mighty lion could not have two mouths or two heads, so the king possessed complete military power in Egypt.

The master musician smiled to himself. Such information, dispensed at the right time and to the right person, could prove invaluable. And Akil, who prided himself on his hard-headed pragmatism, knew this report would have to be presented with the utmost discretion. The mighty Amenhotep would never listen to a lowly musician, but other, more receptive ears had tilted toward Akil in the past. . . .

Tiy would grant him an audience. The queen often asked his opinion and his impressions of the people who visited her throne room, for he was the perfect observer, a mere servant routinely ignored by her guests. More than once after a pompous nobleman had passed out of the queen's chambers, Akil had ended that man's lofty ambitions simply by drizzling gray disapproval. Tiy, marvelous judge of character that she was, trusted him.

For news of impending treason, the queen would be most grateful. And if Akil handled this situation with Jendayi as quickly and quietly as he had others in her past, she would not be affected. She would never even know what had happened to her false friend.

"How do you know this is true, Akil?" Tiy asked, resting her chin upon the dainty tip of her thumb. Her intelligent dark eyes shimmered with light from the torches in her chamber, and Akil found it difficult to find his tongue. No matter how humble her origins, she was a goddess, surely as divine as Pharaoh.

"I heard their conversation with my own ears, my Queen," he said, modestly lowering his forehead to the marble floor where he had prostrated himself. "The vizier's son said he had to return to the desert where the invasion force was training. And so I took a boat at once to bring you word—"

"A military force," the queen echoed, her voice dark and liquid with restrained power. "Pharaoh should be told of this."

"That's what I thought, my Queen." Akil dared to lift his eyes to her magnificent person. "But who am I to tell him? My humble words would be but a buzzing in his ear."

"I will tell him." Tiy's dark hair swung about her proud shoulders as she stood from her chair. Akil bowed his head again, unable to bear the sight of her curving regal figure at so close a distance.

"Thank you, Akil," she said, her voice now coolly impersonal. "Speak of this to no one else, and I will send a message to Pharaoh on the ship that carries you back to Malkata. But I will urge him to do nothing until I have had an opportunity to spy out the matter. If the situation is what it seems, something must be done."

Speechless with admiration, Akil only nodded.

"It is unfortunate, of course, for the young man." Tiy's dark eyes, too hard for beauty, were now as flat and unreadable as stone. "I liked Manasseh. He seemed a great deal more sensible than his brother." She tapped the fingertips of her hands together. "But treason cannot be tolerated from anyone. We would commit a great injustice if we executed our vizier's son without proof of his sedition, so we will give him time, and a little rope, and wait to see whether or not he will hang himself."

What a glorious gift of the gods was this woman! What a song he would write to praise her cunning!

"Now go." Her words echoed along the walls of the empty chamber. "And remember—tell no one."

Buoyed by the knowledge that he had been of service to the queen of his heart, Akil nodded and backed away.

―――――

The inky sky faded to indigo and then to deep purple. The silver stars gradually withdrew into the vault of heaven, leaving Joseph alone with his thoughts. He had left his home before sunrise for several reasons, chief among them his wish to avoid a confrontation with Manasseh. Last night Ani had come into Joseph's chambers and reported that the wayward son had finally returned to the villa. With an uplifted brow the old man had asked the unspoken question—*do you want to see him?*—and Joseph had been forced to admit that he did not.

Why, Manasseh? he questioned, walking silently through the nearly deserted streets. He locked his hands behind his back and kept his eyes intent upon the smooth path beneath his feet. *Why did you embark upon this foolish task without asking for my permission, even my advice? Could we not have discussed your ideas?*

But even as he approached the docks, his mind supplied the answers. Manasseh wouldn't talk to him because he already knew how Joseph would respond: *God is not calling the sons of Israel back to Canaan. I have already decreed that our people will remain in Goshen.* He was a decisive, busy man. He had no patience or time for theory or postulation or suppositions. In over twenty years, in fact, he had had no time for his sons. His time belonged to Amenhotep, to Egypt.

On his loneliest days, in snatched moments between the endless interviews and appointments, Joseph wondered if his burden was too much for one man to bear. But he had been fulfilling these responsibilities for over twenty-seven years, and he was still as strong and capable as any man in Pharaoh's service. He could serve another thirty years if God Shaddai so willed. Amenhotep trusted him, and such confidence was a rare gift.

The stars had completely faded behind a sky of dark blue velvet by the time his felucca reached the palace at Malkata. The guards at the gate bowed and allowed him to pass, and Joseph automatically turned through the halls that would lead him to Pharaoh's bedchamber.

Every morning after the divine pharaoh had been awakened by his hymn-singing priests, perfumed, painted, and bedecked in a spotless kilt and the crowns of upper and lower Egypt, Joseph was the first official to greet him. Today, as the god-king ate his breakfast—the priests' morning sacrifice—Joseph sat before him at a respectful distance and outlined his work of the day before.

On the previous day, he reported, he had interviewed three governors of Egypt's southern nomes, read an assortment of agricultural and tax reports from all the nomarchs, and inspected the king's bodyguard. He had dispatched a detail to investigate a disturbance at one of the northeastern military posts and asked for information from navy officials who commanded forts on the Nile. He had heard accountings from the leading priests of Thebes' temples, received a full report from an assistant in charge of overseeing the valuable timbered lands, and asked for a summary of the Nile's progress from the Nile readers at Elephantine. After completing this work he had returned to his villa where a long line of complainants waited for him to hear their cases and pronounce judgment.

He paused. Amenhotep, who usually ate his breakfast and listened to Joseph's report with few comments, now refused to partake of the banquet spread before him. He sat silently, ignoring the priests' offerings, and gazed at his vizier like a bird staring at a snake.

Supposing that the king had an upset stomach, Joseph continued to read. "Four hundred healthy cattle were gathered in taxes from the city-states of Syria," he said, consulting the scroll in his hand, "with two hundred bushels of grain, three hundred barrels of wine, two hundred of oil, two hundred of honey. And the princes of Mitanni have sent five hundred deben weight of silver to secure your marriage to Astra, daughter of one of their kings."

Ordinarily the mention of a woman would have elicited an exclamation for good or ill, but Amenhotep still said nothing. At the sound of Pharaoh's silence, Joseph lowered the papyrus parchments to his lap. Pharaoh's foul mood hung over him like a dark cloud. "What is troubling you, my lord?" Joseph asked. "By the love I hold for you and the trust you place in me, I beg you to speak freely."

Amenhotep's square jaw tensed visibly. "Last night," Pharaoh said softly, mockingly, "I learned that your son, Manasseh, has been training a secret military force in the wilderness east of Tura."

At the mention of Manasseh, Joseph's whole body tightened, then he forced himself to take a deep breath. Whatever had happened in the desert did not matter now, for Manasseh was home where he belonged. Though Joseph had not yet spoken to his son, the young man was certainly no longer involved with the lunatic scheme to retake Canaan. That escapade—the misadventures of a few hot-blooded Hebrew youths—had been concluded.

Joseph frowned and shook his head. "There are no secret military forces in Egypt, my King. I am your vizier and would know if such a thing were true."

"Do you know every secret, then?" Amenhotep threw the words like stones as he leaned forward. "Does your God tell you everything that goes on in this kingdom?"

"Not everything, Pharaoh." Joseph tipped his head back to better look at Amenhotep. "But He has given me guidance about all matters of importance."

The king's brows flickered a little, and he settled back in his seat. "All matters of importance," he repeated, idly tracing his finger along the curved arm of his gilded chair. "Is your family not important, then? For I have it on good authority that your elder son has been recruiting even my Medjay warriors for a foray into Canaan. He was seen *here*, yesterday, striking hands with my giant! If the rumors are true, he is planning to invade lands that have been under Egypt's authority and defense since the time of Tuthmosis III. How shall I explain to the Canaanite governors that *my* warriors are attacking territories under *my* protection?"

For an instant Joseph could not think. A wave of grayness passed over him, a kind of dark premonition, and his mind reeled with an unruly feeling of disorientation. For though the king's charge was unthinkable, preposterous, he knew with pulse-pounding certainty that Pharaoh spoke the truth. Manasseh was stubborn. He might yet persist in this unreasonable and foolish notion. But would he go so far as to appear at Malkata to brazenly recruit Pharaoh's elite guards?

A wave of bitter sorrow swept over him, then his temper rose. What would make a young man dishonor his father, even the king? Deliberately, consciously, and in full knowledge that he would severely damage his father's reputation, Manasseh had rebelliously plowed through a carefully cultivated character and position.

Joseph lifted his gaze. Pharaoh sat forward in his chair, his eyes large glittering ovals of repudiation. Anger, sorrow, and frustration surged in Joseph's soul, accompanied by a deep sense of shame. If his lack of parental control was obvious to Pharaoh, it would be apparent to the entire kingdom. Word of this mis-adventure would spread throughout the palace by nightfall and be repeated in the nobles' houses by the following sunrise. By week's end, every man and woman in Thebes would know that Zaphenath-paneah had foolishly allowed his son to anger Phar-aoh—

By heaven above, what if Pharaoh cast Joseph off? He would have every right to do so, for Joseph had permitted his son to commit an abominable act. . . .

Joseph lowered himself to the floor, feeling for the first time in his life that he *groveled* before his king. "Forgive me, my lord, for disappointing you and for failing as a father," he whispered, choking on the words. "And forgive my son for his senseless ac-tions. I will remedy the situation immediately. I will do whatever has to be done."

Pharaoh stretched the silence, his eyes icy and unresponsive, then he commanded his vizier to rise. When Joseph stood again before him, the king folded his hands and smiled in a way that only emphasized that he hadn't smiled before. "Find your son," Amenhotep spoke in the tone a father might use to reprimand a child, "and keep him at home. The gods have blessed us since you and your people came here. We have no wish to see you leave. And we will not hold the shame of one son against the other. If your son Manasseh forgoes these foolish plans for battle, your son Ephraim shall marry my daughter Sitamun. And our two houses shall be joined forever."

Intensely humiliated, Joseph could only nod.

"Now, back to your report," Pharaoh said, dipping his hand into a bowl of succulent grapes. "Tell me more about this daugh-ter of the Mitannis."

———

"Did you not stop to think how this action would appear to Pharaoh?" Joseph heard bitterness spill over into his voice, but he did not care. Manasseh stood before him, his hands hanging empty at his side, his eyes closed, his head unbowed. A proud figure who might have swelled Joseph's heart with admiration if the signs of pride had not reminded him so much of himself.

Joseph had chosen to address his wayward son from the authority of the dais in the grand reception hall. The regal height of the chamber only seemed to emphasize his son's solitary figure. Thirty men waited outside in the vestibule, anxious to whine, complain, or beg for justice, but at the moment Joseph had no time or thought for anyone but his own stubborn son.

Manasseh said nothing and Joseph clenched his fist, torn between confrontation and forgiveness. If Manasseh would only confess and apologize, all would be forgiven. Amenhotep could be distracted from this mistake. The wedding plans for Sitamun and Ephraim would provide a pleasant diversion.

Joseph took a deep breath and forced himself to calm down. "Pharaoh has promised to forgive if you abandon this foolhardy venture." He gripped the armrests of his chair. "He has promised that Ephraim will marry Sitamun, thus linking our houses for all time. In a few months, if you please the king, you may be offered one of the younger princesses—"

"I do not want to marry a princess." Manasseh's voice grated harshly in the spacious chamber. He opened his eyes and lifted his gaze to meet Joseph's face. His eyes, cold and proud—oh, how well Joseph understood them!

Joseph forced himself to smile. "Well, then. If the royal women do not suit you, there are yet a hundred noble families in Thebes who would be happy for their daughters to be joined with Zaphenath-paneah's house."

"No." Manasseh's well-formed mouth took on an unpleasant twist. "I love Jendayi, the harpist in Akil's orchestra. I will marry her or no one."

"A slave?" Surprise caught Joseph off guard, then laughter floated up from his throat. "Son, you could no more marry one of Pharaoh's slaves than I could move the sun backward. Why would you hunger for a slave when a princess is within your reach? When you are ready—"

"Father, for a man of understanding, you are incredibly shortsighted." Manasseh's resolute, confident face mocked him. "God has called me to lead our people back to Canaan. I will not marry an Egyptian princess, nor any of the noble Egyptian women. I love Jendayi. If God can lead us to Canaan, He can arrange for her to be my bride."

Joseph had built his career on being patient and slow to

speak, but now a raw and foreign fury rose in his throat and almost choked him. Never had anyone, king or commoner, slave or servant, guard or warrior, dared to speak to him with such determined resistance. And this was his son! The child he had brought into the world, provided for, prayed about, fretted over—

"You will not speak to me in that tone!"

Manasseh's eyes glowed with intelligence and independence of spirit. When had they begun to look so adult?

Manasseh thrust his hands behind his back and looked at the floor. "What tone should I use, Father? I have tried speaking to you in a more humble voice, but you would not listen."

"I always listen to wisdom! But you speak foolishness!"

"I speak what God has told me."

"God has told you nothing! He speaks to *me*!"

Manasseh looked up and the expression in his eyes brought color rushing into Joseph's cheeks.

"Can God not speak to me also?" The young man opened his hands and held them before his chest. "Or must He always speak through Pharaoh's noble vizier?"

"Of course He can speak to others," Joseph said, irritated by his son's mocking tone. "But He would not contradict himself. And He told me that the famine would come, and that we would be preserved in Egypt—"

"Eighteen years ago." Manasseh's eyes darkened with emotion. "God used you, Father, and now the Almighty has chosen to use me. He may choose to use others. Why can you not believe the truth?"

Joseph opened his mouth to speak, but the words died before they reached his tongue. He wanted to reply that *he* was the inheritor of Jacob's blessing of the firstborn and that he was far from dead. His brothers were yet strong and powerful, and Ephraim had received a greater blessing than Manasseh. God Shaddai might have chosen any of a host of deserving, righteous men before calling Manasseh—but then, hadn't Joseph seen that God sometimes chose to work in inexplicable ways?

But God would not, He could not, call the Hebrews out of the Black Land without giving Joseph some sign. Manasseh was mistaken. He was young, and the prospect of war had infected him like a fever.

"You are wrong," Joseph finally said, idly regretting that Manasseh had chosen such a poor opportunity to unveil his latent talent for leadership. "God placed me in a position of authority over the family. If He wanted us to return to Canaan, He would have shown me."

A look of implacable determination remained on Manasseh's face. "God set you apart as ruler in a foreign land," he countered, a hint of inexpressible sadness in his voice. "You are a Hebrew, but you are not of the Hebrews, Father. You have sacrificed yourself in order to save your people, and God Shaddai blessed you for your willingness to obey. But He calls the sons of Israel out now, and He has called them through me, the least of your sons, the least of the Hebrews. And I will obey, though it costs me my life."

"It may." Joseph paused, hoping his words would sink into the fog overpowering his son's reason. "Think, Manasseh! Heed the advice of your elders! No man is so old that he cannot live another year nor so young that he cannot die today. You may think your uncles and I are used up while you are invincible, but men of all ages die in war."

Manasseh shrugged. "If I die, I die following the will of God."

"Enough!" Joseph flung his hands into the air, so furious he could hardly speak. "It is Pharaoh's wish that you stop this nonsense. His word is law. Will you obey it?"

"God's word is more powerful than Pharaoh's," Manasseh answered, his face full of strength. "I am not seeking to injure Pharaoh in any way, but I must obey God before any earthly king."

Frustrated, Joseph searched for another avenue of persuasion. "You say you love this slave girl—then obey Pharaoh for her sake. Remain here in Thebes, forget about Canaan, and I will see what I can do to persuade Pharaoh to allow the marriage. It will not be easy, but perhaps—"

"No, Father." An expression of pain crossed Manasseh's face, but his eyes still shone with a steadfast determination. "I love Jendayi with my life, but even for her I could not remain here when God has called me away. My men are depending on me."

"Then hear me." Joseph felt his flesh color as slowly, suddenly feeling twice his age, he rose from his ornamented chair. "Give this up, Manasseh. Give this up because it is my wish, and I am the father who gave you life. If you won't do it for Pharaoh or this girl you love, do it for me."

Manasseh's mouth twisted, but his dark eyes flashed a warning as he locked his hands behind his back. "Do not ask this, Father."

"But I am asking. I am demanding—no, I am begging you." Joseph held out his hands in entreaty. "Remain here at home with your brother. The others will grow tired of the hardships of war, and in time they will return to Goshen. Their families miss them. They do not approve of this venture, either."

"I can't give up even for you, Father. God told me to lead our people back, and I will."

The last vestige of Joseph's patience vanished. "You are as stubborn as a child! You *are* a child! God did not speak to you!" He glared at Manasseh with a thunderous expression that had quelled weaker men, but Manasseh did not cringe nor waver beneath his gaze. He stood silently in the hall, his posture militant, the shadow of his beard bestowing a manly aura Joseph had never noticed before. The young man's profile spoke of power and ageless strength—by heaven above, when had the man emerged from the boy? Joseph had enjoyed a passing acquaintance with the child, but this man he did not know at all.

He felt the distance between them like a widening space within his soul. Fathers and sons were molded of the same flesh, but now he felt as though his heart had separated from his chest. He had been torn in twain, cut asunder in the space of a few moments.

"We will hear no more of this," Joseph finished weakly, looking away. Best to leave this interview as if he had won, though he knew he had not. He stared at the colorful paintings on the walls of the chamber, occupying his eyes so they would not have to meet his son's gaze. "You will leave me now and say nothing more of a return to Canaan. And we will find a suitable Egyptian family who has a daughter, a girl who would be proud to be part of the household of Zaphenath-paneah."

"I am no longer proud to be part of the household of Zaphenath-paneah." A sudden thin chill hung on the edge of

Manasseh's words. "And if I must leave it in order to obey God Shaddai, I will."

Joseph felt suddenly weak and vulnerable in the face of his son's anger. With stiff brittle dignity he returned to his chair as Manasseh moved confidently out of the reception hall.

The vizier of all Egypt turned and sank onto the woven rush seat. Clinging to the armrests of the gilded throne, he bit his tongue lest he call his son back and surrender.

———

Outside his father's reception hall, Manasseh stood in the courtyard and considered the western sky. The horizon blazed with violent shades of bronze and sapphire. The last gleaming slivers of sunlight clung to the skyline as if reluctant to leave the realms of the living for Anubis' dark abode of night.

Just as he was reluctant to leave his father's house.

He had not been surprised by the passion in his father's plea. Joseph had always been an ardent defender of Amenhotep's position and power. What had surprised him was his father's unwillingness to consider, even for a moment, that God might speak to a lesser man than the noble vizier. How could such a wise man be blind to the truth? Why couldn't he open his mind—even for a moment—to the possibility that God was preparing to do something new?

What could prevent a father from believing in his son?

Manasseh thrust his hands into the fabric belt of his tunic and slumped against a wall, absorbing the familiar sounds and sights of his father's villa. The complex had always hummed with activity at all hours of the day and night. As a boy he had played amidst the wonder of it all, never dreaming that all households did not entertain visiting kings, beautiful women, and sons of Pharaoh. His life had been so full of important people and events and festivals that he had nearly reached maturity before realizing that while he had comfort and excitement, other children had *parents*.

His mother had died while he and Ephraim were young, and his father had always been out of reach. Ani, Tarik, Halima, and a host of other servants had always hovered near to teach, train, and apply ointments to the cuts and bruises gathered by a pair of spirited boys. Going back, picking up the strings of time, Manasseh could remember occasions when he and Ephraim had breakfasted with their mother and father, but even then Joseph had been quick to kiss his little sons and send them out to play.

He was always sending me away. And now I am ready to go.

The shades of night had fallen. Soon the giant Abnu would be outside the gates, ready to fulfill his promise. Straightening, Manasseh lifted his chin and walked briskly toward his chamber to gather his things.

Abnu was a Medjay, and therefore a man of his word, so Manasseh was not surprised when he stepped through the gate and found the giant loitering against a palm tree outside the villa. Over his shoulders the warrior wore a crimson cloak. A finely pleated kilt displayed his lean athletic form and sinewy limbs to intimidating advantage. Red leather sandals with long upward-curving toes shod his feet, a footwear unique to the exalted Nubians. At Manasseh's approach, the warrior whirled and gave a smart salute, his dark reddish brown skin gleaming in the faint light of the moon.

"Peace and prosperity to you, friend." Manasseh flashed the man a smile of thanks. "Are you ready to begin the journey?"

"A Medjay is always ready for adventure," Abnu answered, his deep voice rumbling through the night. His long fingers gripped the iron-tipped spear in his hand. "Lead on, trickster, until I tire of you."

Manasseh extended a hand toward the river, and together they walked silently over the beaten paths. Bittersweet memories rose to haunt him. He and Ephraim had often played along these trails. Ani had taken them fishing on the river, and Tarik had always served as an official escort when they were allowed to stand on shore and observe their father's comings and goings on his magnificent barge.

The reminiscence brought an ache to Manasseh's throat. He didn't want to leave home under a cloud of disapproval, but what other choice did he have? To remain meant to deny the voice of God Shaddai.

The small skiff Manasseh had reserved was waiting at the

docks. He had deliberately chosen a boat small enough to slip through the reeds that hid the entrance to the canal behind Malkata, and he sighed in relief when Abnu did not complain when it became obvious that he and Manasseh would be the only oarsmen.

As he settled into the boat, Manasseh begged Abnu's indulgence and announced that he had to stop at Malkata before proceeding to join the others. "A lady waits and I must say goodbye," he explained as the boat lanced her way out of the still waters of the lagoon and into the river.

"Surely you are not taking me back to the palace!" Abnu grumbled, his bent knees nearly scraping his chin in the small craft. "I have just come from there! And if Pharaoh has heard that I am gone, he may order my Medjay brothers to implore me to stay." He lifted his brows. "Do you hear what I am saying?"

"I hear." Manasseh tossed a grin over his shoulder. "And apparently Pharaoh has already heard rumors. But I do not plan to enter the palace walls. If you remain quiet, all will be well."

The moon, sailing upon a sky of deepest sapphire, cast a narrow bar of silver across the river, leaving the banks in shadow. Manasseh trusted his instincts, turning his boat into the harbor beside the gleaming palace, then allowed the craft to drift along the tall grasses until he spied the gleam of water beyond the curtain of reeds.

The royal docks stood silent. The king's boats bobbed slowly in the gentle wave wash. While Abnu quietly cursed the sharp stalks that razed his arms, Manasseh maneuvered the skiff into the hidden canal, then sent the vessel winging around the curve of the meandering waterway. The only sounds were the soft lap of oars pulling against calm water and the buzz of insects.

A thin rectangle of light poured from the gate where Manasseh had confronted the two guards, but the warriors themselves were not visible. "Insolent curs!" Abnu muttered under his breath. "Lazy beasts! If they were of my squadron I would cuff their ears. I would cut off the ends of their noses for deserting their posts—"

"Then it is good for them that you are with me," Manasseh replied, urging the tiny vessel swiftly past the opening. He had to be quick, for the guards might reappear at any moment. But though he heard the musical murmur of male voices, the warriors did not show their faces. The skiff moved silently past the opening toward the mounded bank outside the secret garden. He did not know if Jendayi would be there, but he had every hope she might appear.

"What are we doing here?" Abnu grumbled, looking around. "It is bad enough that I am sworn to serve you, but if you are up to mischief—"

There! The little door was barely visible inside the wall. "If you are as soft of heart as you are strong of limb," Manasseh interrupted, exhaling in relief, "this may be the most rewarding debt you have ever paid." With a final solid pull on the oars, he seated the bow of the skiff into the thick mud at the edge of the canal, then scrambled out onto the bank. The dry and sandy soil of the upper bank cried out for the refreshing moisture of the inundation. In a few months the river would run full again . . . and so, Manasseh hoped, would his heart.

"What are we doing here?" Abnu's exasperated whisper drifted up to the bank.

"Waiting." Manasseh sank onto a rock.

"For what?"

"A woman. You have said your farewells. Now I must say mine."

"By the stinking wax in Seth's ear," Abnu grumbled, unfurling his long legs and arms as he attempted to lie down. Stretched out upon the skiff, the warrior was nearly longer than the boat. "I agree to fight and now find I must listen to the croonings of lovers."

"I can only hope." Manasseh fastened his eyes to the tiny door in the wall. "Go to sleep, Abnu. I will wake you later."

He crouched on the bank, determined to wait until just before sunrise if necessary. As long as darkness covered the earth, his father would assume Manasseh slept in his chamber. The morning would be half-spent before the servants discovered him missing. At that point, news of Manasseh's defiant departure would be published throughout the house. Tarik would hear of it, and so would Ani. Their hearts would be wounded. They would sorrow for the master and his estranged son. But their grief would be too late. Their mourning should have begun years before.

The land spoke to him from all around. The skiff rocked with gentle sloshing sounds as wavelets lapped against it. Moonlight sifted through the leaves of a tree overhanging the wall, forming strange silvery hieroglyphs upon the ground at Manasseh's feet. What did the shadows say, he wondered idly, studying the moving patterns. Did they promise him victory or foretell his defeat?

A dull wooden clop suddenly disturbed the quiet. The tiny door in the wall, wavering through shifting shadows, creaked open. Manasseh caught his breath, afraid that any sudden sound might frighten Jendayi away. As silently as a cat, he crept over the bank toward the wall.

Little by little in cautious movements, the young harpist's head and shoulders edged through the doorway, seeming to test the silence. Manasseh froze in his place, his heart reveling in open admiration of her beauty and bravery.

"Trickster!" Abnu suddenly called from the boat. "Is the lady coming or not?"

Like a turtle zipping back into its shell, Jendayi's head disappeared behind the door. Manasseh sprang forward to stop her. "Jendayi!" he called in a rough whisper, hoping she had not run back through the garden in a frightened retreat. "It is your friend! Please, there is nothing to fear!"

Silence prevailed for a moment, then the door creaked open once again. Her head, wreathed by a lovely circlet of flowers, appeared and lifted toward him. "Chenzira?" she asked the darkness, her arms and shoulders tensed for flight.

"Yes. Do not fear." He moved smoothly to her side. "You said you came here often, and I wanted to see you before I go."

"You are still going away?" She gave him her hands. He helped her out of the tunnel, and she stood before him, her eyes dark and unfathomable.

Struggling with the sense of confusion her presence always elicited, Manasseh had difficulty finding his tongue. "Yes," he said, acutely aware of the pressure of her hands on his. "I am leaving the vizier's house, and I do not think I shall ever return. But I could not leave without telling you everything. I want to be forthright with you, Jendayi."

"Did you speak to Ephraim?" Her hands struggled to rise like a pair of tethered birds, but he held them tight, strengthening his heart against the sting of Ephraim's name.

"I did not see much of Ephraim in these past two days," he told her truthfully. "He has been spending most of his time at Pharaoh's palace in Thebes. Princess Sitamun is there with her mother, and Ephraim has done his best to charm and entertain the princess."

Jendayi's face fell slightly, but Manasseh clung to her hands. "Jendayi, do not let your heart be troubled—"

"You are kind to be concerned for me." She pulled away from him and took a few steps toward the black water, absently testing each footfall. "But you should not worry so much. What does it matter if Ephraim marries another? As long as he cares enough to ask for me, my future is assured."

Manasseh felt the chasm between them open like a wound. "Why is Ephraim so important to you?" he stammered, not caring what Abnu might hear from the canal beyond. "What gives him the right to your heart? A kiss? A kiss is nothing but an intimation of love. Sometimes there is no truth in it. People kiss one another all the time."

He moved toward her, fully expecting her to launch into an impassioned defense of the man she loved but was surprised when tears spilled from her gray eyes. "Not me," she whispered, her forlorn cry rending his heart. "No one kisses me. In my entire life, I cannot remember any other kiss. Only Ephraim's."

Stunned by her statement, Manasseh took a quick sharp breath. "No one else?" A tremor shook his voice. "Not even your mother, a friend, a sister—"

"I have no mother—at least not one I can remember." Tears glistened on her delicate heart-shaped face. "No friends, no sisters. Akil assigned me a handmaid, but Kesi serves me only because she would be beaten if she did not obey."

"Your master, then," Manasseh suggested, though something in him recoiled at the thought of the old chironomist planting his pruned lips on Jendayi's sweet face. "Surely he has shown some affection for you."

"Akil is a hard taskmaster." She palmed tears from her cheeks. "He cares for me only to please Pharaoh." She sniffed, then wiped her wet hands across the neckline of her gown in a tenderly helpless gesture. "But Ephraim kissed me once, so he must love me. And if my heart does not learn to love, I will die a thousand deaths. I will be eaten by the monster in the underworld. I dream of it and I know it will happen!"

"Jendayi, hear me." Manasseh moved to her side in one swift step. Though she tensed at his sudden approach, he gathered her into his arms and held her in a gentle embrace. "My dear little girl," he said, one hand stroking her cheek while the other held her to him, "you *are* loved. Forget Ephraim. He loves another. Love me. I love you, Jendayi. I would risk my life before Pharaoh himself in order to win your freedom."

She stiffened in his arms, and for an instant Manasseh felt as if he held a statue of the most fragile glass.

"You love me?" In spite of her sorrow a tinge of exasperation entered her voice. "Chenzira, I am not asking for pity."

"I don't pity you! I think you are the most beautiful, the most gifted woman I have ever met."

She shook her head. "You feel sorry for me. I am heartbroken, and alone . . . and blind."

"No! I love you. I have loved you since the day I first saw you."

"Two months ago?" Firmly she placed her hands on his chest and pushed him away. "Your kindness is touching, Chenzira. But you belong to the vizier and I belong to the king. Neither of us has the power to change our fates." Her polite smile faded. "Ephraim once sent word that he was willing to ask for me, but he obviously preferred to ask for the king's daughter."

"That wasn't Ephraim!" Manasseh clenched his fist in frustration and took a deep breath. If ever God had sent an opportunity to tell her the truth, this was it. "The message from Ephraim came while you were in Canaan, after you played for the vizier's guests, right?"

Her brows lifted in an expression of astonishment. "Yes. But why am I surprised? You would know that. You serve in the vizier's house and were probably in Canaan with us."

His lips trembled with the need to laugh. "Yes, I was there! And the message you received came from me."

"But Kesi said she spoke with the captain of the vizier's guard."

"She did." Manasseh's voice was firm, final. "I sent the message, but I did not carry it. Jendayi, I am not the vizier's servant, but his elder son, Manasseh. And you must believe me when I say that I have loved you for years."

She backed away without speaking, one hand over her lips, the familiar mask of aloofness descending like a shadow upon her face. She was retreating inside herself, a frightened slave scurrying away from a nobleman. If he did not catch her—

He rushed on. "I told you my name was Chenzira because I did not think you would confide in me if you knew the truth."

"You were right." She turned from him and faced the river, her head bowed. "It is not right for a slave to share her heart with—a master. But you lied."

He edged forward until he could see her troubled face. "I am not your enemy, Jendayi. I would never hurt you."

She lifted her chin slightly but kept her face toward the water as if she could see a world of mystery in the canal beyond. For a brief moment her face seemed to open, and Manasseh saw a whirl of spinning emotions: bewilderment, a quick flicker of fear, pure and simple agony. Then, with a rush, the mask of detachment descended once again.

"You are the vizier's son." She wrapped her arms around herself as though a chill wind had just blown over her. "Like Ephraim, you will marry a noble woman whether you want to or not. This *love* of yours is not real, but merely a childish fancy. I will not risk this life and the eternal one to come upon the fickleness of a nobleman's heart. I should not even be speaking to you—"

"I am no longer the vizier's son," he said quietly, moving toward her as though being closer would help her understand. "Tonight I left my father's house and everyone in it. My father will disown me, if he has not already. I have no family, no possessions, no support. I came here tonight to tell you the truth and to offer you my love. I must go to war, but when God Shaddai brings me back, I will stand before Pharaoh and give him a portion of the captured spoils as a bride-price. I will redeem you from Pharaoh, Jendayi. My God will arrange it. You will be free to choose your own path."

"You expect a lot of your God," she whispered softly.

"He loves to provide." Manasseh moved to stand between her

and the meandering canal. Carefully, he reached out and placed his hands on her arms, drawing her to him. She did not resist but neither did she relax except to put out a hand to steady herself against his chest.

Her light touch unfurled streamers of sensation that left Manasseh light-headed. "I will return for you." His pulse skittered alarmingly as he felt the movement of her breathing against his skin. "As Pharaoh lives and God Shaddai provides, I will return."

Her face lifted to his then, and beneath the aloof loveliness he saw a suggestion of movement and flowing, as though a hidden spring were trying to break through.

"Chenzira—Manasseh, it is hopeless." Disbelief echoed in the tone of her voice. "I have seen my future. There is no love for me, not here, not anywhere."

"Yes, there is." Manasseh locked her in his embrace. "Give me the opportunity to show you, Jendayi. One chance. That's all I ask of you."

"And if you do not return?" Her chin quivered and she lowered her head, her thick dark lashes fringing her cheek. "If I trust you, believe in you, and you do not return for me, what shall I do then?"

Manasseh cradled her head against his shoulder, not certain how to answer. "I will return," he said finally, releasing her head so that he could study her sweet countenance one final time. "And if you will trust me, your heart will begin to live. Defeat your dream now, Jendayi. Have faith in me . . . and in my God Almighty."

Despite the sorrowful bend of her posture, the corner of her delicate mouth lifted in a half-smile. "You sound so confident. I could almost believe you," she whispered, just before leaving the circle of his arms.

And while the stars sprang out, one by one, from the cobalt dome of the heavens, Manasseh watched her slip back into the palace garden and thought that nothing on earth had ever seemed more breathtaking than the simple grace of his beloved Jendayi.

~~~ Twenty ~~~

AKIL FROWNED AS THE MUSICIANS FINISHED THEIR FI-
nal song for Pharaoh's banquet. Fortunately, the king had not noticed that the oboe and harp consistently clashed in the final ca-
dences of Hathor's hymn of praise, but several of the guests had
unconsciously cringed at the dissonant sounds.

A group of female acrobats took to the open floor, leaping,
twirling, and undulating to the beat of their own drummer, and
Akil nodded to his instrumentalists, granting them permission
to retreat from the king's banquet chamber. He fixed his gaze on
Jendayi as she slipped her arms around her harp and lifted it. A
frown had occupied the space between her delicate brows for the
last several nights, and he wondered again if she had received
some message from the vizier's son. All of Thebes buzzed with
rumors about Manasseh's failure to appear at a recent palace ceremony with his father and brother Ephraim. Pharaoh had been
much displeased. But Queen Tiy had caught Akil's eye and lifted
a confident brow, and he knew she had matters under control.

But perhaps Jendayi was privy to information even the queen
would not know. If Akil could bring that information to the
queen's ear, her estimation of him would rise even higher. Perhaps she would award him with a golden chain or a special suite
of rooms within the palace. . . .

The flautist and oboist pattered out of the chamber. As Jendayi left with her maid, Akil followed them into the hallway,
then caught Kesi's arm. Placing his fingers across his mouth to
signal silence, he pulled her away from the harpist and drew her
into a private alcove.

"What seems to be troubling your mistress?" he asked, painting on the warmest smile he could muster. "She is not herself
these days. Tonight she played with less than her usual brilliance."

"I . . . I don't know," Kesi stammered, tugging at her gown. She paled before his questioning gaze. "I haven't done anything to displease her, I'm certain. Please, master, don't send me away—"

"Hush, foolish girl." Again he forced a smile and relaxed his hold on her arm. "Something is troubling Jendayi. I know her too well to miss the signs of discontent. You must find out what is bothering her."

"Master, she does not often talk to me. She rarely confides in anyone."

"Make her trust you." His breath burned in his throat. Were all slaves as stupid as this girl? But he must control his temper, or like a chattering bird she would fly and warn the harpist. He took a deep breath and smiled again. "Speak to her tonight and draw her into your confidence about something. If you tell her a secret, she will want to confide in you. It is the way of women."

"I don't think it will work, master." The girl's wide eyes clouded with doubt. "She is most withdrawn lately. She does not talk about herself. I never know what she is thinking."

"Then find out." Not bothering to smile this time, he ripped the words impatiently. "Find out or I will send you to the overseer, and he will beat you into obedience. Need I say more?"

"No, Master Akil." A familiar weakness settled about her eyes, the way all women looked just before they cried. "I will try to get her to talk."

"Don't try." Akil released his hold on her arm. "Do it."

~ Twenty-one ~

A SHAFT OF SUN ANGLED DOWN FROM A CLERESTORY window in Pharaoh's chamber, trapping slow convections of dust. Feeling as distant as the stars from the priests who intoned the ritual blessings before Pharaoh, Joseph watched the dancing dust and considered the troublesome matters of his own household.

For two weeks Joseph had said nothing to his servants about Manasseh's defiant departure. No one dared mention the young man's absence to him, correctly sensing that the subject was a delicate and difficult one. Ani, who made it his duty to know everything and everyone who passed through the vizier's villa, went about his work a little more quietly than usual, his face longer and his step slower than it had been in weeks past. And Tarik, that most inspiring of warriors, briefed his men every morning in a voice so dull and dry the words seemed to come from him after a lengthy journey through a desolate wilderness.

But his servants had been wearied by the extra demands of the settlement at Goshen, Joseph told himself. The sons of Israel were busy building proper houses, and Ani had been employed to help the Hebrews procure the necessary workers to form bricks and to bring lumber from Lebanon. And Tarik had not only the safety of the vizier's household to worry about, but also the responsibility of overseeing the caravans that traveled from Thebes to Goshen and back again.

Joseph went about his work as best he could, knowing the situation with Manasseh was a threatening cloud that would hang over his head until it burst. A week after Manasseh left, Joseph had sent out patrols to report the movements and makeup of the Hebrew force. But though Tarik's men had scoured the area between Tura and Goshen, the patrols had not been able to find Manasseh's recruits. Pharaoh had not yet asked how the situation with Manasseh had been resolved, but if the phantom force still existed, the king would soon hear of it. Knowing his stubborn son, Joseph was certain the rogue army was alive, but in hiding.

On his last visit Judah reported that there were now one hundred fifty young men missing from the Hebrew camp. Even a few of the younger women, Judah noted, had grown pensive and wondered aloud if a move back to Canaan might not be in the family's best interest. "But we, your brothers," Judah hastened to add, "believe in your leadership, noble vizier. If you want us to remain here, we will stay. We wrested your dreams of honor and glory from you many years ago, but God Shaddai, all praise to His name, restored them. Who are we to doubt you? Besides, we are content and prosperous. You, noble Joseph, have bountifully provided for our needs. We do not worry about drought, crop failure, or sickness. If disaster strikes, we know the vizier Zaphenath-paneah stands ready to provide for us."

Now, as Joseph sat across the room from Pharaoh and listened to the priests praise the king, he wondered if he had not spoiled his brethren. He loved them and wanted to make up for the many years they had been apart. And he knew God had brought him to Egypt in order to provide for them. Manasseh was right about at least one thing—Joseph had been set apart. Egypt was woven into the texture of his life. He could no more wrest himself from the palace on the Nile than he could divide his soul from his spirit.

Yet a cloud of doubt hovered over his conscience. Years ago, while Joseph lived and worked in Potiphar's house, pride had been the greatest weakness of his life. Had that most subtle and poisonous of evils returned to infect his soul when he least suspected it?

The priests finished their hymn of praise to the divine king, and Pharaoh wordlessly extended his crook, bestowing blessings upon his faithful servants. The worship concluded, Amenhotep stood in one regal motion and uncrossed the crook and flail from before his chest. The crook, a symbol of his duty to shepherd his people, seemed less prominent to Joseph today than the flail, a symbol of the *ladanisterion*, a type of whip used by agricultural workers to gather ladanum, the aromatic shrub that yielded resin when beaten. As Joseph stood and followed his king from the bedchamber, he wondered if Pharaoh had used a sort of *ladanisterion* on him. Ever since Amenhotep had confronted him with news of Manasseh and the alleged uprising, Joseph had felt positively limp with weariness and defeat.

When they had left the king's priests behind, Joseph lengthened his stride, falling into step beside the king. "A large crowd awaits your judgment today," he remarked offhandedly, trying to discern the royal mood. "They are gathered outside in the courtyard."

"Yes." The king's eyes seemed to study the tile floor where they walked. "And after a tiring morning. I don't know why they come to Malkata. Why do they not approach you? Why do they insist upon bothering me?"

Joseph steepled his hands and struggled for a tactful reply. If Pharaoh had been younger, Joseph would have reminded him that kingship offered both privilege and responsibility. But the time for character lessons had passed. Amenhotep's temperament and personality, for good or ill, had already been formed.

"The men who wait to see you are noblemen and deserve an audience with their king." Joseph sighed gently in exasperation. "I have rendered judgment on hundreds of cases in Thebes within the last month. But these men serve you with their lives. They hold important posts throughout the kingdom—"

"They know I will agree with you," Pharaoh interrupted. His smile flashed briefly, dazzling against his olive skin. "You are my teacher, my right hand. How could I not agree with you?"

Joseph smiled, glorying briefly in the intimate moment. Surely there was no better time than this to bring up what was certain to be a disagreeable subject. Pharaoh was relaxed and feeling nostalgic, anticipating the pleasures of his harem.

"My King"—Joseph dipped his head slightly—"I have been considering something of great importance and would like to know your thoughts on the matter."

Amenhotep stopped in the passageway. "You seek my opinion?" A flash of humor crossed his face as he turned to face Joseph. "It must be a troubling matter indeed, since you know everything except for the one subject in which I am expert—"

"The matter has nothing to do with women." Joseph lifted a wagging finger.

Pharaoh's laugh was low and throaty as he crossed his arms. "Speak, then. What is it?"

"My people, the Hebrews." Joseph's gaze swept over the king's face. "You have said you do not approve of a military force to reestablish our home in Canaan, and in those words you have again revealed your wisdom. But if my brothers and their families could return to Canaan in peace, would you allow them to go?"

Amenhotep's eyes widened in concern. "Why should they go? Are they unhappy? Have I not made every allowance for them?"

"Yes, my King, you have been more than generous, and they are prosperous." Joseph smiled gently. "But this is not their land. It is yours. And some of the younger ones are hot-headed. They hear stories of the old days and yearn for glory. Their hearts desire to live in their own Promised Land."

"You must remind them that glory lies in Egypt." Pharaoh nodded with enthusiasm. "No king has been greater than I. No king has fought fewer wars or seen greater contentment among his people. No one has starved during my reign—the land has bountifully brought forth food. The temples I have built shall last throughout eternity."

"Yes, but the younger ones—" Joseph halted, suddenly aware that his king was not listening. Pharaoh stood silent, gazing into private space, and his eyes were those of a bewildered, vulnerable child. Joseph felt his heart constrict in guilt. He had tried to prepare this fatherless boy for the throne, yet his work might never be finished.

"You taught me about life, Zaphenath-paneah." A momentary look of discomfort flitted across Amenhotep's face. "My mother and father both loved you. How could you think of leaving me?"

"I could not consider it, even for a moment," Joseph answered quickly. He bowed slightly to reinforce his sincerity. "As long as I live, I will not leave you. You have my solemn oath."

Though Pharaoh did not answer, the gratified expression on his face spoke for him. He moved ahead toward his throne room, calmly humming the tuneless hymn the priests had sung earlier.

And as they continued through the passageway, Joseph knew

that he would not leave the Black Land alive. God Shaddai often spoke in miraculous ways. Joseph himself had heard God's voice in dreams and visions. So why could He not speak through the voice of a king?

————

The conversation with Amenhotep restored Joseph's confidence in his own reasoning, and with a lighter heart he approached the queen's apartments in the palace at Thebes. An urgent message had been waiting for him when he returned from Malkata, and the queen's messenger said that Tiy would wait for the vizier's appearance, no matter how late the hour.

She has probably imagined some insult from one of the foreign couriers, Joseph thought as he climbed the marble steps that led to the portico outside her chambers. *Since Amenhotep has left her alone in Thebes, she seems to think all men are intent upon slighting her.*

A guard led him to the queen's innermost private chamber. A pair of slaves took his dusty traveling cloak and removed his leather sandals. As he sat on a delicate chair and immersed his dusty feet into a basin of water, he closed his eyes and rested his head upon a luxurious pillow. The day had been long and hot, his work a series of endless and vain repetitions. He hoped the queen's business was not urgent.

A slave dried his feet and urged him to recline on a cushioned couch. Joseph moved to it, pressing the back of his hand over his tired eyes as he savored the sweetly mingled scents of lotus blossoms and incense. Notoriously tardy, the queen might keep him waiting an hour or more.

He had just closed his eyes and drifted into a shallow doze when a hand fell lightly upon his skin. His eyes sprang open. Tiy sat beside him on a couch built for one, her left hand lingering upon his chest. He wondered whether she could feel his discomfort, the sudden banging of his blood.

"My Queen," he whispered, scarcely daring to move.

"My vizier," she answered, her voice no more than a soft purr in the silence of the room. The scent of her heavy perfume assaulted him. Green malachite gleamed from her eyelids, reminding him that just this morning he had jokingly told Pharaoh that most women were not so young as they were painted.

Glancing quickly left and right, he realized that the servants had departed. No guards, no handmaids, no daughters lingered in the chamber. They were quite alone.

"Excuse me." He lifted his head in an attempt to sit up. "I was rude to fall asleep."

Her hand held him to the bench. "I understand and I pardon both your weariness and your deplorable lack of manners. I know that you have spent the greater part of the day at Malkata." She lifted her free hand and gazed idly at her henna-tinted nails. "And how is my husband's harem faring?"

"Everyone at Malkata is well." He lowered his head, tense and tired but not wanting to anger her unnecessarily.

"I know that, too." She turned the full power of her smile upon him. "There is little about you that I do not know, Zaphenath-paneah, known to the Hebrews as Joseph."

The mention of his familiar name sent a warning shiver through him, and his face burned as he remembered another woman, another house, another time. Sagira, Potiphar's wife, had caught him alone in a room decorated much like this one, and she, too, had held the power of his life in her hands. God had preserved Joseph then, though he had suffered mightily for his resistance. But Tiy was not a bundle of raw emotions like Sagira. The queen was an intelligent, pragmatic woman. Surely he could reason with her.

"My Queen," he said firmly, "forgive me if I overstep my authority. But I must beg you to reconsider what our surroundings lead me to believe you intend to suggest."

Her lower lip edged forward in a pretend pout. "Ah, Zaphenath-paneah, you are no fun at all! My husband has a harem filled with women. Why shouldn't the queen be allowed to find love where she can?"

"Because the queen is wise," Joseph answered, daring to take the hand that clung tenaciously to his chest. He lifted it, held it up as if in salute, then dropped it into her lap as he sat upright. "You do not want to do this. Later you would hate me. And such an act would betray the king's trust in both of us."

Though she did not move to touch him again, an invitation lingered in the smoldering depths of her eyes. "Think carefully, my vizier. You have no wife to smell the scent of another woman upon your skin, and I am quite alone here. No one would know. We might take our fill of each other until the dawn—''

"God Shaddai would know," Joseph interrupted, sliding away from her. "And so, I daresay, would those who know me well. A righteous man's eyes, my Queen, look openly upon the world. If he should suddenly build a wall behind those eyes, the people who know him would wonder. My captain, my steward— they would know.''

"I am surprised you did not mention your sons." Tiy quirked an eyebrow. "Particularly the elder, Manasseh. Or do your sons not know you as well as your captain and your steward?''

Joseph flushed, helpless to halt his embarrassment. How much did she know about the situation with Manasseh? She could have spies anywhere, even in his house.

"My people know me." He ignored her question about his sons as he swung his feet to the floor. "If there is no other business here, my Queen, I should be getting back to my villa. I trust that you see the wisdom in this course of action.''

"I suppose"—she shifted slightly upon the couch to see him better—"you are right, as always, noble Zaphenath-paneah. I have offered you the chance to correct an injustice of history, and you have. Tonight you will leave the scorned woman clothed and with your full dignity, not at all like the other time when you ran naked into the stable.''

Mercifully, the dim light of the chamber hid the extent of his humiliation. Her immodest comments, however true, were ill suited to her position. Though he had not smelled beer on her breath, she was behaving like a drunken woman. Tomorrow she would remember . . . and feel shame.

"I give you good night, my Queen," he said, inclining his head.

"Wait." Her hand, like a fist of iron, closed around his wrist. "I did not bring you here to seduce you, most noble vizier. I brought you here to discuss a matter of vast importance for the kingdom.''

"And that is?''

She gave him a smile utterly without humor. "Amenhotep. I love him, Zaphenath-paneah, but though he believes otherwise, he is not the greatest Pharaoh Egypt has ever known. I would be a better one.''

Joseph looked up, startled beyond words.

"Yes.'' She stared at him in deadly concentration. "You know I speak the truth. Amenhotep spends all his time and energy upon his women and his monuments when he could be expanding Egypt's boundaries.''

"Expanding?'' Joseph pressed his hand to his forehead, trying to force his confused thoughts into order.

"Just this week I have heard rumors of unrest in Hatti and Mitanni,'' she went on, her voice like velvet edged with steel. "With troops gathered from our nomarchs, we could send an invasion force and subdue those unruly kings. Pharaoh is always talking about Tuthmosis the great warrior, but he will do nothing to make his own reputation greater than that king's. And yet it could be done. Just as Hatshepsut placed a puppet Pharaoh on the throne while she ruled with her steward's aid, you and I can rule more effectively than Amenhotep.''

"Are you suggesting that we''—the word *murder* would not cross his lips—"get rid of—?''

"Of course not.'' She pulled away and frowned as if he'd suggested something terribly distasteful. "I love my husband. I would not even go as far as Hatshepsut, who eventually took the throne, crown, and royal insignia for herself. But I can rule in private and leave Amenhotep to his adoring public. Together, Zaphenath-paneah, we could do this. If you will sign your name with mine to letters to the governors of the nomarchs, we will simply state our intention to handle all domestic and foreign affairs from the palace at Thebes. In time, when Pharaoh finds out, he will be displeased, but then he will realize that we have acted for his own benefit. He will be king in the peoples' hearts, while we will extend the power of Egypt throughout Canaan, Hatti, and Mitanni.''

The heavy power in her eyes laid hold of something in Joseph's being, and for a moment he found himself caught up in her plans. Amenhotep *was* unsure of himself. He did spend too much time in pleasure and wasteful entertainments, and Tiy had always been the more resourceful and realistic of the two. Who could say that God had not called Joseph to Egypt's throne rooms for this time and purpose? If Egypt's warriors moved through Canaan and subdued the hostile kingdoms there, the sons of Israel could choose from the best lands in the world, while he, Zaphenath-paneah, made every provision for their welfare. . . .

When Joseph looked away, needing a moment to reorient himself, the voice of common sense attacked his grandiose dreams. The queen, he realized, was contemplating treason far worse than anything Manasseh had ever suggested. The priests would consider her words complete and unthinkable foolishness. She was not the supposedly divine Pharaoh. Amenhotep was. She was not even the dynasty heiress. One of Amenhotep's sisters had married him to establish his place in the royal lineage. And Joseph had sworn to serve Amenhotep, Tuya's son, not Tiy.

"My Queen"—he shot her a withering glance—"you cannot do this. I will never agree, never. Pharaoh is the king set apart by God, and you are his queen. Be his supporter, not his enemy."

For a moment her eyes met his with fierce determination, then, perceptibly, she faltered and cast her gaze downward.

Confident that he had corralled a heretical and dangerous notion, Joseph straightened himself with dignity. "Have you spoken of this to anyone else?"

Tiy shook her head.

"Good." Joseph rested his hands on his knees, then stood. "I will say nothing of this to Pharaoh. I think it is best that we forget everything that happened here. Amenhotep is a fine king, content with his kingdom and his people. God has blessed his country. The people are prosperous and happy. Can any king ask for more?"

"No," she whispered, her expression pained.

"My Queen, you are right." He moved toward the doorway and slipped into the darkness before she could say anything else.

Ever since her unpleasant encounter with Zaphenath-paneah, delightfully unpredictable thoughts had bounced in Tiy's head like loose bits of marble after a haphazard blow of the mallet.

The vizier had proven his unshakable steadfastness yet again.

But she was nothing like Sagira, the empty-headed wife of Poti-phar who had attempted to execute her vengeance in one mad accusation. Tiy was wiser, far more temperate, and she knew the vizier well enough to know that the threat of physical destruc-tion would do little to disturb his cursed equanimity. In his life-time he had survived slavery, imprisonment, poverty, and a wife's death. How else could a man be broken?

Resting on her bed, she rolled onto her side and propped her head on her hand. She would accomplish nothing by engineer-ing Zaphenath-paneah's imprisonment or execution. Pharaoh's proud vizier cared nothing for the wealth he had accumulated or his fine villa on the Nile. Unlike other unusually handsome men, he spent very little time consulting with the royal costumers and jewelers. And though he loved his sons and his servants, his pas-sion for Pharaoh overrode everything else.

Father to Pharaoh. The king's most trusted advisor—trusted even more than the Great Wife.

In that title lay the key to the vizier's destruction.

She ran the gilded tip of her fingernail over a pattern in the rich linen bed coverings and felt her lips curve into a smile. Poor Zaphenath-paneah, she could almost pity him. She had tried to appear properly chastised and humbled when he refused her, a difficult challenge when her tongue burned to spew hot defiance in his pious face. She might have overlooked his scorn for her loving attention, but she could not excuse his refusal to aid her quest for authority. For if his overwhelming devotion to Pharaoh should ever urge him to divulge the proposition she had made, *she* would be the outcast, the one exiled from the source and cen-ter of all power.

Zaphenath-paneah, then, would have to go away.

She rolled over onto her stomach and propped her head on her hands. On the morrow she would take a barge to Malkata and speak to her husband. She would not be as foolish and obvious as the notorious wife of Potiphar, but she would destroy the vi-zier nonetheless.

———

"You see how it is, then," Tiy said, regarding Amenhotep with a speculative gaze. She had risen before sunrise and taken her gilded barge to Malkata. Now she sat with her husband in his bedchamber, face-to-face, with no intermediaries or meddling priests about.

"I do." Amenhotep studied her thoughtfully for a moment. "But I shall miss Zaphenath-paneah. He has been the vizier since my father's time! My mother adores him—"

"Queen Tuya has nothing to do with your government of the kingdom." Tiy leaned forward and rested her hand upon his arm. "And the vizier has everything to do with Egypt. Therein lies the problem. The vizier's duties are too much for one man, and Zaphenath-paneah has now lived more than twice as many years as your father. Since Egypt is two kingdoms, appoint a new, younger man to administrate each half. One man shall supervise Lower Egypt from the city of Memphis, another Upper Egypt, from Thebes. And rather than taking your time each morning, they shall report to me at each new moon."

And I will manipulate both.

Amenhotep absently stroked his chin. "There may be wisdom in what you say." He lowered his voice. "I would not admit it to anyone else, but often I have felt like a child who cannot shed his overprotective parent. But what shall we do with Zaphenath-paneah?"

"Have you not noticed the dark smudges of weariness beneath his eyes?" Tiy affectionately placed her hand over her husband's. "I think he is eager for a well-deserved rest. He has a prosperous villa, a reputation for honesty, and two fine sons. Leave him alone, my husband. Let him enjoy the leisure he has earned. Do not call him into your presence. Do not ask his advice on any subject. Leave him in peace to enjoy his people, his home, his sons. That is all he would ask, I think, were he here with you now."

"Yes." Amenhotep tilted his head and smiled with warm spontaneity. "It shall be done."

"Shall you tell him before the court at Malkata this morning?" She held her breath, hoping he would accept her suggestion. Nothing would make her happier than to see Zaphenath-paneah humbled before the Pharaoh he had given his life to serve.

But Amenhotep was too much a coward. "No. I shall send a

messenger to him." He clapped his hands. "Summon a scribe!" he bellowed to the chamberlain who appeared in the doorway. "And a runner! I have an urgent message to be carried at once to my vizier!"

Pharaoh's uncertain eyes sought hers again. "Shall I at least consult him about choosing two new viziers? Zaphenath-paneah is a shrewd judge of character."

"He is not so shrewd as you think," she answered lightly, giving him a careful smile. "He is old. So let him begin his rest today. The honorable and worthy Zaphenath-paneah has served his king well, but no longer shall he enter the palace at Malkata. No longer shall he be required to stand before Pharaoh and report the troubles of an entire kingdom."

Pharaoh nodded slowly, considering. If only her children accepted her ideas this quickly!

"In the name of my father Amon-Re, I think I shall commission a song to honor him." Amenhotep sniffed with satisfaction. Again he clapped his hands. "Send me Akil!" he called to the flustered chamberlain who thrust his head through the curtained doorway. "And waste no time in fetching him!"

Tiy leaned back in her chair and steepled her hands before her chin, well content with the beginning of her revenge.

TIY

The Lord is slow to anger and great in power,
And the Lord will by no means leave the guilty
unpunished.
In whirlwind and storm is His way,
And clouds are the dust beneath His feet.
The Lord is good,
A stronghold in the day of trouble,
And He knows those who take refuge in Him.

Nahum 1:3, 7

~ Twenty-two ~

JOSEPH LOWERED THE PAPYRUS SCROLL TO HIS LAP and stared dumbly at Pharaoh's imprint upon the broken seal. *Dismissed*, the parchment said. Without a word of warning or a hint of displeasure.

Someone had made a grave mistake. He reread the message quickly, searching for some combination of words that his weary eyes could have transposed, some crucial word or phrase his staggered reason might have missed in his first reading. But Pharaoh's message was as clear as it was brutal:

> The Horus Living-of-Births, the Two Ladies Living-of-Births, the King of Upper and Lower Egypt, Amen-ho-tep, Son of Amon-Re, Pharaoh, Living forever unto eternity!
> A decree of the King to the Vizier Zaphenath-paneah:
> Life, health, and prosperity to you, High Vizier of all Egypt, Zaphenath-paneah. Behold, your king and Pharaoh, Amenhotep III, decrees that henceforth from this day, beginning with the rising sail of the sun-bark of Amon-Re, two viziers shall represent my divine throne throughout the double kingdom of Egypt. For today indeed you have begun to grow old and will soon lose your virile powers. Be mindful of the day of burial, of passing to a revered state! A night will one day be assigned for you for oils and wrappings from the hands of Tayit, the goddess of weaving. You will be placed upon a bier, with oxen drawing you and singers going before you, and the mortuary dances will be performed at the door of your tomb.
> Until that day, two younger men, sons of your teaching, shall be appointed in your place as vizier. This is done to give you a well-deserved rest and allow you to take your place of honor while life still pours through your heart. As for you, the king sends his thanks, faithful love, and appreciation for

your outspoken service to the two kingdoms. We shall rest well, knowing that your God will sustain and preserve your coming in and going out as He has from the beginning of your days on earth and in the two kingdoms.

You have begun to grow old. Whatever did Pharaoh mean? Joseph had lost neither the quickness of his mind nor the sharpness of his wit. His hair, or what remained of it under his heavy wig, was streaked with silver, but the hoary head was a sign of wisdom and experience, not weakness. Feathery lines marked his eyes and mouth, but those webbed lines had been etched by his concern over Amenhotep, spun out of love and concern and guardianship.

Old! Young men needed elders, men who were unwilling to become pathetic imitations of younger rivals. What was Amenhotep thinking?

Joseph clenched his fist as ice began to spread through his stomach, then suddenly he remembered that he was not alone. The messenger from the king waited before him, as did Ani, who had been drawn away from his duties by this urgent message from Pharaoh. The steward waited silently, his expression composed, but his bright, birdlike eyes alert to the signs of distress and gravity upon his master's face.

"Pharaoh," Joseph began, dismayed to hear a strained tone in his voice, "will appoint a new vizier—two of them, in fact—very soon. Apparently I have finished my course of service to the king. He wishes me well. In time, perhaps . . ."

Despair rose in his throat, stifling the power of speech. *You have begun to grow old.* Of course he had! He had spent his life in service first to Amenhotep's father, then to the present Pharaoh. He had set aside his own dreams, trusting his estate to Ani and his children to Tarik and a succession of handmaids. Would he be rewarded for that sacrifice like *this*? By means of a simple parchment and a few formal phrases, he had been thrown out like yesterday's vegetables.

Oh, the ingratitude and incivility of the young! Amenhotep's father would never have behaved so rudely. The king's mother, Queen Tuya, would rise up in fury if she had any idea her son had treated his vizier so arrogantly. Joseph had done nothing to deserve being tossed away like a worn and faded garment. Though he was older than most of the king's counselors, he possessed the health and longevity of Jacob. With the blessing of God Shaddai, he would undoubtedly live to see Amenhotep himself entombed, and yet this stripling king had the gall, the unmitigated *audacity*, to cast aside the one who had been his protector and tutor, counselor and father. . . .

In a silent fury that spoke louder than words, Joseph crumpled the royal message, then a wave of remorse swept over him. He was still subject to the king, and he had just demonstrated a spirit of insurrection in front of Pharaoh's messenger. Amenhotep barely tolerated differences of opinion in his counselors, and with ordinary common citizens—which Joseph now was—he had no forbearance at all.

Ani, intuitive soul that he was, understood. As Joseph lowered his eyes to the floor, he heard Ani's voice commanding Pharaoh's slave to depart. The messenger bent to bow on the floor, then caught himself. His face and neck turned a vivid scarlet as he bobbed awkwardly before Zaphenath-paneah, noble *citizen*, then fled the room.

God of my fathers, help me. Joseph smoothed the crumpled papyrus against the linen of his vizier's robe as his blood ran thick with guilt. How could he justify his anger before God? God Shaddai had elevated him from prison to throne overnight. In the past God had demoted him just as suddenly. But though Joseph's previous tribulations had been difficult, at least he had come to understand the reasons for them. By willingly provoking his brothers to jealousy, he had opened the road for their betrayal. By tolerating the dangerous affections of a powerful woman, he had initiated his own confinement in prison. In those situations he had ignored dangerous thunderclouds on the horizon. But in the last few years the horizon of his life had been as clear as the sun.

Or had it? Had he been too involved with Pharaoh's work to even look up?

He looked up now, but his eyes would not focus on the room. Through a blur of tears he saw Ani standing silently, humbly, his hands folded at his waist, his head bent with misery.

A heaviness centered in Joseph's chest as he lifted his gaze to meet his steward's. "I think I would like to be alone," he said, reaching for the solid arm of his gilded chair, the throne from which he had ruled the Black Land for nearly thirty years. That chair seemed the only solid reality in a shifting world, but it too was *old*.

Joseph sat down, wondering for the first time if he had more yesterdays than tomorrows. Had God finished with him, then? Was this parchment the Almighty's way of removing Joseph from the work that counted for all eternity? Perhaps he had made mistakes? Pride had always been his most damaging weakness. But he had tried to do his best for Amenhotep. He had humbly placed Pharaoh and Pharaoh's house above even his own. Joseph had personally tutored the young prince while his own sons learned under Ani's patient teaching. He had spent hour after hour listening to the young king's problems while his own wife pined in lonely silence, feeding the insecurity that ultimately took her life.

Such joys he had sacrificed, and all for Pharaoh! He had not withheld one precious thing from the altar of duty. And now his God-given work was done. Finished. Gone.

Ani gave him a bleak tight-lipped smile, ruefully accepting the terrible truth.

Joseph lowered his head into his hands and kneaded his temples. His head pounded with memories and dire thoughts. Ani did not speak for a long moment—he did not need to. The two men had been master and servant for so long they understood each other completely. The older man held out his hands. "If you truly want to be alone," he said, his dark eyes brimming with tender compassion, "I will go."

Just then the double doors burst open. Tarik hurried into the room and flung himself onto the floor, obviously unaware that he was no longer required to prostrate himself before his master. "Most noble vizier," he called, without stopping to evaluate Joseph's mood, "my scouts have returned. Manasseh and his men have been discovered in the wilderness. By sundown tomorrow I could have a squadron of men at their camp—"

The captain broke off when his gaze met Joseph's, and the jubilant look of satisfaction left his eyes. For a moment he faltered, floundering in confusion as his gaze shifted to meet Ani's, then he finished with a question. "Shall I ride out to bring Manasseh home?"

Joseph heard him through a vague sense of unreality. "Do what you will with the young men," he murmured, rising from his now insignificant gilded chair. "I do not care."

––––––––

Rather than return to Thebes immediately, Tiy lingered in her chambers at Malkata, summoning her coterie and personal servants from Thebes to Pharaoh's pink granite palace. Surprised by her unexpected visit, Pharaoh's flustered chamberlain stood in her chambers now, barking out commands as a host of slaves hastened to freshen the water basins, air the linens, light the tall cones of incense.

Wrapped in a cocoon of indifference, Tiy paced in the center of the hubbub and patiently counted the hours until she might command an audience with one who quite possibly knew more about Pharaoh's palace than Pharaoh himself—Akil. She knew Amenhotep had spent the morning with the musician, fruitlessly trying to appease the creative god who had laid the suggestion of a song upon his pleasure-fogged brain, but the day was now half-spent and Pharaoh would soon be calling for his dinner. Abruptly, she sent a slave to summon the musician, then she dismissed the chamberlain and his servants and settled back to wait.

Tiy's appreciation for Akil had grown dramatically since the chironomist approached her with news of the secret meeting between the vizier's son and the little harpist. A stiff, nearly bloodless individual whom she suspected of being even more clever than she, he was a valuable ally because Pharaoh tended to forget that his musicians had ears and wagging tongues. And Akil adored her. She had discerned that much when the chironomist traveled all the way to Thebes to tell *her*, not Amenhotep, of Manasseh's treachery.

With Zaphenath-paneah out of the picture, Akil could serve as her eyes and ears. If he served her well, she would elevate him as Hatshepsut had exalted her steward Senenmut.

Feeling relaxed and invincible, Tiy smiled when the embroidered curtain to her chamber lifted. The musician entered and promptly prostrated himself on the floor. "Rise, Akil." She languidly pointed to a chair. "You and I are alone, so let us forget formalities. You will sit to talk with me, but you must swear that what I tell you shall never pass your lips."

"You may cut off my tongue if it does." The man rose and moved toward her with abrupt, purposeful strides, then took the seat she offered and clasped his hands upon his knees. Out of long habit, he bowed his head but kept his olive black eyes affixed to hers. "How may I serve you, O Mother of Egypt?"

She gave him a mirthless smile, tight and neat. "I am sure you have realized that Pharaoh is about to appoint two new viziers."

"Oh?" One of his finely plucked eyebrows shot upward. "It is not for me to question the divine Pharaoh, but I wondered why he was so intent upon creating a hymn of praise to honor our noble Zaphenath-paneah."

Tiy made a soft sound of disgust. "Come, Akil, speak plainly. I know you have never liked the vizier. I have read your feelings in your eyes."

The chironomist lifted his shoulders and shrugged, though a suitably shamed look crossed his face. "Alas, the queen knows me too well. And I cannot hide what my heart tells me. The vizier is an opportunist. Can anyone deny that all he has done for Egypt has ultimately been accomplished to provide for the rabble now living in Goshen?"

"You have guessed my concern." Tiy leaned forward. "Since you brought me news of this rebellious Hebrew army, my sleep has not been pleasant. I fear for our people and particularly for my daughter. The sons of Zaphenath-paneah are like their father, attractive and charismatic, and yet we dare not trust them. But my daughter Sitamun has lost her heart to Ephraim, and several of Pharaoh's Medjay warriors have surrendered their loyalty to Manasseh's flattery and cunning."

"The Hebrews are a formidable force," Akil agreed, then held up his pale hand. "But they are not as formidable as Pharaoh's house."

"That remains to be seen." Tiy rested her chin on her hand. "I am concerned. Pharaoh has hidden himself away with his harem, and my son—well, the Crown Prince's will is not as strong as it should be. He is too romantic. He spends altogether too much time with the priests of Aten." She released a nervous laugh. "If Pharaoh had other sons, I might allow him to become a priest. But aside from Neferkheprure' Wa'enre', my womb has brought forth only daughters."

"It is unfortunate," Akil pressed his hands together, "but since your daughters are heiresses of the royal line of Pharaohs, a marriage between Sitamun and the vizier's son might result in a Hebrew rising to the great throne of Egypt. But of course you have considered this—"

"Of course I have," she snapped, cutting him off. She frowned and leaned back in her chair, disturbed that a mere servant had so adroitly expressed her deepest fear. She was the Great Wife, the highest-ranking queen, and therefore Sitamun, as the eldest daughter, would carry the line of succession. If something happened to the Crown Prince, Sitamun's husband or child would inherit the throne of Egypt.

Zaphenath-paneah's grandchild as Pharaoh? The thought tasted like bitter gall on her tongue.

She pressed her hand to her lips, thinking. She had advanced the idea of a royal marriage and even encouraged Manasseh's idiotic flirtation with a slave in order to win influence with the vizier's sons, but they had obviously failed to sway Zaphenath-paneah in her favor. Apparently the opinions of the sons mattered little to the father, and judging by Manasseh's actions in the northern wilderness, the convictions of the father were of no consequence to at least one son.

Ignoring Akil's death-bright eyes, she sat without speaking and toyed with a strand of her wig. An idea had begun to form in her mind, an elusive notion that might prove unpopular in Sitamun's eyes but would certainly be acceptable both to the priests and to the people. And Sitamun, creature of comfort that she was, would be convinced of the plan's wisdom if the attendant benefits were adequately stressed. Ephraim might rage, but who would care? If he behaved inappropriately, he would furnish yet another reason for Pharaoh to banish Zaphenath-paneah and his troublesome sons from court. The three influential Hebrew men had already proven themselves a danger to Egypt's welfare.

"Akil," she turned toward him. "Would you do anything for me?"

"Anything, my Queen." His eyes filled with fierce sparkling.

"Then you will be my spy within the house of Zaphenath-paneah," she announced, girding herself with fresh resolve. Her eyes locked on the musician's. "Since you once lived there, you are the perfect choice. You and your women, your entire orchestra, shall return to the vizier's house. The annals shall record that you are a gift from Pharaoh to the former vizier, a tribute to his work and devotion."

She heard his quick intake of breath. "You would have me leave you?" He managed a tremulous smile. "But Pharaoh—"

"Pharaoh can employ any musician he wishes," Tiy answered, recognizing the sharp light of attraction gleaming from within the man's deep eyes. As the chironomist's expression tightened with strain, Tiy leaned forward and reassuringly placed her hand upon his arm. "Do this for me, Akil, and all will be well with you. Go to the vizier's villa. Make yourself one of the household. Find a weakness I may exploit. Send word to me, and then I will bring you back to Pharaoh's palace and shower you with blessings. You will not regret leaving Malkata."

He smiled in relief. "As you wish, my Queen. My only desire is to serve you."

With careful dignity he rose from his chair and slipped to the floor in a bow.

"Rise and go." Tiy tilted her head as she watched him obey. His eyes did not lift to hers before he turned to shuffle away, and she bit her thumbnail, hoping she had trusted the right man.

"*Who* is going *where*?" Jendayi lifted her head from her bed, not certain she'd heard Kesi correctly. She had been enjoying a nap, a luxury in the middle of the hot afternoon, and Kesi had burst into the servant's quarters babbling about someone moving to a villa.

"Wake up!" Kesi's voice brimmed with excitement amid the soft sounds of garments being pulled from their woven storage baskets and flung onto an empty bed. "We are to pack at once. The master says we will leave Malkata before dark. Can you imagine? We are going to live with the vizier!"

The vizier? Jendayi dropped her head back onto the pillow of her arms, convinced Kesi was nothing but a vivid dream. But when Kissa and Sakmet rushed into the chamber, chattering like excited monkeys, Jendayi lifted her head again and strained to sift through their babble.

"Will someone please tell me exactly what is happening?" She pushed herself to a sitting position. She felt the bedclothes beneath her, the breath of the wind from the open door. This was no dream.

"According to Pharaoh's chamberlain, Zaphenath-paneah has retired," Kesi explained. "Pharaoh will choose two new viziers tomorrow, one to govern Upper Egypt, the other to govern the nomes of Lower Egypt. And to show his gratitude for years of gracious service, the king is returning Akil and his orchestra to the vizier's house." Her voice rose in an excited squeal. "That means us, Jendayi!"

Jendayi caught her breath as the shock of discovery hit her full force. Could this news possibly be true? Zaphenath-paneah had been the one and only vizier since before she had been born. Legends of folklore reported that he had bounced the toddling Pharaoh upon his knee. Paintings of the vizier graced at least a hundred buildings and granaries in Thebes, for the people of the Black Land revered him as Giver of Plenty and the Bread of Life. Zaphenath-paneah was a living legend! He had been blessed by the gods. Some common folk insisted that the spirit of a god rested upon him.

So how could he no longer be vizier? The sun could not stop being the sun, nor could the river pull up its waters and refuse to refresh the land. And just two days ago the women had played at a banquet for the king and his vizier. The voices of both men had echoed with concern and mutual respect. It was neither natural nor logical that Pharaoh should suddenly decree that the time had come for his vizier to go away.

But Pharaoh could be influenced by stronger voices.

Kesi's broad hand fell upon Jendayi's shoulder. "Wake up, little sister!" she whispered, the sickly sweet scent of beer on her breath. "Did you not hear me? We are going to the vizier's house!

You will sleep tonight under the same roof as your beloved Ephraim!"

Manasseh will not be there. For some inexplicable reason, that unsettling thought hurtled through Jendayi's mind. Confused, she blinked up at her maid. "I suppose this is good news," she answered, frowning.

"Of course it is." Kesi sank to Jendayi's side and gripped the harpist's arm with her hot hand. "Do you remember how Ephraim kissed you in his father's garden? Perhaps the gods have answered your prayers. You will come full circle. You will live in his house again, and he will kiss you again. His affection for you, already in bud, will open to the fullness of blossom! He no longer needs to ask Pharaoh to sell you! He must only ask his father's permission to make you a concubine, and surely the vizier would not withhold such a favor from his son. The gods have smiled upon you, my lady."

"Ephraim is going to marry Princess Sitamun," Jendayi remarked dully, wondering why this unexpected miracle did not thrill her. For months she had hoped and prayed for just such a turn of events, but now she could only think of the vizier's house as an incomplete, empty place.

Kesi placed a light finger to Jendayi's cheek. "Those reports of Ephraim's marriage to the princess are only rumors." A teasing tone filled her voice. "Akil says the princess will be married soon, but not to the vizier's son. Our master has already begun to write a song in honor of the wedding."

"Ephraim will not marry?" Jendayi turned her face toward Kesi and clutched the maid's arm.

"Akil says Ephraim will not marry any of Pharaoh's daughters." Kesi patted her mistress's hand with confident pressure. "And Akil is never wrong."

Disturbed, Jendayi turned her face away to consider this new development. Manasseh had certainly been wrong. He had tried his best to convince her to forget Ephraim. He had lied about his name, lied about Ephraim's marriage. Had he lied about *everything*?

Kesi hopped up to continue her packing, and Jendayi sat as motionless as stone while her head swirled with doubts. Why would Manasseh tell her Ephraim did not love her? Did he hate her so much that he was driven to break her heart? Surely not. She was a slave who meant nothing to him. But if he did not hate her, then why would he attempt to—

She pressed her hand over her lips as her mind blew open. *Manasseh hated Ephraim.* She had heard bitterness in his voice when he spoke of his brother—twice. The time he remarked that Ephraim would not join him in the desert, and another time when he'd said that Ephraim was cocky and arrogant, that he gave too much attention to too many different women. And there had been rumors on the caravan from Canaan, stories about a rivalry between the two brothers—something about a family inheritance that should have gone to the firstborn but went instead to the more favored Ephraim.

Of course! Manasseh was jealous of his brother, bitter enough to damage the tender slip of love that had begun to grow in her heart, and ruthless enough to destroy his brother's happiness even as he hurried away from home in disgrace. Manasseh certainly cared nothing for a slave girl. His clumsy efforts to capture her heart had been part of a simple ploy to undermine Ephraim's attempt to redeem her from Pharaoh.

Like a weed among barren desert stones, hope sprouted suddenly in her breast. Somehow, through magic or divine influence, Ephraim had won! Manasseh had been defeated, and Ephraim had managed to arrange for her transfer to his father's house. He, not Manasseh, had sent her the message in Canaan, and he waited now at his father's house to reclaim the love his lips had sealed so many years before.

She sat in delighted surprise for a moment, then stood and reached toward the wall where her harp rested. Let Akil write songs to praise the princess and her future husband. She would write a song herself, one unlike any she had ever written before. It would resonate with hope and love and the sweetness of a fulfilled dream. And when Ephraim heard it, he would know that she had come home to him.

———

Night had spread her sable wings over Malkata by the time Tiy's Medjay spy arrived from the vizier's villa. She received him in her innermost chamber, anxious for any news from

Zaphenath-paneah's house. To her surprise, however, the spy did not bring word of the vizier's reaction to Pharaoh's decree, but news of a different sort.

"We found the rebel camp to the west of Tura," the man reported, pausing to calmly wipe a trickle of sweat from his brow. "They move every night but have circled back to an area just east of Pharaoh's quarry. The captain of the vizier's guard expects Zaphenath-paneah to send us to apprehend them on the morrow—"

"I think not," Tiy interrupted. Resting her chin on her hand, she gave the Medjay warrior a bemused smile. "Remember that you do my bidding, not the vizier's."

"Yes, my Queen." If she had not known him to be as hard as flint, she would have thought he flushed, for two dark spots appeared on his cheeks.

"Besides"—Tiy ignored his possible discomfort—"as of today, the vizier no longer has authority to arrest men in the king's name." She curved her long fingers around the armrest of her chair. "I doubt he is currently in a frame of mind to do anything."

The Nubian frowned in confusion, and Tiy snapped her fingers at the pair of slaves fanning her with ostrich feathers. They whirled and left the chamber, disappearing as quickly as shadows at noonday. Then Tiy propped her chin on her hand and again considered the warrior standing before her. With the craggy look of an unfinished sculpture, he was not the most handsome man she had ever seen, but there was restless energy in his movements and firm strength in the shoulders and arms that gleamed in the soft lamplight. His legs were as brown and firm as cedars, and in his strong features she saw traces of a certain sensuality. His face was as hard as granite, like his eyes.

She raked his body with her gaze, then smiled as he peered at her with the wary look of an untamed animal. This one, she knew, would not be immune to her charms.

"So you are the notorious Hondo?" she asked, steepling her hands at her waist.

Lethal calmness filled his eyes. "Yes, my Queen."

"Even your name means war." She observed him through lowered lashes. He tilted his brow, studying her, and she knew he sensed the ripple of excitement flowing through her blood.

Unlike Zaphenath-paneah, this man would do anything to please her.

She stared at him until he lifted his brows in a silent query, then she spoke again. "Hondo, I must take you into my confidence. Can you be trusted?"

The grooves beside his mouth deepened in a smug smile. "Implicitly, my Queen."

"Good." She rose fluidly from her chair and moved toward him, impelled both by her frustrated passion and by the knowledge that Amenhotep frolicked with his harem only a few paces away. "I need a reliable warrior, a man who will be discreet. Most of all"—she moved so close that her breath softly fanned his face—"I need a man who is willing to die for me."

He stiffened defensively but began to melt when she lifted her finger to trace the shadow above his upper lip. "Of course you will not have to die," she said, noticing that the light of desire now illuminated his tumultuous dark eyes. "I ask only that you are willing to do so."

"I do not fear death, for a man may live forever in a queen's favor," he whispered, pressing the warmth of his palm to her shoulder.

"You are a brave one." She lifted her hand and brought it to the burnished mahogany of his cheek. "For the liberty you took in touching me just now, I could demand your life."

"But you won't."

"No." She regarded him with a lurking smile. "You, Hondo, will not die for touching me, nor for anything else your heart desires tonight. But if you do not do exactly as I tell you regarding Manasseh, the elder son of Zaphenath-paneah, you will most certainly die at Pharaoh's command." Her hand caught his and brought it to her lips. "A most painful and torturous death," she whispered in a breathless voice as she lightly kissed each fingertip. Tilting her head, she gave him a sleepy-eyed smile. "Do you understand, Hondo?"

He had no patience for contemplative thoughts. "I understand," he murmured in the instant before his mouth covered hers.

~ Twenty-three ~

EPHRAIM MOVED THROUGH THE VILLA WITH A LOOSE-boned, easy gait, intent upon finding his father. A full month had passed since Pharaoh had unexpectedly discharged his vizier, but Ephraim had seen no more of his father in the last month than he had when Joseph had been at Pharaoh's constant beck and call. His father used to fill his days and nights with work. Ephraim suspected that he now filled them with regret.

And to think that I once longed for the day when my father would no longer be vizier! I never dreamed his life would empty out into nothingness.

Ani had said that Zaphenath-paneah would doubtless be found in the garden, and Ephraim knew the vast walled sanctuary was one of the few places in the villa that now brought his father any pleasure. The grand reception hall seemed to mock the vizier's former lofty position, and Joseph's own chambers, though spacious, must seem confining and claustrophobic when compared to the wide spaces of Pharaoh's palace. A master had no business in the servants' quarters, stable, or kitchens, so Joseph had begun to haunt the garden. Among the mandrakes, acacia trees, and lotus blossoms, Ephraim suspected Joseph was assuring himself that he and Pharaoh would stand as equals under the sun.

The time of mourning should soon come to an end, however, and Ephraim was determined to pull his father from the cloud of gloom that surrounded him. He did not know exactly what had transpired between Pharaoh and Joseph, but Ephraim knew that the two younger men who had been appointed to fill the vizier's position were already showing signs of strain. Though they were bright and capable, the effort of carrying just half the load of Joseph's job had left them haggard and drawn. Ephraim had heard from a dozen nobles that Amenhotep had already expressed private reservations about the capabilities of his new viziers. But a great deal of responsibility had been placed in Queen Tiy's capable hands, and if she did not complain about her additional duties, the dual vizier system would probably remain in place.

The rising sun had painted a golden glow over everything in the garden, and Ephraim felt his spirits lift as he strolled along the paved path and nodded at the slaves who maneuvered the towering shadufs and watered the plants. Catching sight of his father's dark head beneath the pavilion at the far edge of the garden, Ephraim hurried toward him. He had an idea that he thought his father would approve, a plan to unite the best Egyptian artists and Hebrew builders in order to create a trading center in Goshen, a signature city that would pave the way for others like it. If Joseph warmed to the idea, the work would fill his days, occupy his thoughts, and please both Pharaoh and Joseph's Hebrew brothers.

If he heard Ephraim approaching, Joseph gave no sign of it. He sat motionless in his chair, his elbows planted upon his knees, his eyes drawn into slits as if he concentrated on some vision nearly lost in the past or future. An aura of melancholy radiated from his handsome features like a dark nebula, and for an instant Ephraim slowed his steps, caught up in the fearful reverence that had marked all his childhood meetings with his powerful father.

But he was a child no longer. The tide had turned, and *he* was now the stronger one. Hadn't Jacob foretold this? The old patriarch must have known that Joseph would be incapacitated and Manasseh distracted by dreams of battlefield glory. The mantle of leadership had fallen squarely upon Ephraim's shoulders.

"Father," he called, breaking the spell of silence. He rested one foot on the first step of the pavilion and leaned forward, held back by the old ritual he and Manasseh had been bound to obey since the beginning of their formal education.

His father's lids came swiftly over his eyes as if guarding a secret, but after a moment he turned to measure his son with a cool appraising look. "Do you no longer bow before your father, Ephraim? Or have you joined the thousands who no longer respect me?"

Forever in control, his father was still granting favors, making judgments, reading the will of both God and Pharaoh.

Refusing to prostrate himself on the tile, Ephraim inclined his head in a deep gesture, then looked up and gave his father a warm smile. "I will always respect you as my father." He took another half-step forward. "And I have wanted to speak with you." Clearing his throat, he made an effort to lighten his voice. "You have avoided me these past weeks, but we ought to talk about Pharaoh's decision."

"It is not a subject I want to discuss." Joseph's gaze turned again to that faraway place.

"Why would you avoid it when everyone in Thebes knows what happened? It is not a story, Father, that can be hidden. But neither is the tale of Pharaoh's new viziers. Both of them have already encountered the royal wrath. The king cannot abide them, and the nomarchs are complaining that these men are not able to handle the details of taxation, the temple properties, the rituals of marking boundaries after the flood—"

"Pharaoh will find someone else, then."

"He may." Ephraim lifted his brows, encouraged that his father was still listening. They had never been close, but in the last month Joseph's indifference had extended even to Ani and Tarik, the two most trusted servants in his household. Both men were more like lifetime companions than servants, but Joseph's grief had cut them off completely.

"Father, I can help you." Ephraim decided to be blunt. "I have an idea to build a trading center in Goshen. We will need your knowledge and influence with the governor and merchants of that area. It will be a good work, and I am certain you will enjoy it. Pharaoh will be pleased, and later, when Sitamun and I are married, I will use my influence with Pharaoh to convince him to forgive whatever trouble arose between you."

"There was no trouble." The statement rang with reproach. "None whatsoever between Pharaoh and me. If you have heard otherwise, you are listening to liars."

"So you say," Ephraim answered. The conversation had spun out of his control, and his father's contemptuous tone sparked his own cynicism. "Of course Pharaoh had no problems with you. That's why he dismissed you without warning. That's why he gave your duties to incompetent men."

Joseph did not answer, and Ephraim's mood veered sharply to fury. Would his father never understand that his sons were capable of helping him? Joseph was so arrogantly self-sufficient, so infuriatingly capable! Could he not admit that he had somehow failed Pharaoh? Counselors frequently disagreed with Amenhotep, and if the confrontations were not too severe, they were brought back to court after an apology and a sacrificial offering of praise to the divine king. Why could his father not admit he was human?

"Almost"—Ephraim held tight to the bridled anger in his voice—"I am beginning to understand why Manasseh left this house."

Joseph looked up, his black eyes impaling his son. "Do you understand? Then explain it to me. I do not know why my elder son would rebel. He says he must obey God, and so he disobeys his father and breaks Pharaoh's law. And I, who have struggled always to obey, am the one who is punished." He looked away. His hand, trembling slightly, reached out to nudge a butterfly from the arm of an empty chair. "When I was young, I was told to grow up, to act like a man. Now that I have grown old, I am looked upon as a child, even by my own son."

"Father, I only want what is best for you."

"Then leave me." When Joseph met Ephraim's gaze again, his wise dark eyes had filled with a curious deep longing. "You were never as old as I am, Ephraim, but I was once as young as you are now. You cannot know what is best for me. Only God knows . . . if He has not abandoned us."

Ephraim stepped back, shaken by his father's honesty. Whether he spoke as Joseph the Hebrew or Zaphenath-paneah the Egyptian, his father's proclamations had always been as certain as the sunrise, as sure as the force that pulled objects from the sky to the earth. But the uncertainty in his expression now shook Ephraim to the core.

Without another word, he slipped from the pavilion and retreated through the garden.

———

Jendayi took her seat on the stool against the chamber wall and gently strummed the harp strings to test the tuning she'd just given them. Almost perfect. One string was a little sharp, but she could adjust the pitch by pinching the string at the proper time. The men at this banquet probably wouldn't notice a slight dissonance of tone, but everything had to be perfect in Jendayi's ear, especially when Ephraim was present.

Dinner was Jendayi's favorite hour at the vizier's villa. With dependable regularity she and the others of the orchestra were summoned to the central hall where the aromas of rich foods mingled in a delightful symphony of smells. As her fingers fell into the independent motions forged through long hours of practice, her ears sought the smooth sound of Ephraim's baritone.

Today, like always, she found him. Over the last month she had managed to identify most of the major attendants at Zaphenath-paneah's midday banquet, and she was quietly astounded that so few visitors came to socialize with the esteemed nobleman who had been so illustrious a vizier. She remembered that as a child she had been overwhelmed by the vast crowds who came to consult with the vizier. Every day the banquet hall had echoed with new voices, strange accents, and lilting languages from all over the known world. But now she regularly heard the voices of only four men: Tarik, captain of the guard; Ani, the aged steward; the vizier himself; and Ephraim.

As long as Ephraim was present, she tended to ignore the other three. They did not speak much anyway. But Ephraim held, controlled, and enlivened the conversation. His sparkling wit, the rich timbre of his laughter, the subtle crescendo of his voice as he strove to make a point when debating with the steward or the captain—all these things she noticed. And though she could not see him, she was certain that in moments of strained silence when only her harp spoke, he looked at her . . . and remembered.

The memory of Ephraim's kiss was now stronger than her recollection of Manasseh on the riverbank. The elder son had vanished like a dream at dawn. No one at the vizier's house even spoke of him. She could not discover exactly why his name had been obliterated from all conversations, but though the four men spoke of many things, they never referred to Manasseh's past, present, or future.

She once asked Kesi if she found it odd that the members of the household behaved as if Manasseh had never existed, and the maid only laughed. "Grown men leave home and lead their own lives," she answered flippantly. "You imagine too much, Jendayi."

But Jendayi could see with other than physical eyes, and her spirit could not help but sense the thick cloud of disapproval that filled certain breaks in conversation, unexpected lulls in the laughter, conspicuous gaps in the questions of friends and relatives—all were empty spaces where Manasseh's name should have been.

Perhaps he deserved to be ignored, she told herself. After all, he had lied to her, and he was obviously engaged in serious wrongdoing if the noble Zaphenath-paneah had disowned him.

Yet though she still felt anger for the lies he had told her, another part of Jendayi's heart squeezed in anguish for him as time passed and the obvious public omission of his name opened the door on memories she had tried to lock away. How could the vizier pretend Manasseh did not exist? How could any parent ignore a child? Had *her* mother, whoever she was, blotted out all thoughts of the daughter she birthed and then abandoned? Did she ever stop to sacrifice in the temple for Jendayi's health and prosperity or light a lamp on the anniversary of Jendayi's birth? Did *she* dream of standing in the Hall of the Two Truths and being eaten alive for her lack of love?

Jendayi's breath came raggedly in impotent anger, then she heard the irritated snap of Akil's fingers, signaling she was rushing the beat. She inhaled deeply, forcing herself to slow down, and commanded her fingers to divorce themselves from her feelings. Just as she had ordered her heart not to think about Ephraim.

Ephraim had promised to arrange her release from Pharaoh's house, and he had. But a month had passed and he had not spoken to her or sought out her company. She often took her harp into the garden alone, hoping he would seek her there, but he did not. Though Jendayi followed his voice every day in her blind darkness, she was no closer to being loved than she had been in Pharaoh's palace. Yet here she had to endure the sting of jealousy, for the other female servants talked constantly of Ephraim, praising his charm, his wit, his attractive face and form. They twittered self-consciously when he walked by, while Jendayi sat in silence, awaiting some word of confirmation that he had acted on her behalf . . . and out of love.

But in the uncomfortable silences and dirgelike conversations of the household, she discovered one possible reason for Ephraim's reluctance to approach her: Zaphenath-paneah's household mourned. No one had to tell her that the former vizier had not accepted his fall from grace, for often the atmosphere

LEGACIES OF THE ANCIENT RIVER

within the villa was as heavy and desolate as a tomb. And while the father agonized, she assured herself, the son could not rightly speak of love.

So she would have to wait, even though waiting demanded every ounce of patience Jendayi possessed. Since her return to the vizier's house, her nightmares had intensified. Nearly every night she dreamed of standing before the scales of truth and watching her granite heart sink like a stone opposite the feather of Ma'at.

Just last night the ebony eyes of the jackal god had blazed fire upon her. "You are a waste of flesh and blood!" Anubis' voice ripped through the Hall of the Two Truths like a screaming cyclone. "Why did we give you life? You are nothing. You have loved nothing. You have done nothing but waste the gods' gift."

"What did you want me to do?" she cried. "How do you expect me to find love as a slave? You may as well tell me to count the waves of the Nile. It is impossible!"

Anubis did not defend himself, for he was a god, and Thoth did not offer a word in reply. As Jendayi nervously tested the hold of the treacherous floor upon her bare feet, Ammit crept relentlessly forward, his crocodile head gleaming, his lion's paws thick and heavy upon the shining floor. Iron-willed and hard as steel, he bore down upon her. She thrust her hands before her eyes, coveting her mortal blindness, while a high, shrill, piercing ring deafened her ears—

Her own scream. Kesi had awakened her, prying her from the terrible dream.

Now in the scented banquet hall where blessedly mortal voices wrapped around her, Jendayi caressed the familiar strings of her harp and urged them to speak the secret language of her soul, soft sounds that would woo Ephraim to her side. And more than once, as she played with unusual brilliance, she felt a flush steal over her cheek . . . and knew he was watching.

———

While the other female musicians spent the hot afternoons in sleep or gentle conversation, Jendayi preferred the solitude of the walled garden. The spot was a favorite of Zaphenath-paneah's, but he avoided it during the heat of the day, so she did not worry about disturbing him. After dinner every afternoon, as the engorged guests retreated to their work or their chambers, she picked up her harp and slipped away from Kesi to find her way to the garden.

One of the servants had described the garden's design, so she knew that the reflecting pool lay beyond the portico, and behind the pool stood the master's pavilion. Around the pool, the servant told her, date palms and dom palms had been arranged with clumps of papyrus, while figs and sycamore mingled between those plantings. A host of flowers grew in planters near the water's edge: red poppies and blue cornflowers, purple irises, white lilies, and yellow chrysanthemums.

Jendayi could smell the biting scent of the chrysanthemums as her sandals clapped against the tile of the garden pathway. The servant had not told her that blue lotus blossoms floated in abundance upon the surface of the pool; those blossoms announced their own sweet presence. The lotus, long a symbol of rebirth and beauty in Egypt, was the Queen Mother's favorite flower. Whenever the orchestra had been summoned to play for the regal Queen Tuya, the sweet scent of the flowers seemed to linger with Jendayi for days.

Her questing feet found the pavilion. She carefully managed the stairs and fumbled for the armrest of a chair. After seating herself, she paused a moment to listen. Water splashed near the pool, but those sounds came from the slaves watering the thirsty flowers. Except for the servants, she was alone.

Sweet silence. Nodding to herself, Jendayi pulled her harp to her chest and began to play a tune that had surfaced in her imagination during dinner. Two fanciful melodies had played themselves again and again in her head, and some part of Jendayi knew they were meant to be played together, one voice complementing the other, one rhythm serving as a dynamic contrast to its mate. *Like you and Ephraim,* a little voice spoke in her head. *He will teach you to love, and you will teach him to . . . what?*

Her hand slipped and she frowned, curling her mutinous fingers into a tight ball. Her body wouldn't cooperate. One hand refused to play its melody independently. As a child she had easily managed the old trick of simultaneously patting her head and rubbing her stomach, but commanding one hand to play smoothly while the other plucked out a sharp, bright countermelody seemed as impossible as scratching her ear with her elbow.

"Why the frown, my dear?"

Jendayi flinched, startled. She must have been deep in concentration not to hear the old steward's approach. But though he had surprised her, she was not afraid. His voice, as always, brimmed with tender concern.

"I'm sorry, master." She modestly ducked her head. She tried to rise and bow, but the harp stood in front of her.

"Do not bother with formalities here." The old man sank into the empty chair beside her. His voice sounded tired. "What I heard of your song was lovely. So why do you frown?"

"It wasn't all I meant it to be." She slapped her hand against the strings, risking a small display of temper. "I hear the tune in my head and know how it ought to come out of my fingers, but they will not obey. If I can create it in my head, I ought to be able to play it."

"The gods create us, but they cannot always bend us to their wills," Ani answered, a surprising degree of warmth and concern in his voice. "But they have given you a great gift. Except for the enchanting melodies you put there, no music would dare enter my weary head."

The steward fell silent, and Jendayi felt her polite smile fade. He had not sought her out to talk about music. That was Akil's responsibility. *She* was Akil's responsibility and only indirectly accountable to the steward. So why had he come to her?

Her whole being concentrated on sounds that might give her a clue, but she heard nothing except whispers of foot traffic drifting over the high walls of the garden and the soft lap of irrigation buckets scooping up the pool's calm water.

Ani's hoarse whisper finally broke the silence between them. "I thought you might like to talk about my master's son."

"Ephraim?" Anxiety spurted through her. Had Ani's legendary insight uncovered her hopes? Had she, in an unguarded moment, allowed her face to reveal too much of her heart? She might have looked adoringly at Ephraim. The others might have seen and cast knowing looks toward one another. Perhaps the entire household was laughing at her! One of the worst things about blindness was missing the myriad ways people communicated through nonverbal glances, gestures, expressions. . . .

"Why would I speak to you of Ephraim?" The old steward

spoke in a neutral tone, without inflection, but a warning voice whispered in Jendayi's head. Was this a test?

"He is the only son here in the villa," she answered carefully, her heart beginning to race. "And what I have heard here leads me to believe he is the only living son."

"Bah! You and I both know that the vizier's elder son lives. If he did not, the vizier could not deny him, for one cannot deny the existence of that which does not exist." She heard the steward sigh. "Misery weighs upon my heart like an iron weight, for Manasseh has been like my own son for many years. He has often shared his heart with me, even more than with his father. The vizier, you see, has always been busy with Pharaoh's affairs."

"I don't see," she said, wincing slightly at the tortured sound of his voice, "what this has to do with me."

"Don't you?" His short bark of humor lacked laughter. "Manasseh told me of your . . . *friendship* with him." The cold edge of irony crept into his voice. "He also told me you fancy yourself in love with Ephraim—on account of a kiss given years ago."

Her cheeks burned. "I told him those things in confidence. He should not have told you."

"I am his friend," the old man continued as easily as if he discussed the grain harvest and not the critical state of Jendayi's heart. "I know him better than anyone in this household. And because he considers you his friend, I thought perhaps I could help you."

"How?" Fueled by hopeless anger, a ripple of mirth bubbled into her voice. Manasseh had asked her to have faith in him and his God, and then she had discovered that he was the basest sort of liar. How could this steward change that truth?

"You are an old man," she answered, trying to be respectful. "And though you love Manasseh, he is gone, and you cannot bring him back. Apparently you could not even change his mind about leaving. So how can you help me?"

"I had thought to prevent your heart from being more blind than your eyes." A silken thread of warning laced his voice. "If you truly love Ephraim, well, I cannot hope to command the passions of your heart. I love him myself. But because I have been like a father to both sons of Zaphenath-paneah, I know their natures. And Ephraim will not make you happy, little harpist, no matter what your heart may tell you."

"He will!" she blurted out, scarcely aware of her own voice. "He loves me. He can teach me to love."

"Ah, my child." The aged man's hand came to rest upon the top of her head, and Jendayi fought the impulse to jerk away. "Perhaps you live in an imaginary world. Certainly you hear things I cannot. But you are alone there. If you want to find love, you must come out and seek it as resolutely as Isis sought the coffin of her beloved Osiris."

How? She wanted to scream, but her pride kept her from crying out. She resisted, not speaking, and after a moment the pressure of his hand lifted, and his sandals slowly shuffled away over the marble tiles on the garden path.

How could she seek love? She was as helpless as a plant without water. She owned nothing, not even her freedom. She shuddered as the floodgates opened and her torment found its way out through her tears. She was *a waste of flesh and blood*. Nightly the gods railed at her, foretelling her destruction, and Jendayi could do nothing but agree that they had judged correctly.

———

Ani strolled slowly, blankly watching his sandals fall upon the smooth tiles of the garden path, his thoughts far away. Manasseh had been foolish to lose his heart to such a faithless young girl, but love was often as savage as a chained tiger and as unexpected as a midnight assassin.

In spite of Ani's long-standing resolve not to dwell on the past, inexorably his mind returned to his youth. Long before he had come to Zaphenath-paneah's villa, he had fallen in love with a young slave called Salihah. A slim graceful beauty, she had stolen his heart in just one look. They worked together for weeks, each one shyly loving the other through tender words and teasing glances, until the master took Salihah to his chamber. She resisted his advances, and in his anger he cut her face, marring her loveliness forever. As helpless grief overwhelmed Ani, the steward of the estate took Salihah away and sold her as damaged goods at a slave auction.

Ani never saw or heard from Salihah again. Yet even now, when he had time for introspection, his vision gloomily colored with memories of the woman with whom he had shared only a few words, a score of stolen smiles, and one brief caress as their hands touched. Through the shadow of memory, one terrible, gnawing thought haunted him: had he unwittingly been the instrument of her destruction? Did she resist the master for Ani's sake?

A slave, he decided many restless nights after Salihah's departure, should not risk loving anyone. And because he adored both Ephraim and Manasseh, he did not want either of them to hurt the little harpist and suffer the guilt he had borne for a lifetime.

The sharp smell of burning wood intruded in his thoughts, and Ani lifted his head. Because timber was a rare and valuable commodity, the odor of burning wood usually meant that a clumsy kitchen slave had allowed a grease fire to get out of hand. Stopping, he sniffed the air and frowned. The scent was not coming from the area of the kitchens, but from the front of the villa.

In a zigzag crouch Ani raced to the courtyard. Tarik's guards would certainly have the situation under control, but Ani still wanted to vent his displeasure. The household could not afford to squander valuable materials now. . . .

He rounded the corner, then stared wordlessly across the open space of the courtyard, his heart pounding. The fire was not accidental. Ani had never seen anything like the sight that greeted his bleary eyes.

Zaphenath-paneah stood in the center of the courtyard before a towering formation of lumber piled waist high. Thirsty orange red flames licked the base of the dry wood, tonguing high into the shimmering air. Behind the master, a host of wide-eyed guards stood at attention in wordless wonder. A line of slaves stood to one side, their linen kilts stained with blood, their biceps bulging under the weight of loaded bowls and trays.

Ani was barely able to control his gasp of surprise when, after inching forward, he realized that the servants carried the butchered remains of a bull. The last bowl, he noted with distaste, brimmed with blood alone.

Surprise siphoned words from his tongue, and he pressed his hand over his mouth to keep from wailing mindlessly. Had the master lost his sanity? Though the Egyptian cult of Apis venerated the bull, the priests accomplished all things decently and in accordance with the prescribed order of rituals, not in the center of a courtyard and certainly not in the most extreme heat of the day.

The sacred bulls—those with a white crescent on one side of their bodies or a black lump under their tongues—were considered the offspring of Ptah, born of virgin cows, and destined for a life of service in the temple. The priests of Ptah cared for the bulls for twenty-five years, then quietly drowned and embalmed them.

A rise of panic threatened to choke Ani as he stared at the bloody scene. Never would a priest of Ptah consider such a violent act as this! And Zaphenath-paneah, who devoutly worshiped the invisible and Almighty God of the Hebrews, had never spoken of Ptah or worshiped the Apis bull at Memphis. In fact, the vizier worshiped in no temple at all. In all the winding length of Ani's memory, Zaphenath-paneah had never, ever offered a sacrifice—particularly one as gruesome as this.

"What should we do?"

Startled by Tarik's voice, Ani glanced up. Intense astonishment was also inscribed upon the captain's tanned face.

"He gave you no warning?" Ani whispered, sneaking another glance at his master. "There was no hint of what he had in mind?"

Tarik jerked his chin toward the vizier in a subtle gesture. "This morning he asked for a bull, free from blemish," he answered, calmly locking his hands behind his back. "Then he instructed the kitchen slaves to butcher the entire animal, reserving no part of it for themselves or for dinner. Even the blood has been caught."

"I noticed," Ani remarked, his voice flat.

"Well?" Tarik lifted an eyebrow. "Have you ever seen anything like this? You are a wise and learned man. You should know what he is doing."

"It may be a Hebrew custom, but I know nothing of it." Ani's voice faded to a hushed stillness as the master stepped back and lifted his hands.

A tense silence enveloped the courtyard. Even the nesting birds on the rim of the villa's walls ceased their warbling. Zaphenath-paneah closed his eyes and lifted his face toward the blue vault of heaven. "El Shaddai, God of Abraham, Isaac, and Jacob," he prayed, his voice breaking with huskiness. "Forgive, I beg you, the sins of this household, of my sons. For you have taken your blessing from us, and we are lost without you."

Ani searched anxiously for the meaning behind the words. Zaphenath-paneah was the wisest man in the kingdom. The spirit of a god rested upon him always—everyone said so. So how could he believe that his God had deserted him?

Lowering his hands, the vizier opened his eyes, then took two sizable hunks of raw wounded meat from the first servant's bowl and tossed them into the flames. "Without the shedding of blood there is no pardon of sin." His eyes remained upon the flames as his hands moved again from the bowl to the fire, offering other portions of meat to the sizzling inferno. "And just as I have ordered that the entire bull shall be offered unto you with nothing held back, know that my entire household shall be dedicated to you, O God Shaddai."

The line of servants continued forward, each man bearing his burden in silence as Zaphenath-paneah emptied his tray or bowl onto the altar. The pungent aromas of roasting meat and sizzling fat permeated the air as the master worked. Finally, as the last servant offered the bowl of blood, Zaphenath-paneah took it and held it high above his head for a moment, then moved around the fire, spattering the lower logs with the crimson liquid.

When the last drop of blood had been spilt, the master clasped his bloodstained hands in front of his once spotless robe and bowed his head. "The sacrifice has been offered as Noah and Abraham and Jacob offered it," he said simply. "May God forgive those of my household who have sinned." After a moment of silence, he lifted his head. His powerful dark gaze raked the gathering until he found Ani and Tarik.

"See that no one disturbs the offering," he commanded, moving toward them. "Absolutely nothing is to be eaten. All is to be consumed by the fire."

"Yes, my lord." Tarik lifted his arm in salute.

The master nodded and moved through the crowd, which parted for him, but the nagging fears in the back of Ani's mind refused to be stilled as Zaphenath-paneah walked away.

Three days passed with snail-like slowness while Joseph waited for word of Manasseh's repentance and return. He had offered his sacrifice with every expectation that God would honor a public confession and humiliation, and yet there had been no sign that his erring son had experienced a change of heart.

Why not? Breakfasting in the garden, Joseph waved away the slaves who lingered with fresh wine and steaming loaves of sweet lotus bread. He had not touched the dainties on the tray before him. His appetite had disappeared days before. He wanted nothing more than to be left alone with his thoughts.

The king's disdainful dismissal had left him reeling, but Joseph was now certain the situation was God's call for him to set his house in order. Ephraim had pointed out something Joseph had been too upset to see—trouble *did* exist between Joseph and Amenhotep, and that trouble was Manasseh. This ignoble discharge had to be a direct result of Manasseh's rebellious actions, and once Manasseh had seen the error of his ways, things would certainly be set right. And so Joseph had humbled himself and offered a sacrifice like those of his forefathers, doubtless shocking his household and the nobles of Thebes, but worth every rumor and uplifted eyebrow if God worked and sent Manasseh home to repent. . . .

Tarik's frantic voice nudged Joseph out of his musing.

"Hail to the Mother of Egypt," the captain of the guard called, his voice hoarse with surprise and urgency. "She who is the Most Favored Lady, the Graciousness of the Nile, the Beginning-of-the-Divine-King desires an audience with you, Zaphenath-paneah!"

Tuya! Joseph took a quick breath of utter astonishment and turned toward the portico where Tarik had fallen prostrate on the tile. Two of the palace guards stood there facing each other with the tall graceful figure of Amenhotep's mother, Queen Tuya, between them.

For a moment the sight did not register on Joseph's dazzled senses. The Queen Mother had gone into seclusion after her son's marriage, forfeiting her own enormous popularity in order to allow her son and his wife to hold first place in the peoples' devotion. She rarely left her apartments in the palace, and never went about in the streets of Thebes. But here she was, her luminous eyes fastened on Joseph's face, regarding him with a look that made his breath leave his body.

Joseph suddenly remembered his manners. Tearing his gaze from hers, he rose from his chair and slipped to the floor, a wave of despair crashing over him as he felt the heat of the sun-warmed tiles on his hands and forehead. By heaven above, what had she heard? She must have thought him near death or insanity if urgency had compelled her to come to him.

"Rise, Zaphenath-paneah." Her voice rang with an infinitely compassionate tone, and Joseph's soul shrank from the sound of it. Pity! He had never accepted pity from any man and would not welcome it from a woman, not even one he had loved.

He rose to his feet and stared at her in stony silence. She wore a full short wig, a surprisingly youthful style for a woman of over fifty years, and her graceful figure had ripened to a womanly fullness. Uncommon delicacy and strength mingled in her lovely face. Soft color lingered in her sweetly curving lips. She wore on her pale face the fine lines of her age with a serene elegance. Time had not altered or diminished her vivid beauty.

"Leave us, please," she said, turning to one of the guards. Instantly the pair of warriors moved from the shade of the portico into the house, and after an instant's hesitation, Tarik followed them. The lingering slaves who carried the remains of Joseph's breakfast took their cue from the departing warriors and scurried away like rodents.

Joseph searched for words and could find none. Reading the surprise on his face, Tuya smiled and moved from the portico to the garden pathway. "I am afraid I have put you at a disadvantage." She folded her hands in a pose of tranquillity as she glided over the walkway. "Perhaps I should have sent word that I would come."

"My villa is always open to you." Joseph inclined his head.

"I appreciate the welcome," she answered, moving toward him with the sure grace of a deer. "Though I am not sure you are happy to see me."

She had reached the pavilion, and Joseph awkwardly extended a hand to the empty chair at his side. "Of course I am thrilled that you have come."

"Liar," she whispered, sliding gracefully into the carved chair. She leaned back, allowing the heavy fullness of her wig to tip her chin toward him. "You never could lie, Joseph. That is why Tuthmosis valued you so." One corner of her mouth dipped in a half-frown. "I'm only sorry Amenhotep doesn't value you in the same way. He is a good king, but he is not the man his father was."

Joseph lowered himself to the edge of his chair. "Is that why you are here? To tell me what we both know about Pharaoh?"

"No." She crossed her legs and leaned forward, resting one elbow on the arm of her chair. "You were at my side when Tuthmosis passed into the otherworld, but I was unable to stand by you when your wife died. You were a very public figure then, and I couldn't risk the rumors—"

"There is no need to explain." Joseph cut her off with an uplifted hand. "I know the dangers of palace gossip."

"Of course." She nodded almost imperceptibly. "But I truly believed you did not need me. You had your sons to comfort you, and you had God Shaddai. But now, Joseph, you grieve, and I wonder if you have either your sons or your God."

Her words lacerated him, and Joseph's jaw clenched as he rejected the softly spoken statement. "What do you mean? One son has left my house, just one, and God Shaddai would never leave me!"

Tuya's face emptied of expression, and Joseph felt a sudden icy silence surround her. He had hurt her but he didn't care. Like a scolding mother, she had stepped out of her pristine palace to rebuke and comfort him when he did not need comforting or rebuking.

"God has not left you," she went on in a strangled voice, turning her gaze toward the lotus blossoms in the reflecting pool, "but is it possible that you have left Him? This is not like you, Joseph. I have never seen that look upon your face, that anger in your eyes. I have heard about Manasseh, and I heard about your sacrifice. I thought perhaps you might feel as alone as I often do. . . ."

A weight of sadness lay upon her elegant face, and Joseph shuddered inwardly at the thought that he had put it there. He shook his head in regret. "I am sorry, Tuya, to have caused you pain. Manasseh has done much to hurt all of us, but I believe God will bring him home. And when Manasseh returns, all things will be restored to the order of God's will."

"God's will . . . or yours?" Tuya's dark eyes brimmed with life, pain, and unquenchable warmth as she turned to him. "Think, Joseph, before you believe your own words. And know that I will not cease to pray for you."

Standing, she straightened her shoulders, then moved with regal elegance toward the house, leaving Joseph alone with his thoughts.

～ Twenty-four ～

THE DESERT SUN STOOD PROUD IN THE WHITE BLUE SKY, baking both man and beast in its heat haze. Ephraim shifted upon his camel and slipped the reins from his sweaty left hand to his right. He and a bodyguard had taken one of his father's boats from Thebes to Tura, then led two cantankerous camels from the ship and set off for Manasseh's rebel camp. Tarik's last report placed it somewhere in the wilderness beyond the jagged mountains. Ephraim suspected he would find his errant brother and kinsmen at an oasis five miles south of his father's house at Tura Quarry.

Manasseh was undoubtedly the root cause of their lives' upheaval, and Ephraim was determined to confront him and end the havoc of the last few weeks. Because Manasseh had defied the king and returned to war, Joseph had been dismissed from royal service. And lately it had become clear that because Zaphenath-paneah was vizier no longer, Ephraim would never be allowed to take Sitamun as his wife. Though there had been no formal announcement that Ephraim would not be accepted as a suitor, he knew such a match was inconceivable as long as Manasseh remained outside Pharaoh's will. But if the rebel would come back to Thebes and apologize to Pharaoh, everything could be made right. Pharaoh was truly adamant only in his ambition and in his desire for pleasure. The king could be swayed in matters less important than his monuments or his women.

The camel's jolting gait had reduced Ephraim's muscles to jelly, but he shifted in the saddle again and continued sorting through his thoughts. Manasseh *had* to come to his senses, and the fate of Egypt and the sons of Israel rested upon his decision. The future had begun to unfold the way Ephraim thought it would—his father had withdrawn from leadership, leaving Ephraim firmly in charge, just as Jacob had foretold. Of course Ephraim hadn't realized how quickly his father would falter, or how *publicly* he would lose his grip on reality. Only four days earlier Joseph had demonstrated his deteriorating reason to the entire household. In broad daylight he had ordered the butchering of a perfectly healthy bull, then had offered a sacrifice that blackened the skies over Thebes and attracted every stray dog and cat within ten miles of the villa.

Ephraim had been at a celebration during the unprecedented event, but Ani, Tarik, and a host of other servants had been quick to tell him of their concerns when he returned. Before the day had ended he knew the lower slaves had spread the story at the wells, in the markets, on the streets. All of Thebes, probably all of Egypt, would soon know that the mighty Zaphenath-paneah's wit had broken, and before long people would be praising the divine Pharaoh for having wisdom enough to anticipate the tragedy.

And everything was Manasseh's fault.

Urging his camel into a trot, Ephraim drew a deep breath and forbade himself to lose his temper. He had not set out to quarrel with his brother but to reason with him, to help him see the far-reaching folly of his actions. Perhaps news of the little harpist's arrival at the villa could persuade Manasseh to return to Thebes. If that enticement would not work, then a report of their father's gory sacrifice might spur him homeward. Manasseh imagined himself the deliverer of the Hebrews, after all, but he was doing little to help their cause and reputation by driving Joseph to outmoded sacrificial rites.

Manasseh had to be turned away from his intention of making war. Rumors were rampant. Pharaoh was unhappy, and the family was falling apart.

"There, master!" The guard behind him shouted and pointed toward the horizon. Just above the slope of sterile golden dunes, Ephraim caught sight of movement. The tents had been cleverly disguised to blend in with the sand, but in this heat the dancing image of huddled men proved impossible to ignore.

Ephraim kicked his heels against his mount's side. "Onward, then."

————

"You are fortunate my men didn't kill you." With his hands placed belligerently on his hips, Manasseh paced back and forth, blocking the opening of his tent. "If you insist upon coming, you must send word."

Ephraim clenched his jaw to kill the retort in this throat. *I came here to make peace, not war.* Locking his arms across his chest, he stared steadily at his brother. "It is easier to come than to send a messenger, and my purpose cannot wait."

"Your purpose?" Manasseh abruptly stopped pacing and amusement lurked in his eyes. "What new purpose could send you flying across the desert after me? Nothing has changed. You want me to ignore God's call, and I will not."

"You are flaunting Pharaoh's wishes and breaking our father's heart. He is not himself—"

"So I have heard." Manasseh spoke more quietly, a muscle quivering at his jaw.

"Then come home." Ephraim moved toward his brother in a rush of emotion, extending his hands in a desperate plea. "The way to peace and prosperity is through Egypt. Can't you understand that? We are at peace here, and the Egyptians leave us alone. We can learn from one another. In time we shall be like them—"

"That is the problem! Don't you see?" Sudden anger lit Manasseh's eyes. "You are blind to the truth, Ephraim, and so is our father. God Shaddai brought us here during the famine so that we might be preserved, yes! But not only did He protect us from famine, He brought us to Egypt in order to keep us as the unique people of El Shaddai! We were torn from the idol-worshiping Canaanites—"

"That argument is senseless, for the Egyptians worship idols," Ephraim interrupted, clenching his fists in frustration.

"Not in Goshen," Manasseh countered. "Our people are isolated there, or at least we were until we began to plan cities and build houses of brick. If we persist in remaining here, it is only a matter of time before we adopt Egyptian gods. Today our uncles are building brick houses. Tomorrow they will build brick temples and shrines! We must leave before we bow down to idols, before we forget God Shaddai altogether!"

Ephraim smiled and shook his head. "Well spoken, Manasseh, but you forget that *you* are a son of Egypt, not Goshen, whether you like it or not. You have not forgotten our father's God. And why would God Shaddai call you to lead the sons of

Israel? He set our father aside to bring them to safety, and as long as our father lives, they shall be part of Egypt."

"For an Egyptian, you sound very much like the Hebrews in Goshen." Manasseh raised his voice in a mimicking cry: "As long as Joseph lives, we shall remain here where the grass is rich and the river blesses our fields." He paused, running his hands through his free-flowing hair in a detached motion. "If they are comfortable, they will never leave. When Father dies, they will cling to someone else—you, perhaps. And after you, they will find someone else. And soon they will forget why they are remaining here, and they will hold fast to prosperity and comfort—"

"They will become *powerful* if peace is made," Ephraim interrupted. "And if you will forget this nonsense and return to Thebes, I will be allowed to marry Sitamun—"

"You will never marry Sitamun." Taking a deep unsteady breath, Manasseh lifted a warning finger. "You never will, not even if I surrender and crawl on my knees to declare myself Pharaoh's slave. Can you not see how Queen Tiy fears us? She trembles in Father's presence. She knows a mightier god than Amon-Re has blessed us. She would never allow a Hebrew to marry into the royal family, for the people adore Zaphenath-paneah. If the Egyptians grow disenchanted with Amenhotep's dynasty, they might yearn for Father's descendants to be their leaders. Tiy knows this."

Ephraim snorted in disbelief. "You are dreaming again, brother."

"No." Manasseh crossed his arms and thrust his head forward. "The Egyptians don't care who rules over them as long as they are fed and not overtaxed. When the eastern Hyksos overran this land during the fifteenth dynasty, the Egyptians welcomed them with open arms. As long as the river flooded and the crops grew, they accepted the foreign kings as the gods' will."

Not knowing how to answer, Ephraim fell silent. As always, Manasseh had thoroughly prepared his arguments. But one truth, at least, he could not dispute.

"Father wants you to come home." Ephraim opened his hands in a flourish of triumph. "And because a good son honors his father, you must obey him. Come home."

Manasseh gave him a quick denying glance. "I am doing my best to honor my father." Turning to face the open door of his tent, he placed his hands on his hips. "I am honoring him by following his God. God Shaddai began a work in Joseph, and He calls me to continue it."

I am honoring him by following his God. Manasseh's words froze in Ephraim's brain. From them a thought grew and flowered. "Then all this," Ephraim gestured at the spears, shields, and battle-axes piled around him in the tent, "is to prove yourself a worthy son! You are not here to win Canaan! You care nothing for those miserable Hebrews out there in the heat."

"God called me," Manasseh answered stubbornly.

"No." Ephraim stepped closer as conviction slowly took root within him. "You have always tried to prove yourself. You were always the one who had to demonstrate your lessons, to prove that you could throw a spear farther than me—"

"You are mistaken, brother." Manasseh's voice hardened.

"I don't think so." Ephraim fingered the stubble on his chin. "It is all clear to me now. Jacob gave me the blessing of his right hand, and now you feel you must prove yourself beyond all doubt. Why else would you claim to have heard the voice of God? Your dream was not inspired by the Almighty. Your holy call was nothing but an invention of jealousy!"

"You . . . are . . . wrong!" Manasseh spoke in a thick and unsteady voice, and Ephraim knew his words had struck his brother's heart. Nothing could be gained now by pressing the issue. He would only drive Manasseh to a fury that might prove dangerous for them both.

"War demands a high price of a man," Ephraim whispered, moving close enough to place his hand on his brother's back. Manasseh flinched slightly beneath his touch, but he did not pull away. "Think twice before you risk your life, brother. You may think you are gaining Father's respect, but what will you accomplish if you lose your life? The little harpist will have genuine cause for weeping if you do not return to Thebes. And more is the pity, because she now waits for you in our father's villa."

He caught an expression of mingled wonder and fear upon Manasseh's face, then Ephraim left the tent and mounted his camel for the long ride back to the river.

Alone in his tent, Manasseh slapped his hands to his forehead and railed against Ephraim's timing. Surely his visit was a trick of the Evil One, for on the morrow their band was to make its first foray into enemy lands. They were now a force of four hundred, with two hundred Egyptian warriors and an equal number of Hebrews. Each man had his own reason for joining the force, but most had come for gold, glory, or God.

As Manasseh left his tent and walked among them, every eye gleamed toward him with eagerness. Every warrior's belt held a winking sword that had been polished and honed to the sharpest possible edge. Imposing an iron control on his countenance and his emotions, he returned their salutes with a resolute nod. He could not afford to allow Ephraim or his father to upset him. When next the gold-veiled sunrise crept over the desert, he and his men would no longer be sons and brothers, but warriors on a divine mission, urged forward for God's people and His purpose.

"Sons of Israel and our Egyptian comrades in arms!" Manasseh shouted, climbing atop a smooth rock in the midst of the camp. "Tomorrow is the day! At sunrise we reenter the land of Canaan. We fight at Gerar, and we begin to retake our homeland!"

"Listen to him!" Jokim yelled, hurrying to Manasseh's side as others spilled out of their tents. The men who had been sitting around the cook fires stood and folded their arms to listen as Jokim continued. "The sons of Israel know their true place! The Hebrew homeland is Canaan, the land promised to Abraham, Isaac, and Jacob!"

The Hebrews cheered. The Egyptians and Nubian warriors looked nonplussed. Manasseh caught sight of their confused expressions and smiled. "Never fear, my warrior friends," he said, catching Abnu's eye. That giant alone had been invaluable to their cause, for a mere glimpse of his assuring strength had silenced the quailing of many an anxious heart. "For when we attack on the morrow, the men of Gerar will flee as if before a bear out of the woods! They will run to Gaza with news of our strength, and the men of Gaza will run to Ashkelon and Ashdod till all of Canaan knows that we are coming back to live in the land God promised to Abraham and his descendants. And for you"—he extended his hand toward a knot of soldiers standing nearby—"because your valiant hearts have not feared to join us in this endeavor, you shall be granted first choice among the spoils and captives. The bounty and plunder of Gaza, Ashkelon, and Ashdod shall be yours. Then you shall return home to richly bedeck your wives and your concubines, and all who see you shall marvel at the riches won by your bravery.''

The Egyptians laughed and slapped one another on the back, reveling in their imagined success. Even the reserved faces of Abnu and his Medjay cohorts spread in wide grins, thoroughly enjoying the danger and excitement of the moment. Manasseh had been surprised and a bit alarmed that so many Nubians left Thebes to join them, for Pharaoh's captains must have noticed what was surely an obvious thinning of the royal troops. But if the king could not hold his warriors, he did not deserve them. As long as Amenhotep remained in his pleasure palace at Malkata, the valiant Medjays were as restless as penned bulls. They lived for battle and probably considered this venture a mere exercise to sharpen their skills.

Manasseh paused for a moment, waiting for the riotous merrymaking to cease. ''When the battle is won, all of us shall know that we heard and obeyed the voice of God Shaddai. It is His will that we be holy, and we have kept ourselves pure as we trained here. No women, no idols, and no thievery have been allowed in this camp.''

Shouts of agreement rang from the hills. Even the heathen Nubians nodded in earnest accord.

''It is the will of God that we be submissive,'' Manasseh continued, ''to all the authorities except when they conflict with the voice of God himself. And we have harmed no peaceful citizens of the desert. We have not stolen from the Bedouin in his tent nor from the temple priests who gather the offerings at the river shrines.''

The hurrahs returned with a deafening surge of sound.

''But though Pharaoh and his vizier have asked us to abandon this holy cause,'' Manasseh went on, ''sometimes God wills that we suffer.'' Silence met this statement, followed by a murmur of dissent. Manasseh softened his expression as he looked out upon his men. ''Yes, my brothers,'' he said, his gaze meeting that of Zimri, the gentle youth who had learned how to throw a spear and wield an ax under Jokim's tutelage. ''When we obey God rather than men, we shall have to pay the price. On the morrow it may be that some of us will be injured. It may be that some of us will give our lives in the fields of Gerar, or in days to come, in the streets of Ashkelon or Ashdod. But God is faithful. He will reward our suffering by bringing our wives and children into a green land flowing with milk and honey. That is the unchangeable and unshakable will of God. And all men, be they Hebrew or Nubian or Egyptian, will be blessed if they honor God Shaddai, the Holy One of Israel.''

The cheering began among the Hebrews first, then lifted from the throats of every man present, rising in great waves until the dunes rang with the sound. Manasseh lifted his hands toward heaven in anticipation of victory, then led his men in a dance of praise. He twirled slowly at first, then increased his tempo, hoping to exhaust himself. He knew he would not sleep easily through the night to come.

———

With wary eyes, Hondo watched his dancing companions. Let them cheer and rant and rave. Let them expend their precious energy. They would not live long enough to restore it.

He and the twenty men he had recruited had been living with the rebel force for over a month. Though Hondo had kept to himself, quietly hiding his face from Abnu and the Hebrew leaders, no one had questioned his motives, timing, or skill. He was a Medjay, so they supposed him faithful to Abnu. The foolish Hebrews had not stopped to think that he might actually be loyal to Pharaoh . . . and to his queen.

His brow wrinkled with contemptuous thoughts as Zaphenath-paneah's son trotted by, out of breath and delirious with unbridled energy. That young fool should have known Hondo's face and name, for he was one of the most skilled assassins in the entire Egyptian army. Zaphenath-paneah certainly knew of Hondo's reputation, but apparently the vizier had never discussed the king's special weapon with his son.

He smiled to himself as he studied Manasseh. A shame, really, to cut down such a handsome and passionate youth. A pity that the young man had chosen to follow this ridiculous quest instead of remaining quietly at home like his displaced father.

The young man's dance had spread like a fever. The men around Hondo jostled him, clapping him on the shoulder and moving him into the frantic circle that turned to the inaudible beat of war. Hondo smothered his smile and slapped his arms about his comrade's shoulders, then joined in the frenzy of the dance.

————

Long after sunset, sleep finally came nudging in among Manasseh's thoughts, and he dreamed.

He was a child again, standing in the chamber where his mother and father had often breakfasted. "Come here, my boys," Joseph called, his voice sounding ghostly and faraway, but Manasseh and Ephraim ran to him, crawled up in his lap, and covered his cheeks with kisses.

Asenath, their mother, remonstrated: "You must always bow on the floor before approaching Pharaoh's vizier."

Manasseh looked at his father, hoping for a word of rebuttal, but Joseph only patted him on the head, his eyes distant, his expression aloof. "Go with Ani now, my sons, and study your lessons. Make me proud of you." Manasseh accepted the challenge but left with a heavy heart, knowing he would not see his father again until the morrow.

"Father," he murmured through the embracing folds of sleep. His hands reached out and closed on empty air, then his arm brushed the handle of his battle sword. The cold kiss of metal brought him back to wakefulness.

He was not a child, but a man preparing for battle.

A decidedly non-dreamlike cry suddenly shattered the night. Manasseh fought through the cobwebs of sleep and fumbled for his sword, then sat up and squinted into the night, struggling to focus his eyes in the heavy darkness. For a moment he panicked, not seeing the other tents or campfires, then he remembered that Jokim had insisted that they separate from the others in order to clear their thoughts in preparation for battle. But now, sequestered behind a sand dune, Manasseh felt dangerously isolated.

"Manasseh!" Jokim crouched beside him in the dim moonlight, his sword in hand and a cold hard-pinched expression on his face. "They are upon us!"

"Who?" Manasseh hefted his sword and squatted beside

Jokim. His breath seemed to have solidified in his throat. "Who moves out there in the dark?"

"I can't tell." Jokim flattened himself against the dune that separated them from the camp.

Manasseh joined Jokim upon the dune, and together they crawled upward on their elbows until they peered over the lip of sand. Without speaking they parsed the sounds that came through the night beyond: cries, screams, shrieks of agony. Prickles of cold dread crawled over Manasseh's back.

"Someone is attacking," Jokim mumbled, idiotically stating the obvious. "But who?"

"It matters not." Manasseh stooped to pick up his shield. He thrust his arm through the leather loops that held it to his arm, then turned to look at his cousin. "Our first battle begins tonight. Are you ready?"

Jokim blinked with exhaustion and bafflement, then thrust his jaw forward. "Yes." He bent for his own shield. Like Manasseh, he girded it to his arm, then nodded soberly.

"We should go into the fray together," Manasseh said. "Side by side, the two of us will make a more considerable foe."

"Or a bigger target." Jokim gave Manasseh a humorless smile as he moved out from behind the dune.

The damage had been done by the time they arrived, but there was no sign of whatever marauding foe had passed through the camp. With fearful curiosity Manasseh wondered if an enemy could rise from beneath the sand itself. If not for the viscous pools of blood surrounding the bodies scattered around the campfires, Manasseh would have thought his men asleep. Man after man appeared to doze, their hands folded peacefully across their chests or tucked beneath bearded cheeks. The enemy, whoever they were, had moved confidently at first, swiftly killing with silent strokes of a blade across the jugular. But others of Manasseh's force lay face down on their bellies, their hands extended for swords that had been kicked away, their bare backs opened by an ax.

The heavy darkness, laced now with the smells of blood and fear, seemed to enfold Manasseh like a suffocating blanket. He trembled as fearful images arose in his mind. What enemy had done this? And how could they appear without warning and strike in the dead of night? Whoever they were, they had fled, either to hide or to pursue the survivors who sought escape in the darkness.

"Jokim," Manasseh warily turned to his cousin, "did you know—had you any suspicion something like this might happen? Why did you insist that we not sleep in my tent tonight?"

Jokim opened his mouth in horror. "I cannot believe you would think that I had anything to do with this! By the name of God Shaddai, I swear to you—"

"Do not swear by His name," Manasseh muttered, turning. The silhouette of his tent stood black and awkward at the edge of the clearing, backlit by the moon rising beyond the silvered sands. "At least my tent was empty. For an enemy would search it first, hoping to kill me—"

"By all that is holy, no!" Jokim's hand tightened around his sword. "Zimri! I asked him to sleep there and guard the weapons."

Manasseh darted forward, zigzagging between the bodies on the ground until he reached the tent. The canvas flap that served as a door had been sliced from top to bottom, and an inky puddle marked the rug where Zimri lay.

"I am to blame!" Jokim cried, pushing past Manasseh. He dropped to his knees beside the boy's body. "He is not a warrior. I should never have let him come here. What shall I say to his father? How can I face his mother?"

Keening in sorrow, Jokim scooped up a handful of sand and poured it over his head while Manasseh stepped back to study the scene. Zimri had not been struck while sleeping, for he lay sprawled at an unnatural angle, one leg tucked under him. Blood spangled the sword that lay a few inches from his hand.

"Look there." Manasseh pointed to a mounded shape among the shadows of the tent. Distracted, Jokim stopped wailing and turned.

Manasseh moved to light an oil lamp, then held it aloft and brought it near the stacks of shields and weapons. Another warrior lay on the ground, his eyes glazed in death, his mouth frozen in an eternal spasm.

"I know him." Jokim's voice filled with fresh sorrow. "He was one of the newer arrivals. A Medjay. Alas, even our friends are dying for our people."

Manasseh did not answer but left Jokim in the tent and re-turned to the field, searching for survivors. But in the lurid red glow of smoldering campfires, he found only death. In the space of an hour the army of four hundred men had been transformed to a corps of nearly two hundred corpses.

Engulfed in tides of weariness and despair, Manasseh crouched beside an ashen campfire. Looking around, it seemed to him that there was now more darkness in the darkness, more threat in the world. If God had called him to win Canaan for the Hebrews, why had He allowed this atrocity to befall them just as they prepared to obey?

"Was it men from Gerar?" Jokim's voice startled him from his thoughts. "Spies? Somehow they must have been forewarned of our intention."

"The enemy was not from Gerar," Manasseh answered wood-enly. He looked across the dead fire to the body of a boy scarcely fifteen years old, one of Judah's grandsons. "The killers made no noise. They carried no torches, and they left no animal tracks in the sand around us. These murderers rose up and killed their sleeping neighbors."

Jokim seemed to shiver in the cool night air, then he knelt be-side Manasseh. "Were half our company traitors?" He lowered his voice as if ashamed to speak of such things. "Was it the Nubians?"

"No." Manasseh fought to control his swirling emotions and jerked his thumb over his shoulder. "There, behind me, lies one of Abnu's men. He was one of the first to die, I think. He still wears the smile of contented sleep."

Jokim's head bowed. He remained in an attitude of frozen stillness for a long moment. "The Egyptians, then."

"No." Manasseh shook his head. "For there are as many Egyptian dead as Hebrew."

"But surely there was no conspiracy among the men." Jokim settled back upon his haunches. "You saw them tonight. They were in one accord and ready for battle. They were all willing to fight, to die if necessary."

"Some of them were willing to die, but not for us." Manasseh stood, brushed sand from his knees, then picked up his sword. "Did you look closely at the scene in my tent? Zimri is dead, but he killed the Medjay who lies in the tent with him."

"The Medjay?" Jokim frowned. "But Abnu's men—"

"Not all Medjay are Abnu's men," Manasseh answered. "Most of them have sworn loyalty to Pharaoh. I believe the men who rose up against us tonight were sent from Pharaoh and charged to destroy us before we could venture into Canaan."

"If they were sent to execute traitors," Jokim asked, the line of his mouth tightening a fraction more, "then why are *we* still alive?"

"Because we slept apart," Manasseh answered, moving away from the fire. "They have obviously not finished with us. But neither has God Shaddai."

———

Knowing that their enemy had slipped away under cover of darkness, Manasseh and Jokim crept away from the camp, cowering in shadows, avoiding the wide open patches of moonlight where a man might easily become a target for a silent spear. From time to time they heard movement in the dunes beyond. Once or twice a sharp cry twisted through the silence of the night. Manasseh had no doubts that Pharaoh's guards were tracking survivors in the hills beyond.

After a seemingly endless night, a gentle radiance low on the eastern horizon indicated where the sun would rise. Manasseh and Jokim kept that horizon at their backs, creeping steadfastly toward the river. Once they had reached the Nile, they could either find a boat or beg a ride from a passing barge. If they did not encounter the enemy in the desert, they would reach the river within a day. Within two days they could be back in civilized Thebes where assassins did not work so openly.

At last the horizon's glow spread and brightened until the gleaming sun rose swollen and red above the dunes. Manasseh felt his fear abate in direct proportion to the sun's advent, and by the time the horizon glimmered blue, he felt he could once again stand tall and face any approaching adversary.

He and Jokim talked little on their long walk across the sand. The sun slowly spread its rays over the dunes, baking their skin and parched lips, but neither man dared to speak of his thirst, hunger, or weariness. Any admission of weakness was tantamount to surrender, and Manasseh had given up all he intended to during the previous night of horror. The enemy would have to be content with divesting him of his dreams—for a short time. Once he had regrouped the survivors, he would undertake another incursion into Canaan, even if he had to launch it from Edom or Moab.

If there were any survivors. Guilt, heavy and sharp, avalanched over Manasseh as Zimri's handsome face and deep-set eyes rose in his memory. If not for Manasseh, that young man would not have been in the desert. If not for his dream, none of the Hebrews would have left their homes and families. His relatives would look askance at him now. Mothers would weep at the mention of his name, and fathers would curse the day Manasseh had been born. Even the Egyptians would consider him a pariah, an outcast, a young fool who had flagrantly rebelled against his father and led four hundred men to ignominious deaths in the desert.

A man could die honorably on the field of battle.

No man died honorably sleeping by the fire.

The dead Egyptian warriors, denied both the glory of battle and the satisfaction of willingly risking their lives, would have no funerals or tombs. Some of the wealthier families would undoubtedly send search parties to bring home the mortal remains of their sons, but the poor families would have no way of gathering their loved ones until the desert sun had dried and desiccated the corpses, leaving them to a sorrowful, sandy afterlife with no provision for eternity. . . .

Manasseh swallowed hard, wanting to forget every moment of the last twenty-four hours. What a cruel joke the divine will had played upon him! He had done all he could to please God Shaddai, and yet he had been defeated. How could God allow such a thing to happen? Was He not a God of justice and fairness?

His mind skittered away from that unsolvable dilemma. He could not think about God in his present state. His thoughts scampered around in confusion and made no sense.

"At last," Jokim said, sighing heavily. He paused a step ahead of Manasseh and gestured beyond the rocky hill they were climbing. "I can smell the river," he said, a glimmer of hope in his dark eyes. "We shall make it, cousin."

Manasseh's heart thumped with relief as he lengthened his stride, passing Jokim. But at the top of the rim he thrust out his arm to hold his cousin back.

The narrow river lay as bright as a spill of molten metal across the barren sands, but Manasseh's joy was tempered by the sight of a ship anchored in the small cove south of Tura Quarry. A standard featuring Pharaoh's royal insignia flew from the barge's mast. At least a dozen seamen and warriors wandered over its deck, and another dozen lingered on the shore, their bright blades glinting in the sun. Judging from the amount of ashes in their deep fire pits, Manasseh guessed that they had been situated at this location for several days . . . waiting.

Jokim's eyes widened in alarm.

"Our traitors," Manasseh whispered, dropping to the earth like a stone. Jokim fell beside him and they lay flat on their bellies, peering over the rim of rock toward the water below. Carefree laughter and the taunts of the warriors echoed among the hills. The scent of roasting meat wafted up from their cook fire.

Manasseh's stomach clenched in sudden hunger, and he realized he had not eaten or drunk anything all day. Jokim had to be starving, too, and yet food and water lay within reach.

"What do we do?" Jokim whispered, watching the men below with a keenly observant eye. "If we advance northward we can move around them—"

Manasseh lifted his hand to cut him off. "We take them just as they took us." His surprise yielded quickly to fury. "Their work is done, so why haven't they left? They are obviously waiting for others to rejoin them. So we will lie in wait here, in these hills. I know these rocks. I know the path that leads down to that cove. We will guard it, and any traitor who passes by us is a dead man. And then tonight, if they still remain here, we shall slip among them like shadows. They are guilty of ruthless murder, and so we shall avenge—"

"You shall avenge nothing."

Manasseh lifted his head and felt the sharp bite of a blade against his neck. His gaze moved over to Jokim. He, too, had been pinned to the ground by the sharp point of a spear.

The pressure at Manasseh's neck eased somewhat. "Stand up," came the terse order, and he did, rising slowly from the sand and then turning. Behind him stood a half-dozen men wearing the distinctive kilts and leopard belts of Medjay warriors. Their hungry eyes glittered with battle lust.

The group was dominated by the dark figure of a man, big, powerful, and familiar. The set of his granite chin suggested a stubborn streak, and he folded his powerful arms and smiled slightly. "A very great honor to meet you face-to-face, Manasseh, son of Zaphenath-paneah. It was not even an hour ago that I asked my men of your whereabouts and was dismayed that no one could recall having killed you."

"God Shaddai spared me." Manasseh stiffened at the challenge in the man's voice. "As He will spare me again." He squinted toward his captor, listening to some distant experience, remembering the man's voice and face and form. They had met before, on a winding pathway through the marketplaces of Thebes, but today the barbarian was not drunk.

"You are Hondo." Jokim spat the words in anger. "I remember you. You joined us at Kadesh Barnea."

The warrior smirked in response. "Yes. On direct orders of Queen Tiy, my men and I joined your pitiful band. And I fully intend"—his gaze darted back to Manasseh—"to bring my lovely queen the gift of your head, Manasseh. Though I personally think beheading is rather too merciful a punishment for traitors."

"You are the traitor." Manasseh jerked away as two men stepped forward to bind his arms. "You trained, slept, and ate with us, and then rose in the night to murder your own comrades in combat."

"You are not my comrade, *Hebrew*." Icy contempt flashed in Hondo's eyes. Visibly trembling with suppressed fury, he jerked his thumb toward a narrow path. "Take them down to the river," he said, licking his thin lips. "We shall have some fun with them while we wait for the others."

~ Twenty-five ~

THE TRAITOROUS MEDJAYS DROVE MANASSEH AND Jokim down the narrow path that wound through the rocky cliffs, urging them forward with the points of their spears and an occasional jab of a sword. Breathless and bleeding, they finally arrived at the makeshift camp on the shore where a host of men stared at them with the wide eyes of cowardly conquerors. Hondo barked out an order. Eager servants dragged the Hebrews into the shallows of the drought-wasted river and tied their hands to mooring posts.

Standing in knee-deep water with his hands bound together, Manasseh wondered if Hondo truly intended to take his head back to Thebes or if he would simply leave them in the river as crocodile bait. Nothing, he realized grimly, would be too horrific for Hondo to consider. His actions had already demonstrated that he had no morals, no conscience, and no royal mandate other than to stop the Hebrews. Manasseh lifted his eyes and blinked up at the sky. Now that Zaphenath-paneah no longer served as Pharaoh's vizier, Hondo did not even fear retribution from the second highest throne in the land.

Jokim, overflowing with bravado, poured a steady stream of vituperation upon his captors. Ignoring Jokim's insults, Hondo and his men retreated to the cook fire, and now their blood-stained hands lifted hunks of meat in mock salute to their starving captives.

"Sons of dogs and jackals!" Jokim yelled, struggling against the ropes that held him tight. "If Pharaoh has ordered this, he is the son of a water buffalo! A curse upon all your idolatrous gods! May your wives and mothers bear illegitimate curs! May your daughters marry vile—arraugh!"

One of the warriors, tiring of Jokim's curses, had picked up his bow and sent an arrow winging through the air. It struck

Jokim squarely in the thigh, effectively pinning him to the mooring post. Jokim screamed, then clenched his teeth and looked helplessly at Manasseh as he twisted in a vain effort to move his hands toward the painful spot.

"I am a dead man, cousin," he whispered, sweat beading on his forehead.

"You are not. Don't speak of defeat."

"Yes. We are in the water, and the blood—see, it gushes already, and how it hurts!" He closed his eyes and screwed up his face against the agony.

"Jokim, listen to me," Manasseh commanded. "We are not going to die, not at the hands of these men."

"The others died." Jokim's voice was now a husky whisper. "Why shouldn't we?"

"I don't know," Manasseh admitted. "I don't understand any of this." A cold lump grew in his stomach as he looked at Jokim, and he turned away, frustrated by the niggling guilt of his own inadequacy. When had he ever claimed to have all the answers?

"You said," Jokim's voice scraped terribly, "that God sometimes calls us to suffer."

"Yes," Manasseh answered, looking toward the shore in hope of some miraculous means of deliverance. "Sometimes He does."

He saw nothing. And so, while Hondo and his men ate and drank and occasionally splashed through the shallows to buffet or spit upon their prisoners, the afternoon passed into history.

————

When the sky began to glow red in the west, forecasting the sunset, Hondo moved to the center of the camp and lifted his massive arms. "We are still missing five men," he called, peering through the crowd as if the absent warriors might be hiding among the others. "We can only assume that they have met with misfortune. So load the barge, for we will depart at sunset."

Hanging by the rope that secured him to the mooring post, Manasseh slowly opened his swollen eyes. One warrior had punched his face at least a dozen times, and Manasseh was quite certain that another had broken several of his ribs. At one point during the eternal afternoon, a pair of men had used Jokim and

Manasseh as targets in an archery competition. Though arrows fell in a whistling cloud around the pair for the space of an hour, the wobbly Medjays had been drinking and could not hold their bows steady. One arrow grazed Manasseh's bare arm, leaving a nasty red streak, and Jokim took another arrow in the leg already lacerated. But they were still alive.

Manasseh glanced over at Jokim. Blood from a wound in his forehead had painted his visage into a glistening devil mask. He hung limply from the ropes that held him, weak from the slow seepage of blood from his leg wounds. Manasseh frowned as he looked at the crimson-tinted water. The noise from the men on the beach had apparently kept crocodiles at bay throughout the day, but the creatures were irresistibly drawn to blood, and they would grow more brazen and courageous once darkness fell. Manasseh began to hope that Hondo would choose to take his captives' heads back to Thebes. A quick beheading would be more endurable than being torn apart by battling crocodiles in a feeding frenzy.

Hondo's assemblage of warriors, seamen, and slaves busied themselves now with carrying provisions and weapons back aboard the ship. Their heavy footsteps thudded up and down the narrow gangplank, reverberating like the dull roar of thunder in Manasseh's weary consciousness.

"God Shaddai, they may kill me," he murmured, shivering in the coolness of the water and the fading sunlight. "But let your will be done here today."

His arms, pinched by the constant pressure of the rope around his wrists, had no more feeling. He had the fuzzy impression that he now possessed only a head and chest. He was nothing but a trunk tied to a pole, and soon he would be only a head, stuffed unceremoniously inside a gift basket for Queen Tiy. Would she invite his father to the ceremony during which Hondo would present her with trophies taken from the traitors? *Yes*, a voice inside Manasseh murmured, *she would*. She was a capable and charming queen, but something poisonous lay just beneath the pleasing, polished surface of her personality, something dangerous.

"Men of Egypt, gather around me," Hondo called. Manasseh lifted one battered eyelid. The light was fading fast, color bleeding out of the atmosphere. The sun hovered over the western horizon in a gigantic ball of fire, the last sunset he would ever see. He closed his eyes again and waited for the inevitable.

The gangplank thundered with footsteps, every soul emptied the ship, anxious to be on the scene of Hondo's bloody entertainment. When at last the gangplank stood silent, Manasseh heard the barbarian's bold voice again.

"Today you shall witness the justifiable end of traitors." His words were punctuated by the soft swish of a weapon cutting through the darkening air. Against his will, Manasseh's eyelids lifted. Hondo stood at the edge of the river, surrounded by his men, a gigantic battle-ax in his hand.

Despite his emptiness, Manasseh felt the rise of panic. He had nothing with which to resist: no weapons, no strength, no will. The horror of the previous night and the constant abuse of the day, combined with his anger and thirst, had completely depleted him. And as weak as he was, he knew Jokim was even weaker.

He had no strength in himself. None at all. And no hope. He had been called of God and he had tried to rally his people, but they had not been willing to join him. They had journeyed to the Promised Land and felt its wonderful goodness beneath their feet, but then had turned back for the luxury and empty comforts of Egypt.

But God knew he had been faithful. Manasseh closed his eyes and found strength in knowing that.

A noisy splash told him Hondo had entered the water, ax in hand.

"Are the baskets ready?" the assassin called. Now Manasseh heard the rhythmic slap of the weapon's wooden handle against Hondo's open palm.

"They are asleep! Wake them up!" one of the men jeered, and Hondo laughed. He drew near, so close that Manasseh could smell the rancid sweat of his body. Water splashed in Manasseh's face.

He reflexively thrust out his tongue, hoping to ease his thirst by catching a drop or two, but still he kept his eyes closed. He was not certain his eyes could mask the emotions reeling in his heart, and he would not give Hondo the satisfaction of seeing his fear.

Another splash rained upon his face, then his tormentor's voice dropped in volume. "Open your eyes and give them what they want," he insisted archly, his hand splashing into the water a third time. "Or I shall cut off your companion's arms, then his legs, and finally his head. You may keep your eyes closed, but you will still hear his screams!"

Open your eyes, and you will see my deliverance.

Manasseh's eyes flew open, not at Hondo's threat, but at the urgency in the numinous voice that seemed to come to him from the mountains, through the air, through the water around him. The voice had been so strong, so clear, that he was amazed no one else heard it.

Perhaps someone had. "Jokim?" he called, his blurred eyes focusing on Hondo's malignant face. The warrior pulled the ax back over his shoulder for the swing.

"I heard, Manasseh!" A trace of laughter lined Jokim's weary voice. The sound must have alarmed Hondo, for his eyes widened in midswing. One of his legs suddenly shot forward in the water, and he teetered off balance for a long moment, then screamed and fell into the shallows.

The men on shore laughed, imagining that the warrior had lost his balance, but Manasseh knew better. The hair lifted on his arms; his heart thumped against his rib cage as the water at his feet churned and boiled. Suddenly Hondo reappeared, his clenched hands empty, his face frozen in an expression of primitive horror. "Sobek!" he cried, then another scream clawed in his throat as an unseen force yanked him beneath the surface again.

Recoiling, Manasseh blinked in numb terror. Sobek was the Egyptian god represented as a crocodile. Did Hondo think he had seen the god, or had a crocodile surprised and snagged him?

The men on shore stood in stunned huddles, then one of them shouted and pointed to the water. "Crocodiles!" he yelled, his bony face twitching in a paroxysm of fear. Manasseh swiveled his eyes to follow the man's finger. Beyond the boat, from all directions, the unruffled surface of the quiet cove had dimpled with the horny ridges of crocodile flesh. The river teemed with them, a man could have walked from one shore to the other on their backs without wetting his feet, and they moved steadily toward the men on the sand.

As the water around them blushed with Hondo's blood, Jokim let out a scream that chilled Manasseh to the marrow. Anyone who lived long in the Black Land knew the impossibility of escaping the terrible jaws of crocodiles caught up in the ecstasy of feeding. Energized by the sight of death in another guise, Manasseh strained uselessly at his bonds while the men on shore ran for the narrow gangplank of the barge.

A sense of foreboding descended over Manasseh with a shiver. He caught his breath as a particularly large beast emerged in the water a few feet away. He smelled the sour stench of wetness and rotted flesh caught between the creature's ragged teeth. Warning spasms of alarm erupted within him, and he turned his head away, unwilling to look death in the eye.

But the animal glided past him with a strong side-to-side movement. Manasseh felt the displacement of water as the creature swam by. The mighty tail brushed the benumbed flesh of his leg, and yet the creature seemed unaware of him. Manasseh shivered through fleeting nausea, then turned to look at Jokim. Though coated with blood and as pale as death, he, too, had been spared. A pair of creatures hovered atop the water to Jokim's right, and a gigantic bull crocodile had thrust his pointed eyes up through the water at his left, but none of the animals had harmed him.

But this peculiarity had not been noticed by the panicked men on shore. Screaming and yelling, they hurtled toward the barge, overloading the gangplank until it teetered and tipped over, spilling at least twenty men into waist-deep water. A chilly dew formed on Manasseh's skin as the carnage began in earnest, but a sudden merciful shadow thrown by the setting sun blocked his view of the terror in the water.

The barge shifted, agitated by the death struggles in the river, and the handful of men who had managed to get aboard quickly loosened the mooring ropes and applied themselves to the oars. Thus abandoned, the men remaining on shore ran for the hills as the vicious creatures lumbered out of the water after them. But the towering figure of Abnu appeared from behind a rocky crest, and behind him stood at least a dozen of his fiercely loyal warriors. Hondo's frenzied comrades, bereft now of both weapons and sense, either ran headlong into the Nubians' spears or threw themselves on the ground to beg for mercy.

We are saved. The thought struck Manasseh in an instant of clear understanding, then everything went silent within him as he pitched forward in a faint.

—————

"They must have anchored directly above a crocodile nesting area," Abnu explained after freeing Manasseh and Jokim. He and Manasseh sat now by the fire, while Jokim shivered under a blanket someone had pulled from the sand. The giant clamped his jaw tight and stared at the now silent waters. "It *is* nesting season."

"It was a miracle of God," Manasseh answered, holding his raw hands and wrists up to the warmth of the fire.

Abnu looked down at the ground, then shook his head. "A natural mistake. They should have scouted the area."

"They did. They'd been here for days. We did not see a single crocodile until the first one grabbed Hondo." Manasseh brought his knees to his chest, then folded his arms atop them and smiled at the giant. "If what happened here was not a miracle, then why weren't Jokim and I eaten alive? We were bleeding, and we could not escape."

Abnu shrugged and pushed at a pile of dirt with his enormous foot. "Sometimes strange things happen. I have seen many things that do not make sense."

Manasseh fell silent. He was convinced God Shaddai had worked a miracle to preserve him and Jokim, but why hadn't God spared the others? And why had He allowed the massacre at the camp in the first place? Manasseh suddenly understood why Abnu might have difficulty accepting the wisdom of God Shaddai. Manasseh didn't always understand it himself.

"I do not understand everything God allows." He looked fully into the Nubian's somber eyes. "But it is enough to know that He has a purpose for me. I know it is His will that the children of Abraham return to Canaan. And I know He called me to lead them. But only a few would take the step with me. Most chose not to believe." His eyes gravitated to the roaring fire. "Perhaps they never will align themselves to the will of God. But when they do, He will give them all He has promised."

"Are you giving up?" Abnu frowned, and his expression sharpened. "That is not the way of a warrior. Tarik should have taught you better."

"I am not giving up," Manasseh answered, realizing that he could not. "But right now there are urgent things to consider. Jokim's wounds are serious. He will need a physician, and he cannot travel to Thebes on foot."

"What do you want me to do?"

Manasseh paused, thinking. The danger had not passed. Tiy still wanted him dead, and he was still a fugitive in Pharaoh's eyes. Whom could he trust? Not his father, and certainly not Ephraim. But perhaps there was one. . . .

"You must go quietly to my father's house," he told Abnu, "and ask at the gate for a slave called Jendayi. She is my father's harpist, and she can be trusted. Tell her that I will take Jokim to my father's house at Tura, and she must send a trustworthy physician to me."

"I myself will bring the physician back," Abnu volunteered, his heavy brows rising.

"I had hoped you would." Manasseh's smile widened in approval. He reached out and clapped the other man on the shoulder. "You are a gift from God, friend."

The giant grinned back with no trace of his former animosity. "We shall see," he said, unfolding his long legs as he rose to his feet.

———

"And why," Tiy snapped, her patience rapidly evaporating, "would the river crocodiles attack you and not touch the Hebrews? Perhaps you did not see how your prisoners suffered. Perhaps their legs were eaten away."

"No, my Queen. They stood in the midst of the beasts as if they were invisible." The protesting warrior before her pressed his hands and knees to the floor of her chamber as if he'd been glued there. The trembling fool had been ushered to her quarters as soon as the royal barge had arrived back in Thebes, and she had already interviewed four other infiltrators who survived the skirmish with Manasseh's rebel army. All of them gave the same incredible account, and every man shook before her like a dry palm in a high wind.

She looked away from the senseless man and considered her options. If Manasseh and his comrade still lived, as all five survivors seemed to believe, then they would be hiding someplace, in some safe refuge. And the younger man had been injured, so he would not be fit for travel. Manasseh would need help, food, and supplies from someone he trusted, someone either from Goshen or his father's house. But if many Hebrews had died in the desert, Manasseh would be about as welcome in Goshen as a plague of locusts.

"Get up, you fool," she told the quaking man before her. "Go immediately to the villa of Zaphenath-paneah and ask for Akil, the chironomist. Tell him I have sent you, and that I command him to be alert for one who will come to fetch help for the troublesome son."

"If no one comes—"

"Someone will," she hissed at him. "And when he does, tell Akil to follow him. You bring word to me so that I can send my warriors to aid him." She lifted her hand and waved him away. "Go at once. Your duty is not yet fulfilled."

Gulping in obvious relief that she had not ordered his execution, the man nodded and slunk from the room like a shadow.

Tiy leaned forward and rested her chin on her fingertips. She would never cease to be amazed at the incredible talents of Zaphenath-paneah and his sons. In bygone days the vizier had been able to charm the birds from the trees, and his sons obviously followed in their father's footsteps. Zaphenath-paneah had always claimed that his unique abilities came from his invisible and Almighty God, but Tiy believed them to be the fruit of his intelligence, compassion, and devastating handsomeness. Apparently his sons had inherited the same qualities, for Sitamun had been sincerely smitten by Ephraim, and Manasseh obviously possessed his father's aptitude for leading and motivating men.

A terrifying thought suddenly rose in her consciousness. What if Zaphenath-paneah's special favor *did* come from his God? The Egyptians fondly credited their deities for all sorts of happy daily happenstances, but the survivors of the massacre on the river seemed convinced that they had witnessed a miracle in the midst of the crocodile attack. Could this invisible God wield that kind of force? Would He? And if He could and would, had He set His face against her?

Suddenly she yearned for Amenhotep's company. He would not be able to offer advice or wisdom more valuable than her own, but it would be comforting to rest in his arms and feel the burdens of the throne lifted from her shoulders. But the sun would soon set on what had been another royal wedding day. Amenhotep would sleep tonight with his latest bride, a match Tiy herself had quietly arranged. And though her heart contracted a little to think of that royal couple together, petty heartaches had to be borne in silence.

Tiy was the Great Wife, the reigning queen, and now the power behind the throne. And more than any of her noble predecessors, she understood what the title required . . . for the good of her king and her kingdom.

~ Twenty-six ~

THOUGH JENDAYI COULD NOT SEE THE EXACT MOMENT when the sun slipped behind the western Theban mountains, she knew night had fallen by the way life in the vizier's house subtly gentled. Voices lowered in the night, laughter softened. The stern-voiced guards seemed to relax, for she heard smothered laughter and the clink of weapons as they put their swords, shields, and spears away. Only a quartet of guards remained on duty during the night, and these four manned posts outside the villa's walls, away from the quiet hum of life within.

Once the vizier had been seen to his chamber and provided for, the sweet scents of lily oil streamed through the darkness as the women of the slave house anointed their arms and necks and went forth to entrance the men. Zaphenath-paneah was a more liberal and easygoing master than most—he allowed his slaves to marry, frequently granting them manumission as a wedding present. But no one, slave or free servant, could find a better master than Zaphenath-paneah, and only a few had ever left his service.

Of all locations in the house, Jendayi liked the garden best, but even it seemed different in the night. The ceaseless drone of insects became more melodic in the darkness, and the white lotus blossoms, which hid from the immodest brightness of daylight, generously opened their petals and perfumed the air. Occasionally Jendayi would hear a soft splash and imagine that some cricket or toad had leapt into the reflecting pool. The night sounds never unnerved her, for they belonged to the darkness, and darkness was as familiar as the strings of her harp. Daylight and dreams, she had discovered, brought things far more frightening than the night.

She had just settled down by the edge of the reflecting pool not long after sunset when Kesi came hurrying over the tiled pathway. "Come quickly, Jendayi," the handmaid whispered, a slight tinge of wonder in her voice. "Someone at the gate of the vizier's house asks for you."

Every nerve in Jendayi's body jangled out of tune as she straightened. Who would ask for her? She knew no one outside the circle of this house and Pharaoh's, and it was doubtful that anyone from Malkata would venture here to ask for her. Ephraim was away at some party, as always, so who would seek her out? Unless . . . *her missing mother?*

Her mind retreated from that improbable thought.

"Is it"—her hand went to her throat—"a man or a woman outside the gate?"

"I don't know," Kesi answered impatiently, moving away. "The gatekeeper just sent me to fetch you. But you'd better hurry because he doesn't like visitors after dark."

Jendayi rose to her feet and hurried forward as quickly as she dared, one hand extended to feel her way through the familiar passageways. Within a few moments she felt the courtyard sand under her feet, then she turned in the direction of voices and moved toward the gate.

"I am Jendayi." She spoke to the air.

"You?" The deep voice echoed as if it came from the bottom of a well. Jendayi shivered when she realized she had heard it before—at Malkata, at the center of a duel.

She folded her hands and tried to keep her voice steady. "I am the one you seek. Have you a message for me?"

The man's voice grew closer as it dropped in volume. "Yes. Manasseh and Jokim have been wounded. The planned battle for Canaan has been . . . postponed. But Manasseh bids me tell you that you must send a physician to his father's house at Tura Quarry. Without aid, a man may die."

"Manasseh is wounded?" A strange surge of alarm ripped through her heart, frightening her. Manasseh might be a liar and Ephraim's rival, but he had taken her into his arms when she needed a friend.

"Manasseh will mend, but Jokim has suffered two serious wounds and is in great distress. Do you know a physician?"

Jendayi pressed her fingers to her lips as her mind raced. The priests knew the healing arts, but Zaphenath-paneah employed no priests in his house. He called for his steward whenever one of the servants was ill—

"Ani," she gasped, a little surprised by her leap of logic. "He will know how to help." She whirled toward the house, then turned as an afterthought struck her. "You will wait, won't you?"

"I'll wait, little one," the deep voice growled from a great height. "But hurry. A boat is waiting, but we must be away before daylight."

————

Ani asked no questions when Jendayi told him Manasseh needed help, and if the old man was surprised at her news, he did not remark upon it. He merely told her to wait a moment, then returned to the doorway of his chamber with his feet properly shod in papyrus sandals that made a delicate shooshing sound across the floor. She heard the soft creak of reeds and smelled the bitter tang of herbs. He carried a basket of medicinal plants. "I am ready," he said simply, nudging her with his elbow.

She took his arm gratefully, for her heart was pounding like a drum, and she feared she would move too quickly in her haste and trip over some unexpected object. Within a few moments they had reached the gate, and she heard approval in the giant's words as he greeted the steward. "You are prepared. That is good."

"If Manasseh needs me, we should not delay," Ani answered. The heavy gate creaked, a guard snapped to attention, then Ephraim's oath echoed through the silence of the night.

"By the life of Pharaoh!" Alarm rang in his tone. "What brings a Medjay to my father's house after dark?"

Ani hissed in response, but the warrior said nothing. Jendayi felt her cheeks burning. What must Ephraim think, coming upon her like this, with these men? He would imagine her a troublemaker, a spy, or worse.

"Ani?" All traces of humor vanished from Ephraim's voice. "Tell me why you are dressed for travel and carry your herb basket. And who is this giant?"

"This matter does not concern you, Master Ephraim," Ani said, his tone lightly respectful. "Now let the two of us pass. We have work to do."

"By all the gods, it's Manasseh, isn't it?" Ephraim sounded distracted. "What has happened? He is my brother, Ani, you must tell me! Does he need help? I will give it."

"He might not welcome your company just now."

"Listen, Ani," Ephraim said, his voice raw and harsh. "We may have our disagreements, but Manasseh and I will be brothers until the day we die. If he needs help, you must tell me where he is."

The silence grew tight with tension, then Ani broke the quiet with a long sigh. "I suppose if you are with us you cannot run to Pharaoh." His words were playful but his meaning was not. "Come, then. Your brother is with Jokim, and they are hurt."

"Where are they?"

"That," the giant said, "you will discover when we have reached the place. If you are coming, wipe that arrogant expression from your face and join us."

Still clutching Ani's arm, Jendayi stepped forward as the steward began to move through the gateway.

"No, Jendayi." Ani pulled her hand from his arm. "You must remain here."

Momentarily lost in her own reverie, she hesitated. A startling thought kept repeating in her mind like a haunting melody, and the harder she tried to ignore it, the more it persisted.

"He told me the truth, didn't he?" Though she spoke to Ani, she turned her face toward Ephraim. "He told this warrior to ask for me . . . because he had faith in me." She could not stop herself from pondering the significance of Manasseh's message. "If he had lied, if he had only used me to spite Ephraim, he would not have dared to ask for my help."

"I don't know what you're talking about." Ephraim's voice was calm and clear. "But Ani is right. This is not the journey for a little harpist."

Did he even know her name? "If Manasseh is in trouble, I want to go." She stubbornly lifted her chin. "He won't mind my coming."

"I'm sure he wouldn't." She heard sympathy in Ani's voice. "But this is a dangerous journey."

"The old one is right," the giant affirmed. "A barge escaped us, and the spies have undoubtedly reached Thebes by now.

Manasseh's enemies are powerful, little one."

"Powerful people have nothing to do with me," she insisted, reaching out. Ani had moved his arm away, but she caught the fabric of his cloak and clung to it. "You must let me go."

"No."

"We are wasting time."

Jendayi's heart thrilled to hear Ephraim rise to her defense. Though he would never be what she had dreamed he could be, if he wanted her on the journey he believed she could help.

"Ephraim is right, we haven't time to argue," the warrior broke in. "Already the stars have shifted. We must reach them soon."

"All right," Ani muttered. Jendayi felt his shoulders contract in submission, then she slipped her hand into the crook of his arm and let him lead her through the gateway.

"Not a word of this to my father," Ephraim said to the guard and gatekeeper as they moved away. "He will know soon enough. You will only upset him by telling him of our departure. Say nothing."

By the profound silence that followed, Jendayi knew they would obey.

————

While Abnu had gone to the vizier's house to relay Manasseh's message, one of his companions had slunk along the river, looking for a boat that might be easily unloosed from its moorings. At length he found a narrow felucca with its sail still unfurled. He tied a bit of red scarf atop the high mast, then crouched in the shadows of the railing to wait for Abnu's approach.

Beneath a shining net of stars the quartet found the marked ship and slipped into the boat without a word. Abnu, his Nubian comrade, and Ephraim began to paddle in earnest, while Jendayi sat behind Ani. The warm night breeze caressed her face as she turned to inhale the pungent scents and sounds of the river. The noises of the creaking ship, straining cordage, and flapping sailcloth sent a jet of happiness through her heart. She was on her way, not to entertain faceless nobles and kings, but to help a friend.

She gripped Ani's bony arm and sighed, her soul expanding

with the first real sense of purpose she had known in eighteen years.

As the ship pulled away from the darkened shore, Akil lowered the edge of the tattered cloak from his face and released an anxious cough to signal the warrior a few feet away. The Medjay spy turned and sped away toward the palace, and Akil paused on the bank and glanced longingly toward the crowded city and a row of meager hovels where he might disguise himself as a beggar and be lost for a week or two. Eventually the queen's guards would find him, of course, but at least he would not have to participate in his beloved queen's action against the vizier's son.

Any plan formed against the vizier would not prosper. Akil now understood that truth. The quaking warrior had just told Akil about the episode at Tura Quarry.

Fear of the unknown knotted and writhed in his stomach, fear of the unknown god who could send crocodiles after every man except two Hebrews who stood bloody and broken in the water.

But Tiy's men would hunt him down if he left his post. The Medjay captains had been rational, even *reasonable* under Zaphenath-paneah's command. A runaway servant might have been sentenced to a year or two in prison. But now Tiy commanded the troops at Thebes, and the mistress of malice would order him chopped up into little bits and fed to the crocodiles.

Shuddering, Akil turned his back on the hovels and searched for a small boat he could use to follow the men Tiy sought. *I don't know why I have to follow. The spying warrior will tell her they've gone downriver. And they took a sizable felucca, hard to miss. She really doesn't need me. I'm a musician. What do I know of spying?*

An unexpected splash from the black river sent his heart into sudden shock. A dark premonition held him still for a long moment, then he turned and resolutely walked toward the brightly lit taverns of Thebes.

Let Tiy look for him. With any luck, when she found him he'd be too drunk to care.

The wavelets that had flecked the surface of the river flattened out as the felucca slipped into the sunlit harbor built for hauling stone from Tura Quarry. Ephraim leapt from the boat and splashed his way to shore. He should have known that Manasseh would retreat here, for in their youth they had spent an endless parade of summers at the quarry house. The whitewashed villa offered privacy, comfort, and a warning system, for the quarry overseer might be enlisted to sound the alarm should an enemy approach from the river.

"There's a narrow path leading back to the house," Ephraim called, catching the rope Abnu tossed him. He put it over his shoulder and helped drag the felucca near the muddy bank. "I want to run ahead, so I'll meet you there."

Ani yawned and gathered his things as the two Nubians jumped from the boat into the water and stretched their cramped muscles. But before he departed, Ephraim caught a glimpse of Jendayi's sleepy expression and thought to himself that the little harpist had never looked more beautiful.

"Guard your heart, brother," he murmured as he sprinted up the stony path. "I hope it is strong enough to withstand the shock of surprise."

———

"Manasseh!" Ephraim's voice echoed among the outcroppings of the rocks, but no one answered from inside the house. The villa had not been maintained in several months, and the wide doors at the front entrance hung at an angle as if sprained. But Manasseh would not have hidden in the main reception hall. It was too open. He'd tuck himself in some out-of-the-way corner, perhaps in the servants' quarters or the stables.

Ephraim darted around the house and jogged down a trail that led to the long brick servants' house. "Manasseh!" he cried, a worried note of impatience in his voice. "If you're here, speak up! Ani is with me, and Abnu. Even the little harpist has come along. I know that will please you."

A hot wind blew past him with soft moans, punctuated by the pebbly noises of his companions' approaching footsteps on the gravel path. But the servants' quarters remained as silent as a tomb.

"If this is a trick, I will wipe the ground with your face."

The voice came from behind him, and Ephraim whirled around to see Manasseh standing behind an elaborately carved pillar, a useless bit of courtyard ornamentation that should have been installed in the garden. Manasseh came forward, moving slowly and gingerly, while Ephraim gaped at his brother.

Surely a man could not change so much in such a short time! Manasseh looked ten years older, and his face bore evidence of a severe battering. One eyelid had nearly swollen shut, the area around it green and purple with bruises. The mouth that had been so quick to smile in more carefree days hung unbalanced and puffed in an unnatural thickness above the dark beard, and a rumbling, phlegmy noise punctuated every breath Manasseh drew. An angry red gash ran across his upper arm, and the skin of his wrists was marred by marks of a scablike burgundy.

One corner of the swollen mouth lifted in a smile. "If you think I look bad," Manasseh moved closer, "you should see the ones who didn't get away."

"I heard," Ephraim said, his mind still reeling in shock. "Abnu told us everything on the boat."

Manasseh nodded soberly. "God preserved us, brother. I don't know why, but He did. And now I can only hope that you have come to help."

"Ani is with me." Ephraim jerked his thumb back toward the trail. "And Jendayi. She could not be persuaded to remain behind."

A hopeful glint lit Manasseh's eyes, then the cries of the others distracted him. Ani hurried toward his wounded ward, tears welling in his aged eyes as he lifted his hands to exclaim over Manasseh's battered face. Abnu, Jendayi, and the other Nubian stood at a respectful distance while Ani wept over the vizier's wayward son.

"Manasseh, my boy! How I feared I would never see you again!" Ani cried, exultant tears streaming down his wrinkled cheeks.

Manasseh bore the embrace for a moment, then pulled away. "Jokim is inside, and at this moment he needs you more than I do," he said, leading Ani toward a back entrance to the house. "But I know you will make him well."

"If the God who preserved you will strengthen me, I can try," Ani answered, following Manasseh into the house. "Tell me yourself about the miracle of the crocodiles. These old ears want to hear the truth from your lips, Manasseh."

————

"I believe you *thought* you heard the voice of God," Ephraim said, explaining himself again to his brother. They were sitting together on the floor in the large bedchamber of the villa, a few feet away from the bed where Jokim was being tended by Ani and Jendayi. In a corner near the doorway, Abnu and his companion sat with their backs to the wall, their eyes closed in fitful sleep. The other loyal Medjays had dispersed into the desert to look for survivors of the Hebrew camp.

"But I cannot believe you were following God's will when you went into the desert with an army." Ephraim searched his brother's face for signs of surrender. "Look at the damage you've caused! How many dead? Over two hundred? And what of the ones who ran away? Do you think they all found their way back home? No, many of your Hebrew kinsmen will be cast out for rebelling against their fathers. Others may have died in the desert. You do not know, Manasseh, what destruction you have wrought."

"I did what I had to do." Manasseh clenched his fists. "Can you deny that Canaan is our land? God Shaddai promised it to us. Why, then, should we not go there at once?"

"God willed that Abraham would father Isaac, too, and he and Sarah waited years for the promise to be fulfilled," Ephraim answered. "Yet Abraham became impatient, and fathered Ishmael with the Egyptian handmaid. By rushing ahead and trying to implement God's plan himself, Abraham brought dissension into his own family."

Ephraim grinned as an expression of surprise crossed Manasseh's face. "Yes, I've learned our history. Now that Father has nothing but time, I have enjoyed many dinners with him. And he has talked . . . and taught me many things."

Manasseh's expression grew hard and resentful. "*Now* he has time. For you he has time. But he has not tried to find me, his firstborn."

"You were not willing to be found," Ephraim said, shrugging. He glanced over at Jokim. Their cousin's face was as pale as papyrus parchment, but he had stopped moaning in that pitiful way. Ephraim wasn't certain whether his cousin's silence boded good or ill.

He was about to remark that Manasseh should have taken the time to find their father, but when he turned again, he saw that Manasseh's gaze had shifted to Jendayi's face. Though swollen and bruised, his eyes betrayed his silent ardor.

Shaking his head, Ephraim snapped his fingers to get his brother's attention.

"What?" Manasseh jerked his head around.

"Go to her," Ephraim whispered, aware of the girl's keen hearing. "She is here; you are here. Why are you waiting?"

"No." Manasseh looked at the floor and idly ran his hand over the dusty tile. "She does not love me, brother. I've opened my heart, and she has been forthright with me. She loves someone else."

"Who? Whoever he is, he can't be half the man you are."

Manasseh stared at him for a moment, then burst out in a laugh so loud that Ani screeched in alarm.

"Quiet!" The older man tossed a warning look over his shoulder as he hunched over Jokim. "You boys will wake the dead with your noise!"

Ephraim grinned at his brother, a little mystified by his response but grateful for the gleam of humor in Manasseh's eyes. This moment felt like old times . . . before Jacob's blessing had torn them apart.

"I think you're right." Manasseh carefully ran his hand over his swollen jaw. "I am twice the man. But she knows how I feel. If she changes her mind, she knows I will be waiting."

"Love." Ephraim spat the word like a curse.

"Sitamun?"

"Yes." Ephraim looked away, sighing. "I love her. And I never realized how much until the queen stopped allowing me to see her. After Father's dismissal, my invitations to the palace dried up like a wadi in drought."

"I'm sorry."

"I can't blame you, though I tried to." He managed a choking laugh. "If you hadn't ridden off into the desert, the queen would have found something else wrong with me—or Father, or Reuben, or one of the other uncles."

"I know."

"But it is wrong to hurt Sitamun! I will admit that at first I sought her while thinking of the palace and power, but then I came to know her. She is so bright and beautiful! I would wed Sitamun even if we had to live in a fisherman's hovel."

"You could keep Sitamun in a mud hut about as long as you could stand a bull over a milk bucket!" Manasseh's swollen smile deepened into laughter. "And it would take a brave man to hold either of them in place!"

Ephraim couldn't keep from chuckling. "I'm afraid you're right."

They sat for a moment in companionable quiet, but the brittle sounds of tramping footsteps shattered the silence. The Nubians woke and reached for their swords. Jendayi paled and seemed to fade into the white-washed wall. Manasseh, who was in no condition to fight, pulled a stubby sword from his kilt and held it in his bruised fist as he stared at the doorway.

"Hear me, sons of Zaphenath-paneah!" a voice called from outside the house. "We are the warriors of Pharaoh's guard, and we have surrounded this place. There is no avenue of escape, no hope of recourse unless you return with us to Thebes and face your queen."

Manasseh shot Ephraim an inquiring look, his mouth tight and grim under his beard. "This is not your fight," he said simply. "Let me go out to them. I will surrender, and you can help the others escape after I have gone."

"He said the 'sons of Zaphenath-paneah.' " Ephraim moved to his brother's side. "They know we are together. They know we will defend each other."

"Will we?" Manasseh asked, one eyebrow lifting in inquiry.

"We will." Ephraim pulled his own dagger from his kilt. It was an ornamental blade, not very practical in a duel and even less useful in a situation of war. But if his instincts proved true, Manasseh would not allow this confrontation to end with blows. He would not put the harpist in harm's way.

Manasseh squinted slightly, then turned to look at Jokim and

Jendayi. The wounded man lay as still as if he already slumbered in death's embrace, and the young woman trembled visibly. Only the Nubians and Ani, distracted by his ministrations, seemed unaffected by the situation outside.

"We cannot risk a fight." Manasseh lowered his voice and his sword. "They would kill the others, and I cannot have the blood of Ani and Jendayi on my hands. I would give my life for either of them. I cannot ask them to die on account of my stubbornness."

"That is the wisest thing you have said all day." Ephraim sheathed his own blade, then walked calmly to the doorway and lifted his hands. A dozen warriors waited outside, their swords drawn, their eyes narrowed in suspicion.

"Hail, you of the royal guards," Ephraim called, stepping out into a bright rectangle of sunlight. He frowned, finding it hard to believe that a few weeks ago any one of these men would have given their lives for *him*. "My brother and I surrender to you. Take us to your queen. Only let the others in this house depart in peace."

The commander jerked his head silently toward Ephraim. As half a dozen men came forward with ropes, Ephraim heard labored breathing behind him. Manasseh had joined him on the portico.

"Are you doing this for her?" Ephraim flinched as a pair of warriors tied his bonds too tightly in enthusiastic zeal.

"For her, for Ani, and for you." Sweat beaded on Manasseh's upper lip as the same energy was applied to his wounded flesh.

As soon as the brothers were bound, the commander climbed the steps of the portico and looked into the chamber. "Bring the others, too," he told his men, skipping lightly down the marble steps.

"Not the girl!" Manasseh thrashed in the grips of two burly guards. "My brother and I surrendered. You must let the others go!"

The commander shot a bright grin of amusement over his shoulder. "I made no such promise."

———

A barge transported the prisoners to Malkata instead of to the royal house at Thebes, and Ephraim felt the nauseating sinking of despair as the boat turned into the royal harbor on the western bank of the Nile. He had not spoken to Sitamun in several weeks. All his messages had been ignored or returned, and he doubted that she would be allowed to leave her royal apartments at Thebes if the queen was truly intent upon keeping them apart.

But a constant hope burned in his heart, for surely love could find a way to unite them. With a single private word in Sitamun's ear, he could assure her of his devotion and steadfast heart. Did she still think of him? With a woman as bright and flirtatious as Sitamun, one could never be too sure of oneself, but perhaps even at Malkata he could bribe a guard or servant to carry a message to his love.

He bit his lip as he surveyed the royal harbor. As he had suspected, the queen's barge was tied to the dock. Her royal standard fluttered and snapped imperiously from the highest mast. Farther down the dock, like an ostracized relative, stood the gilded barge that had once hoisted the regal standard of the vizier. His father's boat.

Turning his back to the docks, Ephraim crossed his arms as a new anguish seared his heart. The realization that Joseph would have to observe his sons' trial and disgrace wounded Ephraim as deeply as the thought that he might have to surrender his hope of marrying the love of his life.

Twenty-seven

THEIR FATHER WAITED AT THE PALACE GATE. MANAS-
seh's steps slowed when he recognized Joseph's somber profile
and proud bearing. Even Ephraim seemed to stutter on the path.
Memories opened before Manasseh's eyes as if a curtain had been
ripped aside, and for a moment he and Ephraim were small boys
again, compelled by Ani or Tarik to face their father and suffer
the consequences for some mischief they had committed. Manasseh's knobby knees knocked with fear; Ephraim's chubby face
twisted in a spasm as he bent forward and declared that he would
have to relieve himself before he could go one step farther. . . .

The memory vanished in a sepia haze. If only they could go
back. That childhood fear, as insignificant as a blank spot on the
parchment of life, paled in comparison to the grief and despair
tearing at Manasseh's heart. It was not bad enough that he had
brought his brother back to face Pharaoh, but Jokim still lay on
the boat in Abnu's care, too weak from his injuries to move.

Manasseh lifted his eyes to his father's face. The last weeks
had carved a new series of lines about Joseph's eyes and forehead, diminishing the impression of strength. A muscle
clenched along that chiseled jaw as Joseph's gaze met Manasseh's. He did not speak, but raw hurt and longing lay naked in
his eyes.

"Zaphenath-paneah." One of the guards stepped forward and
bowed his head in a perfunctory salute. "Your sons are commanded to appear before Pharaoh."

"I know."

Manasseh winced. His father's voice, which once rang with
the power to command ten thousand men, now seemed empty
and deflated.

"My sons will appear." Joseph moistened his dry lips. "But
the old man and the girl are of no interest to Pharaoh. The two

slaves are mine. Release them so they may return to my house."

Manasseh looked at the ground, knowing what the guard's answer would be. "I can't do that," the guard snapped, leaning on the security of his spear. "The slaves are runaways. They must be tried with the two malefactors."

"No," Manasseh groaned through stiff lips.

But his protest was useless. The palace gates opened, and without a further word or gesture, Joseph folded his hands and turned, walking forward with a steady and even tread, clothed in his spotless vizier's robe and the rags of his dignity.

The guards who had escorted Manasseh and Ephraim untied their prisoners' hands and fell back, knowing the captives could not run. Ephraim boldly followed Joseph while Manasseh limped beside him. Behind the brothers, a pair of guards pulled Jendayi and Ani forward. As Manasseh moved toward the throne room, he bitterly reflected that his stubbornness might yet result in the destruction of everyone he loved.

Throngs of nobles, supplicants, and visiting kings waited outside in the vestibule, but the sea of sycophants magically parted as Zaphenath-paneah approached the gilded double doors. A pair of trumpets blared, a chamberlain announced the former vizier's presence, and the doors swung open. As one, the waiting supplicants fell to their knees and bowed, lest some ray of the divine Pharaoh's presence fall upon them. Tense with anticipation, Manasseh stumbled forward, walking in the wake of bewildered and curious looks directed at his father.

The long narrow throne room, pillared by columns carefully painted to resemble lotus blossoms on luxurious stems, was lit by high clerestory windows that allowed bright light, not heat, to enter the stone sanctuary. Near the entrance to the king's hall, a lion lounged on the floor like a sleepy tabby cat, an intentional reminder of the remarkable two hundred ten lions this king slew in the first ten years of his reign. The walls of the throne room, which in dynasties past had been painted with scenes of the ruling king's battle exploits, varied from the traditional, for Amenhotep was not fond of war. Aside from a brief uprising in Nubia during the fifth year of his reign, only the two hundred ten lions had felt the murderous fury of his wrath.

Pharaoh's artists had painted his throne room with scenes of

Amenhotep and Queen Tiy in settings of familial bliss: conversing with the gods, entertaining their many children, cavorting in
the garden. As he progressed toward the dais at the end of the
room, Manasseh let his eyes roam over the paintings, wondering
if he would see a representation of Jendayi among the dancers,
musicians, and slaves depicted in service to the royal family. He
sighed in relief when he did not find a harpist pictured on the
wall. Perhaps Pharaoh had forgotten—and would forget—all
about the girl.

Surely the enormous throne room had never been more
crowded. As Zaphenath-paneah and his sons passed by, men and
women stood silent and as still as portraits, their black eyes glittering like polished obsidian. Armed soldiers, nobles, priests,
and scribes stared, watching the Hebrews like a snake watches a
rabbit. The muscles in Manasseh's arms tightened involuntarily
when he thought of those stares fixing upon Jendayi, who followed behind him. Silently he thanked God that she could not
see their darkly accusing eyes.

Finally they reached the platform where Pharaoh perched on
the edge of a chair covered with gold foil, his expression at once
petulant and bored. At Pharaoh's right hand sat Neferkheprure'
Wa'enre', the Crown Prince. Queen Tiy sat in the gilded chair at
his left. Members of the king's bodyguard stood alertly at attention behind the pair of thrones, their spears at the ready. Behind
the queen's guards sat a bevy of her daughters and handmaids.
A similar group of counselors and priests lingered behind the
divine king.

Manasseh had stood in the throne room a dozen times before,
but today the position of the royal family members had changed
remarkably. Sitamun, whose former place had been behind the
queen with the other royal daughters, now stood immediately
behind the king's chair, her hand resting stiffly upon his bronzed
shoulder. Haunted by the suspicion that Tiy wanted to foment
further trouble, Manasseh squinted toward the queen. What
could this mean? Had Sitamun been brought forward in order
merely to provoke Ephraim?

Manasseh cast a quick look at his brother. The significance of
Sitamun's new position was not lost on Ephraim, for his brows
drew together in an agonized expression, then a cold congested

expression settled on his face. He must have felt Manasseh's gaze, for he turned and tried to smile, but his features only flinched uncomfortably.

"She has done it," he whispered in a voice so low only Manasseh could hear. "The queen was too afraid of us, frightened of the people we might become."

"What, exactly, has she done?" Manasseh asked, frowning.

Ephraim stared at the queen, amused resentment evident in the slight curl of his upper lip. "You have been away. You have not heard. Pharaoh took another royal bride a few days ago. The marriage was arranged on Pharaoh's behalf by the Mother of Egypt herself. But I have just realized that the marriage was also arranged by the bride's mother!"

Manasseh shook his head, his thoughts confused and cloudy. "Who is the bride?" he asked, searching for an unfamiliar face among the royal women.

"Don't you see? Tiy is afraid Amenhotep or the Crown Prince will lose the throne if one of her daughters marries an outsider! She's afraid of *us*! So Pharaoh's new bride is Sitamun, his eldest daughter!"

Manasseh blanched. The idea repulsed him. Though it had long been reported that Egyptian royalty approved incestuous marriages in order to avoid diluting the divine royal bloodline, he knew of no such marriages within his lifetime. Until now.

His heart twisted in genuine pity as he looked at Sitamun. He might not live through the day, but at least he had been able to tell Jendayi of his love. But Sitamun, now a royal consort, would never know anything but her father's attentions. At sixteen, she had already experienced all life would offer her. She would never taste anything of the world beyond the royal harem and the palace walls.

The crowd caught its breath in an audible gasp as Pharaoh lowered the ceremonial crook and flail. At this signal, Joseph stepped forward and prostrated himself before Pharaoh.

"Rise, Zaphenath-paneah." There was a note of regret that went beyond nostalgia in Pharaoh's voice, as though he missed an old friend.

Joseph stood and met the king's gaze without speaking, his hands clasped in front of him, his eyes silent pools of appeal.

The Gold of Praise, the ornate chain symbolizing Pharaoh's favor, hung heavily about his neck, a visible reminder that he had once been a valuable counselor, a man worthy of respect.

The king lifted the crook and flail, and silence fell upon the stirring crowd like a dampening cloak. "I have no quarrel with you, Zaphenath-paneah." Pharaoh frowned in exasperation. "It is your elder son who must today answer to my will."

As if on cue, the high priest of Amon-Re stepped forward. "Manasseh! Your king the divine Pharaoh summons you!"

Obeying the command, Manasseh lowered himself to the floor as quickly as his bruised body would allow.

"You, Manasseh, son of Zaphenath-paneah, stand accused of treason," the priest recited as Manasseh lifted his head and shoulders. From lowered lids, Amenhotep shot a commanding look at him, and Manasseh found it hard to believe he knelt before the same man he and his family had dined with so many times. There was nothing of the genial father and host about Amenhotep now. In this room he was king, Pharaoh of Egypt, and nothing else.

"You have conspired to commit acts of war," the priest went on, reading from a parchment scroll. "You have defied the authority of your father Zaphenath-paneah, Egypt's noble vizier. You lured the king's warriors from their places of service. You have waged war and brought death upon loyal Egyptian warriors." The king's glare burned through Manasseh as the priest looked up with one final question. "Have you anything to say in your defense?"

God, give me wisdom. Manasseh licked his swollen lips and looked up through his half-closed eyelids. He wanted to rise to his feet but feared he would fall, so he remained on his knees.

"Life, prosperity, and health to you, mighty Pharaoh!" He felt himself wavering and put a hand out to Ephraim's shoulder for support. "If it please the king, know that I did conspire to return my people to their homeland, but I acted in accordance with a command from God Shaddai, the Almighty God of Israel, whom I must obey before any man on earth. I did ask one Medjay warrior to assist me, and others followed him in hope of spoils. But we did not wage war upon Egyptians. Another enemy rose up in the night and slaughtered half my company. My God and my comrades know that as of this hour I have not turned my sword against any man, not even in self-defense.''

The king's painted eyes remained as expressionless as a hawk's, while the queen regarded Manasseh with impassive coldness. Manasseh inclined his head, knowing they had not finished with him.

"Read the other charge," Tiy commanded, lifting an imperious finger toward the priest.

The bald man shuffled for another scroll, then cleared his throat. "Ephraim, younger son of Zaphenath-paneah," the priest droned, stealing a quick glance at Ephraim's face. "You stand accused of rushing to aid your brother as he did rise up in treason against this throne. You have also taken liberties with a princess of the royal family—"

Sitamun flinched.

"—and conspired with ruthless ambition to take the throne of Egypt for yourself and your posterity."

"Not true!" Ephraim's eyes glowed with a savage inner fire.

"Did you not tell my daughter that Egypt could grow great under the influence of Abraham's offspring?" Tiy hissed, leaning forward.

"And I meant it! But I never did conspire to take the throne! And I journeyed to meet my brother in an attempt to *stop* him, not join him!"

"Silence!" Pharaoh held up his jeweled hand. Behind him, the two young viziers watched, their faces clouded with anxiety.

A murmur of voices, a palpable unease, crept through the room as the king considered his judgment. Manasseh understood Pharaoh's predicament. If the king condemned him for obeying the voice of God Shaddai, Amenhotep would face severe criticism from the priests who claimed that the gods could and did speak to men. And Manasseh had not actually injured any Egyptians, his men had not participated in a single battle. Finally, Pharaoh could not forget that Manasseh was the elder son of Zaphenath-paneah, the Bread of Life, who still enjoyed enormous popularity with the people.

The accusations against Ephraim were as insubstantial as worthless chaff, but his fate would rest on Manasseh's. By marrying his daughter, Pharaoh had eliminated the danger posed by

Ephraim's wooing of Sitamun. And if Pharaoh decided that Manasseh had not committed treason, the charge of conspiracy would be a questionable point.

But Manasseh's heart sank with swift disappointment as he considered an undeniable and dreadful question. How could a divine king acknowledge that a mightier God had the right to command men to disobey the Voice of Egypt, the physical incarnation of Horus and Amon-Re? Pharaoh could not. Admitting that a mightier god than himself existed would be tantamount to admitting Amenhotep was no god at all, only a puffed-up godling with dreams of divinity. . . .

Queen Tiy's voice, velvet-edged but strong, broke the silence. "If I may speak, my King"—she inclined her head toward him in a stiff gesture—"your decision seems to rest upon motive. Did the sons of Zaphenath-paneah act out of a sincere desire to follow their God, or did they choose to indulge in war for the sake of insurrection?"

"You are right." Amenhotep glared at Manasseh from beneath his paint-lined eyelids.

"I know you have already discerned the truth, for you are god." The queen's voice was as cool and clear as ice water. "But if this God of the Hebrews has the power to command men to disobey Pharaoh, why not let Him reveal His will in a physical manifestation? Amon-Re rides across the sky every morning. Hapi pours her floodwaters forth to bless our land. Surely this God Shaddai can do something to reveal Himself to your people."

Manasseh stared at the queen in astonished silence while the chamber buzzed with whispers. What sort of insanity was this? Even Pharaoh's face was as blank as a slab of marble.

Realizing that the king did not understand, Tiy continued. "Your game of Hounds and Jackals," she said, her dusky eyes bathing him in assuring admiration. "The tiles out in the garden. Let the brothers play against each other. Manasseh says he had to obey the powerful God Shaddai. Ephraim says he was trying to stop Manasseh. How could this God send one brother to make war and the other to stop it? One of them lies, so let them play the game. At the conclusion, all who are assembled here will know that the winner spoke the truth."

Pharaoh's face brightened. The idea of sparing one of Zaphenath-paneah's sons obviously appealed to him.

"What shall the winner win?" Sitamun's high, silvery voice rang through the anxious whispers in the room, and Manasseh glanced toward her in surprise. Her wide eyes, filled with longing regret, had fixed upon Ephraim as if she had suddenly realized that she might lose her flattering suitor forever.

"The winner shall save his life," Pharaoh answered, his stentorian voice rumbling through the chamber. "And as an added prize—" He glanced about the room, his bright eyes bobbing for some treasure within his power to bestow, then he thrust out his hand and pointed past Manasseh. "The winner shall have *her*!"

Manasseh felt his heart constrict, knowing that the king pointed to Jendayi. No one had dared to suggest that she and Ani were anything more than slaves obeying their masters' will, but she was still property, and she had belonged to Pharaoh.

Amenhotep turned to Joseph, his finger still stretching toward Jendayi. "Have you any objection, Zaphenath-paneah?" The beginnings of a smile tipped the corners of his mouth. "After all, I did return the girl to you."

Manasseh pressed his lips together as his father slowly shook his head. How could he object? Pharaoh had already stripped Joseph of his life, his calling, and his sons. What did it matter if he repossessed one blind harpist?

"Then that is how it shall be." Pharaoh lowered his finger and folded his hands in satisfaction. "The winner wins his life and the harpist. The loser forfeits his life. And this God of the Hebrews will decide the course of the game . . . which we shall play on the morrow."

He smiled, anticipating the event to come, and Tiy rose to her feet and extended her hand. Taking the hint, Pharaoh stood as well, and the two of them departed the throne room, trailed by a sea of daughters, priests, wives, and counselors.

———

Motivated either by compassion or spite, the captain of Pharaoh's guard put Ephraim and Manasseh into different cells, separated by a far expanse of sandy courtyard. Manasseh thought the arrangement a good idea, for a deep depression had engulfed him after Pharaoh announced the bizarre contest. Ephraim had always enjoyed more luck at games and sporting events than had Manasseh, and he found he had little to say to the brother who would undoubtedly win the game. The comforting words he would have called out across the courtyard would not move past the knot of jealousy in his throat.

So this is the meaning of grandfather Jacob's blessing, Manasseh thought, stretching out on a thread-worn strip of blanket some other prisoner had left behind. *Ephraim shall be the greater nation because Ephraim will live long enough to beget sons and daughters! Whereas I shall die on the morrow, and the last thing my eyes will see is Pharaoh placing Jendayi's hand in Ephraim's.*

His misery was so acute that his heart ached worse than his physical pains, which were considerable. He turned onto his bruised side and moaned, regretting but not surprised that life had boiled down to a choice between him and his brother. They had always been rivals.

A quarter moon the color of dappled bone rose in the sky, and even in that elongated form its light eclipsed the stars and lit the prison yard. From the bars of his cell Manasseh could see that Ephraim seemed to be passing just as troubled a night. He lay stiffly on a small wad of straw someone had tossed into his cage, his face upturned to the thatched roof over his head, his feet beating against each other in an anxious internal rhythm.

Manasseh lowered his head to his arms and sighed. His father would not be sleeping either. Despite his own unhappiness, Manasseh felt a stab of compassion for the man who had risen from slavery to the dizzying heights of power. During the time of famine, Joseph had held the world's survival in his hands. Kings and potentates from every known nation journeyed to the Black Land to buy or beg for food, and Joseph had ably and generously fed the world. The far-flung territories, ordinarily sources of never ending aggravation and trouble for Egypt's kings, had accepted their dependence upon Egypt's grain and grown accustomed to her reins upon their backs. And through Joseph's insightful plan, Pharaoh had gained control of every bit of Egyptian land except that owned by the priests. As a result, Zaphenath-paneah had been granted power, respect, riches, a beautiful wife, two charming sons, even his long lost family.

But the tide had turned. Now Zaphenath-paneah had no wife, no power, and little respect. Would God also take his sons? He had already lost one. Though Joseph had kept his features deceptively composed during the audience with Pharaoh, Manasseh knew the day had been especially agonizing for him when Amenhotep, Joseph's surrogate son, visibly and publicly demonstrated that he cared so little for Zaphenath-paneah's judgment that he would consult a game board before asking advice from the former Father to Pharaoh.

Manasseh closed his eyes and lifted a prayer: "God Shaddai, forgive him for not believing. You have spoken through him for so long, he has found it difficult to accept that you would speak through . . . me." He gulped as a hot tear slipped down his swollen cheek. "I still find it hard to believe myself. You led me into the wilderness where we met with failure. You have led me to Pharaoh's court, where I will probably die on the morrow while my brother lives. But I am willing to do whatever you require. I beg you to make me ready."

Deep within the palace at Malkata, Pharaoh tossed and turned, refusing to be borne to the world of dreams. Beside him, stretched across the spacious bed fit only for a king, Sitamun lay asleep, her gentle snores punctuating the darkness.

Looking at her, Pharaoh frowned. He would never have agreed to marry his daughter if not for the queen's insistence. He knew Tiy's insecurity could be traced to her own humble roots, but sleeping with his daughter was about as thrilling as counting bricks in a pyramid. Once Sitamun had produced an heir, he would send her to the harem and let her live out her days in peace.

Tiy's other suggestion, the game of Hounds and Jackals, had at first struck Amenhotep as delightfully fitting, but now it bothered him. Should a man's destiny be determined by a roll of the knucklebones? Zaphenath-paneah would never agree to adjudicate a case this way, and the former vizier's injured and sorrowful expression had revealed to the entire court just how deeply the queen's idea offended him. Amenhotep knew he should not have wounded Zaphenath-paneah, for the people still revered him and his unseen God. Though very few even knew how to worship this God Shaddai, Amenhotep could not refute the consensus of opinion that an invisible God had blessed the Black Land for the sake of its vizier.

That opinion had grown stronger in the days since Zaphenath-paneah's departure from court. A host of intolerable situations had recently developed: an incurable fungus had blighted the harvest at Opet, a rich vein of black granite had disappeared at the Ibhet Quarry, even the normally easy-to-please harem women had developed a habit of ceaseless squabbling. *Someday soon*, Pharaoh thought, *I might have to bring Zaphenath-paneah back to court. . . .*

Amenhotep could never openly espouse belief in God Shaddai, but having Zaphenath-paneah next to him as a shield had deflected trouble before. He would be wise to restore his old friend to the vizierate, but nothing could be done until this matter of Ephraim and Manasseh had been settled.

But—the contest! It was too late to pardon the young men. He had already publicly declared that he and God Shaddai knew the game's outcome.

Sitamun sobbed softly in a dream, and Amenhotep rolled his eyes and chewed on the edge of his thumbnail. The game would have to be played. One son would live, and one would make his home in the tomb. And after burying one of his sons, Zaphenath-paneah would hear the king's offer to return to the vizierate, spit in Amenhotep's face, and be promptly executed for his effrontery.

Pharaoh covered his face with his hands, tasting defeat for the first time in his life.

"Hush, my girl, don't weep," Ani whispered, his thickened voice rising above the wails of other slaves in Pharaoh's prison. He and Jendayi had been thrust together into the same rank pit, two pieces of property not worthy of any special considerations for modesty or propriety.

Jendayi lifted her face from the matted straw and tried to swallow the sobs that kept rising from her throat. "I can't help it. I don't know what to do. It is too terrible, Ani, too unjust. Manasseh has hurt no one, and Ephraim sought only to help his brother.''

"You speak both their names with affection.'' A slight trace of cynicism lined Ani's voice. "How convenient, since it appears you will leave Malkata tomorrow belonging to one or the other.''

"But I don't want anyone to die!'' Her anguish peaked to shatter the last shreds of her control. "I only want to be loved.''

"My dear girl, don't weep.'' The straw rustled as Ani slid to her side. She felt aged hands upon her head, and he tenderly pulled her to his shoulder, cradling her in his arms. "If you want to be loved, do not fear. I believe you already are.''

"I know,'' she murmured in a despairing whisper. "I see that now. I thought Ephraim loved me, but all the time it was Manasseh, quietly caring, trying not to hurt me—''

"Hush, child.''

"I cannot!'' Bitter laughter bubbled to her lips. "I never knew how blind I was until last night. Manasseh's love was there all along for me to see, to *test*, and Ephraim never gave me any indication that he cared. Oh, I do not fault him, for I imagined and invented every sign of affection I thought I saw. . . .''

She closed her eyes and flung out her hands in simple despair. "I didn't *see* anything! Manasseh asked me to have faith in him, but I couldn't! I could only hear Ephraim's voice. I dwelt on memories of Ephraim's kiss. I put Manasseh out of my mind—''

"No, child, you didn't.'' Ani spoke with cool authority. "You didn't forget him. And when he called for you, you risked everything to answer. Whether you know it or not, you have already made the choice to love.''

Jendayi listened in silence, then gave the old man a grateful kiss on the cheek. Perhaps he was right. Curling up in the straw, she carried the hope in his words back to the bitterly cold caves of her lonely soul.

Could she choose to love? Was the answer to her nightmare really so simple?

Only the gods could tell.

~ Twenty-eight ~

THOUGH ADULTS AND CHILDREN ALIKE ENJOYED THE game of Hounds and Jackals, there was no sign of childish merry-making when a squadron of Pharaoh's warriors escorted Manasseh and Ephraim into the royal garden the next morning. Pharaoh and Queen Tiy had already been seated in tall chairs before the reflecting pool, and a host of curious nobles lounged behind a specially cordoned observation area. A team of archers, Manasseh noticed with a grimace, stood stiffly at the far end of the garden, ready for the execution order. Abnu was not among them. Manasseh had heard from one of the guards that the giant and his loyal comrade had been transferred to the palace at Thebes just after the sick man in their care mysteriously escaped. Pharaoh was not pleased with the Medjays, but he valued them too highly to discipline them harshly.

"Look." Ephraim nodded toward the archers. "Our Pharaoh is not willing to risk criticism in his handling of this matter. The sentence will be carried out before anyone can protest."

"Who could protest?" Manasseh rubbed his stiff arms. "He has already announced that God Shaddai will rule this contest. And so one of us will be dispatched to the otherworld according to the will of Almighty God."

"I am not worried," Ephraim answered, swinging his arms across his chest as if he prepared for a wrestling match. "You think I have no faith in God Shaddai, but I do. And I know Pharaoh is right in at least one thing—the God of Abraham, Isaac, and Jacob *will* prevail here today."

"If you have such faith, why did you not go with me into the desert?" Manasseh lifted a brow. "If you believe in God, you should have believed that Canaan is our home, for it is what He promised—"

"I didn't go with you into the desert because I didn't want to go," Ephraim interrupted, shrugging. He shook out his arms, then slapped his hands on his hips and gave Manasseh an abashed smile. "I hate the desert. I hate sand, and heat, and inferior food. And I hate pain, the kind you felt when someone plastered those bruises on your face. But today, brother, I have no choice but to follow you. And if I have to endure pain, I hope God will be merciful and dispatch me quickly."

"I will never understand you." Baffled, Manasseh stared at the brother he loved more than he cared to admit. Charming Ephraim could tell you his worst faults with a smile, and still you would want to take him home and keep him forever.

Ephraim did not answer but turned away. Respecting his silence, Manasseh lifted his eyes to the sky. The heavens were pure blue from north to south, with no more than a little violet duskiness lingering in the west—a perfect day.

Manasseh's gaze arched slowly back and forth over the crowd until he spied Jendayi, Ani, Joseph, and Tarik. The four of them stood apart from the others in a little knot, united by fear and despair. His father's eyes, large and fierce with pain, were fixed upon nothing, while Tarik looked straight at Manasseh. *Concentrate*, the captain's piercing eyes seemed to say, *take care. Remember all I have taught you.* Jendayi's unseeing eyes were wide, but a look of intense, clear light seemed to pour through them as she nestled against Ani's birdlike chest.

Which brother did she want to win? In either case, she would belong to a man who would take care of her. So why did she cling to Ani as if she were afraid?

Manasseh stepped forward as the king's guard gestured to him. One of the king's new viziers, a portly fellow who only a month before had been a scribe tending to requisitions for the king's tomb, mounted a stand and held up his hands. When the crowd fell silent, his gaze focused upon Ephraim and Manasseh. "You must each choose a representative to roll the knucklebones for you." His brown eyes flickered with roguishness. "Whom shall you choose?"

With the cocky grin of earlier days, Ephraim lifted his head and searched the crowd. Manasseh shook his head in disbelief when his brazen brother flashed a smile at Sitamun. "I would enjoy the honor of having Queen Sitamun cast the bones for me," he said, fixing her in a dark-eyed vise as he suddenly unsmiled.

Murmurs swept through the crowd, but the new queen rose from her chair and moved with fluid strides toward the tray containing the bones.

"And you?" the vizier barked at Manasseh.

Manasseh looked over the crowd again. He could not ask his father to participate in an activity that might condemn Ephraim, and poor Ani would be just as torn between them. But Tarik—he caught the bantam guard's gaze and saw the captain nod slowly. Tarik was a warrior with a heart of steel. His courage would see them through this day.

"I choose Tarik, captain of Zaphenath-paneah's guard." Manasseh shifted his gaze back to the undeserving vizier.

The stout man nodded and rubbed his hands together. "Good. You, Manasseh, will be the hound. You will run this course—" He pointed toward a looping pathway that wound through the eastern half of the garden. "And you, Ephraim, will be the jackal and will run the opposite course."

Ephraim gave the vizier a grudging nod, then positioned himself before the first tile. Manasseh looked at Ephraim and they shared a smile, then Manasseh moved to his starting position and turned toward the small dais where Sitamun stood next to a polished stand.

As Tarik shouldered his way through the crowd, Sitamun gathered the bones from their tray, cast a winning smile at Ephraim, and tossed the knucklebones with a triumphant flourish.

The vizier bent over the pan and read the bones. "Six!" The sixth tile, to which Ephraim proceeded in a burst of energy, was linked to the lower half of the jackal's course. Ephraim paused on the tile and in an instant the bark carriers appeared with the fanciful carved boat of Amon-Re. They lowered it, Ephraim climbed inside, and then, amid a smattering of applause from the observers, the slaves lifted the long poles to their shoulders and carried Ephraim forward to a point only eight tiles away from the end of the course.

Manasseh watched in silence, astounded both by the casual attitude of the staring nobles and his brother's unconcern. He was surprised Ephraim did not wave as the boat passed by.

With a determined quickness in every movement, Tarik stepped to the dais where the vizier held the metal pan containing the knucklebones. Tarik picked them up, jostled them in his palm for an instant, then dropped them clattering into the open container.

"One!" the vizier called out. Manasseh closed his eyes in relief and took a step forward. Though his roll had not been nearly as favorable as Ephraim's, at least he had been able to begin the game. Many times as a child he had sat in morose silence waiting to throw a one or a six while Ephraim gallivanted gaily around the game board.

Bowing deeply from the waist, the vizier presented the metal tray to Sitamun, who cast a longing look at Ephraim as she scooped up the knucklebones and pressed them to her lips for good fortune. Manasseh cast a quick look at Pharaoh to see if he noticed the unspoken language between his wife and the accused criminal, but Pharaoh's eyes were fixed upon the crowd, not the course.

The crowd stilled as Sitamun shook the bones, then released them into the tray.

"One!" the vizier called, his face pinking with eagerness. Sensing that Ephraim was the royal favorite, a few observers applauded as he took the next tile.

Tarik stepped forward again, his chin lifting in iron determination as if he would not allow Manasseh to fail. With vigorous intensity he picked up the bones and clattered them together in his hand, then released them with a vigorous gesture.

"Six!" the vizier called.

A chorus of ahhs rose from the crowd as Manasseh paced out the allotted number of tiles. He had missed linking with the shortcut by one tile, but as he reached the sixth he bellowed in delight. "This tile is marked with the ankh!" he called, rejoicing in the small but satisfying victory. Ephraim's insanely inappropriate gaiety was contagious. "Roll again, Tarik!"

The vizier's mouth spread into a thin-lipped smile as he handed the bones to Tarik again. "Throw them," he said tersely.

Tarik picked up the stones, held them in his hands for a moment, and then did something Manasseh had never seen him do before. In the manner of the Hebrews, Tarik the great Egyptian captain held his hands aloft, lifted his face to heaven, and moved his lips in a silent prayer.

The vizier's eyebrows rose in amazement. "By the power of Hathor's sun disk, what are you doing?" he asked, his voice heavy with sarcasm.

Pharaoh leaned forward in his chair and stared but did not speak until Tarik lowered his head. "Captain," Pharaoh said, his coolly impersonal tone breaking the uncomfortable silence, "if this is some form of protest—"

"It is not, my King." Tarik dipped his head in a formal bow. "But since you said God Shaddai's will should command this event, I thought one of us should ask His blessing upon it."

Pharaoh sank back in his chair and clapped his hand to his cheek, stunned into stillness. Tiy leaned forward, her face marked with loathing. What might she do? Manasseh tensed when Tarik began to shake the bones again.

"Three!" the vizier called when the bones had come to rest in the pan. Manasseh took three giant steps forward, only to grimace when he realized that the third tile connected to a short-cut that would force him backward. The toothless old priest tipped his basket and a pair of cobras slithered forth, ostensibly to chase Manasseh back to the beginning of the shortcut. He re-treated but noticed that the tile where he finally stood was still one ahead of where he had begun at the beginning of his turn. He tossed Tarik a smile of encouragement.

While a pair of shaven priests chased the harmless cobras through the skittish crowd, Sitamun stepped forward to roll the bones again for Ephraim. There was a clatter, a clang, then the vizier yelled "One!" and Ephraim moved forward again.

———

Jendayi grew more uncomfortable with every moment the game progressed. She had scarcely rested at all the previous night. She had not even slept long enough to visit the nether-world of her nightmare. But still the old fears haunted her. She had awakened in a panic, her mind congested with doubts and regrets that had not vanished in the activity of the morning.

Ani had taken her arm and escorted her from the prison to the palace, but exhaustion blurred the scents and sounds in the garden around her, blending her nightmares with reality. Now she stood upon tiles that radiated heat just like the glowing tiles of her dream. And even though she clutched the comforting fabric of Ani's cloak, eerily familiar sounds seeped through her darkness to haunt her. Those in the crowd who rooted for Ephraim were now howling like jackals, giving voice to Anubis and his gleaming ebony eyes. Somewhere in the gathering a papyrus reed scratched across parchment, recording every action just like Thoth the Scribe. And was that sound the clatter of bones or her teeth chattering in fear? The object clanging suddenly in the pan was her own hard heart, the useless and atrophied vessel that would compel her toward the vicious jaws of the One who Eats the Dead.

You have not loved! She had developed an uncanny sense of hearing. Now she heard Anubis' accusation as if it came to her on an inner pulse that had nothing to do with the anxious crowd around her.

"I tried to!" she whispered, wringing her hands. "And I will! If given the chance, I will love him who first loved me!"

Stupid girl! The darkness enveloping her congealed and shifted. Anubis' shadowy face took on shape and thickness. The jackal looked at her with narrow, glinting eyes. *You are too late! Manasseh will die here today, and you will be lost. And so we must surrender you to Ammit.*

"No," she whimpered over her choking, beating heart. "Manasseh will not die. You have no power over him. And he loves me—"

He lies.

"No! He does. I don't know why, but he does."

He will die here, Jendayi. Already he is losing the game. The archers stand ready, and they will shoot at Pharaoh's command. Then you will be given to the one who does not love you.

"No!"

The jackal's curling fangs seemed to lift in a smile. *Perhaps there is a way you and Manasseh can be together. Run, Jendayi, toward the queen's chair. Pharaoh wears a dagger in his belt. Take it and strike the queen. You cannot hope to harm her, for the guards will strike you down as soon as they guess your intention. But you will die in the same hour as your love, and to-*

gether you shall enter into the otherworld. If you love, prove yourself. And thus you may save yourself from Ammit.

Hideously alluring, the jackal's suggestion fluttered through her thoughts. She knew where the royal couple sat, for she could hear Tiy's shrill nasal tones through the voices of the gathering. Anubis was right, the guards would be upon her as soon as she neared the dais, and she would be helpless to fend off any mortal blow. . . .

And Manasseh was losing. She could tell by the low murmurs of the crowd that followed Tarik's toss of the knucklebones. He would die today, so she could precede him into the Hall of the Two Truths.

Quietly, she let her hand fall from Ani's cloak. He didn't seem to notice.

She turned slightly to face the royal pavilion. Her questing fingers felt the cordoning rope, but it was merely decorative. She could slip under it in a heartbeat. If she moved swiftly, she could be upon the steps of the pavilion before Tarik had to take another turn.

A tight knot within her begged for release. Was this not the answer she sought?

Her thoughts turned toward Manasseh. His name echoed in the black stillness of her mind. She recalled the rhapsody of being held in his strong arms, the comfort his words had brought her troubled heart. "If you will trust me, your heart will begin to live," he had promised. "Defeat your dream now, Jendayi. Have faith in me . . . and in my God Almighty."

Defeat your dream now. Your heart will begin to live.

Manasseh would not want her to die. Manasseh had urged her to defeat her nightmare, to believe in his love, to trust that he would return for her. And he had promised that he would, *with the help of his God Almighty.*

If she loved him, she would believe him.

"I will not do this," she whispered, turning back to the dark image of Anubis. "Manasseh worships another god. At the end of my mortal life, I choose to stand before Him."

You are forever a fool. You are truly blind.

Snatches of cheers and the raucous sounds of laughter filled the air, noises from the progressing game, but Jendayi could not tear her inner eyes from the jackal's face.

Manasseh's love is as invisible as the God he serves. Has he ever kissed you like Ephraim?

"No," she admitted in a broken whisper.

Didn't he leave you in Pharaoh's house? He went away to war, not caring what happened to you!

"He went away . . . to obey. He would have come back for me. He did come back."

Yes, as a traitor. Surrender your life to his God, and you are lost to us forever. You shall not again enter the Hall of the Two Truths. You will never pass through these portals into the otherworld.

Suddenly all the formulas, the incantations, and the rituals seemed a senseless and heavy burden. Why not surrender their uncertainty and falseness in exchange for faith in one who loved her?

"Go from me! I will never seek to please you again!"

An indescribable softening took place within her as she uttered the words. She felt as if a warm light had permeated every dark recess of her soul. The feeling lifted her heart and filled her with confidence.

"I will never again place my heart within the pan of your scales, Anubis. Another God shall judge my heart . . . and another man shall claim it."

The darkness before her eyes swirled in a fierce churning of textures, then the figure of Anubis retreated into inky blackness. Shaken, Jendayi reached out, half expecting that the physical world had dissolved away, too, but her groping fingers found Ani's thin arm at her side.

Just then the assembly erupted in a collective groan.

"What has happened?" she asked, afraid to hear the answer.

Ani paused. "Manasseh has been steadily catching up. They are both three tiles away from the shenu square." Awkwardly, he cleared his throat. "Neither player has moved in several turns. Whichever man first rolls a three will win."

Jendayi tightened her grasp on the old man's arm, fully understanding what he had *not* said. Whichever player did not roll a three would die.

Twenty-nine

IT WAS SITAMUN'S TURN TO ROLL, EPHRAIM'S TURN TO move. Smirking in confidence, Pharaoh's newest queen picked up the bones and blew on them for luck. Bored with the lull in the action and fully aware that every eye had focused upon her, she transferred the bones to one hand, then mimicked the vizier's captain and lifted her head and hands as if for a moment of silent prayer.

She heard Pharaoh chuckle behind her. Several of her ladies-in-waiting twittered. Sitamun kept up the pretense, doggedly moving her lips in a nonsense prayer, the bones sharp against the tender palm of her skin.

The crowd began to snicker. Amused, Sitamun lifted one eyelid to peek at her father's former vizier. Beside his steward and the little harpist, Zaphenath-paneah stood as motionless as a statue, his head bowed, his eyes closed. His lips did not move, but Sitamun knew he was praying to his God Shaddai in earnest.

Suddenly she tired of the game. Ephraim had been an irresistible diversion, a pleasant way to aggravate her parents and the stuffy Hebrew vizier. But now she was a queen, and no longer a child—

She would never be a child again.

"For Amon-Re!" she cried bitterly, lowering her head. She opened her hand, and the bones clanged into the pan.

"Two!" called the vizier.

Bored now with Ephraim, the game, and her life, Sitamun crossed her arms and frowned in cold fury.

Manasseh noticed Sitamun's restlessness. So, undoubtedly, had Ephraim. The game was nearly over, and the thin layer of his brother's bravado had worn away. Ephraim might be willing to accept God's will in principle, but Manasseh was certain his brother was not ready to die. And Ephraim would be good to Jendayi, perhaps he would even grant her freedom.

Manasseh lifted his eyes to Tarik and held the captain in his gaze. One of Tarik's brows shot up in a mute question, and Manasseh blinked slowly, signaling his wishes. For a moment Tarik frowned in wordless protest, but Manasseh nodded slightly and tilted his head toward the area where his father stood with Ani and Jendayi.

He would do this for them. And for Ephraim, the favored son who carried Jacob's best and brightest blessing.

Tarik lifted the bones and rattled them in his palm, but Manasseh knew they would not fall into the pan this time. Tarik would do as Manasseh wished and drop them onto the ground, effectively surrendering the game to his opponent.

Perhaps God had spared him in the desert so he could rescue Ephraim now.

Tarik's granite chin quivered. He extended his hand over the pan, then shifted his weight and moved his hand away. Opening his palm, he dropped the bones into the sand at his feet.

"No!" Ephraim's features twisted into a horrified expression of disapproval.

"Manasseh forfeits. Ephraim wins!" the vizier cried, signaling the archers.

———

Tiy stiffened in shock and disappointment as the captain threw the bones to the ground. If she had had a moment's warning, she might have forbidden the man to end the game this way, but she had never expected the captain to sacrifice Zaphenath-paneah's son.

She leaned forward as the archers advanced, then lifted her hand to shade her eyes. The bright sunlight had shifted strangely, casting a pallid light over the gathering. The restless crowd stirred, then an odd coldness settled over the area, a darkly textured sensation like a gust of wind from the otherworld. As voices shrieked in rising confusion and fear, a whirlwind abruptly materialized from the paling sky and towered over the garden in a sullen yellow spout, bellowing over their heads like a river crocodile in mating season.

The claws of the wind snatched wigs and ornaments from the heads of men and women alike, including Pharaoh, forcing a frantic priest to dive for a covering with which to cover the sacred royal head. Across the garden, the sharp and brittle snap of wood cracked through the roaring noise, and Tiy trembled, watching in hypnotized horror as the funnel attacked the archers' bows and arrows, then moved on to snap Pharaoh's beloved acacia trees as easily as toothpicks.

Windblown sand scoured her cheek and blew between her teeth. She opened her lips to scream, but a mouthful of dirt and hot air rushed in to prevent her. Whimpering like a lost child, Tiy threw her arms over her head and sank to the ground, cowering before the fierce presence of the spinning whirlwind. The great current of roaring air drove everyone to their knees, then swirled overhead like an angry warring creature waiting to breathe death upon anyone who dared to stand and defy it.

But two were standing. Whether through terror-induced stamina or sheer courage, Tiy saw that Ephraim and Manasseh remained on their feet, each brother as steady upon his golden tile as if he had been rooted there.

A new kind of fear shook Tiy's body from toe to hair when the whirlwind moved toward the brothers, slowly, purposefully, like a probing finger. The pair stood less than ten feet apart, separated only by the reflecting pool and the shenu symbol. The tip of the whirlwind nosed forward until it hovered over the shenu, mocking Pharaoh's royal insignia. Suddenly, in a vast explosion of noise and color, the undulating column widened. The queen let out a tiny whine of mounting dread as the edges of its hot breath expanded to envelop the two brothers.

A thunderbolt jagged through her as the funnel lifted. Ephraim and Manasseh no longer stood on the tiles, nor were they brokenly sprawled on the ground. The monster wind had swept them up like a gigantic hand.

The whirling cyclone retreated farther into the heavens, shifting and lifting until it metamorphosed into a boiling gray cloud a few feet above the surface of the pool. The cloud hung there, silently, as if it waited for something. From a few feet away, Tiy saw Amenhotep lift his head and gaze upward. The new vizier stared too, slack-mouthed, a tenuous stream of drool dripping from his lips.

Slowly, Pharaoh rose to his hands and knees. When he spoke, his voice was high-pitched and reedy. "What . . . what would you have me do?" he asked the swirling cloud bank.

The dark mass wheeled around its invisible axis, appearing to thicken and congeal. A wild wind hooted, then two human forms fell from the black shadow, landing with loud splashes in the reflecting pool. After depositing its human cargo, the cloud whirled again, and a thousand sparks of diamond light brightened its dark canopy. Still on the ground, Tiy tilted her head, straining to hear the chorus of mellifluous sounds that seemed to emanate from it, voices that could only come from supernatural throats. The strangely melodic song rose and fell, then the cloud spun one final time and lifted, vanishing into a sky of perfect blue.

Wave after wave of shock slapped at her. Tiy lowered her gaze to the pool where Ephraim and Manasseh were laughing and wringing water from their dripping garments. Ephraim looked about the garden with an irresistibly devastating grin on his face. Even Manasseh wore a slow, steady smile of happiness. Though they were wet, Ephraim's wig had not been blown from his head, nor did either brother appear to be injured from the fall. In fact, Tiy noticed, peering intently at them, the bruises that had marked Manasseh's face only a few moments before had inexplicably faded.

Pressing an unsteady hand to her head, she realized that her own wig had been ripped off, leaving her shorn head exposed. Grasping the sheared top of a plant, the only material within reach, she held the mangled greenery to her head and cringed like a scolded dog, keeping one wary eye on the sky.

———

Amenhotep faltered. For a moment he ducked as if he would prostrate himself before the sons of his disgraced vizier. But after a hasty glance upward to make certain the funnel cloud had disappeared, he remembered his own divinity and forced himself to rise.

Pinching his lower lip with his teeth, he turned to the

younger, more easygoing son. "What does this mean?" he asked, his voice low and uncertain.

Ephraim answered with a jaunty shrug and thrust his hands on his hips. "Ask my father. He will know."

Resigned to the inevitable, Amenhotep lifted his chin and turned to Zaphenath-paneah. He and his party had taken cover on the ground, too, but like Ephraim and Manasseh, their clothing and wigs had been no more than ruffled by the vicious claws of the wind.

"I ask you, Zaphenath-paneah," Amenhotep called, uncomfortably aware that his temples had begun to throb. "What has happened here? What does this mean?"

"It means," the former vizier answered, a faint look of amusement on his handsome face as he paused to brush debris from his robe, "that the players reached the oasis pool at the same time. God Shaddai declares that they have both won, my King. Both must be exonerated."

"But the whirlwind . . ." Amenhotep gestured weakly toward the sky, then pressed his hand to his throbbing head and surveyed the damage to his precious garden. "Such power!"

"It is a fearsome thing to trifle with the Almighty God." Zaphenath-paneah folded his hands and dipped his head slightly in a sign of proper respect. "You wanted Him to adjudicate your game, honored Pharaoh, and so He has."

Amenhotep cleared his throat and looked away. "Well," he said, crossing his arms. He frowned at the sight of so many nobles and warriors still cowering on the ground. This was not good. If he did not handle this situation properly, the story would spread like the plague. Rumors would soon have the mighty king of Egypt cowering before a simple desert whirlwind.

He gave his vizier a forgiving smile, determined to be done with the matter. "Your God has decreed that both men are innocent, as I knew He would. But what would He have me do with the prize? The winner was to take possession of the little harpist, and she cannot serve two masters."

"No, my King, she cannot." Zaphenath-paneah turned to the slave girl, who stood silently behind him, her arm linked through the old steward's. "Jendayi," Zaphenath-paneah said, his voice gentle, "you may choose your master today. Whom will you serve most willingly? Manasseh or Ephraim?''

———

Manasseh heard his father's words as if through a thick fog. The events of the last hour had trampled him like a runaway horse, and he needed time to absorb them, to think. But a few feet away the love of his life was being offered the opportunity to choose her future, and he had not had a chance to share his heart with her since that long-ago afternoon at Malkata. She would certainly choose Ephraim, but before she did, he wanted to tell her once and for all that he would always love her.

He staggered forward, his eyes intent upon Jendayi's bright face. But she would not give him time, for she dropped Ani's arm and stepped out without aid. "Thank you, master." Unusual determination rang in her voice. "I am ready to make my choice." Her face lit up with affection and delight—the expression she always wore when speaking of Ephraim.

Gritting his teeth, Manasseh braced himself for disappointment. It was enough that God had spared his life and Ephraim's. He would be asking too much if he expected God to also fulfill his fanciful dreams.

"If God Shaddai wills," Jendayi whispered, the warmth of her voice sending shivers down his spine, "I choose to go with Manasseh."

Manasseh tensed, surprised and more uncertain than ever. She had chosen *him*? Why?

He did not have time to ponder the question, for Ephraim slapped him on the back while Joseph gestured for Manasseh to come forward and claim his prize.

"I wish you every happiness, brother," Ephraim said, sunshine breaking across his face. "Every happiness in the world."

And then Manasseh was standing before Jendayi, and her small hands were upon his arms, her smile beaming for him alone.

———

After a moment Ephraim turned away, unable to bear the sight of his brother's joy while his own heart still ached. He looked toward Pharaoh's dais and caught Sitamun's gaze. Her dark eyes pierced the distance between them. Had she gone willingly to the wedding canopy with her father? Had she been given a choice? He would never know the answers, for now that she was a queen, a great gulf had been fixed between them. The girl he had hoped to wed would never be his.

It was time to face the future.

"Great Pharaoh." His voice echoed above the sounds of the bewildered crowd. "I beg a favor of you!"

"Ask your favor," Pharaoh answered, his arms folded stiffly across his bare chest. Queen Tiy, uncharacteristically silent, rocked behind him on the ground, a handful of greenery pressed over her face.

"If you will," Ephraim said, looking back at Manasseh, "allow me and my brother to dwell from this day forward in the territory of Goshen. Though we have grown up as your loyal servants in Thebes, perhaps it would be best if we raised our families with our kinsmen."

Pharaoh's eyes narrowed in speculation, and Ephraim knew the shrewd king would understand many of the reasons behind his request. If Ephraim left Thebes, he would not have to see Sitamun, nor would he dwell in her thoughts. And if Manasseh wanted to train another military force, at least he would be doing it in the far-off region of Goshen and not under the king's nose.

"Your request is granted." Amenhotep nodded. "You and your brother may live in Goshen, and I wish you well. But your father, my own Zaphenath-paneah, shall not leave Thebes. I will want him by my side for as long as I live."

This announcement brought an immediate hush to the gathering. Tiy's face appeared through the shrubbery, her brows pulled into an affronted frown. The countenances of the two new viziers immediately fell.

"Zaphenath-paneah"—Pharaoh stepped down from his dais and walked toward Joseph—"will you remain in Thebes to serve as my chief counselor? I covet your wisdom above that of all my servants, above my two viziers, above my priests, above my counselors. I value your judgment"—he thrust out his chin—"even above that of the Great Wife, Queen Tiy, who shall from this day be banished to chambers in my harem while a new queen is installed in her place. Remain with me, Zaphenath-paneah, for you and your God have prevailed again."

Ephraim stared after the king, astounded, as his father slipped to the ground and bowed before Amenhotep. "As always, Pharaoh, I am your servant." Joseph looked up at Pharaoh with true affection in his eyes. "God Shaddai has called me to serve you. You may count upon my loyalty until I draw my last breath."

Pharaoh then extended his hand—a truly intimate gesture. Ephraim smiled at the sight but had to blink back unexpected tears as his father rose to press his lips to the royal palm.

———

Upon his barge, where Pharaoh's standard again fluttered from the center mast, Joseph traveled the distance from Malkata to Thebes in a full and satisfying silence. He disembarked at the royal dock and proceeded straightway to the palace, driven by an unaccountable need to see Tuya. "Old wood is the best to burn," he told himself as he climbed the slope to the palace gates. "And old friends are the best to trust."

The palace at Thebes seemed strangely deserted with both the Queen and Pharaoh at Malkata, but the handful of guards on duty at the gates bowed before Joseph and then opened the double doors to the central hall without question.

News travels on the wind, he thought with a wry smile as he moved past them. *How could they have already heard that Zaphenath-paneah is once again in Pharaoh's favor? A servant, perhaps, or one of the seamen from the barge.*

He had not traversed the narrow passageways that led to the House of the Women in years. He was not even certain he would be able to find his way to Tuya's chambers. Turning a corner, he surprised a pair of slave girls in the hall. One of them squeaked, the other immediately fell down and pressed her palms and forehead to the floor.

"Pray tell me which apartment belongs to the Queen Mother," he asked, folding his hands.

The squeaking slave, still too startled to bow, pointed wordlessly down another torch-lit hall. Nodding his thanks, Joseph moved away.

Only one door lay at the end of the hallway where a single

torch hung from an iron bracket and sputtered in the gloom. Timidly lifting his hand, Joseph knocked.

"Enter."

Tuya herself had uttered the command, and as he entered she smiled at him from the security of a delicately carved couch. Long-stemmed and lovely, like a perfect lotus, she looked up. Her exotic eyes tilted catlike toward him and seemed to probe his soul.

She had been waiting.

She had known he would come.

She had always understood him . . . better than he understood himself.

"Tuya," he began, lifting his eyes to the shadows that played flickering games around the high ceiling.

"There is no need to explain, Joseph." She held her arms out to him and in one forward motion he was in her arms, his head pillowed by her softness, his arms clinging to her as if she were a steady raft and he a drowning man.

"What have I done?" he murmured as she stroked his head, the touch of her hand almost unbearable in its tenderness. "I nearly lost my sons! God Shaddai preserved their lives, but for years I should have seen that I was losing their hearts!"

"Fret not, my friend." The sound of her voice was warm in his ear. "God is always at work. How could you forget? Your brothers sold you into slavery, and yet God raised you up. For better or worse, you placed my son above your own, and yet God will bless Ephraim and Manasseh. God works even through human frailty—that is why He is Almighty, and we are as dust."

Her words were a soothing balm to his heart, and for a long interval he said nothing, then his eyes melted into hers. "In my youth days I remembered my God. How could I think He would forget me in my age?"

"I do not know, Joseph." Her hand stroked his hair. "He will not, if you seek him. You offered a sacrifice for your sons. Now it is time to again offer yourself."

In silent agreement, he closed his eyes and pressed his head to her lap, lifting his thoughts to God Shaddai and finding comfort in Tuya's reassuring presence.

~ Thirty ~

THE NEXT MORNING, MANASSEH ROSE FROM HIS OLD bed in his father's villa for what he assumed was the last time. The astonishing and marvelous events of the previous day had irreversibly severed his future from his past. From this day forward he and Ephraim would belong to the Hebrews. But more important, from today on he would belong to Jendayi.

He swung his feet out of bed, splashed his face with water from the washbasin, then patted his face and beard with a linen square. A new robe, a long striped garment designed in the fashion of the Hebrews, draped a stand in his chamber, and Manasseh slipped it over his head, relishing the feel of the fine linen against his skin. The robe had been a gift from Halima, Tarik's wife. This would be his wedding garment, and the old steward suspected Halima knew as much.

He paused in the garden to pluck a fragrant lotus blossom from the reflecting pool, then hurried toward the courtyard. The open space flurried with activity as he entered it. A half-dozen camels had been loaded with provisions for their new start in Goshen, and Ephraim seemed almost happy about making the journey. His bright smile shone on everyone, from Ani, who wept openly, to the slowest slave, and he was directing the preparations for their trip with an unusually efficient air.

Watching his younger brother, Manasseh felt his heart contract in pity. Though Ephraim would not admit it, yesterday in Pharaoh's garden he had abandoned a lifetime of dreams. Neither the glory of Egypt nor its spoiled princess would ever be his. But he still had Jacob's blessing, and now Manasseh actually felt grateful that Jacob had stretched his right hand toward his brother's head. Ephraim had surrendered more than Manasseh. It was only right that God Shaddai honor him with more descendants and blessings.

Jendayi stood with Kesi by the side of a groaning camel, a full traveling cloak billowing about her slim figure. She had chosen to leave her Egyptian wig behind, and her own hair, dark and cropped close to her head, ruffled out in tumultuous waves as the wind blew through it. She was laughing at some secret the girls shared, but as Manasseh approached, Kesi dipped in a bow and shyly retreated.

He expected Jendayi to stiffen in alarm and was pleasantly surprised when she looked up, her gray eyes shining toward him like brilliant stars. "Master Manasseh?" she asked, contentment and joy in her voice.

The sound of her happiness struck a vibrant chord within him. "Yes," he answered, forcing the word over his suddenly shy tongue. He stepped closer and passed the flower just under her nose. "For you."

Smiling her thanks, she reached out to grasp the lotus blossom, then expertly wrapped the long stem about her bare arm. With a quiet confidence that caught him by surprise, she reached out and caught his hand, then fell to one knee before him. "Master, I am so pleased to belong to you! And I am ready for the journey. Kesi has packed my things with the others' possessions, and with your permission, I have asked the servants to place my harp in a basket on my camel—excuse me, *your* camel."

"Of course, do whatever you like, but rise," Manasseh answered, grateful that the noise of the courtyard drowned out the boisterous pounding of his heart. He lifted her to her feet. "Your harp shall go wherever you go, Jendayi. I look forward to hearing you play it every night."

He thought her smile faded a little as she lowered her head. "Yes, my lord. As my master, you may command me at any time."

"You will not play as my slave." Manasseh pulled her toward him, then dropped her hand and gently drew her into his arms. "You will play, only if it is your desire, as my wife." In answer, she nestled against him, her contented heart beating against his.

"Can it be true?" she murmured, lifting her face to his gaze. "I don't deserve such happiness, such freedom. A week ago I was a slave, troubled by nightmares and facing a dim future. Now I sleep as peacefully as a baby, and my heart brims with freedom and joy. Never in a thousand days could I have imagined that I would be free from bondage, and never in ten thousand years would I have dreamed that I could be your wife." A blush of pleasure rose on her lovely face. "You are too good to me, Manasseh. You . . . and your God Shaddai."

"Jendayi." As he said her name she smiled, and a quiver surged through his veins at the sight of her happiness. "I told you I have always loved you. For years I have been waiting—first for you to grow up, then for the opportunity to tell you how much I cared."

"And I was too foolish." A blush ran over her exquisite face and tears trembled on her lashes. "Manasseh, I don't know why you were so patient. I knew I needed to love and be loved. It was all I wanted in the world! But I had been misled by my own ignorance. I didn't know what love was, and I never dreamed that I could be free, that I could be someone's *wife*—"

"God planted my love for you long ago," Manasseh answered, tenderly pulling her head into the hollow between his shoulder and neck. "And as God is eternal, so shall be my love. I would give my life for you, Jendayi. I want to serve you as I serve God."

He might have remained locked in her arms for the rest of the day, but from the corner of his eye Manasseh saw his father approaching from the portico. He released Jendayi, then gestured to Kesi and told her to place her mistress safely within a camel basket. After promising Jendayi that he would speak to her again before they left the villa, he stepped out to exchange farewells with his father.

Joseph waited silently in the center of the courtyard, his beautiful, long-fingered hands folded, his coal black eyes misty and wistful.

Joseph nodded formally. "So you are ready to go, then."

Manasseh felt an odd twinge of disappointment. This was not the parting he had hoped for.

"Yes, we are ready." He lifted his chin. "And I think you should know, Father, that I intend to marry Jendayi as soon as we reach Goshen. I want to take her as my bride among our own people."

Joseph nodded slowly, the light of understanding flickering in his eyes. "I am glad you will not be alone," he said simply.

"Loneliness was the first thing God pronounced not good at creation. I am certain you will make each other very happy."

Manasseh glanced around, then nudged a small mound of sand with his sandal. How tragic that he could think of nothing to say! His father had just denounced loneliness, and yet today both his sons would leave him. Perhaps he would not even notice their absence, for Pharaoh had just thrust himself back into Joseph's life. But though Manasseh had been far closer to Ani and Tarik than he had ever been to his father, still—

He floundered in an agonizing maelstrom of emotion, torn between eagerness to go and the feeling that he ought to stay.

"Manasseh, I know what you are thinking, and you should not deny your own happiness on my account." The corner of Joseph's mouth quirked in a half-smile. "I will not be lonely. As soon as Pharaoh gives his permission, Queen Tuya will be coming to live with me. I will yet take another wife."

"The Queen Mother?" Manasseh burst out, shocked. "Why—how—but you scarcely know her!"

"I know you may not believe me, but I lived a varied and interesting life before you were born," his father answered, one dark eyebrow lifting as he smiled with refreshing candor. "Tuya is an old love, part of my past. We have decided that it would be wise to combine our strengths in order to face the future."

"Well." Manasseh grinned, then relaxed and placed his hands on his hips. "I suppose congratulations are in order. Let me wish *you* every happiness!"

"Thank you." His father rocked slowly back and forth. "Will you try again?" he asked suddenly. "Will you lead our people to Canaan?"

Manasseh sighed and looked away. "I don't know, Father. It would be harder now than before to gather enough men. I don't know if the people have the heart for it. I may be lucky if they even receive me into the camp."

"They'll receive you." Joseph nodded with conviction. "You are family. You are my son."

Manasseh was about to respond, but Joseph held up a quieting hand. He seemed preoccupied for a moment, as if a memory had suddenly surfaced and overshadowed his awareness of their conversation, and when he spoke again his voice was grim. "You asked me once why I did not tell you the stories of Israel," he said, his hand brushing Manasseh's arm. His gaze moved into his son's, but his eyes were as indecipherable as water. "Perhaps I was afraid to speak of things gone by. Before my brothers came to Egypt, I wanted to forget the past, to bury every story I had ever heard. After my family arrived, I was so busy with my responsibilities to Pharaoh and to the Hebrews . . ."

His words trailed away, and Manasseh lowered his gaze, shrinking from the self-accusation in his father's eyes.

"I think I wanted you to understand Egypt first, since that is where God had placed you," Joseph went on, his voice stronger. "But now, Manasseh, it is right that you live as a son of Israel. You have come to understand both worlds, and you have chosen between them." His eyes grew large and liquid. "You have chosen wisely."

"Thank you, Father." Manasseh fumbled for words.

Joseph chuckled softly. "When I was younger I had many dreams. Some of them got me into trouble, just as your dreams brought you face-to-face with adversity. But God spoke to me through dreams, and though He has been silent for many years, He spoke to me again last night."

Manasseh's heart stirred with interest. "What was His message?"

"In my dream I saw a king." Joseph's brow furrowed as he revisited the scene in his memory. "Not an Egyptian king, but one of our own people. He was deathly ill, and God Shaddai willed that he should die and journey on to paradise. But the king begged for his life, and a messenger from God revealed that the Almighty would spare the man for another fifteen years."

Joseph's eyes clung to Manasseh's, waiting for a reaction, but Manasseh shook his head, not understanding. "So—did the king die?"

"Fifteen summers later," Joseph continued, looking at the ground. "But during that fifteen years, the king fathered an evil son who built altars to idols in the holy place dedicated to God Shaddai. He worshiped the stars and spirits. He seduced the children of Israel to commit more evil than the heathen nations around them, then he killed the true prophets of God until the streets ran red with their blood." Fear, stark and vivid, glittered in Joseph's eyes when he looked up. "The son's name was Manasseh."

"This is not me, Father!" Manasseh protested, stepping back.

"I know." Joseph forced a smile. "But God sent me a message . . . for both of us. God chose to take the king to paradise so His people might be spared the evil to come. But the king was not willing to surrender his life, and the nation suffered." He paused a moment and thrust his hands behind his back, holding a powerful emotion in check. "I have come to believe, my son, that it was God's will for you to lead our people back to Canaan. But they were not ready . . . and I was not inclined to let them go."

"Father." Manasseh lowered his head to catch his father's gaze. "Do not blame yourself."

"I must." Joseph's voice was matter-of-fact. "I reached the place where I thought I knew all the answers, but I forgot the questions. I needed the illusion that I still spoke for God. I thought He could speak through no one else. I was foolish, vain, and wrong, and so our people will suffer. Not today, and not while I live, for I shall do all in my power to maintain peace between Pharaoh and the sons of Israel. But we were not willing to obey when God gave the opportunity, and so I am afraid—no, I am certain—we will greatly suffer for our disobedience."

Reaching up, Joseph placed his hand on his son's shoulder. His eyes shone with a tenderness Manasseh had never seen in them before. "You were not a failure, son. God called you to lead, and you obeyed. You cannot be blamed because we would not follow." His hand tightened on Manasseh's neck. "The children of Israel will return to Canaan, for God Shaddai's will is always accomplished. And when they go, whenever they go, let it be known that my bones are to journey with them. God called me to live my life here among the children of the Nile, but I shall sleep with my fathers in the Promised Land."

"Father—" A deep, unaccustomed pain in Manasseh's breast cut off his words. He could only nod in assent.

Joseph smiled, satisfied, and drew his son into the cradle of his arms.

After a long moment, Joseph released him. "Fetch your brother," he said, the glow of his smile warming Manasseh's spirit. "And I will bless you both for the journey."

With a heart too full to speak, Manasseh obeyed.

Epilogue

Joseph, or Zaphenath-paneah, outlived Amenhotep III by thirty years. Shortly after ascending to the throne, the Crown Prince Neferkheprure' Wa'enre', who had never approved of either his father's lifestyle or his halfhearted approach to religion, abandoned Malkata, Thebes, and even his royal name. Calling himself Akhenaten, meaning "He Who Is of Service to Aten," the sun god, the new Pharaoh and his wife, Queen Nefertiti, built a great city in middle Egypt and called it Akhetaten. This Pharaoh, oddly enough, worshiped one invisible and almighty god, Aten.

Akhenaten repudiated everything his father had idolized, attacking the cults of other deities in Egypt and destroying their idols. He confiscated the great estates belonging to the temples of local deities. He reigned only eighteen years, but his impetuous acts vastly undermined Egypt's stability. His major contribution to the Hebrews in Goshen was his simple policy of leaving them alone.

Joseph lived long enough to hold his great-grandchildren from Ephraim, who had married Jokim's sister, Atara. He cradled his great-grandsons from Manasseh, too, and remained so close to his elder son's family that Genesis tells us that the babies born to Machir, Manasseh's son, were "born on Joseph's knees," that is, considered to be his own. On many of his visits to Goshen, a crowd of little ones waited at the harbor for his barge to arrive. Plump young hands tugged at his flowing robe as he made his stately way down the gangplank. Round rosy faces eagerly sought kisses from the Bread of Egypt, the Father to Pharaohs, the Servant of God Shaddai.

As he counted the last of his mortal days, Joseph sent for his brothers. "I am dying," he told them, "but God will take account of you. He will bring you up from this land to the land that He promised to Abraham, to Isaac, and to Jacob.''

And Joseph had the sons of Israel swear that they would carry his bones up from Egypt. So Joseph died at the age of one hundred ten years and was embalmed and placed in a temporary coffin in Egypt.

A rapid succession of Pharaohs followed Amenhotep III: Akhenaten, Smenkhkare', Tut'ankhamun, Aya, and Horemhab. And after Horemhab, who died without an heir, a new dynasty arose, kings whom the Bible describes as those ''who knew not Joseph.''

Author's Note

"It is not a question of whether God is willing to sanctify me," writes Oswald Chambers. "Is it *my* will?" Elsewhere Chambers writes, "Always distinguish between God's order and His permissive will, i.e., His providential purpose towards us. God's order is unchangeable; His permissive will is that with which we must wrestle before Him. It is our reaction to the permissive will of God that enables us to get at His order."[1]

As the wife of a youth pastor, I'm often approached by young people who are struggling to find and follow the will of God. I usually offer guidelines, not hard and fast answers, for I've wrestled to find that most perfect will of God for my own life. Some preachers have it down to a formula: be saved, sanctified, Spirit-filled, willing to suffer, and then follow the desires of your heart!

But it's easier to recite the formula than to apply it. How does a saved, sanctified, Spirit-filled, suffering person choose between good and also-good? Between red and blue? Between going and staying?

At least we aren't alone in our quandaries. As I studied the Genesis account of Joseph's latter years, I was struck by the simple fact that the Israelites *didn't* return to Canaan after the famine. Understanding human nature for what it is, I could easily imagine the forces that held them in Egypt. Still, the idea that they should have returned to their promised homeland seemed a little risky until my theory was bolstered by a passage that one of my former Bible professors faxed to me (thank you, Dr. Harvey Hartman!). The passage, from an old commentary, indicated that I might be following a plausible path:

This interesting little episode gives us a glimpse of the state

---

[1] Oswald Chambers, *My Utmost for His Highest Journal* (Uhrichsville, Ohio: Barbour and Company, Inc., 1935), selections for October 20 and December 16.

of Hebrew society in Egypt; for the occurrence narrated [1 Chronicles 7:20–22] seems to have taken place before the Israelites left that country; and it shows that, looking to Palestine as their proper home, some of them, without waiting the appointed time, attempted prematurely, by dint of their own achievements, to take forcible possession of the Promised Land.[2]

Some of them . . . attempted . . . to take forcible possession of the promised land. Some of them risked their lives to return home!

Was it God's perfect will that man and woman remain in Eden and continue in uncorrupted fellowship with Him? Yes. But God endowed man with free will. If we were not free to make wrong choices, we would not be free to choose *right*.

Was it God's perfect will that the sons of Israel remain in Egypt and forget the God who had miraculously preserved them? I don't think so. But the question is not so much what God willed—for He had already revealed His perfect order—but rather what the Hebrews were willing to choose. They chose to remain in the Black Land and suffered the consequences of that decision—the bondage of Egypt, which focused their need for the deliverer to come . . . Moses.

Just as Eden sharpened our need for a Savior.

It's a variation on the same theme. Every story echoes His Story.

---

[2]Robert Jamieson, A.R. Fausset, and David Brown, "Chronicles," *A Commentary Critical, Experimental, and Practical on the Old and New Testaments* (Grand Rapids: William B. Eerdmans Publishing Company, 1973), p. 468.